GYPSY LOVER

Anna-Maria stared at him, her mouth falling slightly open. The bruising pressure of his lips sent a shiver down her spine and she unconsciously curved her body against his, savoring his male hardness. Ramon laughed, deep in his throat, and began trailing kisses down her face and throat, leaving flames in their wake.

The arching movement forced her breasts upward, temptingly close to Ramon's bent head. Imprisoning her with one hand, he reached up with the other and tore her gown from neckline to waist.

... She felt his strong fingers sliding under her waistband ... With a quick movement he tore her gown from waist to hem ...

TENDER FIRE

Patricia Campbell Horton

TENDER FIRE
A Bantam Book | July 1978

ISBN 0-553-11837-4

Published simultaneously in the United States and Canada

Bantam Books are published by Bantam Books, Inc. Its trade-
mark, consisting of the words "Bantam Books" and the por-
trayal of a bantam, is registered in the United States Patent
Office and in other countries. Marca Registrada. Bantam
Books, Inc., 666 Fifth Avenue, New York, New York 10019.

For Sy "Buddy" Ament with
special thanks for the tender,
loving care he gave me during
the writing of this book.

And for my son,
Kevin Campbell Horton,
because he is
the joy of my life.

One

Anna-Maria leaned out of the coach window, savoring the fragrance of the October air. The wind caught at her long chestnut hair and sent it whipping across her face, tickling her. She laughed softly and brushed the silky strands away from her cheeks. It was wonderful to be going home to Deene, wonderful to be back in England.

Then she suddenly remembered the reason for her journey, and she shivered as fear touched her, the familiar fear that had been her constant companion ever since her mother's letter had arrived, summoning her home from the convent outside Paris. She braced herself against the jolting of the coach and rummaged through her reticule until she found the letter, creased and worn from much rereading. Hastily she scanned the closely written pages. It was obvious that Lady Brudenell had been in a high state of excitement when she had written. Her ornate script was less carefully formed than usual, and in places her pen had spattered, leaving ink blots. Anna-Maria knew that her normally fastidious mother would not have sent such a blotched message unless her excitement had been running high. She had written that Oliver Cromwell was dead. Anna-Maria felt a flash of joy as she reread the words. Too long had the tyrant kept his heavy hand on England. Her family had supported King Charles, whom Cromwell had had beheaded, and as a result they had suffered badly under Cromwell's rule, losing much of their land and the bulk of their vast fortune.

Anna-Maria quickly ran her eyes down the pages, skipping whole paragraphs until she reached the portion of the letter that set her heart to beating rapidly. The earl of Shrewsbury, Lady Brudenell had written, had declared an interest in marrying Anna-Maria.

1

Surely Anna-Maria remembered the earl? He had come to Deene last spring while Anna-Maria had been home on holiday.

For the hundredth time, Anna-Maria knit her brows in concentration. It was terrifying to be journeying toward marriage with a stranger, and she tried desperately to remember him. She would have been grateful for even a scrap of memory—the shade of his hair, the color of his eyes—but it eluded her. He was old, a widower of thirty-five, and no doubt Anna-Maria had dismissed him as one of her father's contemporaries, of no interest to herself. It was maddening; she had taken his hand in greeting, touched him for the first time, with no premonition that he was to be an intimate part of her life.

Anna-Maria sighed and stuffed the creased pages back into her reticule. The earl of Shrewsbury was rich, and this marriage was important to her impoverished parents. Lady Brudenell's joy had been clear on every page of her letter. Anna-Maria wished fervently that she could share her parents' happiness, but fingers of apprehension were tingling her spine.

Her life had changed with bewildering suddenness. Her mother's letter, interrupting the even tenure of her days at the convent, had had the force of a blow, and she still had not recovered. Since the letter's arrival, her dreams had been disturbed. Nightly the faceless figure of the earl had appeared to her. He had unbuttoned her nightgown with easy familiarity, slipped it from her shoulders, and asserted his right to freely caress her breasts. Anna-Maria's dreams had taken her no further than that—she always awoke, trembling. Yet, perhaps, his caresses would prove pleasing. Oh, if only she had been able to select a husband of her own choosing, a young handsome lord who would stir her senses!

I'm acting like a romantic school girl, Anna-Maria thought, impatient with herself. She tried to force herself into some enthusiasm for the match. It would be fine to be the countess of Shrewsbury. She mouthed the title silently, but it brought no sweetness to her lips. I'll be rich! Anna-Maria thought, and felt like bursting into tears.

She looked out the coach window and then straightened in excitement. They were nearly home. She spied a familiar outcropping of rock; and there was the ancient copper beach that had no equal in all of England.

In a few moments she would be home at Deene. Suddenly, to her horror, she realized that she was reluctant to face her parents. They would be full of joy at the earl's proposal, and Anna-Maria would spoil it for them. Loving her, sensitive to her moods, they would realize that she shrank from the idea of this marriage. If only she had more time to compose herself before facing them.

Impulsively, she stood in the swaying coach, bracing herself against the seat, and rapped loudly on the trapdoor in the roof. She could feel the horses slowing, and in a second the panel slid open, and the coachman's face appeared.

Anna-Maria tilted her head to look up at him. "Jim, let me down. I want to walk the rest of the way to the house."

"But your parents will be anxious to lay eyes on you, Miss Anna-Maria," Jim said, his voice hesitant.

Anna-Maria said quickly, "Aye, and I'm anxious to see them. But Jim, the motion of the coach has made me queasy."

A look of mingled consternation and embarrassment crossed Jim's red face, and he pulled his head hastily from the opening. A moment later he was at the coach door, wrestling it open.

Anna-Maria felt a twinge of guilt for deceiving the kind old man. She smiled gratefully at him as she took his hand and stepped from the coach. "Thank you, Jim. Tell my parents that I'll be home within the quarter hour." She could see the rooftops and tall chimneys of Deene ahead.

"Aye, a walk is the very thing for what ails you." Jim doffed his cap and swung nimbly back onto the high seat, drawing the reins into his rough hands.

Anna-Maria stood still, inhaling deeply as she

watched him drive off. Surely the air at Deene was sweeter than anywhere in the world! She began to walk slowly in the direction of Deene, her mind working busily on the problem of marriage to the earl.

Suddenly her attention was caught by a flash of scarlet visible through the copse of trees on her left. She stopped, puzzled. Then she glimpsed a patch of blue and a bit of bright yellow. Her pulse quickened. The gypsies must be at Deene! She knew that every year her father allowed the gypsies to make camp at Deene, but she had always been away during their visits. Lord Brudenell claimed that if he played host to the gypsies, they would do their thieving elsewhere in the neighborhood and leave Deene in peace.

Impulsively, Anna-Maria turned in the direction of the woods. She would put off her confrontation with her parents. The gypsies had skill in foretelling the future, and she would have her palm read. Perhaps, she thought, by the time I face my parents, I'll know better than they what my future will be.

Unbidden, the image of a young man sprang into her mind. He was tall and tanned; his intense blue eyes shone with laughter. Anna-Maria's pulse quickened as she imagined the taste of his lips against her own. Then her mouth curved in a smile. Perhaps there *was* such a man in her future, and the gypsy would have knowledge of him. Before the marriage to the earl took place, this handsome stranger might even appear and claim her.

She walked rapidly through the woods pushing away overhanging branches and jerking impatiently at her cloak when it became entangled on thorns. When she reached the edge of the camp clearing, her spirits rose. How colorful the gypsy wagons were—red, yellow, and blue, sparkling in the sunlight. As Anna-Maria stepped into the clearing, a gypsy woman came walking toward her with a huge bowl balanced on her hip. Anna-Maria stopped, shocked. The woman was wearing a soiled lace blouse that dipped so low over her breasts that her nipples were in danger of popping free. Anna-Maria had never seen a woman's breasts exposed except in the old portraits that lined the walls of Deene and dated back to an older, more licentious age. For a moment she thought of turning back, but then she took a deep breath and moved forward. If she fled now, she would hate herself for her cowardice.

Once she was actually within the camp, it lost a little of its glamour. The paint that looked so bright in the sunlight proved on closer inspection to be old and peeling. Nearby, under a thick clump of trees, was a group of horses. Their coats were pitifully dull and lusterless. Their ribs stuck out in sharp relief, and they were so dispirited that they didn't even flinch away from the flies that were swarming around them in clusters.

A young male gypsy, naked above the waist, looked up from the fire he was building and caught sight of Anna-Maria. His glance moved slowly over her, and he caught his breath sharply. She was arrestingly lovely, tall and slender with chestnut hair that gleamed under the sun. The gypsy felt his flesh tingle. He longed to reach out and run his hand gently down that shining mass of hair, to feel it curl sensuously around his fingers. Her face was a perfect oval with exquisite cheekbones, and her eyes were dark and provocative. Her mouth, he thought, begged to be kissed, and he found his eyes lingering on it as she spoke.

"Can you direct me, please, to someone who has skill in telling fortunes?"

Anna-Maria's tone was imperious, but the gypsy caught the note of nervousness underneath. With grave deference he pointed to a scarlet caravan a few feet away and made a swift bow as Anna-Maria passed him.

He's laughing at me, Anna-Maria thought, horrified. Tilting her chin, she arrogantly swept past.

A woman was hanging clothes on a line outside the scarlet caravan. She turned as Anna-Maria approached and said, "Would you be wanting me?" She was about forty-five years old with dark, swarthy skin and strongly marked eyebrows.

Anna-Maria walked toward her quickly and said, "If you tell fortunes, then you are the one I'm seeking."

The woman dropped the rest of her wash back into

the basket and looked at Anna-Maria with a trace of suspicion. " 'Tis not often in this part of the country that fine ladies seek me out."

"I'm Anna-Maria Brudenell. My father owns this land on which we stand."

"Ah, yes." Rasha nodded, setting her large gold hoop earrings swinging. "Your father has been host to my people for many years. His daughter is welcome. Come inside!" She opened the door of the scarlet caravan and gestured to Anna-Maria to follow her.

Anna-Maria picked up her skirt and quickly mounted the three steps of the ladder. Entering the caravan, she stopped short—the caravan was pitch dark. Her hands held gropingly in front of her, Anna-Maria took a few steps and then stood still, trying to orient herself. The air was foul, smelling of unwashed bodies and decaying food.

Rasha's hearty laugh rang through the gloom. A spark flared, and seconds later Rasha's face outlined by candlelight, swam out of the darkness. "Sit ye down." She gestured with the candle to indicate a straight-backed rush chair that was drawn up to a crude wooden table.

Anna-Maria sat obediently, fighting an impulse to sweep the chair clean first. Rasha seated herself across the table and then smiled, exposing two rotted front teeth. "Well, my lady. And what sort of fortune shall I tell you, eh?"

Anna-Maria managed a smile and made her voice deliberately light and sophisticated. "Oh, the usual things. That I will marry a tall, dark, handsome gentleman. That I will be rich and healthy."

Rasha's grin broadened. She reached across the table and took Anna-Maria's slim hand into her own calloused one. Rasha's strong, square fingernails were ridged with grime, and Anna-Maria had to steel herself not to flinch.

"Your future is written on your palm and is as easy for me to read as a map," Rasha said in a practiced voice. She bent further into the candlelight, examining Anna-Maria's palm more closely. Suddenly her grin faded, and she sucked in her breath with a hiss.

Anna-Maria stiffened. "What is it?"

Rasha's voice was husky. "I've seen few such palms in my life. There is much in store for you. Much." There was a tinge of awe in her voice. "Your name will be on every tongue throughout England."

Anna-Maria felt a flush of pleasure. "Will I marry a great lord?" Perhaps she would become one of the foremost noblewomen of England, famous for her graciousness and lavish entertainments. She bent forward, breathless. If the gypsy mentioned the earl of Shrewsbury, that would settle her doubts forever. If it was written in her palm that she would love the earl, marry the earl, then so be it!

"Aye, you'll marry." Rasha bent closer to Anna-Maria's palm. "You'll have one—two children. Perhaps a third child, but that is blurred." Her lips twisted, and the candle threw a cruel shadow across her face. "All your life there will be a war inside you. You are a pious woman. You wish to serve God and be faithful to your husband. But yours is a hot nature, lustful, and you will crave a man's embraces. The lust in your nature will battle endlessly with that part of you that cries out for goodness."

Anna-Maria could feel herself blushing and was grateful for the concealing darkness. She had never heard the word lust said aloud before. She scarcely understood its meaning. Surely it was evil to have come here—everyone knew the gypsies were immoral!

She was on the point of rising, when Rasha said, "You will have one great love, not your husband. For that man you will give up everything—your marriage, your home, your very reputation!"

Horrified, Anna-Maria tried to pull her hand away, but Rasha tightened her grip. Her eyes intent, she said, "I see blood on your hands. Much blood."

Anna-Maria gave a panic-stricken gasp and stood up abruptly, wrenching herself free from Rasha's grip. Unconsciously she wiped her hand against her skirt as she asked Rasha, in a voice that shook, "What shall I pay you?"

Rasha blinked in the candlelight and refocused her eyes as though she were returning from a long distance.

She waited a moment and then said in her normal tones, "Pay me what you wish."

Fumbling angrily, Anna-Maria opened her reticule and emptied it, tossing the gold coins across the table. She wouldn't put the coins into Rasha's hand, she wouldn't touch that horrible creature again. Anna-Maria's heart was pounding wildly. She felt as though she could not draw a full breath in this evil atmosphere. With a rush of longing, she remembered the cool, sweet-smelling halls of the convent where she had been raised, the hushed peace and the aura of purity and goodness.

Rasha was holding the candle, showing Anna-Maria the way to the door. Her swarthy face seemed harsh and secretive in the candle's glow. "I don't weave stories, my lady. Your fate is written in your palm. I would not have given your father's daughter such a future if it were in my power to change it."

Anna-Maria threw Rasha an anguished look. Brushing past the gypsy, she stumbled a little going down the short ladder, then stood at the bottom taking deep breaths of the cool, sweet air.

It was a sin to come to this accursed place, she thought. She scrubbed her hand against the fabric of her dress and shuddered. Blood. Was she to be a murderess? It was an unforgivable sin. Her soul would be plunged down into the eternal darkness of hell.

Two

The young gypsy caught sight of Anna-Maria and paused in his task. She was running in his direction like someone blinded, her chestnut hair streaming out behind her. Rasha must have told her a bad fortune. But how could that be? A woman so young, so beautiful—life would be good to her. Suddenly a coil of rope hidden in the grass caught Anna-Maria's foot; he sprang to catch her just as she stumbled.

Anna-Maria had just a second to realize she was falling before strong arms clasped her. She was swept up and cradled chest-high while a dark face laughed down into her own. Bewildered, she blinked to clear her eyes of a film of tears. The man's expression was kind, and she unconsciously nestled closer to him for reassurance. Her rapid heartbeat slowed a little, and the mindless panic began to recede. Some of the nightmare sensation faded, but the dreamlike feeling persisted. She looked up into the dark face above her. She had never been this close to any man except her father. She looked at the gypsy with curiosity. His eyes were alight with tenderness, a thick black mustache curled over his sensuous lips. Anna-Maria moved slightly in his arms and suddenly was swept by a feeling of safety. How strong he was! His muscles stood out in bold relief against the bronze skin of his chest, and he held her as lightly as though she were a baby. Anna-Maria relaxed imperceptibly. She had been frightened, and here was comfort. Her arm went up and coiled around his neck, and she burrowed her face against his chest, inhaling with pleasure as she caught the sun-warmed male scent of him.

She missed the quick gleam that appeared in his dark eyes, but a second later she felt his hand under her chin, tilting her face towards his. There was no time to realize his intention before his dark face came closer, and his lips sought hers in a long kiss. At first the pressure of his lips against hers was as light as a butterfly's wings. Then, slowly, he deepened the kiss. Instinctively Anna-Maria parted her lips, and the gypsy's arms tightened around her. A delicious sensation stole over her; she felt as though she were melting in a sweet fire. The heat of his lips was melting her. . . .

"Ramon!" A strange voice cut across the clearing, loud and angry. The intrusion came like a dash of cold water, and Anna-Maria was startled back into reality. Her eyes flew open; she looked with disbelief at the dark face so near her own. Oh, sweet Jesus! She had let a strange man kiss her, and worse, she had liked it.

Humiliated, frightened, she began to struggle in his arms. "Put me down!" Perhaps Rasha had put a curse on her. The gypsy had predicted that she would crave a man's embraces, and only a few moments later she had responded to the sweet fire of male lips. She must get free of this place before she lost her soul entirely. Bursting into tears, she began pounding on the gypsy's bronzed chest.

"Loose me! Put me down at once!"

The gypsy set her on her feet without loosening his grip around her waist. His eyes were mocking, a glint of laughter in their depths. Anna-Maria pushed at his hands, frantic to free herself.

"Ramon!" The sharp voice came again, causing the gypsy's head to swivel in the direction of a young woman about Anna-Maria's age who was striding rapidly toward them, anger clearly written on her face. "Are you mad? Are you trying to bring trouble on all of us?"

Anna-Maria looked over in surprise as the young woman came closer. This was no gypsy. She had clear, white skin with a sprinkling of freckles over an impudent nose, a mass of gold hair, and a pair of blue eyes that were snapping with anger. Her dress was that of the gypsies, a full skirt of gaily patterned calico, but her blouse was fastened discreetly high with a cameo pin. The woman reached Anna-Maria, put a protective arm around her shoulders, and faced Ramon.

"Are you trying to get us turned off this land?" she asked, furious.

Ramon kept his mocking gaze on Anna-Maria as he answered the young woman. "I meant only to give the lady a moment's pleasure, Sarah."

He knows I liked his kiss, Anna-Maria thought and felt a scarlet tide wash over her neck and face. She said quickly, her voice trembling, "I'll tell my father how you handled me, and he'll see that you are turned off this land before nightfall."

"I doubt it," the gypsy drawled lazily. His glance swept over her face and lingered on her trembling red lips. "Surely you will not tell your father that you came to the gypsy camp. That you dared to look into the future. That you were kissed by a man."

Anna-Maria gasped, filled with impotent rage. If she told her father of this morning's escapade, he would be hurt and humiliated by his daughter's unladylike behavior. She shuddered, but found that she could not take her eyes from the gypsy's face. Her body had betrayed her, instinctively melting into his embrace, and it went on betraying her. Her legs would not hold her upright. She began to sway, and Sarah tightened her grip around her shoulders, supporting her. "Come. I'll bathe your face in cold water, and you'll feel better." Her voice was crisp, practical.

Ramon stood aside to let them pass, his eyes still mocking. Anna-Maria leaned gratefully on Sarah's arm as they crossed the clearing. When Sarah indicated a tree stump, Anna-Maria sank gratefully down on it. She turned her face up as docilely as a child as Sarah dampened a rag with cold water and passed it gently over Anna-Maria's forehead.

In a shaking whisper, Anna-Maria began to repeat Rasha's prophecy. Sarah listened quietly, occasionally asking a soft-voiced question until she had a clear picture of the scene that had taken place in the scarlet caravan. When Anna-Maria had finished, Sarah said, in a voice brisk with common sense, "It's all nonsense you know. 'Blood on your hands . . . a lustful nature.' Just the sort of fanciful trash the gypsies like to frighten the gentry with."

Her matter-of-fact tone calmed Anna-Maria, who looked at her with curiosity. "You're not a gypsy."

Sarah laughed and wrung out the rag with a quick, deft movement. "No, but I live with them now. Two years ago I ran away from home, and the gypsies gave me shelter."

Anna-Maria made a shocked exclamation, and Sarah said swiftly, "My father was trying to force me into a marriage with a man I despised. My prospective husband was sixty years old, and his teeth were rotted in his head. I swear he had not bathed since he left his nurse's arms; I gagged every time he approached me."

Anna-Maria shivered. Suppose the earl of Shrewsbury should prove equally repulsive? "But surely your father would not have *forced* you into the marriage, not if he realized how distasteful it was to you."

Sarah said, without a trace of self-pity, "He knew how I felt, but he didn't care. He's never loved me. My mother died giving birth to me, and he remarried a few months later. All his affection went to the sons that my stepmother birthed." She carefully laid the damp rag along the rim of the bucket. "So I ran away and sought a home with the gypsies. I thought it would be an adventure. And it's not a bad life. I've traveled the length and breadth of England." She broke off, and a sadness that belied her words appeared in her blue eyes.

"My parents!" Anna-Maria jumped to her feet. "They will be so worried about me." How lucky she was to have such *loving* parents. Suddenly she wanted nothing so much in the world as to feel their arms enfolding her.

She reached hastily for her reticule saying, "How can I ever repay you?" Then, realizing she had no more money, Anna-Maria looked at Sarah in dismay. "I gave all my gold to that horrible old woman!"

Sarah laughed. "I would not take your money."

"But I must repay your kindness."

Sarah hesitated and then threw a quick glance around the gypsy camp. After a moment she turned to Anna-Maria, seeming to come to a decision. "I wonder—I'm beginning to weary of this life. It's a constant fight against filth. The gypsies don't care you see, they like to be filthy. And they are not really my own people no matter how kind they are to me."

Anna-Maria waited, puzzled. Sarah took a deep breath, hesitated, and then said, in a rush, "I've a mind to go to Deene and ask for work. Would you be willing to recommend me?"

Relief swept over Anna-Maria. How simple it would be to reward Sarah. She smiled. "Of course. Come to Deene with me now. I'll wait while you collect your things."

Anna-Maria stood watching as Sarah walked briskly to a bright yellow caravan on the outskirts of the encampment, one that looked a good bit cleaner than the others. She kept her gaze fixed in the direction that Sarah had gone, fearing that if she looked around the clearing, she might meet Ramon's mocking gaze. For a moment, only a moment, she had actually enjoyed having the gypsy kiss her. While she waited for Sarah, she resolutely shut her eyes and said a string of Hail Mary's, praying fervently that the Blessed Virgin would give Anna-Maria a nature as pure as her own.

Sarah interrupted her in a surprisingly short time. Anna-Maria noted, with pity, that the bundle Sarah was carrying was tiny.

As they walked out of the clearing, Anna-Maria said slowly, "I've been thinking. I've just returned from France, and I have no serving maid for my personal use. Would you like to serve me?"

Sarah nodded, setting her blond curls to bouncing. "Aye, it's more than I hoped for. I have no training, so I thought to be a scullery maid or a laundress." She grinned, wrinkling her freckled nose, "And to tell you the truth I have no stomach for hanging over a tub of scalding laundry."

Anna-Maria smiled back, feeling a quick flash of companionship. "I'll tell my parents that I met you in the meadow as I was returning to Deene and that you asked me for work. I'd rather they didn't know that I've been to the gypsy camp."

Sarah nodded in understanding, and Anna-Maria sighed. She was adding lying to her long list of transgressions, but surely it was a minor sin compared to the others the gypsy had foretold.

As they neared Deene, she began to hasten her stride until Sarah, laughing, was forced into a half run to keep pace. Anna-Maria said impatiently, "Hurry, Sarah. I've not seen my parents in months."

Sarah, instead of obeying, stopped in her tracks and stood staring at the long, impressive facade of Deene. She gasped in amazement. "It's a castle. When I glimpsed it through the woods, I never dreamed it was so vast!"

Anna-Maria explained proudly that Deene was one of the largest private homes in England and had a long history, having been built over one hundred years ago by the first Robert Brudenell who was chief justice to King Henry the Eighth.

Then she picked up her skirts and began running, and in a second Sarah recovered her breath and was on her heels. Anna-Maria flew quickly up the broad stairs and then paused for a moment in front of the door to smooth down her skirts and steady her breathing.

Before she could knock, the door was pulled open. Anna-Maria, catching a glimpse of her parents, rushed past the servant who had opened the door and threw herself into her mother's arms. Her dainty mother reeled a little under the impact, but her arms went swiftly around Anna-Maria. "Darling, it's good to have you home. Are you well? Jim said you were a bit queasy from the jolting of the coach and we were worried because it took you so long to walk here."

Anna-Maria snuggled deep into her mother's arms, loving the scent of verbena that always clung to her mother's clothing. "I'm fine. I sat and rested for a bit, then walked slowly. The walk restored me." She felt a quick prick of guilt and vowed to live her life in such a fashion that she would never have to lie to her mother again.

"Well, daughter. No kiss for me?" Her father's voice was a genial boom. Loosening her grip on her mother, Anna-Maria sped into her father's waiting embrace. Lord Brudenell gave her a hug that nearly forced all the breath out of her body, then held her at arm's length and said, "Let's get a look at you." His quick glance took in Sarah and he asked, "What have we here?"

Anna-Maria flinched. She had forgotten that there would be one more lie to tell. She said quickly, "Father, I've hired a serving woman for my personal use. I met her on my way home. She was coming to Deene to ask for work."

Sarah stood gazing about the Great Hall, silent and demure. Lord Brudenell looked at the young woman dubiously, but knew he could not refuse his daughter anything now. "I'm sure she will be very suitable."

Turning his attention to more important matters, he said, "Anna-Maria, tomorrow the earl of Shrewsbury, Francis Talbot, will be coming here. I assume he has come to a decision at last." There was a gleam of satisfied ambition in his eyes. "Your mother wrote you of his intentions toward you?"

Anna-Maria nodded, hoping that her father would notice nothing amiss in her attitude. Her encounter with the gypsies had only thrown her emotions into further confusion. At the moment she couldn't cope with the problem of the earl and marriage.

Lord Brudenell hesitated uncharacteristically before speaking, nervously rubbing his fleshy red nose. "Anna-Maria, tomorrow when Francis Talbot is here, try to be—well—less French in your speech and mannerisms. Like many Englishmen, the earl detests the French."

Anna-Maria stifled a sigh. From this moment on, for the rest of her life, all her energies must be spent pleasing a man who was at this moment a stranger to her. She felt a quick flare of resentment and was instantly ashamed of herself. Hastily she lowered her eyes. "I'll try, father. May I go to my chamber now? I'm weary and travel stained."

Her father kissed her forehead and gave her an approving smile. Francis Talbot might object to French mannerisms, Lord Brudenell reflected, but there was no doubt that French practicality was a blessing. Anna-Maria had been absorbing a pragmatic attitude toward life since her birth, and she would marry as her father directed without rebellion. He linked his arms through his wife's, and they watched Anna-Maria with affection as she crossed the hall, followed by Sarah.

Anna-Maria, mounting the staircase slowly, felt as though she had aged in a few hours. She would be glad to be in the quiet, familiar surroundings of her bedchamber.

Entering Anna-Maria's room, Sarah's face flushed with pleasure as her eyes traveled over the ornately carved mantel beneath which a cheerful fire glowed, the old, mellow linen-fold paneling, and the intricately embroidered bed curtains and window hangings.

She dropped her bag of possessions down on the floor and moved over to the bed, poking an exploratory finger into the feather mattress. Sighing voluptuously, Sarah glanced around the room with a feeling of homecoming. She had missed the luxuries of life more than she had realized.

Anna-Maria watched her with a stirring of curiosity. When they had talked in the gypsy clearing, she had assumed that Sarah was the daughter of a farmer, perhaps a gentleman farmer. But now—Anna-Maria knitted her brows in puzzlement. Sarah was unconsciously holding her head high on her slender neck, and she moved about the room with easy familiarity, gently touching objects as they caught her fancy. There was the same air of ease and high breeding about her that characterized Anna-Maria herself. Anna-Maria shook her head at the absurdity of the thought. No young woman of her own station would run away and live with the gypsies. Hesitantly she asked, "Sarah, wouldn't it be better for you if you returned to your father's house and begged his mercy?"

Sarah shook her head emphatically. "Never. He'd find some way to barter me in the marriage market for his own gain. When I lie in a man's arms, I want it to be because I am on fire with desire for him, not because gold is trickling into my father's greedy hands."

Anna-Maria blushed. She had felt desire in the gypsy's arms, and the memory embarrassed her. She turned her back hastily to Sarah and swept aside the gleaming masses of her hair. "Please unfasten my gown. I want to wash away the touch of the gypsy's hands." She shivered a little, remembering the way his muscles had rippled under the smooth bronze of his chest.

Sarah looked momentarily startled, then giving a small smile, she obediently reached out and began undoing the intricate hooks at the neck of Anna-Maria's gown. She was silent for a moment and then said suddenly, "All the same, that Ramon is a good-looking animal."

Anna-Maria wanted to ask if Sarah had ever been kissed by Ramon and then was horrified by her own curiosity. She pulled away quickly from Sarah and went to cool her face with handfuls of water from the silver pitcher that sat on a gleaming oak chest. What on earth was wrong with her? It was of no possible interest to her if Sarah and the gypsy had kissed.

She felt a sudden wave of fatigue and threw a longing glance at the feather bed. She needed to be alone, to sort out her thoughts and get control of them. She yawned openly. "Sarah, are you hungry? If you are, go down to the kitchen and tell the cook to cut you a slice from the joint. I'm going to take a nap."

Climbing into bed, Anna-Maria turned her face into the pillow, giving a sigh of comfort. She thought that she was too tired to dream, but images of the gypsy troubled her sleep. Often the gypsy's face merged with a strange one, and she strained in her dream to see it more clearly, realizing that it was the face of the earl. In her sleep she put up her finger and gently traced the outline of her lips, as though she were feeling the pressure of a kiss.

Three

"My lord." Anna-Maria, her delicate chin held proudly high, offered her hand to the earl of Shrewsbury.

As the earl bent to kiss her slender hand, Anna-Maria seized the opportunity to study him. His features were pleasant without being handsome, and, to her relief, he looked younger than she had expected, certainly younger than her father.

The earl raised his head, and Anna-Maria noted

with relief that his brown eyes were kind, his voice gentle. "You are even more beautiful than when I saw you last."

The earl would hardly be flattered if he knew that she had no memory of their last meeting. Quickly, to cover her thoughts, she inclined her head gracefully toward a pair of heavily carved armchairs that were drawn up before a crackling fire. "Will you sit, my lord?"

They were in the smallest of the reception rooms. Light blue silk draperies hung at the windows, and the color was echoed in the furnishings. The earl smiled and sat, stretching his booted legs toward the fire. Anna-Maria busied herself pouring wine from a crystal decanter into two long-stemmed glasses. As she handed the earl one of the glasses, their fingers brushed, and Anna-Maria found herself blushing. Was it possible that this man was to be her husband? That in time his touch would be as familiar to her as the feel of her own hair swinging forward against her cheek? She sat down across from the earl, carefully arranging her new Parisian gown into becoming lines. For a moment she stroked the silk skirt complacently and then was struck by doubt. Surely in this pale blue room an equally pale blue gown had been a poor choice—she might blend into the furniture. But as she looked up, she caught an unmistakable glint of admiration in the earl's eyes. Flustered, she raised her delicate crystal glass and took a sip of the wine, grateful for its quick warmth.

"Was your journey difficult, my lord?"

"No. The roads were dry, and the air is so clear that it acts as a tonic."

God's blood! the earl thought. The girl was exquisite. There was a lilt in her voice that enchanted him, and her smile was more intoxicating than the wine he was sipping.

He leaned forward to bring himself closer to Anna-Maria and said softly, "There is much that we must learn about each other."

Anna-Maria had been well schooled by her father. Raising her long dark lashes, she looked fully at the earl. "I know that you were captain of a horse troop under King Charles and that you served him bravely." She bit back her next words. After the war had been lost, the earl had compromised with Cromwell's government, paying a heavy fine for the privilege of keeping his estates. Anna-Maria would have found it more romantic if the earl had been willing to lose everything for the Royalist cause. Sighing, she pushed the thought away. She wanted very much to like this man.

The earl balanced his wineglass on his knee and twirled it between his blunt fingers. "There is talk that the young prince will be invited to take the throne as Charles the Second." He laughed shortly. "Although he is young no longer, nor am I. He is nearly thirty now, and I am thirty-five."

Anna-Maria stole a covert glance at him. The earl had a sprinkling of gray in his brown hair and beard, and she shivered a little, fancying that Death had already touched him with frosty fingers.

"If the prince takes the throne, my future will be bright. Charles will be grateful for the service I gave his father. I'll be expected to take my place among the powerful men at court." Anna-Maria felt her breath quickening a little. How wonderful to be a member of a royal court, to have the great and noble as your intimate friends.

The earl looked at her for a moment, yearning clearly written in his face. Setting his glass down on a small inlaid table, he reached forward, gently taking Anna-Maria's glass from her slim fingers. He set it down with a decisive click and then drew Anna-Maria's hands into both his own. "Anna-Maria, surely it is no secret why I am here. I want to marry you, and your father is agreeable to the match. Already his lawyers and mine are negotiating." He made a gesture of dismissal as though the details of Anna-Maria's dowry were of no importance to him.

Again Anna-Maria felt a flash of cynicism. The earl was pretending that he had no interest in the financial aspects of their marriage, but if that were true he would have pressed his suit last spring when he was first attracted to her. It had taken the rumor of the king's restoration and the possible return of Anna-Maria's estates to bring him here today. What hypocrites people were.

"Well, Anna-Maria?" The earl's voice was gentle.

Anna-Maria raised her eyes and said quickly, without giving herself time for thought, "I'll be honored to marry you, my lord."

With those words, she had given her future into this stranger's hands. Suddenly she felt like screaming out, "No!" and then fleeing the room, but common sense held her rooted to her chair. The earl's question was a mere formality. Anna-Maria knew that the matter of her marriage had really been settled nearly three hours ago when the earl and her father had been closeted together. If Anna-Maria refused, her father, despite his love for her, would force her into the marriage. The earl, his face lighting with pleasure, drew her out of the chair and into his arms.

How strange. She had been out of the convent scarcely a week, and now twice in two days she was being held in male arms. The earl had none of the musky, sun-warmed scent of the gypsy. His body gave off a faint, clean odor lightly overlaid with a spicy perfume. He was fairly short so that his head was only a few inches above Anna-Maria's. Standing in the circle of his arms, she looked at him with a faint wonder. Yesterday when the gypsy had kissed her, something in her had leaped in response. Only her sense of wrongdoing had made her pull from his arms. But there was nothing wrong in kissing the earl. Indeed, she would be doing it for the rest of her life. In expectation of pleasure, she unconsciously tilted her face toward his, and the earl bent and kissed her fully on the lips.

Instead of feeling pleasure, Anna-Maria wanted to cry. The earl's lips were dry and narrow, and she felt no joy, no response, nothing of what she had felt when the gypsy had kissed her. When the earl released her mouth, she bent her head quickly so that her hair would shield her face. "We'd best rejoin my parents, my lord."

The earl, mistaking her downbent head for maidenly shyness, reminded himself that she was fresh from a convent. Gently he released her. When they emerged into the great hall, Anna-Maria was relieved to find her parents eagerly awaiting them. They walked together into the dining hall.

Lord and Lady Brudenell might be poorer than the earl, but they were determined that he should not find their hospitality wanting. There was buttered shrimp, smoked oysters, flaky crusted meat pies, quail, pheasant, an entire roast lamb, a boar's head with an apple shining between his tusks. The rich odors made Anna-Maria feel slightly nauseated, and she put down her fork in despair.

The meal seemed interminable to her. She sat directly opposite the earl, but fortunately the table was wide, and the heaped dishes formed a partial barrier between them. Her father, in a hearty, expansive frame of mind, engaged most of the earl's attention. Anna-Maria's back ached, and her legs were trembling with fatigue and tension. The entire household had been awake long before dawn this morning in preparation for the earl's arrival. Lady Brudenell had wanted Anna-Maria to sleep late so that she would be fresh when she greeted the earl, but the noise and bustle in the household and Anna-Maria's own inner restlessness had driven her from her bed.

Anna-Maria sighed and tried again to force down a mouthful of food.

The earl looked over at Anna-Maria and caught her attention. He was just biting into a hunk of roast; a rivulet of rich gravy spurted from the meat, trailing down his chin. Snatching up his napkin, he dabbed at the gravy. Anna-Maria sighed in relief. She couldn't have faced life with him if he were careless at the table. She was repulsed when she thought of his kissing her while his beard bore the scents and stains of their latest meal.

Marriage. Anna-Maria picked up her wineglass and looked curiously at her parents. Her mother was leaning forward to speak animatedly to the earl. Had her parents been strangers when they married? They seemed so much a part of each other that she had never thought to ask. And yet, once they had been young. Once her mother must have sat trembling, her fingers gripping the stem of her wineglass too tightly, looking with apprehension at the stranger who sat opposite her, wondering if he would be good to her, wondering what their life would be like together.

Anna-Maria had eaten nothing, and her nerves were strained to the breaking point by the time the meal was finished. Her father was frankly intoxicated now, and even her fastidious mother seemed a bit giddy with wine, laughing frequently in a high-pitched tone that Anna-Maria had never heard before. They both seemed so happy, she thought, feeling a surge of tenderness for them. These past years had been hard for them, and they were relieved that their daughter was to make such a splendid marriage.

At last the earl rose and pushed his chair away from the table. "Your hospitality has been so gracious that I have overstayed myself."

Lord and Lady Brudenell chorused a protest. They had thought he would stay and have supper with them. They had prepared a chamber for him, certain that he would stay the night.

"It would have given me great pleasure, but I have urgent business in London in the morn. And now that I am to be married," he added, smiling at Anna-Maria, "I've much reason to insure that my business affairs are in order."

Grateful that he was leaving, Anna-Maria gave him a smile that warmed her eyes. Instantly he was at her side, picking up her hand and kissing it. His lips had an insistent, intimate pressure. Anna-Maria stared down at his brown hair, wondering what she really felt about him. At this moment she felt only relief that he was leaving. She wanted to be alone with her thoughts. Feeling guilty, she put an excessive warmth into her farewells and was rewarded by seeing a gratified gleam in her father's eyes.

The earl cupped her chin and placed a kiss full on her lips before swinging into his coach. His breath reeked of the rich meal he had just eaten and the various wines he had consumed, and Anna-Maria's delicate nostrils flared in distaste.

As soon as his coach was in motion, Anna-Maria flew into the house and snatched up her cloak. At her mother's startled protest, she explained, "My head is aching. I'm going to walk in the woods until it clears."

Her mother nodded and hugged her. "We're very proud of you, Anna-Maria."

Anna-Maria ran towards the woods, glorying in the freedom of motion after so many long hours sitting cramped at the table. How crisp the October air felt. It was cleansing her, taking her chaotic thoughts and tossing them from her mind, the way it tore the leaves from the trees. She ran until she was winded and then slowed down, laughing aloud with the little breath that was left to her.

After a few moments, however, she sobered, thinking of her impending marriage. She whispered his name, trying it on her tongue. "Francis." How many times would she use it in her lifetime? A million? "Francis, may we hold a small reception on Tuesday fortnight?" "Francis, here is my dressmaker's bill. I fear I've been extravagant again." Or, her breath quickened at the thought, "Francis, we are to have a child."

She bent to pick up a bright gold leaf and began twirling it between her fingers. He *is* nice, she thought. His eyes are kind, and he seemed anxious to please me. She felt a quick regret for something she had never known and then shook her shoulders impatiently. Romantic love existed only between the pages of the novels that the girls had smuggled into the convent to read beneath the bedcovers. In real life, people married and love came later.

Head bent, she began kicking at the spilled leaves covering the path. On either side of her, the century-old trees soared heavenward, making a silent cathedral.

Then a deep laugh rent the air, terrifying her and checking her in her tracks. Heart pounding, she looked up and saw the gypsy, Ramon, just emerging from behind the trunk of a large oak. He stood before her with his hands on his hips.

Anna-Maria stared at him, her mouth falling slightly open. His appearance had been so sudden, so unexpected, that she could not collect her wits.

Ramon's white teeth flashed in his dark face. "We're breaking camp." He jerked his thumb in the direction of the gypsy caravans. " 'Tis good luck that you chose this moment to walk in the woods. In an hour I'll be gone." His sensuous lips curved in a smile. "We've unfinished business, my love."

Anna-Maria stared at him wordlessly, her eyes enormous in the delicate oval of her face. Involuntarily, her senses stirred. He radiated such life and vitality, laughter rich on his face, his bronze skin gleaming in the sun.

Before she could speak, he reached out and pulled her into his arms. Anna-Maria was so surprised that for a moment she fell toward him without resisting. His tanned hands clasped her slim waist and his dark face bent toward hers, blotting out the sun. As his lips met hers, Anna-Maria felt for a moment that she was reliving yesterday's experience. The warm male scent of him, the tantalizing pressure of his lips. Once again she felt the traitorous melting sensation that weakened her limbs, causing her to sway in his arms.

The bruising pressure of his lips sent a shiver down her spine, and unconsciously she curved her body against his, savoring his male hardness. Ramon laughed and began trailing kisses down her face and throat, leaving flames in their wake. Anna-Maria had never felt so vividly alive as she did at this moment, so pleasurably aware of her flesh.

Ramon's hand was on one of her rounded breasts now, leisurely caressing it. The sensation was delicious, and Anna-Maria closed her eyes, feeling the sunlight against her lids.

Then, suddenly horrified by her own emotions, she put her small hands against Ramon's shoulders and sought to push him away. He made an inarticulate sound and pulled her closer, deepening the pressure of his lips against hers. Anna-Maria tore her mouth free and arched against his encircling arm, leaning as far back as she could. "Please stop!" Her voice was breathless.

The arching movement forced her breasts upward, straining against the blue fabric of her gown. They were temptingly close to Ramon's bent head. His eyes began to glisten, a thin film of excitement glazing them. Still imprisoning her with one hand, he reached up with the other and tore her gown from neckline to waist. The delicate white lace of Anna-Maria's busk sprang into view. Impatiently Ramon tangled his strong fingers into the thin fabric and ripped again.

Dazed, uncomprehending, Anna-Maria stared down at the torn material. Ramon's eyes were gazing in fascination at her bared breasts. They were white and rounded, tipped with soft pink nipples. Her narrow rib cage and slender waist made them look even more full by comparison. As the cold October air chilled her naked breasts, her nipples stiffened and pointed. Ramon, thinking it a sign of her passion, gave a husky laugh of triumph and bent his mouth to one pink nipple, lightly grazing it with his tongue.

For a moment, Anna-Maria went limp with terror. Romantic novels, which always ended with a stirring kiss, had not prepared her for this. She was naked to the waist, and a stranger was fondling her breasts as though he had perfect freedom of her body. His hot kisses, his caressing hands seemed to be everywhere on her body creating a warm forbidden pleasure.

Then, frantic to escape his exploring hands and mouth, she began struggling violently, twisting and turning in his arms to free herself. The movements of her slim young body only served to inflame Ramon's passion. Anna-Maria was panting, her lips parted. Catching his hand in Anna-Maria's silky hair, Ramon forced her into a painfully bruising kiss. His tongue probed her mouth until Anna-Maria thought she would faint. She jerked her head from side to side, vainly trying to push words of protest past his probing tongue.

Fire burst in Ramon's loins. Without breaking his

kiss, he lifted Anna-Maria in his arms and deposited her on a bed of leaves. The cold earth shocked her. She tried to speak, but tears were pouring from her eyes, clogging her throat. She whimpered, trying to plead with him, but she knew that she was powerless.

Ramon, his hot gaze on her nakedness, ignored her protests. Standing, he began fumbling with his breeches. Anna-Maria followed the direction of his movements, and her eyes widened. It was as though he had a small animal confined in his breeches, a live thing that leaped and thrust in an attempt to be free. Sudden understanding ripped across her mind, and she closed her eyes, terrified at what she might see if she left them open. One of the girls at the convent had bragged that she had seen her brother's naked male organ. When words proved inadequate to describe it, she had made a rapid drawing on her sketch pad, a thick rodlike shape. Dropping her voice to a whisper, she had said, "They take it and put it into you, *down there.*"

Frantic to escape, Anna-Maria began to scramble to her knees. But the leaves were slippery, and they sent her sprawling. Ramon put out his foot and turned her over with the ease of superior strength. Anna-Maria stared up at him, her eyes growing larger and larger until they were like black pools as she caught sight of his male organ. It quivered above her, and to her terrified gaze it seemed enormous.

She began to gasp, believing that she would strangle on her own trapped breath, and she was glad of it. If only she could die before worse happened to her. Sweet Virgin, she prayed, let me die while I am still without sin, Blessed Virgin . . .

She gave a whimper of terror as she felt his strong fingers sliding under her waistband. With a quick movement he tore her clothing from waist to hem, exposing her slim thighs, her slender, curved hips. At the sound of rending fabric, Anna-Maria screamed. Instantly Ramon's dark hand was over her mouth, forcing the scream back into her throat. Anna-Maria frantically whipped her head from side to side, sending her chestnut hair streaming over the red and gold leaves. The wind was playing across her naked body, chilling her and driving home the knowledge that she was totally exposed to the gypsy's gaze.

Suddenly Ramon was on top of her, pinning down her writhing body, pressing her deeper into the leaves. Anna-Maria felt a hardness pressing against her thigh. It leaped and moved, and suddenly the full extent of her danger burst upon her. She moaned in frantic protest, but he swiftly took her mouth in a passionate kiss, muffling her cries.

Ramon's loins were on fire, and he was scarcely aware of Anna-Maria as a human being. She was silky, fragrant hair that teased his nostrils, rounded breasts that molded against his cupped hands, a fire-warmed belly, and soft, slender hips. His desire mounting, he reached down and, with one swift movement, parted her soft thighs. Anna-Maria instinctively tried to cross her legs, but he was too strong for her. With humiliating ease, he forced her legs apart. For a moment he lifted his body from hers, and Anna-Maria felt a quick relief. The next moment she felt his hot breath on her face, his male organ thrusting between her thighs.

"No, no, no." She writhed and kicked, desperately trying to rake his tanned face with her fingernails. He laughed and caught both her slender wrists in one of his strong hands, pinning her arms over her head. Tears of helplessness spilled from her eyes.

Ramon was between her thighs now, painfully assaulting her. Suddenly he gave an exultant animal cry and pressed against her with renewed force. Sweet Jesu, he had torn her! She had been ripped open by the force of his thrusting. A burning pain seared her loins, and she thrashed wildly to escape it.

Ramon checked his movements, looking down at Anna-Maria with shock in his eyes. Then he began thrusting even more deeply, his passion so great that he could not contain himself.

Shocked, dazed, and humiliated, Anna-Maria could no longer fight. She lay limp and unresisting while he thrust again and again, his movements rhythmic. Finally he gave a low cry and collapsed against her. His weight was suffocating, but it didn't matter. Nothing mattered. Dully, Anna-Maria waited to see what he would do with her next.

Ramon's ragged breathing gradually slowed. Reluctantly, he rose from Anna-Maria and began rearranging his clothing. His eyes narrowing, he stared at a spot of blood visible on a gold leaf between Anna-Maria's parted thighs. As he watched, Anna-Maria sat up and looked wonderingly at the blood. Then she fainted.

Ramon leaped forward, staring down at her in dismay. Her oval face was deathly white, her slim, curved body sprawled lifelessly. Ramon knelt down and began arranging her clothing. Her torn gown gave her scant covering, so Ramon carefully drew her cloak tightly around her naked limbs. She lay without stirring, and suddenly he was frightened. He must rejoin the caravan and leave these parts before she awakened. To rape the highborn daughter of the manor house was a serious business indeed. It could cost him his life. Surely she would regain consciousness within minutes. He gently grazed her cold lips with a farewell kiss, his senses stirring again as he touched her. In a moment he was gone, racing lightly through the woods toward the departing gypsies.

Cold. She was so cold. Her body ached. Bewildered, Anna-Maria opened her eyes and found herself staring into a darkening sky, the trees looming blackly above her. For a moment she was puzzled; then memories flooded in, and she turned her head, frantically fearful of seeing the gypsy's dark face. Relief at finding him gone was followed by intense humiliation as she remembered what had happened.

Painfully she rose and stood shakily, trying to force life back into her body. She must get back to Deene, must scrub the gypsy's touch from her bruised flesh. Moving slowly, like an old woman, she began her journey. How often she had run lightly through these woods, and yet now each step was a painful effort. Was her penance for her sin to journey forever in the

direction of Deene and never reach it? Tears spilled
down her cheeks, wetting her cloak, but she was entirely unaware of them. She drew a deep, shaking
breath as she emerged from the woods and onto the
lawn. Moving furtively, she tried to walk across the
open space without being seen. She could not bear any
eyes upon her, any witness to her shameful state. Deep
inside her there was a longing to seek out her mother
and throw herself into her arms as she had done when
she was a child, but not until she had soaked in a hot
bath and scrubbed away the gypsy's touch.

Reaching the manor house, she kept close to the
wall, turned a corner, and slipped through a rear entrance. Her heart lurched painfully when she spied a
buxom figure. The housemaid, Maggie, was staring at
Anna-Maria in horror, her hands flung up in surprise.

"My lady! Whatever has happened to you?"

Anna-Maria's dazed mind worked more quickly
than she would have thought possible. "I fell in the
woods, but I'm not hurt. Maggie, I need a bath. Send
the maids up with hot water as quickly as you can."

She stood by passively while three young serving
maids carried a tub into her chamber and filled it with
pitcher after pitcher of steaming hot water. When her
bath was ready, she sent them all out of the room, refusing assistance. She could let no one see her bruised
body.

She slipped into the tub while the water was still
so hot that it turned her fair skin a fiery pink. Instantly it began its magic, soothing her aches, and Anna-
Maria leaned her head against the rim of the tub,
wishing that she could lie here forever. If only she
could simply enjoy the creature comforts of life, without ever having to think.

There was a quick tap on the door, and then Sarah
entered without waiting for permission. "What happened to you? Maggie says that you fell in the woods."

As she came closer, her jaw dropped open in astonishment. Anna-Maria had not yet washed her hair,
and it was still caught with twigs and shreds of leaves,
but what caused Sarah to narrow her eyes in suspicion

were the numerous small bruises on Anna-Maria's throat and breasts, traces of kisses. "A fall in the woods caused this damage?"

"I climbed on a rock and—" Anna-Maria suddenly broke off her lie and burst into tears. "Sarah, he deflowered me!"

"Who?"

Anna-Maria felt that to say Ramon's name would betray her guilty intimacy. "The gypsy."

Sarah swiftly knelt by the tub and put a comforting arm around Anna-Maria's slippery wet shoulders. "He's an animal. He'll hang for this day's work!" Then she sat back on her heels, a look of dismay crossing her freckled face. "Nay, he'll not hang because we must keep his secret. To punish him is to shout to all the world that you are no longer virgin."

"Everyone will know soon enough." Anna-Maria flinched at the thought. Only a few hours ago she had left this house a virgin, betrothed to be married. Now, such a short time later, her life was ruined. No one would ever marry her. She could not even enter a convent except as a lay nun, one of those women who, having lost her virginity, was allowed to do only the menial tasks of the convent and could not join the other nuns in the more spiritual duties.

"No one need ever know!" Sarah's voice was passionate. "Anna-Maria, you must swear never to tell, or your life will be ruined."

"Sarah, won't the earl know that I am no longer a virgin?"

Sarah shook her head emphatically. "You are not wanton. Your timidity, your shyness will convince him that you are a virgin. As for the membrane, many women rupture it when riding horseback."

Anna-Maria flinched, remembering the searing pain in her loins when the gypsy had entered her. "Sarah, does it always hurt so much?" She would have endless nights in bed with the earl.

Sarah shrugged. "I don't know. My mother said that a woman must put up with lovemaking because men set such great store by it."

Anna-Maria sighed. She would endure whatever came.

Anna-Maria sank back into the warm, soothing water, her eyes closed. Sarah's reassuring conversation gradually faded, and she began remembering the afternoon. She had *liked* the gypsy's kiss, had wanted that sweet sensation to go on forever. Even when he had first touched her breast, she had not wanted him to stop because the sensation had been so pleasurable. She flushed guiltily remembering how she had melted in the gypsy's arms, had curved her body to fit his. Suddenly the gypsy woman's words sprang into her mind. "Yours is a hot nature, lustful, and all your life you will crave a man's embraces." Resolutely Anna-Maria tightened her trembling lips. She was *not* wanton. She would be a loving and faithful wife and never again—never!—would she abandon herself in a man's arms as she had done today.

Four

For her parents' sake, Anna-Maria threw herself into the wedding preparations. She knew that the truth would be devastating to them. If she refused to marry, Anna-Maria would have no choice but to remain at home and be a lifelong burden on her parents or to enter a convent.

Sometimes she felt that if it were not for Sarah she would go mad. With everyone else she had to wear a mask, to pretend to be a happy, carefree bride. It was only with Sarah—who knew her secret and did not condemn her—that she could drop her pretense and pour out the worries and fears that plagued her. Their friendship deepened daily. Anna-Maria unconsciously found herself treating Sarah as an equal instead of a serving woman. And indeed, there was a nagging odd-

ity about Sarah. She performed her duties as a serving woman quickly and deftly, but there was an air
of playacting about her actions, as though she had
set herself a role and was acting it to perfection. Sometimes Anna-Maria found herself stealing covert glances
at Sarah, noting the delicacy of her wrists and ankles
and the grace of her movements, and wondered about
her origins. Once, unthinkingly, Anna-Maria had
spoken to her in French, and Sarah had replied swiftly
in the same language, then caught herself and fell
silent, biting her lips in vexation. Anna-Maria tactfully smoothed over the moment and stifled the questions she was longing to voice. She could not repay
Sarah's kindness by invading her privacy.

One evening, as Sarah was brushing her hair, Anna-
Maria said, "Sarah, I don't know what I would do
without you. My secret weighs so heavily on my conscience that if I did not have you to confide in, I
could not bear it."

Sarah was silent for a moment, bringing the brush
in long, smooth strokes down Anna-Maria's chestnut
hair. Then she came to a decision. "Aye, a secret is a
lonely burden. I've been carrying one myself, and now
our friendship has reached such a point that I've a
mind to confide in you. If you wish to hear it?" She
looked at Anna-Maria questioningly, their eyes meeting in the mirror.

Anna-Maria nodded gravely. "I'll keep your secret
faithfully." She swung around on the dressing stool
to face Sarah and then waited.

Sarah took a deep breath and then said quietly,
"I'm Lady Sarah Devon."

Anna-Maria gasped, and then her eyes lit. "I suspected it. But Sarah, then how could you bear to live
among the gypsies? And how can you humiliate yourself by acting as my serving woman?"

Sarah smiled affectionately. " 'Tis hardly a *humiliation* to be serving you. You have ever treated me as a
friend. And living among the gypsies—even with all
their filth and coarseness—was better than spending
my wedding night in the arms of a man I loathed."
She shuddered slightly. "My father was trying to force

me into marriage with a neighbor of ours, a repulsive old man with vicious habits. I was sickened everytime his glance swept over me." Her mouth twisted bitterly. "But he was vastly rich, and my father coveted his fortune. My father lost most of his fortune supporting the king during the civil war. Since then we've been on the verge of poverty. About all we have left is a manor house in Kent—and the roof needs mending, the brick work is crumbling."

Anna-Maria felt instant sympathy. Sarah's situation was similar to her own. And yet her father was vastly different from Sarah's. And although she didn't love the earl yet, she didn't fear and loathe him. She shuddered slightly, thinking how much worse her own situation might have been, and then she jumped to her feet and hugged Sarah sympathetically. "Sarah, I'm so glad you have told me. We can tell my parents at once, and they will treat you as our honored guest."

Sarah stiffened and pulled away slightly, her voice cool. "You promised to keep my secret."

Anna-Maria let her arms drop. "Aye, and I will if you bid me to do so. But Sarah, if you let me tell my parents, you can resume your title and live here as my friend instead of as a servant."

A cynical smile touched Sarah's lips. "Can you imagine the gossip?" Suddenly she did an uncannily accurate imitation of one old dowager gossiping to another. "Have you heard, my dear? Lady Sarah Devon is staying with Lord and Lady Brudenell. I hear that the little minx ran away from home, and Lord Devon has been scouring the countryside for her." She dropped her imitation and said dispiritedly, " 'Tis no use. My father would come to reclaim me, and he'd force me into marriage."

Anna-Maria's dark eyes were troubled as she searched Sarah's face. "Then what's to be done?"

"Nothing. I want to go on as before. As your serving maid."

"But your future? How can you marry a man of your own rank if you go about disguised as a serving maid?"

Sarah shrugged and said with a coolness that took

Anna-Maria's breath away, "Perhaps my father will die." A shadow crossed Sarah's face as she remembered a lifetime of cruelty at her father's hand. Then she abruptly shook off her mood and pretended gaiety as she swept Anna-Maria a deep curtsy. "Lady Sarah Devon at your service. Will you accept me as your serving maid?"

Anna-Maria laughed shakily, so full of pity for Sarah that she was on the verge of tears. "I'll accept you as my dear *friend*. And I'll continue to pretend that you are my serving maid if you wish."

Sarah smiled her thanks, her eyes bright with unshed tears, and then gestured with the brush. "Then sit down again so I can finish brushing your hair."

Anna-Maria sat obediently, her thoughts in a turmoil, seeking a way out of Sarah's plight.

Sarah angrily told tale after tale of her father's neglect and cruelty. "If my mother had lived, my life would have been different. Often I feel a sense of loss —of envy—when I see how your mother loves you."

Anna-Maria's heart ached with pity. In the days that followed, she encouraged Sarah to pour out her pent-up bitterness and noted that the telling seemed to relieve Sarah. Often Sarah returned to the theme of her mother's death.

Anna-Maria nodded. She could not imagine what her life would have been without her mother's steady love. "It is only for my mother's sake that I am going through with my marriage. Otherwise I would run away as you did, although I lack your courage. But Sarah, I can't hurt my mother. She is so happy these days!"

She had watched her mother going about the wedding preparations with a look of deep contentment on her face, humming as she performed her tasks. The sight of her mother's happiness strengthened Anna-Maria's resolution.

One morning Lady Brudenell took Anna-Maria's face between her cool, verbena-scented hands and said softly, "You are so fortunate, my darling. And I'm so happy for you! Time goes by so quickly. It seems but yesterday that you were a babe." She smoothed back a tendril of Anna-Maria's hair. " 'Tis strange to think that on the same day you are to become both a wife and mother."

Lady Brudenell saw her daughter's surprised expression and asked, "Anna-Maria, did the earl neglect to tell you?" She clicked her tongue in exasperation. "Men can be so thoughtless, so impractical."

"Tell me what?" Anna-Maria had seen the earl but once. Since then he had been busy in London arranging his affairs.

"That you are to be a stepmother. He has a little daughter by his dead wife. The child is about three years old now."

"Oh, I wish he *had* told me. I'd have been so pleased." Anna-Maria's face flamed into radiance. It was more than she could have hoped for, a miracle. For the first time in weeks, she felt a genuine surge of happiness.

Lady Brudenell made a dismissing gesture of forgiveness. "He is so besotted with you, poor man, that he can scarce be blamed for forgetting his wits."

The approaching wedding took on new meaning for Anna-Maria now that she had learned she was to be a mother as well as a wife. There was an air of frenzied preparation at Deene, and Anna-Maria occasionally found herself humming as she went about her tasks, the thought of the child warming her.

She was still troubled, though, about Sarah and worried because she could see no solution to Sarah's difficulty. Sarah protested, laughing, "But Anna-Maria, I'm perfectly happy. I take each day as it comes without fretting too much about the future. Someday I'm sure that I'll want to be Lady Sarah Devon again, but right now I'm content as plain Sarah, the serving woman." She teased, "Don't you want me to go with you when you get married?"

"Selfishly yes," Anna-Maria admitted. "I think I would die if you did not. I've come to rely on you so."

"Then stop fretting about matters you cannot

change," Sarah advised practically. "I'm quite convinced that something wonderful is going to happen to me someday, and I'm content to wait."

Anna-Maria tried to follow Sarah's advice and busy herself with the wedding preparations, but many of the arrangements were out of her hands. Her father was frequently closeted with the earl's lawyers, working out the details of Anna-Maria's dowry and calculating to the last farthing the amount of her jointure—the money and land that was to be hers if the earl died before her. He emerged from these meetings triumphant, boasting of his astuteness, and Anna-Maria was called on only to listen to the details and heap him with praise.

Lady Brudenell was preparing Anna-Maria's trousseau, the linens, bedcoverings, and wardrobe that she must take into her marriage. Even though time pressed, Lady Brudenell was determined that the trousseau should not shame them, and she kept the maids at their sewing until they were red-eyed and on the point of tears.

The tension eased a little when Anna-Maria's half-sister, Mary, returned home. Anna-Maria had been longing to see Mary again. Mary was Robert Brudenell's daughter by his first marriage, but Anna-Maria and Mary had been as close as full sisters. When Mary's mother had died and her father had remarried, she had shown no signs of jealousy of her stepmother, and when Anna-Maria was born Mary had been delighted.

When the sound of Mary's coach was heard approaching Deene, Anna-Maria flew out the door and caught Mary in her arms just as she alighted. "I've missed you so! How dare you be away when I came home?"

Mary, reeling a little under the force of Anna-Maria's embrace, laughed, "Darling, I didn't want to be away, but Cousin Elizabeth was ill and she sent for me."

Anna-Maria clung to her hand affectionately. "I'm

so glad that you are here now. There are a million preparations to be made and we need you."

Lady Brudenell was waiting to greet her stepdaughter and the two women exchanged a look of deep regard before embracing. Watching them, Anna-Maria was suddenly struck by an idea. Eagerly she told Mary, "When I marry I will also find myself the mother of a stepdaughter named Polly, just as my mother did. I hope that we will love each other the way you two do."

Mary touched her cheek gently, "I'm sure you will. Be your normal, loving self, Anna-Maria, and the child will adore you."

Mary was famous for her needlework, and she was delighted to take on the finer sewing for Anna-Maria's dowry chest. She sat late by candlelight, taking infinitely painstaking stitches. Her special joy was sewing hundreds of blue-ribbon love knots onto Anna-Maria's white wedding gown. Each was fastened by a single stitch, to make it easier for the exuberant wedding guests to tear them from the gown after the wedding ceremony.

The old wedding customs had been forbidden by the Rump Parliament who decreed that only a brief civil ceremony was needed. During the drab civil ceremony, at the Church of St. Giles in London, Anna-Maria would be forced to wear a plain brown gown. But later, Mary's eyes sparkled at the thought, there would be a *real* wedding, performed by a priest at the earl of Shrewsbury's home, Grafton Manor.

Mary held up the plain brown gown and inspected it critically. "Thank God you are so beautiful, Anna-Maria. Even this plain gown will not be able to dim your beauty." She bit off her thread neatly and then said anxiously, "But you must remember to pinch your cheeks just before the ceremony. You need color in your face when you are wearing this shade."

Anna-Maria laughed. "You must remember for me. No doubt I'll be too nervous."

Faithful to her word, on the day of the wedding, Mary pinched Anna-Maria's cheeks until she protested. They were standing outside the Church of St. Giles in the Fields, London, waiting for the civil ceremony to begin. Anna-Maria was so nervous that she had difficulty in catching her breath, and she kept reminding herself that this was a mere legal formality and not a real wedding at all. She must look like a little brown wren in this drab dress, with her hair tucked back in a demure knot. Reading her thoughts, Mary said quickly, "You look lovely," and gave Anna-Maria's hand an affectionate squeeze.

The door opened, and the justice of the peace, Peter Bradshaw, beckoned them inside. Anna-Maria gave her parents and Mary a smile, hoping that they would not notice the trembling of her lips, and then stepped into the dim interior. There was no music, no banked flowers, only the earl standing before the altar looking at Anna-Maria with tenderness in his eyes. Just a few people were present. Most of their guests had scorned the civil ceremony, preferring to wait for the religious one later in the day.

The earl, dressed in a simple suit of gray, his brown hair pulled back in a queue, reached out for Anna-Maria's hand. She swallowed nervously and put her hand into his. Suppose she were to blurt out right now, "I am not what you think me. I am not a virgin." It was hard to keep a still tongue when she looked into his honest brown eyes. But if she spoke, the quiet happiness in his eyes would turn swiftly to pain. Both her own reputation and that of her parents would be ruined. She took a deep breath, willed her heart to stop its erratic pounding, and gave the earl a quiet smile.

Peter Bradshaw, bulky and somewhat coarse looking, cleared his throat self-importantly. "I am ready to begin."

Anna-Maria was acutely conscious of the earl's hand enfolding hers. It was dry and warm and held hers so firmly that she began to feel secure.

The earl's face was grave as he listened to Peter Bradshaw read the brief ceremony. When it was time to make his vows, his voice was calm and strong. "I, Francis Talbot, do here in the presence of God, take thee, Anna-Maria, for my lawful wedded wife. . . ."

Oh, I'll be safe with this man, Anna-Maria thought. Safe and happy. No man will ever dare ravage me while I am under his protection.

Her own voice was shaking as she repeated the vows, but her eyes were grateful as she turned a tender glance on the earl. After the ceremony, the earl, anxious to be alone with Anna-Maria, made short work of the congratulations, saying he hoped to see the guests later at Grafton Manor. Then he bundled Anna-Maria into his coach. They had a fairly long ride ahead of them, into Worcestershire, and as Anna-Maria stepped into the coach, she noted that he had made every preparation for her comfort. There were heavy fur rugs to cover their legs, two burning braziers for their feet, and a wicker basket that looked promisingly stuffed with delicacies.

She wanted to say something special, her first words alone to him as his wife, but she found her tongue suddenly silent.

Francis came to her rescue, tilting her chin and looking down into her face. "No man has ever been more fortunate in his choice of a wife, Anna-Maria. I'm deeply honored that you accepted me."

"I'll be a good wife to you," Anna-Maria said, with the intensity of a vow.

She would spend her life pleasing this man, rearing good, strong children, and eventually she would feel clean and whole again. The incident in the woods with the handsome gypsy would begin to fade from her memory, and by the time she was an old and respected lady, it would be entirely gone.

The earl cupped her chin and raised her face toward his. He sought her lips, and Anna-Maria willed herself to respond. Because of her experience, a male touch frightened her, but this was her husband, and she must give no sign of her fear.

The earl kissed her deeply and then held her away from him. "Your loveliness excites me, and I fear I'll forget myself during our long journey. We will not really be married until this evening when the priest speaks the words over us."

He leaned forward and began unpacking the con-

tents of the wicker basket. "I have a surprise for you."
He pulled out two crystal glasses and then unwound a
napkin from a chilled bottle of champagne. Although
tense, she was delighted with the surprise.

After three glasses of champagne, she began to relax
a little and to enjoy listening to Francis, who was full
of plans for their future. "We'll work together for the
king's return. And then, Anna-Maria, what a glorious
future we'll have!"

The future—within a few hours she would be mistress of a large manor house and the mother of a small
child. Soon she would also have a prestigious place at
court. She wondered if she would be able to fulfill
her role as the countess of Shrewsbury.

But she could not worry about it now. The day
had been fraught with nervous excitement, and the
wine was taking its toll. Despite her determination to
stay awake, she nestled, childlike, against the earl,
put her head on his shoulder, and drifted off to
sleep.

She was awakened by the earl's insistent shaking
of her arm. "We're approaching Grafton Manor now,
and already our guests are arriving."

Feeling a quickened heartbeat, Anna-Maria sat up
and peered out the coach window, anxious to catch
her first glimpse of Grafton Manor. Would it ever be
home to her? Would she come to love it as passionately
as she loved Deene? It was dusk, and already the windows of Grafton Manor were ablaze; there must be
a thousand candles burning inside.

Shrieks of laughter and good-natured joking split
the air. Ahead of them, pulled up before the studded
oak door, were three coaches, discharging their pas-
sengers. Anna-Maria began to make a hasty toilette,
anxious to make a good impression on Francis's friends
and neighbors. Unfortunately, while she had been
sleeping, her hair had pulled loose from its severe knot
and was tumbling down her shoulders. She despaired
of ever putting it in order without Sarah's nimble-fin-
gered aid.

The earl touched her bright chestnut locks and

smiled. "Leave it as it is. I prefer it flowing free like this."

Her eyes bright with nervousness, Anna-Maria began to smooth her hair with her hands. She was fluffing out her skirt when the coach suddenly drew to a stop and a bright, impish face appeared at the window. "Hoy, Talbot! Let me get a look at this new wife of yours. I hear that she is a beauty."

Francis whispered laughingly in Anna-Maria's ear, "My neighbor, Sir Peter."

Sir Peter wrenched the coach door open and put in his hand to help Anna-Maria alight. As she stepped into the flare of the torches, he let out a long, low whistle of admiration and clasped his hand dramatically over his heart. "I am overcome. Rumor failed to do you justice!"

Anna-Maria smiled at him, and he turned swiftly and addressed Francis, who was getting out of the coach. "Talbot, it is not seemly that a doddering old man like yourself should marry such a young and beautiful woman. I shall take her for myself."

Turning to Anna-Maria, he gave her an elaborate bow. "You are not truly married until after this night's ceremony. There is still time to marry me instead."

Anna-Maria was laughing, charmed by his nonsense. She was on the point of returning his banter when she suddenly checked herself and looked questioningly at Francis. It would not do to make him jealous so early in their marriage.

Francis was grinning at Sir Peter. "You deal with this rascal," he said to Anna-Maria. "His impudence defeats me."

Anna-Maria laughed, a clear bell-like laugh, and put her perfumed, gloved hand into Sir Peter's firm grip. "Thank you, my lord. I vow that if my husband beats me or is stingy with my dress allowance, I will run away to you at once."

Her spirits soared. This was a good omen. She was entering her new home with laughter on her lips.

Five

As she entered the vast entrance hall, a knot of guests broke apart and moved toward her. Anna-Maria smiled and put out her hand in greeting as Francis introduced each one, but her free hand went to her hair, and she touched it nervously, conscious of her disarray. Francis noticed the gesture and put his arm around her protectively. "My wife needs time to herself to wash away the stains of the journey and dress herself for tonight's ceremony."

The guests murmured in quick understanding and parted to let Anna-Maria and Francis pass. Anna-Maria walked for the first time up the curving staircase of her new home, and she found herself wondering how many times and in how many varied moods she would climb these stairs. Her heartbeat quickened a little as she thought of her children racing carelessly up and down the staircase. She gave Francis a smile so tender that he caught his breath sharply and tightened his grip around her waist.

"You grace Grafton Manor as no woman has ever done," he said softly.

The room he led her into was large and comfortably appointed, although the furnishings were somewhat old-fashioned. Francis looked around it and said apologetically, "It may not please your taste. You must make whatever changes you like."

"It's lovely," Anna-Maria said, trying to sound convincing. She felt awkward and uncertain. No doubt the chamber had been furnished by her predecessor, Francis's first wife. Anna-Maria disliked the dark green velvet draperies at the windows and the bedhangings, but to criticize it would be to criticize the dead woman's taste. Moving swiftly across the room, she stood warming her hands at the fire, which was crackling briskly beneath a white, elaborately carved marble mantle. Above the fireplace the pale green damask-hung wall showed a faint rectangle, and Anna-Maria realized, with a little shiver, that a portrait of the former countess of Shrewsbury must have hung there until recently. I *will* redo this room, she thought. I'll make it bright and gay and cheerful.

Francis came up behind her and slid his arms around her waist, gently kissing the back of her head. "Why don't you rest for a short while? Shall I send a maid up to you?"

Anna-Maria turned her head and smiled at him over her shoulder, fighting down the uneasy feeling that his dead wife's ghost was watching them. "Thank you. I'd love to rest for a bit. But please don't send me a maid. I'd rather wait for Sarah. She can't be far behind us."

Francis cupped her chin and gave her a swift kiss on the lips. "I'll see that no one disturbs you until Sarah arrives."

After he was gone, Anna-Maria moved over to the bed and drew back the thickly embroidered coverlet. As she pulled the despised brown gown over her head and unfastened the tight laces of her busk, she looked apprehensively at the crisp white sheets of the bed. In this bed her predecessor had lain with Francis. Here she had conceived her child. Anna-Maria shivered. Perhaps it was in this very bed that she had died. Anna-Maria shook her head, impatient with her morbid thoughts. She must put all such thoughts behind her.

She finished undressing, then slowly climbed into the bed and pulled the eiderdown up to her chin, staring at the ebony wood of the underside of the canopy. The first countess and Francis had been young together and had probably romped in this bed like two healthy young animals, loving and caressing. Surely the countess would disapprove of this new marriage. With the ease that spirits possess, she would be able to look into Anna-Maria's heart and find only respect and liking for Francis there, but she would search in vain for love. She might even be resentful for Francis's sake and revenge herself on Anna-Maria.

Feeling suddenly deathly cold, Anna-Maria pulled the eiderdown more closely about her and chided herself for her runaway imagination. The truth was that she was frightened of the marriage bed. She was terrified of the responses of her own body. The gypsy's touch had evoked an Anna-Maria that she had never known before, a mindless creature who, for a few moments, was at the mercy of delicious bodily sensations. Only later had pain and humiliation followed.

It was impossible to sleep with such thoughts crowding in upon her. Impatiently Anna-Maria thrust aside the eiderdown, sat up, and put her feet on the floor. Without bothering to replace her busk, she pulled the brown gown over her head and fastened it as best she could. She paced the room, longing desperately for the security of her parents' arms. What was she doing in this strange bed, in this strange house? Her breath came short as she experienced an intense panic, as though she were caught in a senseless nightmare from which there was no awakening. Someone should have stopped her from this marriage! Someone who loved her. Images of her father and mother rose strongly before her eyes. But although they loved her, they were no help. It was for *their* sake that she had made her marriage vows. She remembered her mother's pleasure at the marriage, the look of relief and delight on her face. She remembered a talk she had had with her mother a few weeks ago. "Anna-Maria, I want to prepare you for the marriage bed. It was many years before I learned to experience any pleasure in your father's embraces. I dreaded the fall of night, dreaded his touch. But once you resulted from our union, I saw beauty in our lovemaking."

The thought of having a child stopped Anna-Maria's agitated pacing. She had almost forgotten that she was a mother already! Suddenly she felt a longing to see her little stepdaughter, and she quickly went out into the long upper hallway. A young, rosy-cheeked maid was in the hall, a pile of bed linens over her arm. She paled and then flushed at the unexpected sight of her new mistress and dropped into a deep curtsy.

Anna-Maria smiled at her reassuringly. "Please don't

tell anyone that I am awake and about. I don't want to see my guests right now, but I am longing for the sight of my new stepdaughter. Is she asleep already?"

The maid grinned broadly. She was devoted to three-year-old Polly and was delighted at this evidence of concern from Polly's new stepmother. "She be in the kitchen. She's a great favorite with the cook."

"Can you show me the way? A back way so I don't meet anyone?"

Obligingly the maid led Anna-Maria to the top of the staircase leading to the kitchen. "The cook will be in a fair state when she meets you," she warned. "She's already beside herself with excitement because of the preparations for the wedding."

"I'll try not to distress her," Anna-Maria promised and carefully pulled up her long skirt before setting her foot on the first step of the winding stairway. The candles threw little light, and Anna-Maria promised herself that as soon as she was fully in control of the household she would see that the servants had enough light on the stairway to insure their safe footing.

Reaching the kitchen, she stepped out into the brightness and met the astonished gaze of the florid-faced, wide-eyed cook.

Anna-Maria said with composure, "Good evening. I'm the countess of Shrewsbury. I've heard that my stepdaughter is with you, and I'm eager to meet her."

The cook gulped, wiped her red hands on her stained apron, and dropped into an awkward curtsy. "She be there." She gestured. Anna-Maria followed her motion and saw Polly perched on a stool next to the kitchen table eating a fresh slice of bread dripping with honey.

Instantly Anna-Maria lost her heart to her. Kneeling on the flagging stone floor, she said, "Come here, darling."

Polly took a quick look at Anna-Maria and then smiled. Climbing down from her perch, she bent her head shyly, her blond curls falling forward, and slowly walked to Anna-Maria.

Anna-Maria reached out her arms and tightly hugged the chubby little girl. On the tip of her tongue were the words, "I'm your new mother, sweet," but she restrained them, fearing that the child, young as she was, might remember her own mother and resent an intruder. Quickly she substituted, "I've come to take care of you."

The inner door to the kitchen swung open suddenly, and the earl stepped inside, sending a wave of tense excitement through the kitchen staff. He stopped abruptly when he spotted Anna-Maria with his daughter in her arms. For a moment he was too startled to take it in, but then his dark brown eyes lit with warmth and approval.

Anna-Maria pulled the child closer to her and smiled at the earl over the child's curly head. A wave of joy swept over her. I'll be a *good* wife and mother, she thought. I'll be the warm center of my family, the way the hearth is the center of this kitchen.

She stood, still clasping the child to her, and held out her hand to the earl without a trace of self-consciousness. For a long moment the three stood together, a family circle, and Anna-Maria's heart sang with the knowledge that she had taken the first step into wifehood and motherhood and found it easy.

The earl looked as if he were about to make an intimate remark, but then surveyed the breathlessly intent kitchen staff and checked himself. "We must find Polly's nursemaid. 'Tis long past her bedtime. And you will want to prepare yourself for the ceremony. Sarah has arrived."

Anna-Maria kissed Polly's soft cheek, and then rose reluctantly. "I'll see you in the morning, poppet."

Polly looked up at the woman who was suddenly so tall above her. "Are you to stay here? You won't go away?"

"Never!" Anna-Maria bent to kiss Polly's blond curls. "From now on I'll be here when you wake, and I'll play with you all day, and when you are sleepy, I'll tuck you in and tell you stories of when I was a little girl."

When Anna-Maria returned to the bedchamber, she found Sarah already there, pursing her lips disapprovingly at the dark, elaborate furniture and heavy, dark green hangings. "I hope the earl is not stingy. You'll be needing a great many changes to make this cheerful."

Anna-Maria hugged her. "Oh, Sarah, I've seen my daughter, and she's all that the angels could have asked for. Beautiful and sweet. And I think she liked me!"

Sarah smiled and returned Anna-Maria's hug. "It warms my heart to see you so happy. I worried about you during the whole journey here. Many brides are beset by fears on their wedding day."

"Not I." Anna-Maria had completely forgotten about her earlier fears. "I know that I have made the right decision, and I mean to stick by it."

Sarah smiled approvingly and then went into the hall and called for maids to bring a steaming tub of hot water. She was asserting immediately her position of importance in this new household and enjoying it immensely, but when the maids carried in the slipper-shaped tub, she dismissed them and bathed Anna-Maria herself.

As she squeezed a sponge over Anna-Maria's perfectly shaped shoulders she asked softly, "You have no fears, then?" And Anna-Maria, flicking a soap bubble with her fingers, said firmly, "None!" But inside, she felt a flicker of panic. As though she were invoking a charm, she deliberately remembered her mother's words, "At the end of that—*act*—they put a living child in your arms, Anna-Maria, and you know it has all been worthwhile."

She stretched herself luxuriously in the bath. "Imagine, Sarah, I am already a mother without any of the pain and the discomfort."

She was out of the bath, and Sarah was drying her with fleecy white towels when Mary burst into the room, breathless. "Our coach lost a wheel, and they were forever repairing it. Mother and I were in despair that we would miss the ceremony until I remembered that we carried your wedding gown with us."

Anna-Maria smiled. "Calm yourself. I would never

agree to be married if you and our parents weren't here!"

Mary burst into an uncharacteristic torrent of words. "I'm stunned at the notables who wait below for your marriage. I knew that the earl was wealthy, but I had no idea that he was so *important*. All the really impressive Catholic families are represented here tonight."

Mary began to tick the names off on her slender fingers, but Anna-Maria found it difficult to listen. What did she care about social position? She would attain it only to please her parents. What she really cared about was leading an honorable life so that one day she could die and face God bravely without sin on her soul. She cared about the chubby, sweet-scented Polly in her arms. She cared that at the end of her life she would see that same look of tender admiration in Francis's eyes that she had seen today.

She ignored Mary and Sarah's chatter as they powdered and perfumed her, then put her into her white wedding dress. The skirt billowed out, making Anna-Maria's waist appear even tinier than it was. The low-cut neckline exposed the swell of Anna-Maria's breasts and the soft whiteness of her shoulders. Sarah clapped her hands in admiration and stepped back to survey Anna-Maria with satisfaction. Mary coaxed forward a tendril of Anna-Maria's hair, and then Anna-Maria said, through pale lips, "Tell Francis that I am ready to begin the ceremony."

Mary, obedient as always, walked down the stairway and whispered in the earl's ear. Francis immediately began assembling his guests in the chapel and notified his house priest, Father William Johnson, that the ceremony was about to begin.

Upstairs Sarah picked up Anna-Maria's missal and handed it to her just as Mary returned. Together the three of them followed a servant to the chapel. At the chapel door, the three young women paused for a moment. Sarah, her eyes misted with tears, gave Anna-Maria a quick kiss and then went into the chapel and slipped into a rear pew.

Mary took a deep breath and smiled shakily at

Anna-Maria. "I'm so nervous that I could cry. You must be even more so." Mary was to walk down the aisle ahead of Anna-Maria, and she flinched at the thought of strangers staring at her.

Anna-Maria gave Mary's hand a reassuring squeeze. " 'Tis best to start quickly before you have time to become even more frightened." She gave Mary a gentle push, and Mary, collecting her poise with a visible effort, began her journey down the aisle.

Anna-Maria counted to three and then followed Mary, her head held high. As though from a distance, she heard the quick indrawn breaths of the wedding guests and the whispered comments. "Isn't she exquisite!" "Francis has outdone himself this time."

Anna-Maria fastened her gaze on the altar. Her heart began to beat more rapidly. Now, truly, she was to be married in the presence of God, and she would be linked to Francis for all eternity.

Francis was standing before the altar, looking almost handsome in a suit of sky blue satin, lace cuffs at his wrists. He gave Anna-Maria a look of deep pride, and she attempted to smile at him but found that her lips were trembling.

For relief she looked at the priest, Father William Johnson. How wonderful to see a priest again! Occasionally over the years, wandering priests had sought a night's refuge at Deene, but she had not seen a priest since she had left the convent in France.

When she reached the altar rail, she knelt down gracefully and bent her head for Father Johnson's blessing. As she received the blessing, Francis joined her, kneeling by her side. Father Johnson put his hand on top of Francis's bent head and murmured a blessing, calling Francis "My son" in a voice that was warm with respect. He was indebted to Francis, who had given him shelter during the years of Cromwell's rule.

When he had completed the blessing, he turned toward the altar and began the mass. The familiar Latin intonations fell sweetly on Anna-Maria's ears, and she felt herself relaxing and becoming very quiet, as though a terrible tension had finally been eased. The sweet, heavy smell of incense made her senses swim pleasantly, and when Francis put his hand out to hers, she gripped it with a rush of friendliness.

Anna-Maria and Francis repeatedly rose and knelt together, following the order of the mass, their voices mingling as they gave the Latin reponses to the priest, and Anna-Maria's sense of closeness to Francis deepened. When they took communion, Anna-Maria stole a sideways glance at Francis from under her lashes and saw from his expression that he found it as awesome as she did.

At the conclusion of the mass, there was a rustle as the wedding guests settled back into their pews. Father Johnson spoke gravely for a moment to Anna-Maria and Francis in a voice that was inaudible to the guests, reminding them of the sanctity of marriage. Then, his voice deep and resonant, he began leading them in their marriage vows. Anna-Maria's voice rang out without a tremble of fear, "I, Anna-Maria, take thee Francis. . . ."

As they turned from the altar after the ceremony, Anna-Maria slipped her hand into Francis's with a feeling of perfect confidence in him and was rewarded by the look of quick pleasure that lit his face.

As Anna-Maria and Francis moved down the aisle, the guests, released from the solemnity of the mass, began to stir in their pews. They were eager now to laugh, talk, and revel.

At the door to the reception room, Anna-Maria paused for a moment and said softly to Francis, "How lovely!" The room was banked with greens, and fires roared in the fireplaces on either side of the long chamber. Several young pages were softly playing harps, and masses of candles blazed. Anna-Maria smiled with delight and then suddenly felt a pang of nervousness. Tonight she was caught in a position somewhere between a guest and the mistress of the house. She had not been responsible for tonight's entertainment and indeed, knew nothing of the workings of her new, large household. Tomorrow she would begin her duties, and all her skills would be put to the test.

Before she had time to think about her apprehension, her parents were in the room, her mother's eyes still moist. "Darling, you looked so beautiful!"

Her father, his eyes also suspiciously moist, tried to cover his emotion with great heartiness, clapping the earl on the shoulder and jocularly calling him "son."

Anna-Maria felt a twinge of distaste that she hastily forced down. The earl and her father were too close in age for the "son" to be appropriate. She stole a look at Francis, saw him flinch, and felt a quick flood of sympathy for him. She vowed that never, by word or gesture, would she make him self-conscious about the difference in their ages.

The other guests were pressing around now, demanding a kiss from the bride. After embracing a series of people she had never before met, she urged her guests toward the long banquet tables. Already footmen were heaping the tables with steaming platters. Anna-Maria, with a little sigh of relief, sank into a heavily carved chair next to Francis at the head of one of the tables.

When she picked up her fork she found that she could not eat. Her only thought was that later she and Francis must share the marital bed. Her stomach contracted, and to hide her apprehension, she turned to her neighbor on her right and pasting a dazzling smile on her face said, "Forgive me, but I did not hear your name when Francis introduced us earlier."

The woman leaned forward with a friendly smile that exposed long teeth. "I'm Lady Framingham, your closest neighbor." She gestured vaguely to her right, as though Anna-Maria's glance could penetrate solid walls. "Lord Framingham and I have known Francis since—" She broke off, looking disconcerted, and took a rapid bite of food.

Anna-Maria realized that she had been on the point of saying, "Since his first marriage," and she felt a warm sympathy for her neighbor's embarrassment. So she broke the silence before it could grow more embarrassing. "Do you have children?"

Lady Framingham smiled with pleasure and answered. "Aye, five girls. Lord Framingham says that the dowries for five females will be the ruin of him. Still"—she brightened optimistically and speared a steaming oyster with her fork—"things are looking up for us now that there is talk of the king's return."

For a moment Anna-Maria was startled to hear her speak so freely on the forbidden subject, but then she glanced around the room and realized that in this vast candlelit chamber, it was perfectly safe. She was surrounded by friends and neighbors, all Roman Catholics, all Royalists. Never before in England had she been surrounded by so many of her own kind, and she suddenly felt vastly exhilarated. How wonderful to live without fear, to speak impulsively without having to guard one's tongue.

The feeling of being in a safe place lasted all through the three-hour-long meal, and although she was unable to eat, she drank several glasses of wine and found herself entertained by her neighbors' sallies. At the conclusion of the meal, Anna-Maria felt slightly giddy from the wine, and she found that most of her apprehension had slipped away. The faces of her guests began to look familiar to her now, although she could not put names to many of the faces.

After the tables were cleared away, the harpists struck up their music again, and the guests began to crowd around Anna-Maria, eager to be the first to snatch one of the blue-ribbon love knots from her wedding gown. "Wait," Anna-Maria laughed and warded them off. "I want Mary to be first, for luck."

Mary stepped forward, blushing at the sudden attention and pulled firmly on one of the blue-ribbon love knots. As she did so, Anna-Maria remembered the long, patient hours that Mary had spent sewing them on, and she said a fervent prayer that Mary would find a man who would appreciate her kindness and housewifely skills.

The ribbon pulled loose easily, and Mary, holding her prize tightly against the folds of her dress, stepped back into the crowd, and the others pressed forward. Laughing, Anna-Maria was spun from one pair of arms to another as eager hands pulled at the ribbons.

But her lighthearted pleasure vanished when a

coarse-faced nobleman, clearly drunk, shouted, "Let's revive the old customs. We'll bed Francis and his lovely bride in the old way." He seized Anna-Maria by the waist, his thick fingers biting painfully into her delicate flesh. His protuberant brown eyes moved boldly over her shoulders and breasts, his expression lustful. Anna-Maria gasped and blushed, suddenly remembering the old, ribald custom in which the wedding guests stripped the bride and groom and put them into bed naked, amid coarse jesting. Her face flamed as he bent closer to her, his breath foul, his wet lips seeking to plant a kiss on her trembling mouth. She recoiled and looked about, frantically seeking help. For a long moment no one moved to her aid, and time seemed to stand still. She could feel that several of the other male guests were openly staring at her, and she was terrified.

Just as a small sob escaped her, Francis suddenly clapped his hand on her captor's shoulder and said disgustedly, "I had not expected such conduct from a guest of mine!" At his icy tone, the man released his hold on Anna-Maria's waist, muttering drunken apologies. Anna-Maria swayed and would have fallen if Francis had not quickly steadied her. She was sickened by the looks that were just fading from the faces of the men. Even more embarrassing were the covert looks of sympathy that the women were sending in her direction.

Francis bent close to her ear. "I regret that a few of my more boisterous guests are becoming coarse. I'll send them home as tactfully as possible, but there is no reason that you have to endure more of this. Make your escape to our chamber now, and I'll join you as soon as possible."

Anna-Maria pressed his hand in gratitude and slipped through the crowd, feeling as though she were escaping a pack of wild beasts.

She moved slowly up the great staircase, too tired to hurry. When she entered her bedroom, she found Sarah already there, and her eyes filled with quick tears of gratitude. "Sarah, I'm in sore need of your comforting. 'Tis a terrifying thing to be a bride and have people examine you as freely as they would a cow at auction. At times I expected one or two of them to pry open my jaw and demand to inspect my teeth!"

Sarah laughed sympathetically. "And yet I'll warrant not one of them could find a single flaw in you!"

Anna-Maria smiled at her, grateful for Sarah's stout friendship. "It was a beautiful wedding, Sarah, and yet I can't help feeling that marriage ought to be more of a *private* affair. I was uncomfortable knowing that everyone present knew that Francis and I would be bedding tonight and speculating about it. When I followed their thoughts, I found my mind rushing ahead to this moment, and now it has come and, Sarah, I'm frightened!"

Sarah held out her arms, and Anna-Maria rushed into them and held Sarah tightly for comfort. In all the world only Sarah understood her plight, knew that she was going to her marriage bed no longer a virgin.

"Hush, hush." Sarah was stroking her hair gently. "I promise you that it will be all right." She held Anna-Maria a little away from her and shook her gently. "I'm going to put you into a hot bath and then give you a calming brew that the gypsies taught me to prepare. I swear that after you drink this, nothing will frighten you."

By the time Sarah had finished bathing her and Anna-Maria had drunk the last drop of the herbal brew, she felt strangely calm. The hard edges of reality had softened into a blur.

Sarah helped her into her nightgown and then stepped back and looked at her with satisfaction. "You're the perfect bride!"

"I wish I felt more bridelike," Anna-Maria sighed. As Sarah tucked her into the vast bed, she said wistfully, "I do so want to be a good wife to Francis. This morning, during our wedding ceremony in the chapel, I felt so committed to him. It all seemed easy then. But now—"

Sarah gave her a quick kiss on the forehead. "I'll pray for you throughout the night, and in the morning you and I will laugh together at your fears."

Sarah moved softly about the room, blowing out all the candles except those nearest the bed. "Lie back and relax now until the earl joins you." She slipped through the doorway before Anna-Maria could protest.

Anna-Maria lay back against the high-banked pillows and found her thoughts darting in too many directions for her to grasp them. The idea crossed her mind that it was not too late to find Francis, throw herself on her knees, and confess her sin to him. But the drink Sarah had given her made her too lazy to move. She knew that in a few minutes Francis would penetrate her body, and although she had committed herself to him before God and man, the act still seemed strange. How little she knew of Francis, other than that he was a good and gentle man. She knew nothing of his habits, his preferences in food and drink, his taste in literature. When she squeezed her eyelids shut, she could not even summon his image to her mind. Dear God! She was not even comfortable saying Francis, yet in a few minutes she would be expected to murmur words of love to him.

Francis entered the bedchamber quietly, still fully dressed. Anna-Maria felt her heart leap and begin to beat erratically, but she managed to smile at him without any evidence of fear.

For a long moment Francis simply stood and gazed at her, his eyes lighting. Anna-Maria lay with her chestnut hair spilling out over the white pillows, the candles picking out gold highlights in the curling masses. Her oval face was pale but that served only to accent the dark beauty of her eyes. Francis's eyes fell to the white ruffled nightgown, and he caught his breath. Anna-Maria's young breasts were straining against the soft fabric, and the ruffles over her bosom fluttered with her rapid breathing.

Francis forced himself to calmly approach the bed. Sitting carefully on the edge, he took Anna-Maria's small hand into his and said gently, "Don't be afraid, Anna-Maria."

"I'm not." Anna-Maria's tone denied her brave words, and Francis smiled.

He stood and began blowing out the candles near

the bed. As the room was plunged into darkness, Anna-Maria gave a startled exclamation. Instantly she felt Francis graze her cheek with a kiss. " 'Tis for your sake, my sweet. For my part, I confess I would love to feast my eyes on your young charms. But often a virgin is frightened by her first sight of a naked male. I would spare you that until you are more accustomed to our lovemaking."

How kind he was! Guilt pierced Anna-Maria, and she was on the point of confessing, but a sob escaped her, and Francis covered her lips with his own before she could speak. "I'll be gentle with you."

He rose, and Anna-Maria heard faint rustlings as he removed his clothing. In a moment he joined her, stretching full length beside her on the bed. She stiffened involuntarily, and Francis instantly began stroking her hair, murmuring soft, soothing words. As she began to relax a little under his touch, he untied the ribbon on her nightgown and he moved his hand to her breast, curving his palm to its fullness. Anna-Maria caught her breath, expecting to feel the sharp, sweet sensation the gypsy had aroused in her. She half longed for the sensation, half feared it. Her reaction was a mingling of disappointment and relief when she found that Francis's touch evoked no response in her at all. She was aware of his hand, and then his mouth, at her breast, but she felt nothing except the slight pressure of his touch. Francis's breathing was coming more rapidly now, and he groaned as he raised his head from Anna-Maria's breast. In a soft murmur, he told her what he was going to do next, ending tenderly, "It may hurt slightly, my sweet, but that is a necessary part of deflowering. I'll be as gentle as possible." He was softly stroking her inner thighs, his fingers trembling a little in his desire to possess her fully.

Anna-Maria bit her lower lip until it hurt, so moved by his kindness that shame overwhelmed her. Perhaps there was no need for her to confess her sin. Despite Sarah's reassurances, she was sure that men had mysterious ways of knowing whether a woman was a virgin or not.

Francis was parting her thighs now, and Anna-

Maria stiffened, waiting for his cry of outrage. How could she ever face this gentle man once the knowledge of her sin was written on his face!

Francis, panting heavily now, took the tip of his male organ and gently began inserting it. How different it was from the gypsy's bold, careless thrust. And yet as terrifying in its way. Anna-Maria trembled as he entered her, conscious of the burning heat of his naked skin through the thin material of her nightgown, of his male hardness moving into her.

Suddenly she realized that her body would never again belong wholly to herself. It was as much Francis's possession as his house, furniture, and lands. At the realization that her privacy had been lost to her forever, she let out a cry, and Francis, thinking that he had hurt her, paused in his gentle stroking. "Try to relax, my sweet. It will not hurt much longer."

Suddenly he thrust swiftly and boldly. The move startled Anna-Maria into an outcry, and Francis, thinking that he had deflowered her, bent to kiss her deeply on the lips. It was only by a strong effort of will that he made his strokes even and gentle. His words coming out in little pants, he murmured, "Now you are no longer a virgin, my darling. And from now on you will find pleasure in our lovemaking."

Anna-Maria, sobbing softly from a bewildering array of emotions, clasped him about the shoulders and pulled him more closely to her. This was her husband in the sight of God and man, and surely he was the best of men. She kissed him gently on the cheek.

He began thrusting more rapidly, but still with controlled gentleness, and then a second later, he collapsed against her, spent. Anna-Maria stroked his damp hair and stared into the darkness.

Six

As Anna-Maria went about her household tasks in the months that followed, she sometimes, unexpectedly, found the gypsy's words, "Yours is a hot nature, lustful," intruding into her thoughts. Each time she would laugh with a mixture of regret and relief. Only once, in the early moments in Ramon's arms, had she felt any passion and that, no doubt, had been caused by the gypsy's curse. Certainly she felt no stirring of her senses in Francis's arms. He only claimed her for twenty minutes or so, three or four times a week, and always, as on the first night, his lovemaking was gentle. Although Anna-Maria got no pleasure from it, she was pleased to satisfy Francis. She wished fervently that a child would result from their union, but her monthly flow came on with grim regularity, and once she wailed to Sarah, " 'Tis my punishment for my sin with the gypsy."

Whenever Anna-Maria was upset about her childlessness, Sarah would hasten to find Polly and put the child in Anna-Maria's arms. The relationship between mother and stepdaughter had deepened over the past months, and Polly had come to look on Anna-Maria as her true mother.

Francis, although as eager for a son as Anna-Maria, was not as preoccupied with the matter as she was, his mind being engaged with the great events that were taking place in England. Often he rode to London and was gone for three and four days at a stretch, conferring with other Royalists who were scheming to put the exiled Prince Charles on the throne.

He would return splattered with mud from his journey and as talkative as a schoolboy. As everyone had expected, Richard Cromwell had been unable to fill his father's shoes and had resigned as lord pro-

tector of England. Now the army ruled in England,
which Francis was strongly against.

Each time Francis returned home to Anna-Maria,
however, he was more heartened by the news he
brought. "The people will not stand for this much
longer! Already tempers are rising against the arro-
gance of the army officers. Even the peasants are beginning to call for the return of the monarchy. They
always loved Prince Charles when he was a young boy.
Their quarrel was with his father, not him!"

One evening he arrived at dusk, his horse's hoofs
pounding on the cobblestones as he rode into the
stableyard, waving his hat and shouting. "General
Monck has arrived! He's come down from Scotland
with an army at his back to settle our affairs."

Anna-Maria, frightened by the shouting, dropped
her embroidery frame and rushed into the courtyard.
"What's amiss?"

"Amiss?" Francis threw back his head and gave a
clear, ringing laugh of sheer triumph. "Best ask me
what's *right,* my sweet! God's in his heaven, and justice will triumph."

Anna-Maria, thinking him drunk, although she had
never known him to overindulge in spirits, urged him
down from his horse. "Come into the house, Francis.
You can tell me your news as you bathe and change."

As he swung to the ground beside her and caught
her in an exuberant hug, she wrinkled her nose in
puzzlement. There was no odor of spirits about him,
and yet his behavior was that of a man crazed by
drink. He lifted her into the air and swung her by the
waist as easily as if she were Polly.

Carrying her, he began to run toward the house,
and Anna-Maria forced herself to relax, afraid that if
she struggled, she would prove too heavy for him.
Once inside Francis set her down and bellowed for
someone to bring him brandy. "Several bottles of our
finest French brandy. We must toast one of the greatest events in our life!"

Anna-Maria tugged at his sleeve. "Francis, what is
it?" But Francis, his dark eyes gleaming, refused to
satisfy her curiosity until they were seated in front of

the fireplace, their glasses brimming with brandy. Then he rose, stood with his back to the mantle, and raised his glass. "General Monck has landed in England with an army at his back!" He downed the brandy in one gulp, turned, and threw the glass into the fireplace.

Anna-Maria jumped to her feet, her hands to her throat. "But that means fighting. War! Francis, why are you so *happy?*"

Francis laughed and seized her hands. "Sit down, Anna-Maria. 'Tis good news, I promise you."

Her eyes dark, Anna-Maria obediently sank back into her chair while Francis, his hands still clasping hers, sat on a footstool at her feet. Forcing himself to be calm, he began speaking slowly. "Well, George Monck, bless his brave heart, who is opposed to army rule too, has ridden down from Scotland with a hand-picked army at his back to set matters right here in England."

"But who *is* he?"

Francis stared at her. "Sometimes I forget that you are so young and that you spent so many years away from England. Monck fought bravely for Charles the First. He was one of the staunchest of the Royalists."

"Then he is one of us?" Anna-Maria asked, beginning to understand.

"Yes! Except that—" Francis hesitated and shook his head. "These are tangled times, Anna-Maria, so the tale I tell you must of necessity be slightly complicated."

He drew a deep breath. "When Charles the First was defeated and then beheaded, Monck turned his support to Oliver Cromwell."

Anna-Maria gasped in indignation and snatched her hands from Francis's grip. "A traitor!"

Francis sighed. "Monck is a good man, darling, and he did what he thought best for England. He knew that Oliver Cromwell would be a strong ruler. He felt that Prince Charles was too young at the time to rule England effectively. But now that Cromwell is dead and Charles is a man of thirty, the entire complexion of matters has changed! Monck has declared that he cannot stomach England being ruled by the sword. He is sweeping down into England with soldiers who are loyal to him. And I've no doubt that he'll support our cause and invite Charles to take the throne."

Anna-Maria leaped to her feet, as excited as he was. "Oh, Francis! To have the monarchy restored at last!"

Francis laughed and picked up her brandy glass, taking a hearty swallow. "I predict that Charles will be on the throne of England before the summer of 1660."

He began to pace excitedly about the room. "Anna-Maria, we must find a house in London immediately. Already I find myself in sore need of one, spending as much time as I do there."

For a fleeting moment Anna-Maria felt a pang. Grafton Manor was so lovely. And yet, there was a power and excitement to be found in London that existed nowhere else in the world.

The next time Francis rode to London, Anna-Maria went with him and spent nearly two weeks searching for a house that would suit their needs. Knowing that he would often be at court once the king arrived, Francis stressed that the house must be convenient to Whitehall Palace. In addition, it must be large enough and fashionable enough for them to do the entertaining that would be required of them.

Because there had been a scarcity of money in her girlhood, Anna-Maria had difficulty in spending vast sums. She knew that Francis was wealthy, but at Grafton Manor she had had very little occasion to spend money, and the full extent of his wealth had not occurred to her. None of the houses that she showed Francis pleased him, and finally he said in exasperation, "Anna-Maria, we are not paupers you know."

Casting caution aside, Anna-Maria found a house on the fashionable Strand, a mansion whose gardens ran down to the Thames River. Francis surveyed the location with approval, strode through the vast rooms with their graceful moldings and parquet floors and declared himself satisfied. "We'll furnish it only moderately at first, though," he said. "No doubt when the king returns, fashions will change, and I want the most up-to-date furniture."

Never before had Anna-Maria had the responsibility of choosing and placing new furniture, and she found it delightful. At times she felt like a young child playing house and at others like a very mature and sophisticated matron.

She and Francis rode so frequently between Grafton Manor and London that when she began to feel uncharacteristically fatigued, she attributed it to her pace of life. But then her monthly flow didn't come, and she and Sarah stared at each other hopefully. Another month passed, and Sarah took Anna-Maria to visit a midwife in the village who confirmed their expectations.

Anna-Maria was able to tell Francis that when the king rode into London to claim his throne, he would find a new subject waiting for him.

Seven

Anna-Maria, with Francis by her side, stood outside their house on the Strand, craning her neck to catch a glimpse of the approaching procession. Today the king was riding into London to take his throne, and the streets were massed with people eager to catch their first glimpse of him. All of the London houses were bedecked with flowers or streamers. Many of the people had been up for nearly four hours, anxious to secure a good position from which to watch the procession, and many of them were already drunk from wine. False reports of, "I see the procession, the king is coming now," flew from mouth to mouth, causing the excitement to briefly reach a fever pitch, and then die down in disappointment.

Anna-Maria settled back on her heels and looked at

Francis, a smile playing at the corners of her mouth. "I fear I sadly miscalculated. I promised you that when the king rode into London, we would have a new subject to greet him." She put a tender, reverent hand on the swelling of her belly. This was May thirtieth, and the midwife had predicted that the baby would be born at the end of June. She flashed Francis a teasing glance from under her long dark lashes. "Is the king early, or the baby late?"

Francis laughed. "Don't put my loyalties to the test. To decide who is in the wrong, my king or my son, is more than a man should be asked."

As he looked at Anna-Maria, his smile faded. Unconsciously her hand had gone to the small of her back, and she was rubbing it as though it pained her.

"Anna-Maria, this is madness to stand in the street this way. We are fortunate enough to have a house directly on the procession route. Why don't we take advantage of it and comfortably watch the procession from our windows?"

Anna-Maria protested. "I don't want to be *above* the procession looking down at the king's head. I want to be able to really *see* him. And I like being down here among the crowds, feeling the excitement."

Suddenly she squeezed Francis's arm and stood on tiptoe. "Oh, Francis, I think he is truly coming now."

The sounds of the crowd had swelled into a vast roar, and Anna-Maria could see the bright trappings of the first horses in the distance. Bells had been pealing in London all morning, but now they seemed so loud that Anna-Maria clapped her hands over her ears and, laughing, looked up at Francis.

In a moment the cavalcade had reached them, and Anna-Maria felt her heart begin to pound. It was the soldiers of Monck's army who came first, their faces proud despite the fatigue of the march and the heat of the May morning. Who better than they had the right to lead their triumphant king into his city?

For a time Anna-Maria was spellbound by the color and excitement, but then as the procession went endlessly by for nearly an hour without a sign of the king, she began to weary, moving restlessly from foot to foot in an attempt to ease her unaccustomed weight. "When will the king come?" she asked Francis.

He was looking away from her, over the heads of the crowd. "I think he is coming now."

Anna-Maria followed the direction of his gaze and saw a dark-haired man, resplendent in a suit of white and silver, sitting on a pure white horse. As she watched, he caught a flower in midair and pulled off his plumed hat in an exuberant gesture, bowing to the woman who had thrown it. His face was dark, his teeth gleaming white against his tan as he smiled. He was not handsome, and for a moment Anna-Maria felt a sting of disappointment. But still, there was something about him that caught and held the eye. Perhaps it was the easy grace with which he sat on his horse, or the almost palpable air of masculinity that emanated from him.

Anna-Maria's attention was caught by a movement directly behind the king. She looked, and then everything within her seemed to become perfectly still as she stared in amazement. She had never seen, never dreamed of, a man as handsome as the one who rode behind the king. He looked like a golden god, his rich blond hair falling to his shoulders, his blue eyes the color of the sky. Under his blond mustache, his lips were perfectly formed, sensitive and yet sensual, and as Anna-Maria watched, they parted in a smile, exposing strong white teeth.

Francis followed the direction of her gaze. "That's George Villiers, the duke of Buckingham. He'll be an important man in the king's court. He was raised as a playmate to the king, and when civil war came, he and the king escaped England with a price on their heads."

Anna-Maria barely heard him, so absorbed was she in watching the duke, marveling at the play of expression across his handsome features, the careless grace of his movements as he waved to the people.

When he drew abreast of them, Anna-Maria stood totally still, scarce daring to draw a breath, her eager eyes drinking in every detail of his face and form. His horse wheeled, frightened by the roar of the crowd. The duke controlled him with laughing ease, and as he brought his horse to a standstill, his glance fell on Anna-Maria. She had her face tilted toward him. The duke's glance took in the delicate beauty of her face, and he grinned appreciatively.

As their eyes met fully, Anna-Maria felt a strange stirring deep inside her. The moment when their glances met and held seemed timeless. Perfect contentment settled over her. She could go on for eternity simply staring at this man.

The duke was jostled by the horseman directly behind him, and it broke his gaze. As he turned, Anna-Maria felt a pang of loss, and a cry of protest rose to her lips. As though he had heard her, the duke turned back, rose a little in his stirrups, and tossed her a flower. Anna-Maria reached up and caught the flower as it fell towards her, brushed its smooth petals against her lips and watched the duke ride out of sight.

After he had gone, it seemed as if the day had darkened. The procession was no longer exciting. Anna-Maria was conscious of a nagging ache and a great fatigue. Turning to Francis, she said, "Let's go inside. Now that the king has passed there is nothing else of importance to see."

Francis gave her a glance of approval, gratified that the duke had singled her out for attention. Anna-Maria would be a great help in furthering his ambitions at court.

Slipping a gentle arm around her bulky waist, he led her inside. "Ah, darling, I wish that the baby were born already so that you could go to Whitehall with me tonight."

There were to be splendid entertainments at Whitehall that evening, and all who had supported the king's cause would be there, reveling in their triumph. Anna-Maria smiled, "I care only that the baby be born healthy. There will be time for me to go to Whitehall."

But that night, as she lay in bed, she could not help but feel a quick tinge of envy of Francis. How fortunate men were—they could move freely in the world and have all the joy of children, without having to bear a single moment of discomfort or miss one evening of entertainment.

Then superstitious fear overcame her, and she said a quick Hail Mary begging the mother of God to forgive her for her careless, selfish thoughts. Lovingly she stroked her swollen belly. Poor Francis would never experience the breathless wonder of feeling life move inside his body as she did now. She kissed the tips of her fingers and placed the kiss on the mound of her stomach. "Be born, soon, little one. I'm anxious to hold you in my arms."

Happy now, she turned over, but sleep eluded her. Tantalizing images crept into her mind. Suddenly a delicious shiver ran down her body as she remembered the duke's blond hair and intense blue eyes. If he was at Whitehall tonight, he might speak to her or even—she caught her breath at the thought—ask her to dance.

In the morning she pressed Francis for details of the evening's entertainment at Whitehall and drank in his descriptions with vicarious pleasure. Soon the baby would be born, and she would see all that splendor with her own eyes.

The days of June dragged for her. She was so large now that she took little pleasure in motion, fearing that she might fall and injure the child. She preferred to sit in a wide, heavily cushioned oak chair and embroider smocks for the baby. The sheer tininess of the garments awed her. "Amazing," she said, holding out one for Sarah's inspection, "to think that a living creature could be so small."

Sarah gave her a bright smile, her eyes on the delicate garment. "I can't wait to see those sleeves filled with tiny, wiggling arms." Then her face clouded, and she rose and moved restlessly over to the window. Throwing the casement wide, she leaned out into the mild June sunshine, letting the air play against her cheeks.

Anna-Maria looked after her, a worried frown on her face. It wasn't fair for someone as alive and responsive as Sarah to be denied the joys of wifehood and motherhood. Sarah must often ache with frustration, wondering if all her experiences must come secondhand, through sharing Anna-Maria's life. Anna-Maria sighed and plunged her needle into the fabric so fiercely that she pricked her finger. She sucked angrily at the drop of blood, feeling helpless and frustrated. There was so little she could do for Sarah.

Sarah was inhaling deeply, and Anna-Maria realized suddenly that Sarah, energetic Sarah, had not been outdoors for days. Appalled at her selfishness in having let Sarah share her confinement, she raised her voice and called, "Sarah, I'm sore in need of some pale blue ribbon. Would you mind going to the Royal Exchange for me?"

Sarah turned, her face suddenly alight, and hastened to fetch her cloak. When she returned from the Royal Exchange, she was glowing with renewed vigor, and from then on Anna-Maria made a point of inventing some small errand every day to send Sarah out. She missed Sarah during the short absences, but Sarah always came back with diverting bits of gossip or a lively account of the comical sights of the London streets.

One afternoon when Sarah returned from an errand, Anna-Maria looked up from her sewing, expecting Sarah to be bubbling over with laughter and a new tale. But what she saw frightened her. Sarah was ashen faced, her eyes dilated with fright, and she stood for a moment trying to quiet her breathing before she spoke. "My father is in London!"

Anna-Maria's sewing dropped from her suddenly numbed fingers. "Oh, no!"

"I was just emerging from the Royal Exchange—his coach nearly ran me over," Sarah gasped. "It was only inches from my nose. When I recognized the Devon crest, Anna-Maria, I thought I would faint right there in the street."

She began pulling distractedly at the ribbons of her hood. "Then I looked inside and saw *him,* but he was looking straight ahead, and I doubt he spied me. But Anna-Maria, he must have traced me to London."

Anna-Maria rose with difficulty and then put her arms around Sarah. "Hush. He may have business in London that has nothing to do with you."

"He hates London. I thought it was the one place

where I need not fear meeting him." Sarah looked around wildly like a hunted animal. "Where can I go now?"

Anna-Maria had been thinking rapidly. She gave Sarah a reassuring squeeze. "The first place you are going is to your bed to lie down until your fright has passed. I'll send a footman to find out where your father is staying and watch his movements. When he reports that your father is coming here, it will be time enough to run then."

Sarah, dazed, obeyed with uncharacteristic meekness.

Anna-Maria rang for a footman and gave him rapid, explicit instructions to find Lord Devon and secretly watch all his movements while he was in London and then report immediately when he left the city.

He returned briefly later in the day to report that Lord Devon was in London for four days, deeply involved in business transactions.

For those four days, Sarah clung like a shadow to Anna-Maria. Even after the footman reported that Lord Devon had returned home, Sarah, still shaken by her experience, was reluctant to leave the house. She made the excuse that she hated to leave Anna-Maria when the birth could take place any minute, but Anna-Maria detected the underlying nervousness. Often, as she sewed, her mind was on Sarah.

Sarah's life was being ruined by her father's cruelty and indifference. Her plight made Anna-Maria more keenly aware than ever of the responsibilities of parenthood and she prayed frequently for the wisdom and understanding that she would need in her role of mother.

One day Anna-Maria was hemming a small garment when she suddenly felt a wetness seeping between her legs. She was ashamed and said to Sarah, "I've disgraced myself like a young child."

Sarah smiled and said reassuringly, "Your water broke. 'Tis a sign that the baby is on his way."

For months Anna-Maria had been planning for the birth of the baby, yet now she found herself startled that it was actually to take place. It had been more like a daydream that would go on and on forever. To think that within hours she would hold new life in her arms—that she was actually to be a mother. "Call Francis."

Francis had been dressing to go to Whitehall, and he ran into the room with his shirt awry, his hair standing comically on end. "Anna-Maria, is it true what Sarah tells me? The baby is to be born today?"

Anna-Maria nodded.

Francis's face suddenly darkened with rage. "Sarah is a fool! What is she thinking of to leave you like this while she brought me the news? You should be in bed." He sprang for the bellcord and pulled frantically on it, and then, lest the bell not be sufficient summons, he began bellowing for the servants.

Anna-Maria smiled, feeling suddenly very wise and mature. She felt motherly even toward Francis who, despite his age, was acting like a child. Suddenly a pain hit her, and she gasped involuntarily, startled by the force of it. Francis sprang to her side, fearful as he saw the sweat beginning to stand out in beads on her face.

"Sarah! Damn you, Sarah! Where are you?"

Sarah came into the room at a run, panting, "I went to fetch the midwife. I thought it best she be on hand."

The pain was ebbing now, and Anna-Maria, slightly breathless, said, "Francis, I want you to go to Whitehall and go about your business. The midwife tells me that a first birth is always a prolonged affair, and I don't want you here to suffer needlessly. At Whitehall you'll be distracted."

Francis protested and knelt by her side, smoothing the damp hair back from her face. Then Sarah asked to speak to him. Pulling him aside, she whispered, "It will be a kindness if you obey her, my lord. If you are at home, she will stifle her screams for your sake."

Francis nodded, his eyes on Anna-Maria's sweating white face. "You may be right," he said reluctantly. "Will you swear to send me a messenger the moment the baby is born?"

"You can be certain that I will." Sarah smiled at him reassuringly.

Francis went over to Anna-Maria, lifted her gently from her chair, and deposited her on the bed. Bending over her he said softly, "Since Sarah and you both command it, I will go to Whitehall. But my thoughts will be here with you."

Another pain struck her, and Anna-Maria found herself unable to speak. Pressing Francis's hand, she managed a wan smile. He groaned and left the room, nearly bumping into the midwife who was just entering. Sarah, knowing nothing of London midwives and darkly suspicious of them, had insisted on bringing Mrs. Thompson from the village near Grafton Manor, and several weeks before, she had been ensconced in a room in the house. A sparkling clean, rosy-faced woman of forty-five, she had been practicing her midwifery skills for nearly twenty-five years. Bobbing her gray head, she smiled happily at Anna-Maria. "So the baby has decided to be born, has he?"

Anna-Maria laughed weakly. "We all speak of the baby as 'he.' Suppose the baby chooses to be a girl?"

Mrs. Thompson smiled cheerfully. "Then we'll have a fine new life in the world, won't we? And the *next* child can be a boy."

She pressed delicately on Anna-Maria's stomach, assessing the contractions and then sent Sarah out of the room. When Sarah returned with a pot of sweet-smelling butter, she dipped her fingers in it and carefully oiled her hands. Then she lifted Anna-Maria's gown and began a gently probing examination.

At its conclusion, she washed her hands and announced with satisfaction, "Everything is progressing well. But it will be a few hours yet before the baby —he or she—" she threw a twinkling glance at Anna-Maria, "—arrives."

She bustled over to the bed. "Best we get you as comfortable as possible."

She and Sarah helped Anna-Maria into her nightdress and then bathed her hands and face with cool water. Mrs. Thompson began tying a strong white cloth to the knob of the bedpost, and Anna-Maria craned her head, following the movements with curiosity. "What is that for?"

"To pull on when the pain is bad."

Hours later Anna-Maria writhed on the bed, fully tasting pain for the first time. She had never dreamed that pain like this existed in all the world. Surely when pain was this intense, death must follow. She would have liked to have questioned Mrs. Thompson, but her breath was coming in short pants, and she had none to spare for speech. Sarah would see her condition and send for a priest. She didn't want to die unshriven. But dying in the act of giving life might be an act of contrition in itself.

"Oh, Jesus, Blessed Virgin. Let me live long enough to hold my baby in my arms," she prayed. Sweat was streaming down her forehead, mingling with the tears that poured unchecked down her cheeks.

She desperately wanted to be brave, but despite her best intentions, she felt herself straining against the white cloth tied to the bedpost, involuntary screams coming from her lips.

Through the dark haze of pain, she dimly heard Mrs. Thompson whispering to Sarah, "She's as narrow and slender as a child. It goes badly with her. I feared this."

Sarah's answering voice was a whispered hiss of rage. "Why didn't you *tell* us?"

"It would have served no purpose to frighten the countess. The baby was already in her womb. I had hoped that it would be born early, when it was still small enough to slip out easily."

Sobbing, Sarah turned away. Another pain had seized Anna-Maria now, and she was helpless under its assault. In a moment Sarah was by her side, her face streaked with tears. "Anna-Maria, *push down*. You must push to help the baby from the womb. Push! Push!" Over and over Sarah and Mrs. Thompson commanded her to push, and Anna-Maria tried valiantly to obey for the baby's sake, but there was no respite between pains now, and she was dangerously exhausted.

Once she fainted, but Sarah held a burnt feather under her nose and slapped her repeatedly across the face. Anna-Maria's tear-dark eyes reproached her. Was this the act of a friend? To bring her back into relentless pain? Sarah flinched, but leaning close against Anna-Maria's ear, she said fiercely, "It's for the baby's sake! Do you understand? If you faint you cannot help the baby." Instinctively she knew that the only way to reach Anna-Maria now was through her concern for the baby. Anna-Maria might allow herself to die, but not until the child lived.

Anna-Maria, her eyes clinging to Sarah's, nodded. She forced herself to push again.

"Good!" Sarah's voice was strong with encouragement. "Again!"

Oh, God, she couldn't do it again. The temptation to slip away into unconsciousness was almost unbearable. Anna-Maria forced herself to think of the baby. The baby was even more weak and helpless than she, trusting her as its mother. If she died, she couldn't face eternity knowing that she had failed her child.

She bit into her lip and tasted blood. She pushed again, her face growing red with the strain, her hands frantically twisting the cloth knotted to the bedpost.

Suddenly Mrs. Thompson shouted, "The baby is emerging! Push!"

A swell of joy rose in Anna-Maria, and she pushed with renewed vigor. She could feel her body expelling its burden and a sensation of awe swept over her. A new life was suddenly in the world, and she was dazed with the wonder of it.

Mrs. Thompson and Sarah were both working busily now, their words rapid and excited. Anna-Maria attempted to raise herself to see, but Mrs. Thompson pushed her gently backward. A second later Sarah triumphantly held up the baby so that Anna-Maria could view it. "A boy. A fine lusty boy!"

Anna-Maria attempted to see through the tears that were filling her eyes. She began to laugh weakly, a laugh that turned into a feeble cough. It was not the pink-skinned, chubby baby of her dreams. This mite of a stranger was dark red and coated with mucus. But he was alive, was unquestionably alive, his red legs flailing, his thin arms waving. As she watched, he let out a piercing cry, and the sound was the sweetest music Anna-Maria had ever heard. Smiling, she sank into unconsciousness.

Eight

Anna-Maria hung over her child's cradle, tickling his nose. "You're a very special baby, do you know that? You're the first godchild of the king, the first baby to be born after his restoration to the throne, and you bear his name."

Picking up the baby, she held him over head, laughing up at him. He yawned, and a milky bubble formed on his lips. Anna-Maria laughed and hugged him to her. "Don't you *care* that you are named after a king and that he stood sponsor to you?"

She sat down in a chair and laid him in her lap, examining him closely, just as she had done over and over during the two months since his birth. His perfection never ceased to amaze her. She picked up his small hand, kissing it. "I've heard that some of the ladies of the court have their noses out of joint because *they* wanted to be the first to produce a godchild for the king."

Charles waved his free fist in the air and looked at her intently, and Anna-Maria smiled. "I know you can't *really* understand what I'm saying, and since you can't, I'll confide a secret to you. This afternoon I'm to go to court for the first time, and I'm *frightened*." Anna-Maria bent closer. "No doubt I'm being foolish. I'm as highborn as any at court. But they all *know* each other, and I know no one. I'm sure that they are all very fashionable, and they will think me a plain country wren."

Sarah came into the room with a pile of baby garments over her arm and laughed when she found Anna-Maria talking so seriously. "You're going to spoil him. Are you telling him again that he is the most beautiful charming baby ever born on this earth?"

Anna-Maria made a rueful face. "You'll scarce credit this, but I'm confiding my problems to him."

"And what problems do you have, pray? A devoted husband, a beautiful child, an assured position at court!"

Anna-Maria sighed and rose to put Charles back in his cradle. "I know it's ungrateful of me, Sarah. But in truth I'm worried about how I will be received at court. I know scarcely anyone there, and Francis tells me that they are very close-knit. And they are all very clever, always ready with a quip on their tongues to entertain the king."

Sarah looked indignant. "You are as quick-witted as anyone I've ever known! And certainly your beauty will outshine that of any woman at court."

Anna-Maria smiled. "The king, because of the years he spent in exile in France, is enchanted with everything French. It may be to my advantage that I was educated in France." She began to laugh. "Isn't life strange? Just before I met Francis, my father warned me not to be too French in my accent and mannerisms because Englishmen hate the French."

"The average Englishman still does," Sarah said grimly. "But if the French are fashionable at court, then I suggest that you give free rein to your French accent."

"Oui, madame!" Anna-Maria grinned impishly at Sarah and made a little pirouette. Then she stopped and looked at the ornate Venetian clock on the mantel. "Do you think it is time for me to start dressing?"

" 'Tis nearly three hours yet until you are due at Whitehall. But it may be best to start your toilette now, since you are too excited to do anything else."

They chatted and giggled as Anna-Maria dressed, and Anna-Maria could feel some of her nervousness slipping away. It was a shame that Sarah was a servant and could not come to court with her. It would be wonderful to have a close friend of her own rank.

Anna-Maria and Sarah fussed for nearly an hour over her hair, pulling it into a large soft swirl on the top of her head with a few tendrils escaping forward toward her cheeks.

When the last wisp was in place, Anna-Maria raced eagerly to fetch one of the gowns that she had had made recently by a London dressmaker who vowed that it was the latest word in fashion. Anna-Maria thought it exquisitely pretty but inappropriate for afternoon wear. The bodice was cut perilously low, so low that her nipples were in danger of popping free. And indeed, when she took a deep breath, the soft pink of her nipples showed through the gauze ruffle that edged the bodice. Anna-Maria tugged at the neckline, modestly trying to raise it, but Sarah stopped her. "The dressmaker swore that this is the fashion. Leave it be."

Anna-Maria's slender figure had returned to normal after the birth of Charles, except that her normally nineteen-inch waist now measured an implacable twenty inches no matter how much Sarah strained to tighten the lace of her busk. Anna-Maria laughed, a bit breathlessly because of the constriction. "No matter. At least laced this tightly, I'll be in no danger of breathing deeply, and my nipples will remain modestly hidden."

Sarah stepped back to look at Anna-Maria and clapped her hands in admiration.

The gown was of a deep leaf green, and the full skirt was pulled back and held in place with bows of a lighter shade of green, revealing an underskirt of spring green.

Anna-Maria peered anxiously at herself in the mirror and then nodded slowly. "I think that Francis will not be ashamed to introduce me at court."

When Francis walked into the room a few moments later, he looked at her and said, "I'll be a proud man today, wearing you on my arm like an ornament. I've already been besieged by courtiers who have heard rumors of your beauty and are anxious to catch a glimpse of you."

The thought of strangers peering at her made Anna-Maria flinch. She would rather have been able to creep into court and remain unnoticed for a time. But picking up her fan, she raised her chin bravely. "I'm ready, Francis."

Whitehall Palace was a far cry from the peace and serenity of Deene or Grafton Manor. One after another, coaches rattled across the cobblestones, discharging elegantly dressed men and women. Anna-Maria looked at Francis quizzically. "Does everyone in the world come to Whitehall?"

Francis laughed shortly. "There are many who are eager for the king's favor. He is besieged day and night by Royalists who want their lands restored. Poor man, he gets no peace."

Anna-Maria sat forward eagerly. "But surely, Francis, the king will be happy to restore their lands to those who worked so long and hard in his service! Why, I should think it would be the first thing he would want to do on returning home."

Francis shook his head ruefully. " 'Tis not such an easy matter, my sweet. Think of the complications. Often those lands were sold over and over, each sale legal. To do justice to one is to harm another innocent person."

Suddenly Anna-Maria's attention was caught by two figures a few yards away. "Isn't that the king?"

King Charles, his black head thrown back in laughter, was striding rapidly along, his arm thrown carelessly over the shoulders of his male companion. Anna-Maria felt her heart skip a beat as she stared at the back of the king's companion. The man's hair was golden in the sunshine, and his stride was as rapid and graceful as the king's.

Francis leaned forward, "Aye. And the duke of Buckingham is with him, as usual. No doubt they are headed for the Stone Gallery. We'll catch up with them there."

Anna-Maria leaned back against the cushions and closed her eyes, blaming her queer breathlessness and the erratic beating of her heart on her tight lacing.

As their coach bumped to a stop, Francis sprang from it with the alacrity of a young boy, anxious to display his beautiful wife to the courtiers and equally anxious to have Anna-Maria see his importance at court.

Anna-Maria, numbed, tucked her arm under Francis's and followed him obediently.

She was stunned at her first sight of the Stone Gallery. It seemed to stretch endlessly, one wall broken at intervals by red velvet curtains concealing doorways to various apartments in the palace. For a moment she pulled back, confused by the throng of people, the din of many conversations being carried on simultaneously, the sudden onslaught of scents and colors.

Francis bent close to her ear. "This is a favorite meeting place." His expression was disapproving. "The king surrounds himself with wastrels!"

Anna-Maria was too busy drinking in the fascinating scene before her to listen to him. As she watched, one woman laughed at the man she was standing with and then tapped him reprovingly on his nose, the gesture charmingly flirtatious. Was it her husband? Anna-Maria wondered. Surely it must be. No woman would be so bold with a man to whom she was not married.

The heat and press of bodies was stifling, and Anna-Maria wished she had enough room to raise her fan and cool herself. Snatches of conversation reached her ears, and she listened avidly to a light, feminine voice. "Had I known you would make so bold, my lord, I would not have agreed to this meeting today." Anna-Maria stopped, tempted to eavesdrop, but Francis relentlessly urged her on.

She pulled at his sleeve to get his attention. "Where are we going?"

Francis looked down at her and said briefly, "To find the king."

Finally they reached the outskirts of the group surrounding the king. A few in the outer circle turned as Francis and Anna-Maria arrived. Anna-Maria flinched under their frank scrutiny.

Surely it was rude to stare so, she thought indignantly. And why was that blond woman looking at her with such disdain? Her indignation melted suddenly under a wave of uncomfortable shyness. Oh, she wished she were back in her own room playing with her baby. One courtier, a short man with spindly legs, examined her as though she were a horse offered for auction and then gave a low, soundless whistle of approval. Anna-Maria gasped and looked at Francis, hoping that he would chastise the gentleman for his rudeness. But Francis had not noticed the byplay. He was looking toward the king, eager to catch his attention. Anna-Maria stood by his side, feeling naked and defenseless. She was appalled to see open hostility in the faces of the women who were appraising her. In her innocence and modesty, she didn't realize that they were jealous of any beautiful newcomer to court. She thought the fault must be within herself.

Suddenly she blushed as she realized that her elaborate, fashionable dress was not enough. Her face and coiffure gave her away as a country bumpkin! The other women had painted their faces, and a few wore imaginative beauty patches to point up their best features. The blond who had first looked so disdainfully at Anna-Maria had a small cupid pasted near her right eye. Anna-Maria nervously put her hand to the nape of her neck. She was the only woman wearing her hair on the top of her head. The others had elaborate cascades of curls massed at the back of their necks and small curls framing their foreheads and cheeks.

For a moment she wanted to turn and run, but the king had already spotted Francis at the back of the crowd. "Hoy! Shrewsbury!" The king had a natural talent for friendship, for making each man feel he was important.

Francis, his face alight with gratification, was moving toward the king, drawing Anna-Maria with him. Reluctantly the crowd parted to let them through.

The king clapped Francis heartily on the shoulder and then bent over Anna-Maria's hand with a courtly gesture. "It is good to see your lovely face at court, countess. Too long have you kept us waiting."

What charm this man has, Anna-Maria thought. She could almost believe that the king had been waiting impatiently, feeling his court incomplete until she arrived.

The king put his arm around an older man, drawing him forward to be presented to Anna-Maria. "My good friend, Thomas Killigrew."

Killigrew, lean and aristocratic of face, stepped forward and bent over Anna-Maria's hand. "I'm charmed to make your acquaintance." His kiss on her hand was exactly right, she thought, neither too wetly lingering nor too perfunctory.

"I claim the same privilege as my father!" A laughing voice caught their attention, and Anna-Maria looked up to find a man of twenty-six or so elbowing his way through the crowd toward them. He had light brown hair and dark, mischievous eyes.

"My son, Henry," Thomas Killigrew murmured to Anna-Maria. There was a wry look on his face.

Henry Killigrew, flushed with triumph, succeeded in reaching them and looked at the king boldly. "Well, Charles, am I to be presented to our newest ornament at court?"

The king grinned. "I'll be doing the countess of Shrewsbury no service, Henry!"

"Countess of Shrewsbury, may I present Henry Killigrew, the wildest rascal in all of England."

"At your service!" Henry Killigrew bent over Anna-Maria's hand, his light brown mustache tickling her as he lingered over his kiss. When he raised his head, Anna-Maria saw that he had the same narrow, aristocratic face as his father.

Henry Killigrew nodded at Francis. "Shrewsbury, I congratulate you on your choice of a wife."

Francis nodded back frostily. Henry Killigrew was a notorious wastrel. The king valued Killigrew for his boisterous wit and his wild tongue, but Francis despised him because he was usually embroiled in one unsavory mess or another. Killigrew was rumored to visit the lowest of brothels nightly, and it sickened Francis to see his wife's slim hand in Killigrew's.

The king had an arm around each of the Killigrews now. Talking to both Francis and Anna-Maria, he said, "They are costing me a pretty penny, these two. They are building me a new theatre."

Tom Killigrew started to protest, but the king cut

him off with a laugh. "I but jest, Tom. I trust you with my pocketbook as I would trust you with my life."

Thomas Killigrew, gratified, began to describe the theatre he was building to Francis, who listened attentively.

Henry Killigrew was silent, staring at Anna-Maria, his glance sweeping down her body as though he were attempting to penetrate her clothing.

Nervously she broke the silence. "It appears that both you and your father are great friends of the king."

Killigrew nodded absently, his gaze on her breasts. "My father has been appointed groom of the bedchamber to the king, and I to the duke of York."

Anna-Maria flushed and was casting about in her mind for another remark when the king caught her attention. "Buckingham! Over here!"

Killigrew's eyes narrowed angrily as Anna-Maria turned from him. She was watching intently, scarcely breathing, as the duke of Buckingham made his way toward them. The duke was taller than any of the other men at court. Was easily visible as he moved through the crowd. In deference to his importance, the courtiers fell back to give him passage.

The king clapped Buckingham on the shoulder, but before he could say anything, Tom Killigrew said, "Shrewsbury has just raised an interesting point about the cupola for the theatre." Immediately absorbed, the king forgot to introduce Buckingham to Anna-Maria.

Amused, Buckingham looked down at Anna-Maria. "It seems that we must make ourselves known to one another without formality."

Anna-Maria was staring at him entranced, her lips slightly parted. He had lost none of his godlike quality up close. His skin was unmarked, his lips sensuous beneath his blond mustache.

The amusement in Buckingham's blue eyes changed to puzzlement, then suddenly his eyes lit with recollection. Once before he had seen this oval face, these dark eyes with their thick fringe of lashes.

"I tossed you a flower once." His voice was deep and tender, sending shivers down Anna-Maria's spine.

She intended to say, "You are kind to remember, my lord." But instead she said simply, "Yes, I have it still."

The crowds in the room seemed to fade away as they stood looking at each other. Then Henry Killigrew's voice jolted Anna-Maria back to reality. "Perhaps *I* may have the honor of presenting you to each other, since the king is remiss. My lord, duke of Buckingham, this is Anna-Maria, countess of Shrewsbury, *wife* of Francis Talbot."

Anna-Maria stood mute, her senses in a turmoil. She was scarcely aware of Henry Killigrew's persistent attention, scarcely noticing as he picked up the gold cross that dangled between her breasts, affecting to admire it, but in reality stealing the opportunity to graze the creamy mounds that swelled above her low-cut bodice.

Buckingham noted the gesture with distaste, and his fine eyebrows arched. Kindly he bent his head and spoke to Anna-Maria in a low, intimate tone. "You bring to my mind a young lamb set down among a pack of ravenous wolves. You'd best be careful at court."

Anna-Maria looked up at him uncomprehendingly, and the purity of her face stirred his heart. He smiled down at her. "I don't mean to frighten you. Only to warn you that your innocence will not protect you here at court. It will only serve to inflame wastrels such as Killigrew."

Anna-Maria looked at him in bewilderment.

He groaned and said softly, "God's blood! Your beauty and sweetness would stir any man's senses." He seemed on the point of speaking further, but then he checked himself, made an abrupt bow, and walked away, leaving Anna-Maria staring after him, her lips slightly parted.

Nine

Anna-Maria was often bewildered at court. She felt that she had been thrust abruptly on stage to act in a play where all the others knew their lines and only she was stumbling through without a script. One night as she sat at her dressing table, limp with fatigue, she suddenly threw the brush down violently, buried her face in her hands, and let the tears flow unchecked.

Francis, who was sitting in a chair near the fireplace checking over the contents of the black dispatch box that was always at his side, got up, bewildered. He had never seen Anna-Maria cry, and he had congratulated himself that she was not like other women, prone to depressions.

Anna-Maria turned and threw her arms about his waist, burying her face in the slight paunch of his stomach, hoping for comfort. "Oh, Francis, I'm so *tired*," she wailed. A slight look of distaste crossed his features. He, too, was tired. He had been up since dawn and busy all day on the king's business. Surely Anna-Maria, who had nothing but pleasures to occupy her day, had no right to complain of fatigue. Nevertheless, he put a soothing hand on her bent head and rubbed it with the rough affection that one would give a favored dog.

At his touch Anna-Maria raised her head, her dark eyes luminous beneath a film of tears. "Oh, Francis, I scarce have time to play with the baby any longer. And I'll vow Polly thinks that *Sarah* is her real mother."

Anna-Maria's face was white with strain. She had been in attendance at court all day, ridden in Hyde Park in the afternoon, and attended a ball that night. She had danced until her legs ached and been besieged by a series of courtiers who had begged her for a smile, a word, a lock of her hair. She had smiled until her jaw hurt, and all the time she had been longing for the comfort of her clean white sheets. Francis had refused to attend the ball, preferring as he usually did to stay at home, a glass of brandy at his hand, pouring over the contents of his black dispatch case.

He moved his hand abruptly from her bright head. His voice was frosty. "I can scarce credit that you are complaining because I ask you to spend your days in pleasure."

Anna-Maria flinched at his tone but held her head up defiantly. "Don't you see that pleasure is no longer pleasure when it becomes a fatiguing duty? Having nothing but pleasures is like stuffing oneself with too many sweetmeats."

Francis was certain that many of the courtiers thought him foolish to allow Anna-Maria to go so frequently to court without him. Already her beauty had created a sensation, but Francis trusted implicitly in her innocence and her innate good sense.

"Let's sit together by the fire and talk this over." After helping her to a chair, he sat down in his own chair, his hand moving unconsciously to the black dispatch box resting on the table next to the chair arm. Anna-Maria, noting the gesture, felt a quick prick of resentment. That box had taken the place of wife, child, and family for Francis she thought, and then was instantly ashamed of her pettiness. It was true, though, that Francis was seldom tender with her now, as he had been in the early part of their marriage. He treated her with an offhand affection, the exact amount that a gentleman of honor must accord his wife, no more, no less.

Her head thrown back, she watched Francis from under her lashes as he placed his hands together, forming a tent with them, collecting his thoughts. Finally he said slowly, "It's true, Anna-Maria, that you have always been accustomed to a quiet life—the convent, the slow pace of the country at Deene and Grafton Manor. But Anna-Maria" he said, leaning forward now, his elbows propped on his knees, "you're scarcely twenty-two years old and should be brimming with energy. Most young women your age would be delirious with joy to be part of the court of Charles the Second. It's said to be the most exciting court in all of Europe!" Francis's mouth pulled in distaste although he was quick to hide his expression from Anna-Maria.

"Francis, you've changed since we've come to London."

Francis looked annoyed. "I've not changed at all, Anna-Maria. I've always been an ambitious man. Now I have an opportunity to give full rein to my ambition." He gestured toward the dispatch box. "I work hard for the good of England."

Anna-Maria nodded, "I know that you do but—"

Francis broke in, "Anna-Maria, all I ask of you is that you be my true helpmeet. I cannot waste my time with the frivolities at court. It is important that you go in my stead." He sighed, a look of scorn crossing his face. "Unfortunately, the king is a frivolous man, and often the way to his favor is to share his pleasures. It is not my nature to be the kind of companion that the king enjoys. I'm not quick with a jest, I am not ribald."

Anna-Maria felt a quick pang of sympathy for him. At the same time she was bewildered and a little frightened. "But what are you suggesting? Surely *I* cannot be a companion for the king?" The king already had a reputation for bedding with any pretty young woman of the court who took his fancy.

At the look of horror on Anna-Maria's face, Francis leaned forward and took her hands in his. "Anna-Maria, I am suggesting nothing immoral. Merely that the king see the countess of Shrewsbury constantly at court, adding to the merriment. I ask only that he enjoy the sight of your pretty face. It will warm his heart toward our family." He sighed, his brows knitted. "I often question whether or not the king appreciates the vast amount of time I give to his business. You will bring me to his attention, and then my work will receive the rewards it deserves."

"What is it that you want?" Anna-Maria asked with curiosity. Francis often seemed to be a driven man.

"Nothing selfish," Francis said quickly. "I'm working for your family's good as well. I've hopes to have your father made earl of Cardigan before the year is out."

Despite her fatigue, Anna-Maria sat forward. How pleased her father would be!

Francis seized the moment. "You see? All I ask is that you enjoy yourself at court. No more. And you will be helping your father, as well as me."

Anna-Maria reached forward and lifted Francis's brandy glass, which was on the table by his side. There was a scant inch of the dark liquid left. She raised the glass to her lips and quickly drained the glass, hoping it would quicken her brain. It made no sense to her that if she were seen at court, laughing, flirting, helping to devise masques, it would aid her father in becoming the earl of Cardigan. Still she was ignorant of the ways of politics, and Francis knew what he was about.

She forced herself to smile at him. "No doubt I can accustom myself to ceaseless pleasure." As she spoke, a sudden image of their wedding in the chapel rose to her mind. She had vowed to stand always by this man's side, supporting him in every way possible. At the time she thought her duties would be to raise a flock of children and to manage a vast household with grace and ease. Life took strange turns indeed.

Setting the glass back on the table, she said, "If I'm to help you, Francis, then I'd best sleep now. I must be up early to be fitted by the dressmaker."

As she turned, Anna-Maria noted the gleam in Francis's eyes, and her heart sank. For a moment she wanted to rebel—she craved sleep so desperately that she was on the point of tears. Francis was out of his chair now, his hand already on her breast, and Anna-Maria forced herself not to pull away. It was a sin for a wife to deny herself to her husband. This might be the night on which a child was conceived, and if she denied Francis, she would be denying life itself. She bit her lip as Francis lifted her into his arms and crossed the room to lay her on the bed. If only God had devised another method for bringing children into the world. Men seemed to set great store by the act of lovemaking, but for a woman it was a matter of lying rigid, fighting down the urge to push the man away, until he had had his pleasure and collapsed against her. Then, she could turn her face to the wall and find the sleep she had been craving. She lay back, resigned to doing her duty.

She was up early the next morning, determined to begin her task of turning herself into a fashionable lady of the court of Charles the Second. In the past she had been fairly modest in her dress expenses, feeling that it was almost sinful to spend exorbitant sums on personal adornment. She had been amazed—and a little amused—by the women at court who vowed themselves ashamed to be seen in the same gown twice. Now, while the dressmaker watched in astonishment, she recklessly began selecting fabric after fabric, rich satin, purest silk, the finest of laces.

The dressmaker's eyes gleamed, and she began counting up the unexpected riches that had befallen her, her hands hidden in the folds of her dress as she reckoned on her fingers. Pray God that Lady Shrewsbury's uncharacteristic mood of extravagance continued. She was a rare pleasure to dress. Her slim waist and full bosom made each garment she wore a splendid advertisement for her dressmaker.

Anna-Maria held a length of red satin under her chin, tossed it onto the heap of colorful fabric, and laughed a bit breathlessly as she surveyed the pile. Then she gently picked up a piece of primrose yellow silk, her slim fingers caressing the delicate material, and said, "Please make this up for my daughter." Her face glowed as she thought of how sweet Polly would look in the diminutive gown.

Later, as Sarah was dressing her, Anna-Maria said, "I've picked out a great number of new fabrics for Mrs. Muggs to make up. I vow I'm going to be the most fashionably dressed lady at the court."

Worried, Sarah looked at Anna-Maria. She seemed very high strung today.

"Francis has made clear to me that it is my *duty* as

his wife to be immensely fashionable and popular at court. Instead of being reluctant to join in the frivolities, I am going to throw myself into it with all my energy."

In the months that followed, Anna-Maria became one of the most sought-after beauties at court, constantly pursued by a string of suitors. Her beauty attracted them, but it was her maddening virtue and tricks of flirtation that kept them at her heels. She had studied the coquettes at court, and from them had picked up a whole repertoire of flirtatious mannerisms. She became devastatingly skillful at glancing up and sideways at a suitor from under her long dark lashes, pouting prettily, and producing a low, seductive laugh at the proper moment.

She had started it merely as a game to please Francis, but soon she found that her success was exhilarating. It was exciting to stand in the Stone Gallery surrounded by a group of attractive, entertaining gentlemen who vied with each other to get a special glance from her or a private word of favor. She laughed prettily, her vanity tickled, when several of the gentlemen begged for locks of her chestnut hair to be made into bracelets. She gave them readily, and soon more and more were begging for a similar favor until she complained to Sarah that she was in danger of becoming bald.

Life at court was hectic, but she was adjusting to the pace, able to ride at a fashionable hour in the morning, attend the theatre in the afternoon, and then dance all night.

Henry Jermyn, master of the horse to the duke of York, the king's brother, was one of her most persistent suitors. Henry amused her, and she allowed him to escort her more frequently than any of her other admirers. He was short, scarcely a quarter inch taller than she was, and his spindly legs were his private despair. Still, he was considered extremely handsome with his dark eyes and sensual mouth. His success with women was legion at court, and he frequently complained to Anna-Maria, "You are the only woman who has ever remained cold to me. I fear that I must go to my grave longing for you."

Anna-Maria would laugh at him. "I'm *not* cold to you, Henry. I'm more kind to you than to any other man at court." Henry, with his irreverent wit and never-ending fund of gossip was excellent company. Occasionally his persistent attempts to seduce her would become annoying. "I'm *married*, Henry," she would say firmly and then be cool to him for a few days until he meekly came to her, begging her forgiveness.

During her first months at court, she believed that the constant flirtations between the beauties and courtiers were merely harmless pastimes, a matter of words and empty gestures. It was Jane Middleton, the closest she had to a friend among the women, who enlightened her one day.

She and Jane were strolling along Birdcage Walk in St. James Park. The air was mellow, and the chirping of the birds formed a pleasant background for conversation. Many of the courtiers were taking advantage of the beauty of the day, and shouts of laughter and snatches of conversation were audible on the clear air.

Jane was talking idly of the play they had seen the day before. Anna-Maria appeared to be paying attention to Jane, but in reality her mind was wandering. Jane's conversation was frankly tedious. She had flirted so hectically during the play that she had caught very little of the performance, and it was ludicrous that she should be attempting to criticize it now.

Bored, Anna-Maria wandered off the path, hoping that Jane would fear to soil the hem of her gown on the damp grass and would refuse to follow her. But Jane plunged into the bushes beside Anna-Maria, still talking affectedly. Suddenly Anna-Maria tensed and Jane broke off abruptly, puzzled at Anna-Maria's strangeness.

Anna-Maria was staring into a dense clump of thick foliage. A soft, quickly suppressed laugh caught Jane's attention, and she narrowed her eyes, focusing. Then laughing and giving a shrug, she turned to Anna-Maria. " 'Tis only Elizabeth—Lady Chesterfield."

"But what is she *doing?*" Anna-Maria's lips were

parted, and her large eyes were dark with shock. Elizabeth was lying on the earth, her bodice open, her huge breasts spilling loose. An auburn-haired man was lying next to her, fondling her breasts. The scene reminded Anna-Maria of the day she had lain on the cold earth with the gypsy leaning above her, and she instinctively moved to go to Elizabeth's defense. Then, as she watched, Elizabeth gave a low, smothered laugh and tangled her hand in the back of the man's hair, pulling his lips down to hers.

Anna-Maria gave a shocked gasp. Jane, who had been looking on with frank interest, laughed. "Elizabeth has caught herself a youth fresh up from the country. He only arrived but yesterday." She began to walk on, carelessly indifferent.

But Anna-Maria did not move. Turning, Jane asked, "Had you an eye on him for yourself? Be patient. Elizabeth is notoriously fickle. No doubt she'll be finished with him once she has lain with him a time or two."

Anna-Maria stared at her. "An eye for him myself! Jane, I would never do such a thing!"

Jane stared at Anna-Maria, her eyes narrowing. Then she tossed her head and tapped Anna-Maria reprovingly with her fan. "I vow you play the innocent so well that you should be on the stage." She knew that half the men at court were wearing bracelets made of Anna-Maria's chestnut locks, and a woman only bestowed such a trophy on a man after he had enjoyed her favors.

Anna-Maria looked bewildered. "But Elizabeth is *married.*"

Jane nodded. "Aye, but she hates Phillip because of his affair with Barbara Palmer, and she takes her pleasure elsewhere."

Anna-Maria's senses were reeling. Barbara Palmer was the beautiful red-haired mistress of the king. Could she be lying with Lord Chesterfield as well? "But Jane, lovemaking is no *pleasure* for a woman. She does it only to please her husband and to have children."

Abruptly Jane dropped her carefully cultivated pose. "Are you mad? Lovemaking is our very reason for existence. I vow I could not survive a night if I did not have a hot-blooded lover in my arms."

Anna-Maria was blushing, her expression dazed. Jane stared at her for a moment, her eyes narrowed. Then she threw back her head and laughed. Anna-Maria was the most provocative flirt at court, and yet the truth was that she was cold. The courtiers who boasted of her favors were nothing but lying braggarts. Privately, Jane thought that Anna-Maria must be mad if she did not quicken to a man's embrace, but she had a sudden feeling of genuine warmth for the girl. If she were cold, she was no longer a rival. She took Anna-Maria's arm. "Come, let us walk if the sight disturbs you."

Anna-Maria let herself be led by Jane, her senses in turmoil. The scene she had just witnessed was too disturbing a reminder of the day in the woods with the gypsy. Once she *had* been stirred by a man's hot, sweet kisses, and no doubt that was what Elizabeth was experiencing now. For a moment she felt again the sweet fire that had run through her veins at the touch of the gypsy's kiss, and she felt a quick pang of envy of Elizabeth. Trying to escape her sinful thoughts, she quickened her pace. Jane followed, protesting.

At a curve in the path, they nearly collided with the duke of Buckingham. He moved aside gracefully, laughing. Taking off his hat, he swept down in a deep bow. "And what, pray, causes two such lovely ladies to rush so? A forgotten appointment with the dressmaker? News that a new hairstyle has been introduced?"

Buckingham was wearing a suit of deep plum color, and the tight-fitting breeches were molded closely to his legs. Jane's eyes lit appreciatively, but Anna-Maria was embarrassed at the sudden encounter. In recent months she had come to feel very relaxed with the duke of Buckingham. He was invariably tender and kind to her, and she had come to look upon him as a friend at court. Now, simply because he was a man and her thoughts were in turmoil, old memories were revived, and she found herself unable to look at him.

Buckingham noted her downcast eyes. Anna-Maria never failed to stir some deep well of tenderness in him, as no other woman had ever done. Putting a gentle finger under Anna-Maria's chin, he raised her head. "What's amiss, Anna-Maria?"

Under the gentle pressure of his finger, Anna-Maria tipped her head and looked deeply into his eyes. At the kindness there, she felt a sudden flash of pleasure go through her body that left her weak and trembling. As their glances held, she completely forgot that Jane was at her side, forgot everything except the intense blueness of his eyes.

For a moment she was tempted to reveal her thoughts to him as she would have done to no one in the world except Sarah. Then Jane's high-pitched giggle broke the spell. "She was but fretting because there were no handsome gentlemen about. Your arrival has remedied the difficulty, my lord." Reluctantly, the duke turned courteously to Jane. Anna-Maria stood by numbly while Jane flirted brazenly with the duke. Once, when Jane made a particularly inane remark, the duke's eyes met Anna-Maria's, and they smiled at each other in shared recognition of the joke. It was a moment of intimacy, and Anna-Maria felt a breathless delight.

When Buckingham finally made a bow and parted from them Jane gave an exaggerated sigh. "I vow that Buckingham is the most handsome man at court. When he looks at me with those blue eyes of his I swear I could swoon."

Anna-Maria breathed deeply, trying to quiet the bewildering excitement that always seized her when she was near Buckingham. She watched him as he strode down the path, her pulse quickening at the grace of his masculine stride, the way the sunlight crested off his golden head. "Yes," she said softly, "he is very handsome." Then she turned abruptly and began walking in the opposite direction, moving rapidly in an attempt to outdistance her bewildering, turbulent emotions.

Ten

When she got home, she immediately sought out Sarah and poured out the events of the day, as well as her confusion about them. Sarah probably knew more about the love affairs of the nobility than she herself. There were no secrets from servants, and they had ample opportunities for gossiping. The court of Charles the Second was the most licentious in all of Europe, and the love affairs of the king and his courtiers provided endless juicy morsels of gossip for the lower classes.

Sarah was relieved that Anna-Maria had confided in her, for she had often wondered, in the past months, if she ought to warn Anna-Maria that the flirtations she thought so harmless were in reality serious. But always she had put it off, thinking that Anna-Maria's innocence was her best shield.

Sarah had carefully guarded her own virginity, but recently she had fallen in love with young Sir Joseph Phillips, a distant cousin of Francis's, who was acting as secretary to Sir John Talbot. Soon, she knew, she must trust him with the secret of her noble birth. When he knew that her blood was as fine as his own he might even offer to marry her, even though she lacked a dowry. If not, Sarah feared she would succumb to her increasing desires and find herself in his bed, marriage or not.

She chose her words carefully. "There *are* women, Anna-Maria, who enjoy the pleasure of a man's body. It is possible that because your first experience of lovemaking was unpleasant, the part of you that was destined to thrill to a man's touch died." Inwardly Sarah cursed the gypsy. Who knew what lifelong damage he had done to Anna-Maria by raping her?

Anna-Maria picked up a brush and began stroking her long, gleaming hair. "It would be wonderful to en-

92

joy a husband's lovemaking." She thought of Francis and herself in bed and shrank from the memory. "But, Sarah, I'm talking about adultery—sin! Jane Middleton takes it so lightly."

Sarah replied, "You know well that the king encourages it."

Anna-Maria bit her lips. "I love the king, and it is difficult to criticize him. But after all he is a man, and men's passions run high. But Sarah, it is the *women* I don't understand. Oh, I can see why a woman would consent to share the king's bed. It is an honor, and no doubt she feels that she is doing it for the good of her family, to further their fortunes."

Sarah smiled. The king was an appealingly handsome man, and even Sarah had sometimes found his lean, dark face stealing into her dreams at night.

Anna-Maria continued, "But women like Jane Middleton and Lady Chesterfield don't make love for honor and glory. They do it for their own pleasure. Or so Jane says."

Sarah decided she must tell her mistress the truth. "Those courtiers who pursue you constantly are not merely exchanging pleasantries. They truly have hopes to take you to their beds."

Anna-Maria gasped and swung around on the stool. "I give them no reason to dream of such a thing!" Then she stopped, horrified. All the tricks of flirtation that she had studied in the beauties at court and imitated no doubt meant something entirely different from what she had intended.

Sarah nodded. "Your husband has set you a difficult task. In order to be popular at court as he demands, you *must* flirt. If you are overly meek and virtuous, you'll put a pall over the court, and you'll soon find yourself unwelcome."

Tears filled Anna-Maria's eyes, and her head began to ache. "What shall I do?"

"Exactly as you have been doing," Sarah said firmly. "You are already established as one of the most sought-after beauties at court. You must continue to flirt and be gay. The only difference is now you are aware that the courtiers are serious in their intent." She sighed. "I don't know whether innocence or knowledge serves you better in your situation."

The next time she went to court, Anna-Maria was stiff and uncomfortable. When Tom Howard bent over her hand, his jet black hair glinting like a raven's wing in the sun, she had to force herself not to pull her hand away. His dark eyes were filled with a hot light that she fully understood for the first time. She could no longer act spontaneously.

Henry Killigrew and Henry Jermyn were becoming more persistent in their attentions to her. Anna-Maria responded with practiced flirtatiousness, but there was a new wariness in her manner. Cheerful Jermyn seemed to notice nothing amiss, but she often caught Killigrew looking at her with speculation in his intelligent eyes. Fortunately, it was easy these days to divert the conversation from herself by mentioning the forthcoming coronation. Already London was ringing to the sound of scaffolds being built, and ambitious noblemen were in a fever of excitement because the king would celebrate his coronation by creating new peerages and bestowing honors on his favorites.

As March moved into April, Francis was scarcely at home, coming in merely to fling off his clothing, bathe, and change. By ancestral right he was to bear the second sword at the coronation and—despite his protests that the preparations were far too elaborate and costly for England's slim purse—his gratification was apparent on his face. At times it seemed to Anna-Maria that his ambition was making him physically ill. His skin had a grayish cast, and he often rubbed irritably at his eyes as though they were constantly tired. However, he seemed to take on renewed energy one afternoon when he told her that the king had just made him earl of Waterford in Ireland and was also giving him the post of housekeeper of Hampton Court.

Anna-Maria, pleased for his sake, ran to find the children and returned leading Polly by the hand, with Charles in her arms. "Children," she said ceremoniously, "I wish to present to you your father, the earl of Shrewsbury, earl of Waterford and housekeeper of Hampton Court."

Polly, delighted by the game, smiled, and Anna-Maria bent and swiftly whispered to her. The child nodded and then swept an elaborate curtsy to her father, her blond curls bobbing. Francis's tired face lit with pleasure, and he caught his daughter in his arms. Then, speaking over her head, he said to Anna-Maria, "Your father has been made earl of Cardigan."

Quick joy flamed in Anna-Maria as she thought of her father's happiness. Oh, she had been *right* to marry Francis. Guilt assailed her as she remembered how often she had silently reproached him for his ambition, and yet he truly meant only to provide for the children and herself—and her family.

As the time grew nearer to the coronation, Anna-Maria became increasingly concerned about Francis's health. She coaxed him to eat regular meals and get adequate sleep. On the night before the coronation, she persuaded him to go to bed early, knowing that the next day would be long and strenuous.

Francis obediently went to bed but he protested that he would be unable to sleep and Anna-Maria found that she too was keyed up with excitement. She tossed and turned fitfully and dawn was streaking the windows before she slept.

She woke to the sound of bells pealing wildly throughout London. Rushing to the window, she saw that the cobblestoned streets were strewn with flowers. As she watched, a burly farmer ducked his head under a fountain running with wine and drank deeply, shaking himself like a puppy when he was done, drops of red wine streaming down his broad face.

Anna-Maria remembered last year at this time when she had watched the king riding into London. So much had happened in such a short time; her whole life changed. Last year she had been awaiting the birth of her son. If only she would get pregnant again. Sighing, she turned from the window and roused Francis. " 'Tis the day of the coronation."

Six hours later she watched proudly as Francis bore the second sword at the coronation. The king, followed by Francis, the duke of Buckingham, and the other highest nobles of the land, walked on foot upon a blue cloth laid down from Westminster hall to Westminster Abbey, where the throne had been erected. Anna-Maria found herself mentally calculating the cost of the blue cloth. No wonder Francis had moaned about the extravagance of the coronation. The cloth, soiled by muddy feet and pierced by boot heels, would be in shreds by this evening, fit only for the trash.

Westminster Abbey, in its majesty and grandeur, never failed to awe her. Kings of England, stretching back to the time of William the Conquerer, were buried under the paving stones beneath her feet. It was with a sense of breathless awe at being part of history that Anna-Maria watched the king as he took his oath before the altar, vowing to maintain the religion, the Magna Carta, and the laws of the land. As William Juxon, the archbishop of Canterbury, moved to place the crown on Charles's head, Anna-Maria held her breath. Her knuckles turned white as she clutched the back of the pew. There was a sense of God watching this moment, this awesome moment when a man became an anointed king.

When the crown was firmly on Charles's dark head, shouts of "God save the King!" rose all over the great cathedral, and Anna-Maria found herself shouting with the rest. It was a welcome release after the solemnity of the ritual. Outside the cathedral, the cannons of the Tower boomed, and the sound seemed to reverberate through Anna-Maria's veins. She had the heady sense of living in an exciting time and suddenly she felt grateful to Francis. It was indeed wonderful to be an intimate member of the court of Charles the Second.

The court had barely settled down from the excitement of the coronation when it was rocked by further news. The king was to be married.

Henry Killigrew gave Anna-Maria the news as she was riding in Hyde Park. She had just quarreled with Jermyn and sent him on his way because he was being over-persistent in his wooing, his advances more bold. Henry Killigrew's eyes lit when he caught sight of her riding alone, and he drew abreast of her, reaching for the halter of her mare to bring her to a standstill. "This is a rare find! You are usually so surrounded by smitten swains that it is a day's journey to reach your side."

Anna-Maria laughed. "How are matters at the theatre?" Henry's special pride was the King's Theatre built by his father, Tom Killigrew. It was a dusty, drafty building that nevertheless drew the courtiers almost daily.

Henry smiled. "I've just promoted one of the orange girls to actress, the most beautiful little creature you've ever seen—Nell Gwyn." He laughed. "She's naught but a street urchin, raised in Coleyard, her mother a drunken slut. And yet she has a charm about her, an impish quality that I think will please our audience."

Anna-Maria smiled. "All women are born actresses." She thought wryly of the role she played daily at court, the role she was playing now.

Henry started to talk about a play and then suddenly broke off. "What a dolt I am, chattering about trivialities when I've far more important news. The king is to be married!"

Anna-Maria leaned forward eagerly. "To Barbara Palmer?" The king's red-haired mistress had just been made Lady Castlemaine and had just borne the king a child, a little girl.

Henry threw her a look of masculine exasperation. "Anna-Maria, kings don't *marry* their mistresses. Besides she is already married. Charles is in sore need of money, and his marriage will be with a princess who will bring him a generous dowry—in *gold*." Henry's eyes sparkled. Charles was a generous man, and Henry had no doubt that some of the gold would eventually trickle into Henry's outstretched palm.

Anna-Maria asked eagerly, "But who is she?"

"Catherine of Braganza, the daughter of the queen of Portugal. Portugal is anxious to make an alliance with us since they need our sea power against the might of Spain."

Anna-Maria wanted no explanation of foreign wars and alliances. "What is she like?"

Henry shrugged. "Probably ugly. Most princesses are, although Hyde has assured Charles that she is not uncomely. I only know that she was raised in a convent and has but recently returned to her mother's court."

Anna-Maria felt a quick joy suffuse her. "A Catholic!" And convent bred. Oh, they would be friends, she and the queen.

Henry made a wry face. "Her Catholicism will be difficult for Charles to force down the Englishmen's throats. But no doubt it will go down more easily, sweetened by all that gold."

Anna-Maria scarcely heard him. How wonderful it would be to have a queen at court, and a Catholic queen at that. It was natural that the court of a bachelor king should be licentious, but all that would change once the king was married.

Hope flooded Anna-Maria. The queen would set a model of virtue and decorum for the court and Anna-Maria would no longer have to flirt ceaselessly, walking the knife edge of danger. Without thinking, so practiced was she now in the art of flirtation, she swept up her dark lashes and gave Killigrew a radiant smile that caused him to catch his breath sharply. She spurred her horse into motion and raced off, leaving Killigrew to follow her.

Eleven

The months seemed to move so swiftly that they blurred in Anna-Maria's memory. Christmas came and went and still the negotiations went on for the king's marriage. The queen of Portugal insisted that Charles and Catherine be married by proxy because she refused to send her daughter into England without the protection of marriage. The proxy marriage took place and then England awaited the arrival of their new queen.

When spring came, Anna-Maria threw Mrs. Muggs, who was now calling herself Madame Julie, into a tizzy by ordering an entire new wardrobe in preparation for the queen's arrival.

The gowns were finished in mid-May, just as the king was riding off to greet his bride as she landed by ship at Portsmouth. As soon as the king had set off, Anna-Maria and Francis packed and rode to Hampton Court. The king had decided not to bring his young bride directly to Whitehall, feeling that the comparative quiet and peace of Hampton Court Palace was more suitable for a honeymoon. Francis had been housekeeper of Hampton Court Palace since before the king's coronation, but it was an honorary post and had never demanded his presence before. Now he and Anna-Maria must be on hand to greet the new queen.

The first sight of Hampton Court Palace enchanted Anna-Maria. It was a graceful, exquisite brick building. Cardinal Wolsey had built it in the reign of Henry the Eighth, and had built it with such exquisite taste that the corpulent monarch had immediately demanded that it be turned over to him. Anna-Maria could understand Henry's greed as she feasted her eyes on the lovely lines of the building. What a perfect place for a honeymoon!

Everyone worked to prepare the palace for the king's arrival. Anna-Maria ordered that so many fresh flowers be put in every room in the palace that Francis finally protested that she was denuding the gardens.

Anna-Maria was standing under Anne Boleyn's gate when King Charles finally rode in with his bride, the new queen, by his side.

Anna-Maria's heart skipped a beat as the resplendent procession came into view. The sunlight gleamed off the royal coach which was followed by a long line of coaches carrying the queen's retinue, the Portuguese ladies in waiting and monks who were following her to England to serve her. Behind them were a seemingly endless string of farm wagons carrying their personal possessions.

The king's coach came to a stop just beyond the Anne Boleyn gate and Anna-Maria moved forward, her pulses pounding. It was May 29th, the king's birthday as well as his bride's homecoming, and she hoped fervently that her preparations would please him.

Anna-Maria watched as the king leaped swiftly from the coach and then turned to help his bride alight. He caught sight of Anna-Maria and a grin split his face. He doffed his hat at her and then led the queen over to her. Anna-Maria spared a thought for Francis, wishing she could catch the eye of a messenger to send to find him, but there was no time. The king and queen were already standing before her.

Anna-Maria searched the queen's face eagerly, and her heart lifted. She looked kind, very young and sweet, and she was obviously in love with her husband. Her head was tilted to him adoringly as he tenderly spoke to her. When Charles introduced Catherine to Anna-Maria, he said gently, "Speak slowly and distinctly. The queen knows very little English."

Catherine, her small face lit with a smile, put her hand into Anna-Maria's. "I am so happy to know you."

Anna-Maria smiled back warmly. "Welcome to England, Your Majesty." How tiny the queen was, scarcely bigger than a child. Anna-Maria found herself looking down at her protectively. The queen was not pretty, although her eyes were lovely—dark and luminous. When the queen smiled, Anna-Maria saw that her teeth protruded just the slightest bit. Her figure was slim, her breasts barely discernible under the odd garment she wore. Puzzled, Anna-Maria stared at the bulky, oddly distorted skirt of the queen's gown, and then her brow cleared. The queen was wearing an old-fashioned farthingale, a metal understructure to prop out her skirts. No doubt her figure would be prettier once she assumed the softer English fashions. Anna-Maria found her fingers twitching, so eager was she to rearrange the queen's coiffure. The hair on the queen's head was pulled flat against her skull, and on either side of her face hideous corkscrew curls bunched out.

Charles turned to Anna-Maria. "I've told the queen that your husband is the housekeeper of Hampton Court. I've also told her that you are Catholic, and she invites you to attend mass with her in her chapel."

"Oh, I would so love that!" Anna-Maria spoke directly to her and saw by the warmth in Catherine's eyes that she understood the tone if not the words.

The king bustled the queen away to inspect her bedchamber and to rest, and Anna-Maria went to find Francis. He was in despair, clutching his forehead, his normal composure totally lost. He gestured toward a wagon piled high with odd-shaped packages wrapped in muslin. "Now I know why the king was so long delayed in riding from Portsmouth. They had to find extra wagons to transport those farthingales." His mouth twisted on the word.

"The queen has also brought a pack of silly, babbling Portuguese serving women in her train, and they are impossible to deal with."

He was furious because he had meant to be on hand to greet the king, but preparations had detained him and now he had a host of unexpected problems on his hands. "They refuse to sleep in any bed that a man has *ever* slept in! I doubt that there's a single bed in all of Hampton Court that some man hasn't slept in at some time." He spread his hands in a gesture of despair. "And in any case, how am I to know? Do civilized people go around carving their names in bedposts? May 22, 1662. Slept here. Francis Talbot."

"Lie to them, then."

"What?" Francis looked at her, startled.

"Lie to them," Anna-Maria repeated even more firmly. "There are certain circumstances in which only a lie will serve. It's only practical."

"Your wife is right, Shrewsbury." They turned to find the duke of Buckingham smiling and standing a few feet away, a plain, brown-haired woman by his side. "Assure those silly women that a man has never despoiled the bed, and they will sleep dreamless at night."

He crossed the few feet, bringing the woman with

him, and looked down at Anna-Maria with the familiar tenderness in his eyes. "Even God forgives such small harmless lies, doesn't he, Anna-Maria?"

She nodded dumbly, thinking only of how tender and sensitive his mouth was. She often lost the sense of what he was saying because she was so engrossed in watching the movements of his lips. He must think her a dolt.

To distract herself, she looked at his woman companion, realizing for the first time that this was his wife, Mary Villiers.

Anna-Maria had known that the duke of Buckingham would be in one of the coaches following the king but she had not expected his wife to be accompanying him. Anna-Maria studied her with curiosity. The duchess of Buckingham seldom came to court, and Anna-Maria had glimpsed her only a few times. She knew that she had been Mary Fairfax, the daughter of one of the Parliamentarians under Cromwell. It had been Fairfax who had gained most of Buckingham's vast estates and, during the time that Charles had been in exile, Buckingham had come back to England for a short time, wooed Mary Fairfax, and recouped not only his own estates but an additional great fortune. Some had reviled him for marrying an enemy's daughter, and others had praised his practicality.

Mary Villier's Puritan upbringing was visible even now. Her gown was of a deep, dark green, very plainly and demurely cut. Her skin was clear and fresh, innocent of cosmetics, and her brown hair was drawn in a smooth bun. She seemed an odd mate for so handsome a man, but when her hazel eyes rested adoringly on her husband's face, it was clear that on her part at least, this marriage was a love match.

Like Anna-Maria she seemed to have difficulty taking her eyes from the duke's face. She was watching him with a look of longing, and she turned reluctantly when Anna-Maria spoke to her. "Will you be staying at Hampton Court?"

"Aye. My husband feels that the queen will have need of my services immediately, even though she has all her Portuguese ladies-in-waiting with her." As soon as the queen was acclimated to her new country, the Portuguese women would be sent home, replaced by the English ladies who were to have the honor of serving the queen. "I understand that you are to be one of Her Majesty's ladies-in-waiting."

Anna-Maria nodded. "Yes, we will be seeing much of one another."

Mary Villiers smiled, her mouth curving sweetly. "It will give me much pleasure." She had heard that Anna-Maria was a notorious flirt, but she had never heard her name linked with Buckingham's. It was seldom that Mary could speak with a woman without feeling jealous bile rise in her throat, wondering how recently the woman had lain in Buckingham's arms. As she studied Anna-Maria more closely, she realized that the girl looked fresh and sweet, her eyes clear, her face touching in its purity. She began to discount the stories she had heard as so much idle court gossip.

In the days that followed, the two women were often together, and Anna-Maria found herself relying on the other woman's quiet wit and never-failing good humor. "The king seems to genuinely love his new bride, does he not?" Mary asked one day. Her eyes were wistful.

She and Anna-Maria had spread a quilt on the lawn and were taking a much-needed rest. They were watching the king and queen, who had taken a boat out on the river. The king had rolled up his white sleeves and taken the oars himself, his muscled arms visible even at this distance. The queen's excited little shrieks of laughter carried across the river, and Anna-Maria smiled at the happiness in the sound.

"I think that he is quite taken with her. He is by her side constantly. And did you notice how tender he is with her?"

Mary nodded slowly, and her eyes were sad. "A happy marriage is the most beautiful of God's creations, but it is given to only a few." She turned to Anna-Maria and broke her normal reticence. "Are you happy in your marriage, Anna-Maria?"

A little startled, Anna-Maria nodded. "Yes, I suppose so. I rarely question whether I am or not."

Mary, her head bent, was pulling at blades of grass. Slowly she said, "Your husband is faithful."

Anna-Maria had a burning desire to know what it was like to be married to the duke of Buckingham. She felt that her curiosity was shameless, sinful, but Mary had given her an opening, and she could not resist the opportunity. "And you, Mary? Are you happy in your marriage?"

Mary looked up slowly, and her gaze met Anna-Maria's fully. "You are so much at court. You must know that my husband is not faithful to me."

Anna-Maria stared at her, feeling a strange sense of loss. She knew that many women of the court angled shamelessly for the duke's attention, but he was seen frequently with many women, never singling out one. She had assumed that he was like herself, flirtatious, but faithful to his marriage vows. She felt a sense of betrayal and was aware of faint pangs in her stomach.

Mary had her head thrown back. She said intensely, "You'll think me a fool, Anna-Maria, many think me a fool, but I *am* happy. I love Buckingham, and for me it is a rare pleasure merely to be in the same room with him, to watch his gestures, hear the sound of his voice. I am willing to share him with all women, as long as I can have those moments. And after all, I *am* his wife, something that no other woman is." She broke off abruptly. "You think me a fool without pride."

Anna-Maria said softly, "I think you are a woman who loves greatly."

Mary picked up a clump of grass and brushed at the dirt clinging to it. "But with all my love, I have failed him. I cannot give him a living child."

Anna-Maria felt a quick rush of sympathy toward her. She had reason to suspect that she was pregnant again, and it hurt her that Mary had never known such joy. She reached her hand toward Mary's and was on the point of speaking, when a shadow fell over them.

The duke of Buckingham was standing over them, his blond hair making a halo of gold in the sunlight. He dropped to the grass next to them, stretching his long legs out in front of him. As he settled himself into a comfortable position, his hand grazed Anna-Maria's. She felt a flash of pleasure, and she snatched her hand hastily away, as though she had been scalded. When she could force herself to look up, the duke was watching her with a thoughtful expression in his eyes.

Twelve

"Virtue," Mary Villiers said bitterly, "has *no* reward."

Anna-Marie looked up from her embroidery. They were in a small sitting room at Hampton Court working on their tapestries. Slowly she bit off a gold thread and asked Mary softly, "What's wrong?"

Mary jabbed her needle angrily, not noticing that she was still using a deep crimson thread, although she was now working on a patch of sky. "I suppose that I am thinking partially of my own marriage," she admitted. "But at the moment I am chiefly angry for the queen's sake."

She threw her tapestry abruptly aside and began pacing. "Life is simply not fair, Anna-Maria. Nothing is as we think it will be. Nothing is as we were taught. I myself was raised as a Puritan, and you were raised Catholic—it is much the same thing. We were both taught to be virtuous. It was the chief value a woman could have. And now we are grown and faced with real life, and what do we find? Men want nothing of virtuous women. They find them as pallid as porridge without salt!"

Anna-Maria was stitching more slowly now. There was much sense in what Mary said. Would she herself be so popular at court were it not for her practiced flirting?

She looked at Mary with curiosity. "Why do you speak of the queen?"

"Because," Mary said angrily, "her honeymoon is

over, although the poor queen doesn't know it yet. This morning the king rode off to visit with his whore."

Anna-Maria gasped and dropped the tapestry.

"Aye." Mary's face was twisted in disdain. "Word came that Lady Castlemaine was delivered of another of the king's whelps, a boy this time, and nothing would do but that he fling himself on his horse and go to her."

Anna-Maria bit her lip and was silent. Barbara Palmer, Lady Castlemaine, was a cousin of the duke of Buckingham and thus Mary's cousin by marriage, but Mary hated her both for her beauty and her wantonness. Anna-Maria herself had no dislike for the king's mistress. Barbara was so beautiful that even women had to smile when they looked upon her, and she had been unfailingly pleasant to Anna-Maria, for Anna-Maria had never sought the king's attention.

"Lady Castlemaine went nearly insane at the news of the king's marriage, and she threatened to come here to Hampton Court to give birth to the baby right under the eyes of the queen, didn't she?"

Mary laughed. " 'Twould be like her."

Anna-Maria shook her head. "I think she spoke out of pain, Mary. It must be a deep grief to love a man you cannot marry."

Mary stopped her angry pacing. "You give her credit for more sensibility than she has. I doubt that she loves the king. She is ambitious and wants only the favors he can give her."

"Ah, no," Anna-Maria said softly. "I've seen her eyes upon him when they were dancing. There is no mistaking the love there." Suddenly a thought struck her. "Surely the queen doesn't know about her."

"Aye, she does." Mary nodded heavily. "She told me that her mother informed her of the situation before she left Portugal and warned her never to receive Lady Castlemaine at court."

"But the king has promised Barbara that she is to be one of the queen's ladies-in-waiting," Anna-Maria protested.

"The king is going to find himself in a pretty predicament. The queen is a soft little thing but determined where her religion and honor are involved. I think that the king has not realized that yet. She will not disobey her mother and allow the king's mistress to attend her. She would feel it a sin, that she was condoning her husband's adultery and jeopardizing his soul." Mary's voice was sad. She herself had condoned her husband's adulteries over and over again, merely for the pitiful reward of keeping his good will.

"And Barbara is not a woman to retire gracefully from court."

Mary laughed shortly. "That she is not. She's quarreled with her husband and moved out of his house, taking all her plate and furniture, as well as the king's babies to her uncle's house in Richmond. No doubt she will inform the king that she has nothing in the world except his kindness to sustain her."

Three days later Mary and Anna-Maria learned that the king had stood sponsor to his new child and had promised Lady Castlemaine that he would soon acknowledge him as his son.

When he returned to Hampton Court he presented Catherine with a list of the Englishwomen who were to serve her, and to his astonishment she struck out the name Castlemaine before returning the list to him. The walls of Hampton Court rang with gossip about their quarrel. The king was appalled to discover that his shy young bride was not as ignorant and pliable as he had thought.

"The king is furious!" Mary reported to Anna-Maria.

"Well," Anna-Maria said reasonably, "it is a humiliating situation for him. In all honor he must make some provision for Lady Castlemaine." Unlike Mary, who identified with the queen, Anna-Maria could look at both sides of the situation.

The king and queen had still not resolved their quarrel a few days later when a bevy of noblemen and women rode out from London to be presented to their new queen. Everyone was anxious to boast that they had made the acquaintance of the queen even before her official arrival at Whitehall.

Anna-Maria found herself greeting friends that she had not seen for several weeks and was surprised to find that she had missed them. Henry Jermyn told her that he had not slept or eaten for missing her, and Captain Tom Howard flicked his tongue against the back of Anna-Maria's hand as he was kissing it, and she was not as horrified as she would ordinarily have been. It was fun to be back among festivity and excitement. Even the little queen seemed heartened by the merriment. Her cheeks glowed pink, and she looked almost pretty. The king had dropped his quarrel with her for the day and stayed constantly by her side. Catherine kept looking up at him with open adoration that was almost painful to see.

Anna-Maria was shocked to the point of speechlessness when Lady Castlemaine suddenly appeared, and the king brazenly presented her to the queen as Barbara Palmer, carefully omitting her title.

Anna-Maria stood, a part of the frozen tableau, waiting to see what the queen would do. Innocently, the queen was holding out her hand to be kissed. Then one of her Portuguese serving women, Donna Elvira, leaned forward and whispered Lady Castlemaine's true identity to the queen.

The queen snatched back her hand and jumped to her feet, her hand groping for the arm of the throne. Blood began to stream from her nose, and she fainted.

Anna-Maria rushed from the reception room on the heels of the king, who was carrying the queen to the State Bedroom, fury clearly marked on his face. He dumped the queen on the great crimson and silver bed with scant ceremony and then strode from the room.

Anna-Maria, surrounded by the queen's Portuguese serving women, bent over the frail, pale figure. She slapped gently at the queen's cheeks, wondering as she did so if it was really a kindness to restore the queen to consciousness.

As soon as Catherine was fully conscious, she

clutched Anna-Maria's hands gratefully. "You who are Catholic like myself, you understand me, as many of these Englishwomen do not. I am pleased that you are to be one of my serving women. I have need of good friends."

Both Anna-Maria and Mary stayed almost constantly by Catherine's side in the days that followed, although they were still not officially her ladies-in-waiting. No official appointment could be made until the list was agreed upon by both the king and queen. Nothing could be done until the quarrel over Lady Castlemaine was resolved.

When the king and queen made their official state entry into London via the Thames River, Anna-Maria and Francis rode with the duke and duchess of Buckingham in the barge directly behind the royal barge. The duke was in high spirits and kept the rest of them laughing with his quick jests.

Anna-Maria's spirits soared so high that she could almost fancy herself a bird skimming above the Thames, marveling at the pageantry below. Thousands of craft both large and small were on the Thames today, all flying colors to welcome the new queen. Scaffolds had been erected in London, along the banks of the river, so that people could catch a glimpse of her as she sailed into her capital city.

The duke of Buckingham was standing with his back to the bow, and Anna-Maria shielded her eyes from the sun so she could look up at him. For a moment, she found herself longing to reach out and stroke his cheek. Appalled at her thoughts, she blushed and buried her hand in the folds of her skirts. Her long chestnut hair was loose, blowing in the wind, and she made an attractive picture outlined against the blue sky. The duke looked down at her and bent forward so that his words were for her ears alone. "Are you happy today, Anna-Maria?" The tone of his voice was like a caress, and Anna-Maria shivered.

"Yes, my lord." Her tone was as low and intimate as his own. She had the unreal feeling that the words they actually spoke were of little importance. The real message was being sent as their eyes met. For a long moment she was lost in the sensation, and then she shook herself, breaking the spell, and turned to Francis. "It will be good to be back in London. I sorely miss Polly and little Charles. And Sarah, dear Sarah."

Francis smiled and patted her hand affectionately. "And to think that you carry another child within your womb. We are indeed blessed, Anna-Maria."

She nodded and tilted her head back, watching a lazy cloud scuttle across the sky. It was easy to pray, to thank God with a full heart on such a day.

Her mood of elation was still with her when she and Francis reached their home on the Strand. She knelt to receive Polly's hug and tightly held the child to her, wondering how she had endured the long absence. She hoisted Polly in her arms and went to look at Charles, who was sleeping peacefully in his bed, one rosy hand tucked under his cheek. Leaning over him, she inhaled his clean scent, then turning to Polly, she said softly, "You are going to have a new brother or sister soon." Polly glowed with excitement and kept chattering about the new arrival all the time Anna-Maria was tucking her into bed. Anna-Maria tried to explain that the interval before the baby arrived would seem very long to a young child, but Polly went to sleep convinced that a new baby would be there when she awoke in the morn.

Thirteen

There was a new element at court now that the queen had arrived, and Anna-Maria was aware for the first time of the strain of cruelty that ran in many of the courtier's natures. Many mocked the queen for refusing to accept Lady Castlemaine, and the court was being divided into two factions. Anna-Maria tried to make her open friendship for the queen apparent without being embroiled in the quarrel. Francis had warned her to take a neutral attitude. The king was not to be offended.

Anna-Maria was glad to see that her popularity had not waned during her absence. Both Tom Howard and Henry Jermyn wooed her with renewed vigor, and Henry Killigrew made every excuse to be at her side. Anna-Maria fell into the familiar pattern of going to the Stone Gallery in the morning to hear the latest gossip, riding in the park in the afternoon, and attending the latest play. Masques, balls, and private suppers were even more numerous now, and she often found herself with more invitations than she could accept. Often she was fatigued, particularly because of her new pregnancy, but Francis beamed approval at her success and urged her to continue her effort.

The one thing Anna-Maria avoided was participating in the gambling that went on nightly at the groom porter's lodge or at private parties. The large sums of money that changed hands so carelessly shocked her, and she could not understand the reckless fever that seemed to possess the gamblers. She felt that the gambling instinct was a form of sickness, and indeed, the glittering eyes and sweat-drenched brows of the players often made them look ill.

She was relieved to escape the groom porter's lodge one evening when Tom Howard invited her to go to the Spring Garden, a popular resort at the east end of St. James Park. It was a beautiful summer evening, she thought, much too lovely to spend locked in watching the gamblers toss a fortune away. She accepted with alacrity, putting her hand on Howard's arm and giving him her sweetest smile. Henry Jermyn, who had been standing nearby had overheard the invitation. Anna-Maria had not noticed him and so missed his angry expression.

She and Howard were seated at a small table, sipping wine and listening with appreciation to the music being played by a string quartet when Henry Jermyn strolled into the Garden. Affecting surprise at seeing them, he hastened over to their table. Anna-Maria smiled a welcome at him. Howard had become uncomfortably bold in his efforts to seduce her, saying that he had never waited so long for a woman before and that his patience was wearing thin. Anna-Maria was glad to avoid a further tête-à-tête with him.

When Howard caught sight of Jermyn making his way toward them, he scowled. "That spindle-shanked little whelp. It sickens me to think that you lie in his arms while you deny your favors to me."

Anna-Maria turned to him, shocked. "Why, you don't think—" She broke off because Jermyn was standing above them now, a mocking grin on his face. Without asking permission, he pulled a chair from another table, swung it around and sat down, straddling it. Propping his chin on the chair back, he ignored Howard and grinned at Anna-Maria. "I've no doubt but that you are vastly relieved at my appearance. I know that Howard has no fund of small talk. You must have been mightily bored trying to make conversation with him this past hour. For my part, I'd as soon try to communicate with a deaf mute."

Howard clapped his hand to his sword and sat fiddling with it. Anna-Maria felt him glowering dangerously at her side, but she refused to turn and look at him or attempt to placate him. She knew that he would not draw his sword in this public place and she was pleased at his discomfiture. How *dare* he make such bold advances to her. And worse, brazenly proclaim that he knew she had taken Jermyn to her bed.

So she laughed and flirted with Jermyn, totally ignoring Howard. Although Jermyn had often brought Anna-Maria to the Spring Gardens, now he jeered at Howard's choice of entertainment, ridiculing the music and pronouncing the wine of inferior quality. Normally, Anna-Maria's innate politeness would have prevented her from being party to such rudeness, but now she was delighted with each thrust at Howard. No man had ever spoken to her so coarsely before, and she was seething with humiliation.

When the evening's entertainment was over, Henry Jermyn offered to escort Anna-Maria home in company with Howard, and she quickly accepted. Howard's expression was black, and Anna-Maria smiled to herself as she slipped one hand under Jermyn's arm and one under Howard's. Howard would learn that he could not question her virtue without being punished.

"After all," she said sweetly, "I'm much safer being seen in two men's company than one. Even the worst of gossips cannot suggest that I am playing my husband false with both of you at once."

To her horror, she learned the next day that that was *exactly* what the gossips were saying. After leaving Anna-Maria at her door, Howard had gone straight home and penned an angry note to Jermyn, challenging him to a duel. Mary Villiers heard of the challenge before daybreak and took her coach and hastened to Anna-Maria's home to give her the news.

"Howard has a notoriously bad temper and a taste for murder," Mary said. "I fear for Jermyn's life."

"Oh, no!" Anna-Maria pressed the back of her hand to her shaking lips. " 'Tis all my fault. Howard made me angry last night, and I provoked him to this." Not even to Mary would she repeat Howard's words.

She pulled Mary after her to her bedchamber and began putting on clothes with reckless haste. "I must stop this somehow!"

"It's too late." Mary shook her head. "Jermyn has already accepted Howard's challenge. He has no choice. It was either that or be branded a coward and leave court."

"But dueling is forbidden by law." Even as Anna-Maria said the words, she knew how foolish they were. Gentlemen dueled on the slightest provocation and then threw themselves on the king's mercy.

Francis was still sleeping, and Anna-Maria decided not to wake him. He would worry needlessly. She might be able to avert this tragedy, and he need never know about it. She piled her hair on top of her head and skewered it with a pair of gold bodkins, never noticing that it began to slip almost immediately, tumbling about her flushed cheeks.

Together, the two women quickly left the house and got into Mary's coach. Mary leaned her head out of

the coach window, shouting for the coachman to whip
up the horses.

Anna-Maria fairly raced from the cobblestoned
courtyard into the Stone Gallery. Titters and sly comments followed in her wake, but she scarcely heard
them. The news of the duel was the talk of the gallery
this morning, and the courtiers were amused by the
sight of the normally fastidious countess of Shrewsbury
arriving unpainted and disheveled, worry clear on her
face. Her expression brightened when she saw Jermyn
standing a little distance away, safe and unmarked.
She had been picturing him torn and bleeding, his eyes
already glazed with death.

She rushed over to him and laid a hand on his arm.
"Henry!"

He looked at her feverishly bright eyes, the way her
bosom rose and fell with her rapid breathing and
grinned. "I think your feelings for me have under-
gone a change since last evening. If having my life
threatened is the path to your favors, then I'll face danger gladly."

"Henry, don't play the fool! It was I who provoked
Tom Howard last night, and I won't allow you to duel
with him."

Jermyn arched one dark eyebrow and smiled at her.
"Duels are a man's private business, my sweet. Women,
no matter how lovely, cannot interfere." He was pleasurably aware that the courtiers had fallen silent,
watching them closely. No doubt this little scene
would convince them that he had truly enjoyed the
countess's most intimate favors. At this moment she
was giving the perfect performance of a woman in love,
her fingers biting into his sleeve, her face tilted to his
beseechingly.

Then he looked into her tear-bright eyes and relented. "In truth, I have no desire to end my life on the
point of Howard's sword." He grinned. "I accepted his
challenge because my honor demanded it. But I have
the privilege of selecting the time and place, and I've
not done so yet." His eyes lit with mischief. "I in-

tend to keep out of Howard's way for the next week or so until his hot temper cools. No doubt the matter will blow over without a sword ever being raised."

"Oh, thank God." Anna-Maria went weak with relief and swayed against Jermyn for support. His arm went readily around her waist, and she leaned against it gratefully for a moment. Then she straightened and became aware of the locks of hair tumbling about her face and her disheveled gown. She laughed a bit shakily. "I had best go home and make a proper toilette. I can hardly attend the queen in this condition."

Jermyn curbed an impulse to kiss her. If he took such a liberty now, he would lose all the ground he had gained with Anna-Maria. Instead he dropped a fervent kiss on her hand. "Your concern for me has made me deeply happy."

Anna-Maria went home to bathe and change, relieved that the matter had been settled so sensibly. She was equally relieved in the next few days not to see Tom Howard at court because she would have had difficulty being civil to him, and she feared to provoke him further.

She attended the queen, who was sad and dispirited since she saw little of the king these days. He spent much of his time with Lady Castlemaine, who was as much in evidence at court as ever. She might be forbidden to enter the queen's apartments, but there was nowhere else she could not go at court, and the king was always at her side.

Anna-Maria was sitting in the window seat of the queen's apartment, reading slowly to the queen to improve her English, when a shout from below caught her attention. "Howard and Jermyn are dueling!"

"Oh, God, no!" Anna-Maria stood abruptly, sending the book to the floor with a crash. She ran out of the chamber without a word of explanation to the startled queen.

When she reached the dueling ground, she saw a subdued knot of courtiers looking down somberly at two figures prone on the ground. For a moment her senses swam, and the whole scene seemed unreal. It was such a bright August day, the sun smiling from the heavens—surely death could not have struck in such an atmosphere. She saw Tom Howard wearing a sword-proof leather jerkin. His heavy dueling sword at his side was crimson with blood. Anna-Maria gagged at the sight, but determined and willful, she began to beat her way through the crowd. When the crowd recognized her, they moved silently to let her pass. Their silence was terrifying.

Breaking out of the knotted crowd, she saw two bodies lying on the ground. One she recognized as Giles Rawlins, a special friend of Henry Jermyn's. Rawlins's sensitive face was frozen, his open eyes staring sightlessly up at the burning August sky. A sob broke from Anna-Maria's throat, and tears began raining down her cheeks. Only yesterday she had been laughing at a careless remark he had made. Now she would never hear his voice again.

Suddenly she was seized by guilt. It was her careless flirtations that had led to this! Rawlins's death was *her* fault, and she was sickened by the memory of the provocative glances she had given Howard and Jermyn, the way she had teased and flirted, pleased by her popularity. And yet she had meant no harm; she had merely been doing her husband's bidding.

She dreaded going near the other body. She couldn't bear to see all the laughter gone from Henry's face. There were two surgeons bent over Henry's body, conferring in low voices. Perhaps he still lived then! Slowly, scarcely breathing, she moved forward, then stopped abruptly in horror. There were two wounds in Henry's side, and another in his thigh, all streaming blood. The sweet, cloying odor of the blood wafted to Anna-Maria's nostrils, and she gagged.

As she watched, Henry turned his head and caught sight of her. He lived! Thank God, he lived! A sob of joy broke from her throat, and she rushed to kneel by his side, catching his sweat-soaked dark head into her lap. One of the surgeons spoke to her sharply, warning her away, but Henry said weakly, "Leave her be! She's all the medicine I need."

As Anna-Maria pulled him closer into her arms, cradling him as she would a child, he looked up at her with a ghost of his former mischief. "So I finally feel your breasts crushed against my lips, my sweet." His mouth was at her bosom. " 'Twas a painful way to win your favors, but I vow it was worth it."

Tears spilled from Anna-Maria's eyes. "Henry, hush. You should not speak so when—" She broke off with a sob.

"When I am going to die, my sweet?" Henry smiled wryly. "I have no intention of dying. Mark my words, I'll be up and about in no time."

The surgeon was pulling urgently at Anna-Maria's shoulder now, and she rose reluctantly, her eyes clinging to Henry's face.

"Here, I'll take her." At the sound of that familiar, stirring voice, Anna-Maria turned and found the duke of Buckingham at her side. She looked up at him in bewilderment, and his eyes were scornful as he looked down at her. It was the first time that he had ever looked at her with anything but tenderness, and it frightened her. "My lord?" Her voice was timid, low.

He said shortly, "I'll take you home. You've done enough damage for one day." He put his arm around her waist and set off with long, angry strides, and she had to half run to keep up with him. For a time she attempted to meet his pace, but then she stopped and dug in her heels mutinously. "My lord, I demand to know what happened. Henry had not planned to duel with Tom Howard."

The duke stopped and raked her with a glance, and she found herself shivering at the intense scorn in his eyes. The duke was white-lipped with fury. His loins had stirred at his first glimpse of Anna-Maria, he had wanted her from the first time he met her. But he had respected her virtue, accorded her a respect he had given to no other woman. And now he had clear proof that she was a wanton. No man would be fool enough to get himself killed in a duel over a woman unless he had enjoyed her most intimate favors. What a fool she had made of him with her pansylike innocent eyes and soft mouth. For a moment he had an impulse to throw her to the ground and take her right here and now.

Instead he said, "You should learn not to bestow your favors so carelessly, my sweet. A hot-tempered man like Tom Howard does not like to share his woman."

Anna-Maria stared at him, her eyes growing large and dark with hurt. Words of protest rose to her lips, but the duke continued. "Jermyn and Rawlins were unprepared when Howard and his second, Dillon, set upon them. Howard had provided himself with a sword-proof leather jerkin and a heavy dueling sword, but Jermyn and Rawlins had only light dress swords.

"A fine gentleman, your Tom Howard. He barred Jermyn and Rawlins from leaving and demanded that they fight then and there. Rawlins and Jermyn protested that they had only light dress swords and asked at least to exchange swords with their footmen, but Howard refused and charged upon them without another word. He killed Rawlins with the first thrust. Rawlins's bodkin had no chance at all against Howard's heavy sword." The duke's blue eyes darkened angrily. He had liked Rawlins a good deal.

"While Howard was murdering Rawlins, Dillon exchanged a few sword thrusts with Jermyn, but I think myself that he had no stomach for such butchery. He made no move to wound Jermyn, merely engaged him until Howard was free. Then Howard ran upon Jermyn and skewered him three times and left him for dead."

"Will he die?" Anna-Maria forced the question through lips that were bone-dry with fear.

The duke looked at her with angry impatience. "Am I a surgeon? I don't like the look of his wounds, nor the way his blood spills so freely, but I've seen men recover from worse."

He shook himself angrily. Damn his eyes! He despised her now, and yet he found himself stirred by her face, the trembling of her delicate lips. Impatiently he seized her arm. "I'll take you home to your husband. I hope he learns to control you so that more good men don't spill their blood needlessly because of you."

Fourteen

Anna-Maria was caught in a nightmare from which there was no escaping. Henry Jermyn still lived and was said to be recovering. Howard, with Dillon by his side, had ridden to the nearest seaport immediately after the duel, and had taken a ship for France. Anna-Maria hoped that he would find an ignominious and lingering death in France.

To her shocked horror, Francis had been furious with her when he learned of the duel. "You have ruined your reputation, Anna-Maria. I don't know how I'll be able to hold up my head at court after this."

When the first wave of shock had passed, Anna-Maria became angry in turn. "I don't see how I can be blamed for Tom Howard's actions. The man is a criminal. Perhaps insane."

Francis whirled from the fireplace and faced her angrily. "Aye, and you inflamed his madness with your pretty tricks."

Anna-Maria could not have been more shocked if he had hit her. "I did only what you bade me do. Flirt a little so that I would be popular at court and the king would look with favor upon us."

"Favor!" Francis spat the word, and he looked suddenly very old. "Do you think that the king is going to *thank* us for this day's work? He's forbidden dueling because it's a needless waste of young lives."

Anna-Maria, thinking of Rawlins's lifeless body sprawled on the ground, nodded, tears filling her eyes.

Francis picked up his wineglass, drained it without

stopping, and then wiped his mouth. "You realize that no one at court will believe that you were not bestowing your favors on both Howard and Jermyn."

Anna-Maria caught her breath and almost sobbed. "Surely Francis, *you* don't believe that!"

Francis's eyes had been narrowed suspiciously, but now his brow cleared a little. He knew Anna-Maria, knew her convent upbringing, her coldness in bed. He relented a little and thrust the wineglass toward her, saying with an approach at kindness, "Drink this. It will calm you." Anna-Maria was carrying his child, and he didn't want the baby to be harmed.

She gulped the warming drink gratefully. "Francis, you *don't* believe that, do you?"

"No," Francis said, hesitating slightly. "I merely think that you have badly mismanaged your affairs. A more sophisticated woman would not have found herself in this unsavory mess."

Stung, Anna-Maria retorted, "You took me straight from the convent. You could hardly have expected to find me sophisticated." She spat the last word at him and then flung out of the room without waiting for him to reply.

She spent a sleepless night, choosing one of the unused bedrooms because she could not bear to be near Francis. At the core of Anna-Maria's pain was the memory of the duke's cold eyes as he had raked her with his scornful glance.

Finally she sobbed herself to sleep and woke in the morning with swollen eyes and a leaden head. She knew that she must go to court immediately, or she would never dare face it again.

She spent a long time putting cold compresses on her eyes to reduce the swelling, then carefully painted her face. She took care in selecting a gown. She wanted no hint of mourning, no demureness that bespoke a feeling of guilt. On the other hand, she didn't wish a wanton display of her charms. Finally she selected a gown of deep rose that lent some color to her pale cheeks.

For many months Anna-Maria had made the journey to Whitehall Palace daily. Now the familiar route seemed strange and very long. A buzz of excited comment rose when she appeared in the Stone Gallery, but she tossed her head back and sailed through the crowd, nodding and smiling coolly to those she passed.

She went straight to the sanctuary of the queen's apartments, knowing that the Englishwomen who befriended the queen were those of a more serious turn of mind, not given to idle gossip.

As she entered the queen's apartments, sudden silence fell. Anna-Maria met eight pairs of speculative eyes, and she suddenly felt uneasy. Her eyes went immediately to the queen, who was looking at her solemnly. "Come to me, countess." The queen reached out a thin white hand and beckoned to Anna-Maria. She turned to the waiting women and said, "You may leave us."

Anna-Maria went swiftly to the queen and sank into a deep bow. "Good morning, Your Majesty." She could feel her heart beating so rapidly that she thought she might die of it.

The queen motioned to a nearby chair. "You may sit." The queen looked at Anna-Maria in silence for a moment, her thin face pensive. "You have disappointed me, countess. I thought you virtuous—a truly devout Roman Catholic like myself."

Anna-Maria leaned forward. "Your Majesty, I *am* virtuous!"

The queen was shaking her head, and Anna-Maria remembered how stubborn the queen was being about the king's mistress, and her heart sank.

The queen said slowly, in her halting English, "I've had reports of the duel yesterday. Rawlins, one of the finest of our English youths dead to no purpose. He was not even one of your lovers, was he?" Without waiting for Anna-Maria's reply, she went on, "I am having masses said for his soul."

"Your Majesty, I *have* no lovers. None at all. I'm a Catholic. I was married to my husband in a nuptial mass. I've been faithful to him—and I will be all my life!" Her voice was frantic, trembling.

The queen looked thoughtfully at her for a moment. She had felt a true affection for Anna-Maria and had been shocked when her Portuguese attendants had reported the court gossip, calling Anna-Maria "the notorious countess of Shrewsbury."

She sighed and rose, going over to a rosewood desk at one corner of the room. She came back with a long white parchment in her small hand and turned it so Anna-Maria could read it. It was the list of proposed ladies-in-waiting for the queen. Near the top, the countess of Castlemaine's name had been inked out.

Anna-Maria's eyes dropped lower, and she gasped. Her own name had a thick black ink mark drawn through it. When she found her tongue, she protested, "But Your Majesty, this is unjust. I swear on the Blessed Virgin that I am innocent."

Pity rose in the queen's eyes, and she put out her hand to Anna-Maria. "Perhaps you are. Already I am learning that this court of my husband is a tangled affair, and it is difficult to sort truth from lies." She sighed deeply. "But you must understand. I cannot have even the *appearance* of evil among the ladies who serve me.

"I am refusing to have the countess of Castlemaine serve because of her bad reputation. My husband and I are quarreling about it. You must see that I cannot accept you as my lady-in-waiting. You—innocent or not —are as notorious as Lady Castlemaine. My husband would be quick to seize on your appointment to turn it to his advantage."

Anna-Maria felt nauseated, and her hand flew to cover her mouth. To be compared to one of the most flagrantly promiscuous women in the Kingdom!

Her hand still covering her mouth, muffling her words, she said, "Your Majesty, I beg to be excused." She turned and fled. She did not care that the queen had not given her permission to leave and might be angry with her. What more could the queen do to her now?

Francis was pale-lipped with fury at her dismissal by the queen, and Anna-Maria came close to hating him for it. She longed for a comforting pair of arms to embrace her and was bewildered and angry at Francis's rejection. Hadn't she been his true helpmeet, standing by his side always and doing whatever he asked of her? And now, when *she* needed *him,* he failed her. She would still have her unsullied reputation, her spotless name, were it not for him.

She locked herself in an unused bedroom, refusing Francis admittance. For two days she remained confined in the room, refusing to see him, but finally, on the third day, she felt that she was behaving childishly, and she answered Francis's summons. He was in their bedroom. He rose when she entered and came over and took her hands in his in a gesture of conciliation. "Anna-Maria, sit down, my dear. You look ill."

"I've good cause to look ill," she said resentfully. She found the touch of Francis's hand unpleasant and pulled away.

He said slowly, "My dear, I've spoken to the king about your difficulty."

Anna-Maria felt her temper flare at his choice of words. Why couldn't he have said *"our* difficulty"? She listened quietly, carefully showing no emotion as he continued. "The king believes that you have been treated unfairly. He believes in your innocence, but he is reluctant to approach the queen about your appointment. You can understand why."

Anna-Maria nodded.

"However, the king says that there is no reason why you cannot continue to enjoy life at court as you did before. Only a handful of women are appointed to serve the queen, and the rest seem to manage very well without the honor."

"Enjoy!" Anna-Maria leaped to her feet. "How can I possibly *enjoy* myself at court with people mocking me? Everywhere I go I'll be followed by their sly whispers. And Francis, it is so unjust! I've done nothing wrong."

Francis leaned back in his chair and stretched his legs. "We have both exaggerated this matter out of proportion, Anna-Maria. Your reputation is very important to you, and I can understand your humiliation. But examine the matter realistically. Most of the women at court are of light virtue, and although they may enjoy gossiping about you for a time, in reality they don't think less of you for taking lovers."

Anna-Maria clenched her teeth so tightly that her jaw hurt. "I did not *take* lovers."

Francis looked at her with the beginning of sympathy. "You'll waste your energies, Anna-Maria, in a futile wish to have the truth known. There is no court of justice for lost reputations. Women are tried and condemned by idle tongues, and that's the end of it."

Anna-Maria stared at him. For the first time it crossed her mind that Francis might actually believe the rumors about her. It would account for his failure to take her in his arms and comfort her. She forced a question through trembling lips. "Francis, do *you* believe that I am innocent?"

Francis laughed shortly, his lips twisted unpleasantly. "My dear, I above all men know that you are singularly lacking in passion. I do not question your virtue—only your discretion." He paused and looked at her levelly. "To my mind, lack of discretion is the greater of the sins. Certainly you have not advanced my position at court."

For a moment Anna-Maria was too stunned to react. Then anger replaced the shock. Her virtue mattered nothing to this man who was her husband, her lawful protecter. She mattered only to him as a pawn in his game at court. Too choked with rage to speak, she looked at him for a long moment, her eyes large and nearly pitch-black. Then she turned on her heel and quit the room.

Within a week, Anna-Maria was going to court again, partly because the household ran so smoothly that there was really very little for her to do at home and in part because of her pride. Let those vicious scandalmongers see that they had not been able to drive the countess of Shrewsbury away from court.

Mary Villiers was warmly sympathetic and spent as much time as she could by Anna-Maria's side, although she was most often attending the queen. "I feel that you've been done a grave injustice, Anna-Maria, and I hope to eventually influence the queen in your favor."

Anna-Maria pressed her hand, tears springing to her eyes at the kindness. "I wish that I did not care about the gossip, Mary, but I do. *God* knows that I am innocent and that should be enough for me, but somehow it is not. It is good to know that I have your friendship." She sighed. "Perhaps it is my pregnancy that makes me so sensitive."

She saw a shadow fall across Mary's face and instantly felt a twinge of sorrow for her childless friend. How tactless she had been. Before she could think of another remark, Mary excused herself, saying that the queen awaited her, but she kissed Anna-Maria lightly on the cheek before departing.

Jane Middleton professed her undying friendship and support of Anna-Maria, while managing to wound her repeatedly with the dexterity of an expert swordsman. "I think it is a shame to blacken your name so. The courtiers are taking bets as to whether your baby will have Henry Jermyn's spindly legs or Tom Howard's black brows."

What a cruel world in which to bring a baby, Anna-Maria thought. She wondered if doubt about his paternity would follow him all his life.

Black rage settled over her, seeming to seep like an evil mist into her bone and blood. She trusted no one now, save Sarah and Mary Villiers.

Francis was courteous to her but remote, and she sensed that he was still displeased that her name had been struck from the list of the queen's ladies-in-waiting. The king, however, was bestowing more honors and responsibilities upon Francis, and he was busy from morning to night.

Anna-Maria began more and more to accept invitations to supper parties in private apartments at Whitehall, and occasionally three or four days passed without her and Francis exchanging more than a few words.

In the autumn, when her pregnancy had advanced into the fifth month, she asked Francis to sleep in an unused bedchamber, claiming that his restless sleep disturbed her and was bad for the baby. In truth it was she who was restless, often lying awake hour after hour, staring into the darkness. When she shifted position, brushing against Francis, she felt no desire to be in his arms, knowing that she would find no comfort there.

One morning, after a long night of prayer, she rose and went into the room where Francis lay. She touched him softly on the cheek, and he woke, instantly awake as was his habit. "Anna-Maria!" They had moved so far from intimacy that he was startled to find her by his bed.

She felt a moment's pang of shyness. She had never been totally at ease with Francis, never able to pour out her thoughts and feelings to him spontaneously. Always there had been an element of formality in their relationship, and she had assumed that it was a natural state between men and women. Now she found herself wishing that she could talk to him as easily as she did to Sarah.

Francis sat up and swung his legs over the side of the bed. "What's wrong?"

"Francis, I want to speak to you about our life." Anna-Maria pulled up a small, embroidered footstool and sat down on it, her blue satin dressing gown billowing out around her. Francis cast a look out the window. The first streaks of dawn were just lighting the sky.

"Our life? At this early hour?" He laughed shortly. "You pick a very serious topic for so early in the morn."

"I couldn't sleep," she said simply. "I've been awake all night, thinking and praying." Her lovely face suddenly took on an intensity that would have moved him in the early days of their marriage. Now he simply looked about for his dressing gown. "I think, Francis, that we ought to move back to Grafton Manor, to live quietly in the country."

Francis's jaw dropped. He rubbed uneasily at his unshaven cheeks. "Anna-Maria, it is sleeplessness that puts such fancies in your head. Have Sarah make you one of her gypsy brews and sleep today. You'll injure the baby if you lie awake spinning senseless schemes."

Anna-Maria leaned toward him pleadingly. The bodice of her dressing gown gaped open, exposing her breasts, which were even fuller now because of her pregnancy. Francis looked at them longingly. It was a month now since he had laid with her. Reaching out, he stroked her hair. As she realized his intention, she paled, her hand going up to clutch his, to stop his insistent stroking.

"Francis, you must listen to me. I can see nothing ahead at court but more pain and heartbreak for us." For a moment she was tempted to tell him that the courtiers were placing wagers as to the paternity of the child she was carrying, but as she hesitated, he reached down and began caressing her partially exposed breast.

"No, Francis." Frantically she pushed at his hand, trying to fasten the gap in her dressing gown. He easily fended off her hand and bent his mouth to one soft pink nipple.

She threw her head back and shut her eyes, feeling a shudder of despair ripple down her spine. It had been a mistake to come to his bedroom, a mistake to try to reason with him. Tears were seeping from under the corner of her eyelids as Francis lifted her and laid her on his bed.

He pulled back her dressing gown. Even after several years of marriage, her body never failed to excite him. He even found the swell of her belly exciting and paused for a moment to caress it before lowering himself on top of her.

Anna-Maria lay rigid, her heart pounding with repugnance. After he had finished, she rose and threw her dressing gown around her and left the room in silence. Never again would she tell Francis what was in her heart and mind.

Fifteen

New scandals rocked the court, and as Anna-Maria found that her own affairs were stale gossip now, she began to relax a little. Then, just before Christmas, Henry Jermyn returned to court, fully recovered. Anna-Maria was relieved to see him, but she feared that his reappearance on the scene might rekindle the gossip. Her fears proved groundless. Henry still treated her with the old gallantry and made outrageous attempts to seduce her, but there was an absent-minded quality to his attention now. His eyes were constantly following the king's beautiful, red-haired mistress.

Then the rumor swept the court that the king had caught Henry and Barbara in bed together and had banished Henry in a fit of rage. Anna-Maria, having no time alone with Henry for a private word, was inclined to dismiss the rumor, knowing how little truth there had been in the rumors about her. True, Henry was barred from court, but the king might only have been irritated at his open and insolent attentions to Lady Castlemaine. Barbara was clearly madly in love with the king, and Anna-Maria seriously doubted that she had taken Jermyn to her bed. Although she was sorry for Barbara, she couldn't help feeling selfish relief. Jermyn was now identified as Lady Castlemaine's lover, not the countess of Shrewsbury's, and the old scandal was receding further and further into the recesses of everyone's memories.

Anna-Maria was furious when Tom Howard and Dillon came back to England and threw themselves on the mercy of the court. She ground her teeth in fury when Howard was formally acquitted of the charge of manslaughter and began to be in attendance at Whitehall again. She refused to acknowledge his presence even when they met face to face at small, intimate dinner parties, and he, on his part, seemed to have lost all his infatuation with her.

Anna-Maria felt life an increasing strain. She was always keyed up, always self-consciously watching her every word and gesture lest she give further cause for scandal. At court her laughter was deliberate, contrived, but a clever ear could have heard the underlying tension in it. It was only when she played with her children that she laughed spontaneously, the sound ringing out, clear and bell-like.

The duke of Buckingham had virtually ignored her at court ever since the duel, and each time that he brushed past her with a perfunctory nod, she felt a pang of wistful emptiness.

Often she checked an impulse to delay him as he hurried past her. If she could talk to him alone for a quarter hour, she might be able to convince him of her innocence. But each time she stopped herself.

One night, shortly before the baby was due, she found herself dancing opposite him at a ball. As their hands brushed in the steps of the dance, Anna-Maria shivered and the duke, thinking she was ill, looked at her with quick concern.

At the end of the dance, he led her solicitously to a quiet alcove. "It is madness for you to be here tonight when it is so close to your lying-in."

Anna-Maria blushed crimson. It was not seemly for a man to mention a woman's pregnancy, even when she was so close to her time. Anna-Maria had been entertaining the false notion that her full skirts concealed her condition. Suddenly she wondered if the duke knew that the court was speculating about the child's paternity.

He handed her a glass of chilled wine, saying gently, "Let the glass warm in your hand for a moment. Chilled wine might sit uneasily on your stomach." The old note of concern and tenderness was back in his voice, and Anna-Maria felt her heart flutter. She realized now that she had been starving for that sound, and she looked up at him with naked emotion in her eyes.

He caught his breath involuntarily. Even now, when he knew that she was as wanton as the other courtesans, he felt the old, protective tenderness for her, and he was angry at himself. He had been bedding women since he was a lad of fourteen and congratulated himself that he knew the breed well. Now, in his maturity, he found himself as helpless as a schoolboy, succumbing to this woman's wiles. How easily she had deceived him! Her total air of innocence had made him yearn to cherish her. She must have been secretly laughing at his gullibility while she bestowed her favors on worthless scoundrels like Howard and Jermyn.

Roughly, to cover his emotion, he said, "Tom Howard has just become betrothed to my sister, Mary." He expected Howard's name to wound her and was rewarded when she saw a look of dark pain leap into her eyes.

She was looking up at him indignantly, her head tilted back because of his greater height. "Tom Howard is no suitor of.mine, nor ever was!" There was an unaccustomed sharpness in her soft voice. "Indeed, my lord, your sister has my sympathy because I think the man is insane."

She had never spoken to him angrily before, and for a moment they both stared at each other, wordless with surprise.

Anna-Maria recovered first and put her hand on his sleeve, beseechingly. "My lord, may we sit a moment? I've been craving a quiet moment with you."

The duke looked down at the small white hand lying on his blue sleeve, as light as a butterfly's caress. He could refuse her nothing.

Her voice was so low as to be almost inaudible, and he had to lean forward to catch the sound. "My lord, I have ever felt you to be my friend here at court. And yet in the past months you have turned a cold face to me, and I have been desolate. Your wife has proved a good friend to me. She believes in my innocence. Cannot you believe as well?"

She leaned toward him and touched his knee lightly and then was immediately sorry that she had done so because it created sensations within her that bewildered her.

Their eyes met, and he stared into her eyes as though he were attempting to read her very soul. Suddenly the tension went out of his body, and he smiled. Anna-Maria nearly wept with relief.

"No doubt you have been more foolish than wanton," he said. Now that he was sitting so close to her, looking fully into her pure face, it was impossible to imagine her, as he had done on sleepless nights, in the arms of either Jermyn or Howard. Their coarse hands could not have stroked that slender white body, lingered in the bright, gleaming masses of her hair.

The duke leaned forward and drew one of her hands into his own, and her heart sang at the touch. "Anna-Maria, why weren't you more cautious of your reputation? I warned you the first day you arrived that you were like a lamb among wolves. And yet you flirt too readily, you come too frequently to court without your husband."

Anna-Maria said simply, "My husband bids me come, my lord." Slowly, taking sips of wine between words, she told him of Francis's ambition and his desire that she be seen frequently at court since he disliked coming himself.

The duke's face darkened in an expression that men under his command had learned to fear. Shrewsbury was either a knave or a fool. At that moment of rage he wished that he had a sword in his hand and could run Shrewsbury through, for placing his wife in such a dangerous position.

He took Anna-Maria's wineglass from her unresisting fingers and set it on a table. "You are very sweet, my dear. I beg your forgiveness for doubting you. And now I'm going to escort you home. You should be tucked up in your own bed, not straining yourself here at court."

As Anna-Maria rose at his bidding, she realized that she would like to put her entire life in this man's hands and do his bidding for the rest of her days. His integrity, his cool head, and his deep strengths would be a rock on which to build her life.

They rode in silence to Anna-Maria's house on the Strand. It had lightened the duke's heart to believe Anna-Maria innocent once again. And yet it went contrary to his deepest desires. Had he been able to believe her wanton, he would have no scruples about seizing her now in the darkness of the coach and covering her with hot kisses as his senses cried out for him to do.

Anna-Maria's hand lay on the leather seat between them, only inches from the duke's thigh. She wanted desperately to move her hand that small fraction of space and touch him, and she could not understand her longing.

She knew that when he bade her goodnight he would take her hand in farewell, and she found herself straining ahead to that moment, craving it. What foolishness was this? To crave a casual touch with such intensity that her pulses were racing!

As they drew up in front of the house, the flare of the torches outside the doorway illuminated his face. Anna-Maria realized suddenly that she was aching with a desire to reach up and cup his face between her hands, her palms warm against his cheeks. She wanted—oh, God!—she wanted to press her lips very lightly against his tender, sensitive mouth.

Appalled at her thoughts, she was confused and perfunctory in her farewell. When he finally took her hand, she snatched it away and raced into the house, calling a breathless, "Good night, my lord," over her shoulder.

For the next few days, she was restless and moody, and Sarah attributed it to the impending birth of the baby. "Don't fret so," she advised. "The midwife assures me that the second birth is always an easy one."

But Anna-Maria, her thoughts in a turmoil, had no fear of the impending birth. Her mind was constantly on the duke. No thought of lovemaking intruded into her mind. Lovemaking was an unpleasant duty and had no link with the sensations the duke aroused in her. Her imagination dealt only with someday being kissed by him, and she grew faint with pleasure at the thought.

It was almost a relief when her pains started and she knew the baby was on its way. She lay staring out the window at the chill February day, watching one naked tree limb etched against the sky until it was engraved on her memory. The pains were not so intense this time, nor so frightening. The last time her labor had resulted in the birth of a healthy child, and she was confident that this birth would go well.

Shortly after midnight, the baby's head appeared, and Anna-Maria, straining to release the small body, felt a flash of ecstasy. If only she could give birth to a child each year! When the small, squirming body was put into her arms, slow tears of gratitude crept down her sweat-damp cheeks. She hugged the infant to her and put a gentle kiss on his damp black head. "We'll call you John," she said softly. Suddenly she remembered the rumors about this child's parentage, and her arms tightened around him protectively. "Nothing in this world shall ever hurt you," she vowed.

Sixteen

"Sarah! Why are you such a slugabed?" Anna-Maria, fully dressed, stood in the doorway of Sarah's bedchamber looking impatiently at Sarah, who was lying in leaden misery under a pile of bedcovers.

Sarah moaned and dug her blond head deeper into the pillow. " 'Tis my time of month."

"Oh!" A quick look of sympathy crossed Anna-Maria's face. Normally Sarah gloried in being a woman, but once a month she took to her bed cursing the fate that had made her female. Anna-Maria was used to dealing with the situation. She moved swiftly across the room and gently laid her hand on Sarah's damp forehead. "I'll tell Martha to bring you a posset heavily laced with wine. It will make you sleep."

Sarah moved the bedcovers down a little so that one of her bright blue eyes peeked out. "What are you planning to do today?"

Anna-Maria's subdued manner, which she had assumed out of sympathy for Sarah, dropped as abruptly as a cloak. "Oh, Sarah, it's such a glorious day. I'm going to take the coach and go for a ride. It's a day for picking wild flowers—" She broke off. "But it's unkind of me to chatter when you are unwell." She straightened the bedcovers, tucking them firmly around Sarah's shoulders and said softly, "Go to sleep. I'll bring you a present when I return."

Anna-Maria donned a heavily plumed hat, then ran

quickly down the stairs to the waiting coachman. As she settled into the coach, she had a sudden impulse: she wanted the smell of the sea in her nostrils. Giving the coachman a radiant smile, she said, "John, drive down to the docks. I have a fancy to see the ships come in."

She settled back happily as the coach lumbered into motion. The docks never failed to fascinate her. She thrilled with pride as she watched ships come in from all over the world, silent, white-sailed testimony to England's proud place as the foremost maritime nation. They came with an air of mystery, bringing exotic cargoes—rare silks, spices, ivory—from countries that Anna-Maria would never see.

Salt breezes wafted into the coach as they neared the docks, and Anna-Maria sat forward eagerly. The unpaved road was thick with mud, and sighing, she settled back. It would be slow progress from now on. Suddenly the seat tilted, and she was thrown to the far side of the coach, landing up against the door with a jolt. Dizzy with the shock of it, she straightened slowly, clinging to the window jamb and rubbing her shoulder, which had taken the worst of the blow.

The coach door was wrenched open, and John said apologetically, "I'm sorry, my lady. We went into a ditch and one of the wheels—" He broke off as a hand was clapped on his shoulder, a narrow, pale hand covered with a profusion of jeweled rings. Suddenly Henry Killigrew thrust his head in next to the coachman's and looked at Anna-Maria. "Here's a pretty find!"

Anna-Maria blushed, slightly uneasy. Ever since Jermyn and Howard had ruined her reputation by their duel, she had avoided being alone with Henry. His abrupt appearance on the scene found her unprepared.

Henry gave her a knowing grin and turned his attention to the coachman. In a moment Henry thrust his head back through the door and said, "Come, Anna-Maria. I'll ply you with refreshments at that tavern over there while John makes his repairs."

Anna-Maria looked at him dubiously. She didn't want an uncomfortable tête-à-tête with Henry, to sit opposite him while he expertly flirted with her. No doubt, he, like others at court, thought that she had given Jermyn and Howard good cause for their duel. "Thank you, no," she said crisply. "I'm perfectly comfortable here."

"Nonsense." Henry's aristocratic face was filled with delight. He had been angling for nearly two months to get Anna-Maria alone again, and here was a rare opportunity. He'd be damned if he'd let it slip past him.

The coachman said slowly, "Best go with him, my lady. This is a rough neighborhood, and I doubt my ability to protect you singlehanded if we are set upon by thieves."

Anna-Maria looked out the window and hesitated. It was indeed a rough neighborhood. The buildings were shabby, neglected, and looked in danger of falling down. The tavern Henry spoke of looked just as bad, but there would be a good fire and hot wine.

Henry took advantage of her hesitation. Leaning into the coach, he swept her into his arms. "Henry, don't play the fool! I can walk."

Henry laughed at her outburst and gripped her more tightly. "I'll not have it said that I allowed a lady to spoil her new French boots in a sea of mud." He carried her across the mud and into the tavern.

"Faugh!" Anna-Maria wrinkled her nose in disgust and hastily put her hand to her nose so that the perfume from her gloves would mask the stench. The tavern was a small, mean hovel. Several sailors were visible through the gloom, looking up curiously at the finely dressed pair in the doorway. The sailor at the nearest table put down his pewter mug of ale and stared intently at the narrow gold cross that hung from Anna-Maria's neck. He grinned, exposing rotted teeth. "Here's pretty pickings. And it's fallen into my hands like a gift from the gods."

Anna-Maria shrank back into Henry's arms, certain that the sailor's coarse hands would be fumbling at her neck at any moment. Henry whispered in her ear, "Pay no mind to him. He's full of wind. He knows well that he's no match for my sword."

He raised his voice and shouted for the barmaid. She came quickly from behind the wooden counter, knowing that these two could afford to pay well for the finest she had.

"We want your best room, a roaring fire and a bottle of port. Decent port," Henry said with good humor. Swiftly he added to Anna-Maria, "Best that we hire a private room. You can't stay among this rabble."

Anna-Maria nodded. Even in the better taverns, the nobility rarely sat in the public rooms. Before Anna-Maria could slip from Henry's arms and regain her feet, he was carrying her quickly up the stairs, following the barmaid.

The chamber was narrow and dusty, but the barmaid presented it with a flourish of pride. She quickly lit the fire and blew on it to coax it into life.

Anna-Maria stood in the center of the room watching her and feeling acutely uncomfortable. A large bed dominated the room, and she carefully averted her eyes from it. She feared meeting Henry's flirtatious gaze even more now than previously. She could rush past him and down the stairs, but Henry had given her no excuse for such action. She could imagine the hoots of laughter that would go up at court if he repeated the story. "Damme, I meant but to give the countess of Shrewsbury a glass of wine, and a few moments of company while her coach was being repaired, but the lady so overestimates her charms that she was certain I was bent on an assignation. She fled the room like a frightened child!"

Anna-Maria slowly took off her plumed hat and moved closer to the fire, determined to conduct herself like a lady of sophistication. She used her perfumed leather glove to dust the seat of a chair, then sat down, demurely smiling at Henry as the barmaid bustled off to get the wine. "Thank you, my lord. This is much more pleasant than being mired in mud."

Henry unbuckled his sword and tossed it onto the table. "It was a happy chance that brought me in this direction. What are you doing in such a neighborhood?"

"I wanted to go down to the docks and watch the ships come in. I find it endlessly exciting—they come from such far-off, romantic places."

Henry smiled. "You can find romance right at home. Even in such a mean-spirited room as this, if the right people are together." His hazel eyes swept over her face and neck with an unmistakable gleam of desire.

As Anna-Maria opened her mouth to protest, the barmaid arrived, proudly displaying an apron full of dusty bottles. "Tis the best in our cellar, my lord."

Henry plucked one of the bottles from her apron, blew off the dust, and inspected it critically. "It will do."

Pressing a gold coin into her hand, he said, "I'll shout down if I want anything further." A look passed between the two, and she nodded in understanding before quiting the room.

She thinks that we are lovers, Anna-Maria thought indignantly. Restless, she moved quickly to the fire and held out her hands, wondering how long it would take John to repair the wheel. Surely he would be done within the quarter hour, and she would be out of this troublesome situation.

Henry came up behind her, momentarily startling her, and pressed a glass of wine into her hand. Anna-Maria took a sip and smiled at him over the rim, hoping that she looked sophisticated and composed. "And what is the latest gossip at court, Henry?" Killigrew's wild tongue and flights of fancy usually made him an amusing gossip.

Henry shrugged. At the moment his attention was not on the antics at court. "There are new love affairs daily but no new duels recently." His eyes were intent on Anna-Maria's face.

Anna-Maria gasped. "For shame, Henry! That duel between Jermyn and Howard was no fault of mine."

Henry's face was flushed, and his speech slightly thick, although he had only drunk half a glass of wine. "Not your fault, my sweet? You drive a man half mad with your pretty tricks and then deny your responsibility when he is inflamed by desire?"

Anna-Maria, angry and now a little frightened,

started to move past him, but Henry grabbed her by the waist and pulled her to him, pressing his hand against the small of her back until her body was curved tightly against his. The state of his arousal was obvious even through the thickness of her skirts. Filled with panic, Anna-Maria began to struggle, but he silenced her protests by covering her mouth with his demanding lips. Anna-Maria tried to keep her mouth unyielding, but his lips forced hers apart, and her cries were muffled in her throat. She twisted her head futilely, her long hair spilling loose. She was sure her waist would crack if he didn't loosen his grip.

Wild anger at her helplessness filled her. Desperate, she beat at his shoulder with the hand holding the wineglass, sending wine spilling over his shoulders.

He laughed, a soft growl of a laugh, and thrust his tongue between her parted lips. Tears began streaming down Anna-Maria's face, but she could make no sound because once again his kiss was muffling her cries. Past caring about dignity, she attacked him with sudden savagery, feeling a primitive satisfaction as she violently scratched his face.

With an involuntary yelp of pain, Killigrew released her for a second, and she sprang back from his arms. "You forget yourself. I'm not Lady Bennett or one of her harlots."

Henry's eyes were dark with anger. He was breathing unevenly, but his words cut at her. "There are more harlots at Whitehall than ever graced a brothel. And you, my sweet countess, are the greatest harlot of them all!"

Anna-Maria was stunned into silence. Henry, charming, suave Henry, who had bandied pretty words with her on candlelit evenings at court had disappeared, and in his place was this angry stranger, a stranger who was clearly a madman.

He reached out with the swiftness of a striking snake, his fingers biting into Anna-Maria's wrist. "How many men wear bracelets made from locks of your hair? Chestnut-hued trophies of a successful hunt. They flaunt them so that all the world may see that they have bedded the countess of Shrewsbury."

"Oh, sweet Jesu!" Anna-Maria gave a soft moan and pressed her free hand to her trembling lips. She had been flattered when various courtiers had begged for locks of her hair. She had thought it a pretty conceit, harmless.

"I'll not be made a fool of!" Henry shouted, enraged. "You've driven me near mad with your teasing ways. I'll not be the only man at Whitehall who fails to taste your charms." He reached out and seized her roughly, and before she could catch her breath he had dragged her across the room and thrown her on the bed.

"No, Henry!" Anna-Maria screamed. His hand swiftly covered her mouth. She writhed, and kicked desperately, frantically trying to claw his face.

Only a few hours ago, the day had been full of sunlight and sweet promise, and now she was caught in a nightmare. It wasn't possible that she could be lying on this crude bed, fighting like an animal for her virtue. Surely this unspeakable thing could not happen. She needed but a moment's peace, and then she could coax him back into sanity. But already Henry was impatiently pulling off his breeches, and like a mindless animal, she fought against a savage beast who sought to satisfy a burning, primitive urge.

She struggled to sit upright, but he slammed her back against the bed with the full force of his weight. Reaching down, he tore at her busk and petticoats, and they fell away from her with the sound of tearing silk.

Henry's hands were between her legs. Anna-Maria tensed her thigh muscles, but Henry, seemingly with no effort, succeeded in pushing her legs apart. Oh, God, this couldn't be happening!

She was still mouthing a frantic denial when Henry entered her. She was dry, and his entrance hurt so badly that Anna-Maria almost fainted from the pain. She went white, and the sweat stood out on her face in a thin film. Henry moaned with pleasure and deepened his kiss, thrusting strongly. Anna-Maria's whole body was rigid with denial. She wished passionately that she could faint so that she could escape the sight of his sweaty face, escape his painful thrusts.

There was a star-shaped stain on the ceiling, and Anna-Maria found herself staring at it as though it were the only point of reality in a world gone mad. The shape of that star would be imprinted on her mind forever.

His penetration of her body had knocked all the animal fight out of her. She was almost indifferent as she felt his lips on her full, pink-tipped breasts. Anna-Maria thought suddenly of how her babies' mouths felt, contentedly sucking those same nipples, and a gush of helpless tears welled up in her eyes.

"God's blood!" Henry's voice came in short, muffled pants. "I've never tasted flesh as sweet as yours."

Anna-Maria felt anger sear through her. It was intolerable that he should be deriving such pleasure from her pain and humiliation. She could hear herself whimpering, but the sounds seemed to be coming from a distance. Henry stiffened suddenly and then, with a hoarse cry of triumph, climaxed inside her.

Henry moved slightly, and Anna-Maria looked at him listlessly. We are not human at this moment, Anna-Maria thought disgustedly. He has reduced us both to the level of animals.

Henry flushed and moved his body away from hers. Sitting on the edge of the bed, he spoke to her over his shoulder. "I had not thought to find you so cold." His voice was a parody of his normal, sophisticated tone. She wondered if he were still civilized enough to feel shame.

She lay on the bed, too dispirited to move, while he pulled on his breeches and tugged his clothing back into position. She felt as if some essential part of her had died during the last quarter hour's degradation and she would never be able to resume normal life again—would never laugh with her children, plan menus, dance at Whitehall. The Anna-Maria who had done those things seemed separated from her by a vast distance of time and experience.

Henry surveyed her from head to toe and laughed shortly. "I should have been less careless about ripping your clothes, but passion leaves no room for clear thinking." Grabbing Anna-Maria's cloak, he tossed it at her. "Cover yourself with this—unless you want those sailors below filling their eyes with your charms." His eyes were on her naked breasts.

I'll kill him, Anna-Maria thought dully. I'll wait till he is off guard and then I'll grab his sword and run him through.

But she knew that she could not. The sword would be too heavy for her slender arms; Henry would wrest it from her before she could raise it. And even if she succeeded in lifting it, she would probably falter at the thought of taking a life.

Henry pulled her roughly to her feet. "I've no taste for lingering after I've done with lovemaking."

Anna-Maria fastened her cloak with numb fingers and, head down, followed Henry from the room, shrinking from the faces that turned toward her as they crossed the tavern. Outside John caught sight of her and raced across the muddy road, worry clearly written on his face.

Henry handed her into the coachman's arms saying smoothly, "The countess is feeling a bit unwell. If the coach is ready now, I suggest you take her home as swiftly as possible."

John took her arm firmly under his, and, making soothing sounds, led her across the road and into the coach. "I'll soon have you home."

Anna-Maria huddled against the leather seat and shut her eyes.

Henry thrust his head through the coach window and doffed his hat mockingly. "I thank you for the pleasure of your company."

Anna-Maria began to sob without restraint. But through her tears she threatened, "My husband will avenge me!"

Seventeen

When they reached home, she jumped from the coach without waiting for the coachman's assistance and twisted her ankle as she landed. She heard John's startled outcry behind her as she wrenched open the heavy oak door herself and brushed past the footman. She was frantic to find Sarah, and despite the pain in her ankle, she ran up the stairs. Sarah was deep in a posset-induced sleep, and Anna-Maria had to shake her vigorously.

"Wha—?" Sarah looked up to find Anna-Maria bending over her, shaking with sobs that seemed to be torn from the very center of her being. "Is it one of the children?" Sarah struggled up on one elbow, her face pale with alarm. Surely nothing else except the death of one of the children would cause Anna-Maria such terrible grief.

"Oh, Sarah, Sarah. Help me!" Anna-Maria flung herself, sobbing, into Sarah's arms. Sarah put her arms about her and held her with fierce protectiveness. "Hush. Hush. Try to tell me the trouble."

Anna-Maria sat up and tried to tell Sarah as coherently as she could, but she could barely talk between sobs. Sarah pieced together the story from the incoherent fragments, and her face darkened with anger. "This is one knave who shall not go unpunished!" It had been impossible to punish Ramon without shouting to all the world that Anna-Maria was no longer a virgin, but now that she was married, the situation was entirely different.

"I'd like to kill myself." Anna-Maria's voice broke on a fresh gust of sobs. "Oh, Sarah, if you could only see the way he handled me. As though I were not human. Not a woman. Only an *object* for his pleasure."

142

When Sarah heard Francis in the hall sharply rebuking a footman, she flung back the bedcovers and jumped out of bed. Running into the hall, she seized Francis by the arm. "My lord, you must come with me at once."

Alarmed, Francis stared down at her. Sarah was in a faded nightdress, her blond hair snarled as if from sleep, her blue eyes frantic.

"Has the countess been injured?" Francis had a quick image of an overturned coach, Anna-Maria's body lying broken beside it.

"Yes, and badly," Sarah said abruptly. "She's in my chamber. You must come at once." She was pulling at his sleeve, but he tore free, running ahead of her into the bedchamber.

Anna-Maria was lying on the bed, deep sobs racking her slim body. Francis ran over and gathered her up, searching for bruises and injuries.

She turned with a wail and flung herself against his chest. "Oh, Francis, he raped me. Killigrew raped me!"

Francis suddenly went very still, and Anna-Maria could feel the tension of his muscles under her fingers. Brokenly, between sobs, she repeated the story.

Francis's eyes never left her tear-stained face. His expression rapidly darkened, and by the time she had finished, he looked disgusted. Abruptly he removed her fingers from his arms and thrust her toward Sarah. "Take care of your mistress."

Anna-Maria stared at him uncomprehendingly as he rose from her side. He had spoken no word of comfort to her, had vowed no revenge. He stopped in the doorway, his back turned to them, the lines of his shoulders rigid, and said, "We will talk of this later, Anna-Maria, when you are more restored."

Sarah was shocked but sought to reassure her mistress. "He's sorely upset, poor man. 'Tis a hideous thing for a man to learn that his wife has been violated."

Anna-Maria sat up and pushed her hair from her face, her sobs subsiding a little. Suddenly her face hardened. "I shall insist on being present when he runs his sword through Killigrew."

Anna-Maria, who wept at the sight of a dog run over in the streets of London, now seemed cold and bitter. Sarah was afraid.

Still, Sarah thought, I've no knowledge of what it feels like to be violated by a man. It might ruin one's very nature.

She took refuge in practicality, helping Anna-Maria out of her torn gown and gently soaking her twisted ankle. She brought her a steaming drink which she said would calm her, but Anna-Maria pushed it away.

"I want nothing to addle my thoughts. I must speak to Francis."

Slowly, favoring her injured ankle, she made her way to the small, private chamber that Francis used as an office. He was sitting at his desk, his graying head clutched in his hands, staring dully at some papers spread before him.

"Francis."

He looked up reluctantly at the sound of her voice and then stood slowly. "Come sit by the fire. Did Killigrew injure your ankle?"

"Nay." Anna-Maria carefully made her way to the chair. "I hurt it when I jumped too quickly from the coach." The flat, carefully noncommittal tone of Francis's voice disturbed her. She had expected him to be nearly mad with rage, angrily penning a challenge to Killigrew. Instead he was looking at her with a remote expression on his face.

She gripped the arms of her chair so tightly that her knuckles turned white. "Francis, I don't care when or where you duel with Killigrew, but I insist on being there. I want his last sight on earth to be my face!"

Francis turned abruptly and began fiddling with a silver quill on his desk. Quietly he said, "I have no intention of dueling with Killigrew, Anna-Maria."

She leaped to her feet, forgetting her injured ankle and then winced with pain. "What do you mean?" She thought that perhaps he meant to have Killigrew set upon by footpads and murdered quietly, but then Killigrew would never know that he was dying for the injury he had done her.

Francis, normally so careful of his property, was jabbing angrily into the fine surface of his desk with the point of the quill. His voice steady, he repeated, "I have no intention of dueling with Killigrew."

"How then will you avenge me?" Anna-Maria could feel the blood pounding in her veins, throbbing behind her eyes.

Francis dropped the quill and looked her fully in the eyes. "I don't intend to avenge you."

Anna-Maria sank back into the chair, staring at him wordlessly. For a moment she thought that she had not understood him. Then, very quietly, very patiently, as though she were talking to one of the children, she said, "But you *must* avenge me. I'm your wife, and Killigrew violated me."

Suddenly her control snapped, and she screamed, "Don't you understand? He raped me!" The memory of her humiliation returned in full force, and she sobbed in anguish.

Francis looked at her with open distaste. "If you will control yourself, Anna-Maria, we can talk about this calmly."

He made a move as though to seat himself in the chair facing hers, but then checked himself and sat in the chair behind his desk, increasing the distance between them. Reaching forward, he began shuffling a pile of papers, aligning the edges neatly. Anna-Maria watched his motions in silence, waiting for his explanation.

"In the first place the king has forbidden dueling, and I have no wish to incur his displeasure."

"You would put your ambition ahead of me?" Her eyes fell on the black dispatch box resting on the edge of the desk, and she suddenly stood, walked over to the desk, and violently swept the box to the floor with a quick thrust of her hand. "Your ambition is an illness, Francis. No man of honor would let his wife go unavenged."

Francis had involuntarily risen as the dispatch box fell to the floor, but now he sank back in his chair, visibly fighting for control. When he spoke again, his voice was even, uninflected.

"A man of honor avenges his wife when she is virtuous. You have given Killigrew—and every man at court—the right to think that you can be taken easily. The fault is yours, Anna-Maria, not mine. I have given this much thought, and I've decided that I am not willing to die over a matter that is essentially of your own doing."

If the heavens had opened and thundered forth fire, Anna-Maria could not have been more dumbfounded. She stared at Francis, and her voice was very low when she asked, "You are saying that you will not kill Henry Killigrew?"

Francis shot her a quick look. The fight seemed to have gone out of her. No doubt she was prepared to be sensible. "Exactly. And it is to your benefit as well, Anna-Maria. Look at the scandal that followed when Jermyn and Howard dueled over you. If I attempt to avenge you with Killigrew, it will only damage your reputation further. Everyone at court will say that you and Killigrew are lovers and that I challenged him in a fit of jealousy."

Anna-Maria was standing very rigid, her hands in tight fists at her sides. Her stillness and the expression in her eyes frightened him, and he said, with an attempt at kindness, "It will be best if we ignore the matter. Even if Killigrew shouts to the world that he has enjoyed your favors, there are many who will not believe him. Remember that he is known as a liar, and people believe only a fraction of his wild tales."

Anna-Maria still had not moved, and when she finally looked fully into his eyes, it was as though she were returning from a long distance. She surveyed him with a look of withering contempt. "When I married you, I thought myself safe. And yet you are a coward!"

Francis half rose in his chair, bracing himself by holding onto the desk. "And you, madame, have earned the reputation of being wanton, even if you have not performed the act itself."

Anna-Maria raised her hand as though to strike him, then looked at her fist and dropped it to her side. She had learned earlier in the day that her physical strength was no match for a man's.

With the intensity of one taking a vow, she said, "You claim my body through a marriage of convenience. Killigrew took it through brute force. I swear to you that no man shall ever touch me again!"

Her head was thrown back, and her eyes were luminous as she stood facing him defiantly. Francis's anger dropped away as he felt a stirring in his loins. She was magnificent in her anger, and he wanted her at this moment as he had never wanted her before.

He moved swiftly from behind the desk and came toward her, his arms outstretched. Anna-Maria saw the unmistakable signs of his arousal, and for a moment, disbelief swept over her. Then an expression of mingled contempt and deep anger crossed her delicate features. She made no attempt to flee, merely stood looking at him until he noticed her expression and faltered. Then she said, with dangerous quietude, "If you attempt to touch me, I shall kill you!"

She held his eyes for a long moment and then swept out of the room, her exit dignified despite her slight limp.

Only a few days after the rape, Anna-Maria went to court.

"Are you not frightened?" Sarah blurted, without thinking. It was likely that Killigrew, who was a notorious braggart, had boasted to everyone at court that he had enjoyed the favors of the countess of Shrewsbury.

Anna-Maria was sitting at the dressing table, brushing her hair. She stopped, the brush poised above her head, and looked at Sarah curiously. There was a blank expression in her eyes. "Why should I be frightened? The worst that can happen to a woman has already befallen me. I have nothing left in life to fear." Picking up a gleaming strand of hair, she absentmindedly brushed it.

Sarah felt a queer clutching in her stomach. "A woman without fear," she said slowly, "is a dangerous creature. Dangerous to herself and others."

Anna-Maria laughed shortly, and the sound was unpleasant. "Fear is a luxury that can only be afforded by women who have husbands to protect them. I *have* no husband, so it's fortunate that I am no longer subject to fear."

Eighteen

"Anna-Maria!" The duke of Buckingham had just caught sight of her slim form ahead of him in St. James Park, and he hurried to catch up with her.

At the sound of his voice, she turned and stood quietly waiting for him. Her face was shaded by her heavily plumed hat, and he could not read her expression.

As he drew within earshot, she said quietly, "Good morning, my lord." Her voice was totally without inflection. He wondered what had caused the loss of the lilt in her voice that he had always found so charming.

Standing before her, he bowed, his eyes on her face. His expression grew grave. "Anna-Maria, are you ill?"

Anna-Maria gave a brittle laugh. "My lord, I fear you will ruin your reputation for gallantry. I expected a pretty compliment from you, not an accusation that I look ill." She pirouetted for his inspection. "Isn't my gown becoming? It's the latest rage from Paris."

Buckingham seized her arm angrily. "Don't play the coquette with me." Her brittle manner and the sudden loss of the intimacy between them irritated him to the point of wanting to shake her.

His fingers gripped her arm so tightly that she winced and for a moment looked at him in the old way, her expression open and unguarded. Then a tightening passed over her features, and she said quietly, "You are hurting me, my lord."

Muttering an apology, he dropped her arm, his eyes still on her face. Indeed, she did look as though she were suffering from a prolonged illness. Her delicate cheekbones stood out in sharp relief against her smooth skin, and her mouth and eyes had a hardness about them.

"You've been avoiding me these past few weeks," he said, desperately anxious about her.

"Have I, my lord? 'Twas not deliberate." She bent and plucked a lush pink rose, then held it to her nostrils, feigning indifference. She wanted to fling herself into the duke's strong arms and melt with tears against his chest, but she knew she must disguise her longing.

The duke spoke angrily. "Ever since you came back to court after the birth of your son, you've been changed. And I dislike the difference."

"Changed, my lord? How?" She twirled the rose in her slim fingers and watched it carefully, not daring to look up at him.

"You're brittle. Cold. Your laugh has no real mirth in it. And no man is safe from your flirtations." Suddenly he snatched the rose from her fingers and dashed it to the ground. "Anna-Maria, look at me!"

Reluctantly she raised her face, and he felt a pang when he saw that there were tears in her lovely dark eyes. Taking her chin, he gently cupped it in his hand. At his touch she became rigid but didn't move away from him.

"Anna-Maria, once you begged me to believe that all those rumors about you were false. And I *did* believe you. I trusted in your innocence and sweetness. And yet now your conduct gives the lie to your words. There's not a man at court who doesn't have hopes of winning you someday, and it is you who gives him such hope."

Abruptly she pulled away from him. "They are false hopes, my lord. No man will ever touch me again."

The word *again* inflamed the duke. She was virtually admitting that men had enjoyed her favors in the past. Cruelly he said, "Henry Killigrew gives proof that he has known you intimately. He tells me—indeed he tells all who will listen—that you have a beauty mark on the underside of your right breast."

Instinctively, Anna-Maria's hand flew to cover the spot he had mentioned, and the duke angrily clenched his jaw.

"So it is true!"

"Aye, it's true." Anna-Maria's voice was a bitter whisper. "Killigrew speaks with authority when he describes me intimately."

The duke's bright blue eyes were blazing with anger, and his hand came up with a sudden motion, as though he intended to strike her. Then Anna-Maria's icy composure, which had carried her through the past few weeks, deserted her, and she began to cry, deep wrenching sobs that racked her slender body.

Suddenly there were the sounds of people approaching on the path behind them, light laughter mingling with deeper masculine tones, and the duke seized Anna-Maria's arm and looked about for privacy. Quickly he pulled her into a thick clump of trees that bordered the path. He was fiercely angry, and yet, mingled with his anger, was an urge to protect this beautiful young woman.

Anna-Maria went with him numbly, the tears flowing ever more freely in blessed relief. When they had reached the sanctuary of an overspreading elm, the duke pulled a handkerchief from beneath his lacey sleeve. Holding it to her nose, he spoke to her as he would to a child. "Blow."

Anna-Maria blew obediently, but her sobs were still coming unchecked, and she almost choked. Groaning, the duke pulled her into his arms. "Hush, darling. Nothing is so bad that I cannot set it right for you."

Her hair was fragrant against his nostrils, her slim body sweet and pliant, and he felt a moment of intense joy. He suddenly realized how keenly he had been longing for this moment. No other woman had ever stirred him as Anna-Maria did. For no woman had he waited so long.

Instinctively she moved closer into his embrace, her tears subsiding as she gave a long sigh of contentment. Not since her father had held her when she was a young child had she had such a feeling of safety. She nestled closer into his arms, then instinctively raised her face toward his, her red lips parted in delight, her eyes soft with happiness.

The duke groaned and bent his head, taking Anna-Maria's lips in a kiss. She had been watching his mouth as she always did, and now she felt a flash of incredulous joy as she realized that she was to feel its touch at last.

As his lips met hers, she experienced a piercing sweetness, and she swayed toward him, limp with happiness. At first his kisses were very light, exploring, as though his mouth were greeting hers, softly making its acquaintance. There was such tenderness, such a contrast from Francis's perfunctory kisses, that Anna-Maria felt faint. The duke's lips were grazing hers, tracing the shape of the curves, tasting the texture. A swell of desire swelled up in Anna-Maria, and just as she felt that she could bear no more, that she would die if he didn't increase the pressure, he suddenly pulled her closer, his kiss intensifying. Her body was liquid fire now, weightless, and all of her being was concentrated in her lips, which were tasting a sweetness that made her senses swim. The duke's tongue was moving into her mouth now, and Anna-Maria welcomed it, longing for deeper contact.

Her abdomen, pressed against the duke's taut stomach, suddenly burst into flame, the sweet heat building with the rhythm of his breathing. She let out a cry and pressed closer, all aching desire now.

She felt the pain of loss when the duke reluctantly pushed her away a little. He had no patience with the randy noblemen who bedded in the open like animals in heat. "Not here, darling."

Anna-Maria looked at him in bewilderment, her cameo face soft with desire.

He moaned softly and then picked her up in his arms and sat down on a mossy bank, cradling her as though she were a child. Tears still stained her cheeks, and he bent and gently kissed her. "Why are you crying, my darling?"

She had always loved the deep timbre of his voice, and now she nestled closer to his chest, feeling pure joy because she could feel the source of his beloved voice, feel it building beneath her ear before he spoke. For the moment the sense of his question eluded her. She was so happy in this moment that her pain and tears seemed to have happened in another lifetime.

He grazed her mouth lightly with a kiss and repeated the question. She looked at him hopefully for a moment, wishing that he would kiss her again, but then she stirred and tried to collect her thoughts.

"Killigrew raped me." At this moment it scarcely seemed to matter. The scent of flowers was wafting from the garden, the glade was cool, pierced by shafts of sunlight, and she lay in the duke's arms, her slender hand on his chest.

She was startled when he tensed at her words. Tersely he pressed her for the details, and haltingly she told him of the broken coach, of Killigrew's invitation, of the terrifying half hour in the tavern bedroom. "And Francis refuses to avenge me," she concluded.

The duke swore a string of oaths that would have put a common seaman to shame. "The coward!"

"He says that he is not." Anna-Maria was tracing the line of the duke's chin with a slim forefinger. "He says that I have been careless and thus ruined my reputation and there is no reason for him to risk his life for my foolishness."

The duke's face looked as though it were carved from stone. "Then *I* will avenge you! Killigrew will die on the point of my sword before night falls."

Here at last was the strong male championship that she had been craving. For a moment she nestled closer in his arms, looking up at him, gratitude shining from her eyes, but then she sobered. "It would not help me," she said sadly. "People would merely say that *you* were my lover, as well as Killigrew."

The duke scowled. "Then I will set upon him in ambush. In any case he'll die for what he has done to you."

"But that would stain your honor." Anna-Maria let her finger trail lightly across his lips. "I could not bear that."

His arms tightened about her. "Then what would you have me do?"

"Nothing." At this moment Anna-Maria cared little about revenging herself on Killigrew. She was deliciously happy and had no room for any other emotion. "There is nothing you *can* do. I would not have you violate your honor by ambush, nor do I want the gossips saying that you are my lover."

He pulled her more tightly into his arms. "Am I not your lover, my darling?" His voice was infinitely tender.

"Oh, no." Anna-Maria looked at him seriously. "I can never have a lover. I cannot bear a man's touch."

Buckingham turned his head to hide a smile, fearing he would upset her more. She was lying seductively in his arms, her face already upturned in expectation of another kiss. Anna-Maria had been subject to her husband's unimaginative embraces and had been brutally raped by Killigrew. No doubt the art of kissing was a novelty to her, and she had not yet made the link between kissing and serious lovemaking.

His loins were on fire now, his pulses pounding. She was all soft warmth within his arms, her fragrant hair tickling his nostrils, her sweet mouth a font of purest pleasure. And yet, for her sake, he must restrain himself lest he frighten her.

He looked down into her upturned face and realized that, for the first time in his life, he was in love. He had gone unscathed for so many years that he had thought himself immune, and for a moment the emotion frightened him. Then he squared his broad shoulders. This woman was his now, his to love and to cherish, and for her sake he must fight down his desires. Gently, very gently, he bent and pressed his mouth against hers, speaking softly as he brushed against her lips. "There is nothing more to be frightened of, my love."

The sensation delighted Anna-Maria. When he raised his head, she begged, "Do that again, please. Speak to me with your lips against mine."

He laughed and bent his head whispering, as he moved his mouth gently across her lips, "I love you."

Anna-Maria could feel her very soul reaching out to him, wishing urgently to mingle with his. "I think I loved you from the first day I saw you," she said simply, "and I will love you all my life."

Nineteen

Anna-Maria was blindly happy, her days illuminated by the duke of Buckingham. Life seemed to be made of some soft, delicious substance, with no hard edges, and she walked through it radiantly. Tasks that had seemed wearisome before now took on a new ease, and she found herself singing as she checked her dressmaker's bill or went over the day's menu with the housekeeper.

She saw little of Francis, but when they met she was courteous to him in an aloof fashion. He seemed scarcely real to her now. Indeed, everyone except the duke seemed a little unreal.

No longer did they meet by accident. Now they conferred at the end of each evening at Whitehall and planned their schedules to coincide so they could meet as frequently as possible. Buckingham was as busy on government business as Francis, yet he always had time for Anna-Maria. Her cheeks glowed, and her senses were heightened as she anticipated their stolen embraces.

Once he entered a room unexpectedly, and she, unprepared, felt her body melting and flowing until she blushed and turned away, certain that everyone in the room had read her feelings.

In truth, neither she nor Buckingham was very successful in concealing their love. Although she tried to control it, Anna-Maria could feel her face grow soft with longing every time she looked at him, and her eyes openly betrayed her emotions. The courtiers were soon buzzing about the scandal, but Anna-Maria neither knew nor cared. When they were in a crowd, she and Buckingham sought each other's glances often, and each time, Anna-Maria realized that she had been searching for something all her life without ever knowing what it was that she had pursued. Now she knew. The delight in eye meeting eye, the shared recognition of a joke, the delicious sensation of hand touching hand in a stolen caress.

Buckingham was unfailingly tender with her, but sometimes he tilted back her head and looked deeply into her eyes and said, "Darling, I want to hold you all night long in my arms. I want to make love to you."

She would give him her life if he demanded it, but this one thing she could not do. He would find her cold, and it would be the end of his love for her. She could not bear to lose him.

When with great gentleness he pressed for an answer, she would say simply, "I cannot," then turn away so that he would not see the tears stinging her eyes.

Once Jane Middleton made flagrant advances toward the duke while Anna-Maria stood by, white with shock. She would have liked to have leaped at Jane, throwing her to the ground and pummeling her silly face. Then her anger turned inward on herself. Jane was a silly, feckless creature, but she was a true woman, passionate and giving, while she herself was nothing but a wooden doll, cold and lifeless.

She began to fear every other woman at court, her eyes alert now to the way they preened and pirouetted for the duke, blatantly exposing their charms. It was only a matter of time, she knew, before one of them would capture his interest. Jealousy was a new emotion for her, and she grew pale with the strain of it, feeling as though some small animal was constantly gnawing at her vital organs, draining the life from her.

One day she was so pale that the duke questioned her about it, and, giving a wail, she threw herself against his chest. "I hate every woman who makes advances to you. I think I must be going insane because I have the most terrifying thoughts. When I see a woman flirting with you, I'd like to pull a golden bodkin from my hair and stab her face with it until she is scarred and no longer appeals to you."

The duke laughed, delighted with her jealousy. "Do

you think I love you only for your beautiful face, my sweet? I love you for the thoughts that are within this small skull." He pressed her head gently, as though feeling the shape of her thoughts. Then he moved one hand and traced a gentle outline on her breast, over her fast-beating heart. "And I love you for what lies here, your goodness, your honesty."

Anna-Maria looked up, her love shining in her eyes, and he said, "Don't ever fear that my love will fail you, Anna-Maria. No other woman tempts me, nor ever will." He sighed unconsciously, feeling the pressure in his loins that was almost constant now.

Anna-Maria, understanding, felt a prick of guilt and a sudden onrush of fear. Despite his reassuring words, she doubted that he was capable of loving for a lifetime a woman who denied him release from his passion. There was a queer, shamed look in her eyes.

Pity stirred in him, and he kissed her gently. "I love you. That's all that's of importance." He gave her a playful little shake and laughed, trying to lighten the mood. "Hurry and make repairs to yourself. I'm going to take you to the theatre today. Nell Gwyn, that little orange girl turned actress, is going to play Cydaria in Dryden's *Indian Emperor*."

For a moment Anna-Maria's brow clouded, and Buckingham looked at her, puzzled. "What's amiss?"

Anna-Maria shrugged and managed a light laugh. " 'Tis nothing. Only that it was Killigrew who first spoke to me of Nell Gwyn."

Buckingham scowled and then forced himself to calmness. He wanted to cheer Anna-Maria, and dwelling on that scoundrel would not serve his purpose. "She's a nice little thing; I've taken a fancy to her."

At the sudden flash of resentment in Anna-Maria's eyes, he raised his hand, laughing. "Nay, darling, not in that sense. I have no eyes for any woman save you. I meant merely that she is a gay companion—witty, outspoken. She makes a good friend. In fact, I've a mind to introduce you to her after the theatre."

He bullied and coaxed Anna-Maria into hurrying, and before she could catch her breath, they were seated side by side in a box at the King's Theatre. It was stifling, and Anna-Maria kept her fan in rapid motion. The King's Theatre was rarely comfortable. In winter the chinks between the wooden walls and the large glazed cupola overhead made it drafty. In warm weather like this, the press of bodies and the heat from the candles that flamed on the walls and lit the stage made it unbearably hot. To distract herself, Anna-Maria leaned forward and peered into the pits where the seats cost two shillings and sixpence. As always it was a lively scene, often more entertaining than the action that was to follow on stage. Courtiers and apprentices who wished to be mistaken for courtiers bought seats in the pit and flirted with masked prostitutes. The orange girls moved constantly among them, holding out oranges and making risqué quips. The girls were chosen as much for their wit as their beauty, and they knew it was their job to keep the gentlemen amused until the curtain parted.

Anna-Maria looked around curiously to see who of the court was at the theatre today. The king was just entering his box with the queen at his side. It was unusual for the queen to attend the theatre, and Anna-Maria looked at her thoughtfully. She had heard that the king had recently taken a new mistress, Moll Davies, an actress from a rival theatre, the Duke's Theatre, and she wondered if the queen had heard the rumor and was wounded by it. When the king spied Buckingham and Anna-Maria together, his mouth twitched in a conspiratorial smile, and he gave them a hearty wave. The queen followed the direction of his movement, and, even at this distance, Anna-Maria could see the look of distaste that passed over her thin face. She winced. Now, indeed, she was guilty of all, save the final act, and were she to plead her innocence before the queen now, she would be lying. It was not morals, but the knowledge of her own inadequacy that kept her from the duke's embrace. She flushed and looked away, relieved that the play was about to begin.

When Nell Gwyn came on stage, Buckingham nudged Anna-Maria, and she leaned forward for a better look. She saw a small, charming figure with a mop of chestnut curls and a tilted, impudent nose. Nell's own personality triumphed over the part she was playing, and Anna-Maria found her gaiety and charm immensely appealing.

She found herself straining forward in her seat as Nell, playing Cydaria, met Cortez. She herself had looked and felt exactly the same when she had first seen the duke riding in the procession. She scarcely breathed, living the part with Nell, as Nell fell passionately in love at first sight. She was deliciously aware of Buckingham sitting next to her, his sleeve brushing her arm. When Nell described her emotions as, "Thick breath, quick pulse, and beating of my heart," Anna-Maria realized that that was exactly how she felt everytime Buckingham was close to her. Suddenly she envied Dryden his skill with words. How wonderful to take formless emotions and shape them so that others could share them.

At the conclusion of the play, she turned to Buckingham, limp with emotion, her eyes shining. "Nell Gwyn is wonderful!"

Buckingham smiled down at her. "Do you want to meet her? We can take her out for supper if you like."

"Oh, yes! Do you think she will come?"

Buckingham smiled. "I think she will be honored."

Nell Gwyn seemed to have a very good sense of her own worth and was not at all awed by the company in which she found herself. She teased Buckingham with perfect confidence, her quips ready and telling. But she treated him without the least sign of flirtatiousness, and Anna-Maria gave a sigh of relief; she had feared she might be jealous of Nell. The actress chattered happily to Anna-Maria, and it was clear that she was offering her friendship if the countess of Shrewsbury wanted it. In her openness and honesty she reminded Anna-Maria a little of Sarah, and Anna-Maria warmed to her instantly.

They sat in an upper room of the Hare and Hounds with a bushel of steaming oysters between them, and Nell cracked them open with frank greed, pausing at times to take a drink of wine. "Acting is thirsty, hungry work," she said, grinning.

Nell entertained them with backstage gossip of the theatre, and Anna-Maria realized, with amusement, that it was not so different from life at court. There were assignations, rivalries, jealousies, seductions. At court people fought over obtaining favors from the king, and in the theatre they scrambled to obtain the best roles.

Anna-Maria sat with her hand cupped under her chin, the lace on her sleeves falling back to expose her slim white arms. The duke gently touched the tip of her nose with his finger, pleased that she was so entertained by Nell's company. Anna-Maria smiled at him and then asked Nell curiously, "Tell me. Is it true that the king has been lying with Moll Davies?"

A shadow crossed Nell's bright face. "Aye, it's true enough." Juice spurted from the oyster shell she was opening, showering over her slim fingers. She gave an exclamation of annoyance and casually wiped her fingers on the bodice of her gown.

She popped an oyster into her mouth, then looked from Anna-Maria to the duke. With a great show of casualness, she said, "The king sent for *me* a fortnight ago, and I've been there twice since." Suddenly her impish face softened, and her eyes grew warm with remembering. "He is like no other man on earth. I never thought to find myself in love, and yet now I confess that I live for the moments when he summons me."

Anna-Maria and Buckingham exchanged a look. Buckingham's blue gaze was bright with amusement, but Anna-Maria felt a quick surge of pity. Surely this little orange girl turned actress was going to have her heart broken if she loved the king.

Nell laughed suddenly, a clear bell-like peal. "You should have seen me when the king summoned me the first time. It was immediately after the performance and suddenly Progers—you know the king's gentleman-of-the-backstairs?" Anna-Maria nodded. Progers was well known for his discreet conduct of the king's private love affairs.

"Well, Progers suddenly appeared backstage and told me to make myself ready immediately, that the king had sent for me." Nell shook her head despairingly. "I was a fair sight, greasepaint staining my face, and I'd thought I was going straight home after the theatre, so I had only one old gown with me."

Anna-Maria's mouth twitched. The gown Nell was wearing now was liberally stained with oyster juice, the lace torn in spots, although it had been fresh when the evening started. She thought of the many hours ladies at court spent in preparing their elaborate toilettes to please the king's eye and had difficulty in not laughing aloud. Nell, with her stained gown and disheveled hair, must have made an amusing contrast to the fastidious and bejeweled women that the king was used to. And yet Nell's grace of movement and pretty face would enhance the shabbiest of garments.

Nell took a quick deep drink of wine, then wiped her mouth with the back of her hand and gave a sigh of satisfaction. Turning to Anna-Maria she said, "I envy you. You are about the court all day and can see the king as often as you like."

Anna-Maria smiled and covered Nell's hand with her own. With impulsive kindness she said, "He often seems distracted this past fortnight. No doubt his thoughts are with you, and he finds life at court irksome because it keeps him from your side."

Buckingham's gaze was tender upon her, his eyes approving her kindness, and Nell gave her a wide smile. " 'Tis nice to have the friendship of a woman who is not a rival at the theatre. Would you like to visit me in my apartments tomorrow? I live in Drury Lane near the theatre." She shrugged suddenly, her brow knitting. " 'Tis not much of a place, but such as it is, there will always be hospitality for you."

Anna-Maria gave Nell's small hand a quick squeeze. "I'd love to come, Nelly."

She could eat no more, but Nell and the duke shared a steaming mutton pie, and the evening went by swiftly, Nell and the duke capping each other's jokes, the talk becoming increasingly lighthearted and boisterous. When the evening was over, Nell insisted on going home in a hired coach, and as Anna-Maria and the duke got into his coach, he smiled at her. "I'm glad you liked Nelly so well. I often think that you are lonely at court."

Anna-Maria nodded, her face sobering. "Many of the women are so—artificial. And they feel that all women are natural enemies, all rivals for the attention of men. 'Tis rare that I meet a woman of wit and honesty like Nell."

The duke was thinking that Anna-Maria would need a staunch friend if their affair progressed and became known.

Anna-Maria said thoughtfully, hesitating a little, "Another woman that I like well is your wife, Mary. She and I have been fast friends since our time at Hampton Court."

By unspoken agreement she and the duke rarely mentioned either Mary or Francis, but of late Anna-Maria's conscience had been troubling her. And yet she and the duke had committed no sin, had not broken their marriage vows.

"Mary returns your liking. She speaks of you often and with affection." The duke chose his words carefully. "Anna-Maria, I think no matter what the circumstances, Mary would remain loyal to her friendship for you." Anna-Maria started to reply and then checked herself. Not for all the world would she have deliberately fallen in love with the husband of a friend and she was bitter at fate that it should have happened to her. She wanted to tell the whole world of her love for Buckingham, but it was a secret that she must keep locked inside herself. Except for him. She could tell him. For the blessed relief of saying it aloud, she moved closer to him and said, "I love you more than I have ever loved anyone and I shall love you until I die."

The next morning Mary noticed Anna-Maria's unaccustomed silence as they shopped together at the Royal Exchange. As they were turning over a heap of colorful ribbons at one of the smaller stalls, Mary broke off a remark and turned to Anna-Maria with a worried frown. "Is something amiss, Anna-Maria?"

Anna-Maria shook herself out of her reverie and forced a smile. "No, nothing."

As usual Mary had been chattering about Buckingham, her eyes keen, as she and Anna-Maria made their way through the stalls, to find items that would please him. Already she had purchased an inlaid mother-of-pearl snuff box and a length of shining gray satin to be made into a coat for him. Anna-Maria was trying to stifle pangs of envy. It would be such sweet pleasure to be shopping for the duke herself, to have the freedom to say as Mary did, "He'll like this," anticipating the light in his eyes when she bestowed the gift.

It was a constant nagging pain to love a man she had no right to love. And yet, Anna-Maria stole a glance at Mary's absorbed face, to be a wife was not necessarily to have your husband's love. She sighed, her hand going unconsciously to her forehead.

Mary was immediately concerned. "Anna-Maria, you *are* unwell. Come. I'll take you home immediately."

Anna-Maria let herself be helped into Mary's coach, her headache becoming genuine now as she tried to sort out her confused emotions. She felt a tender regard for Mary, a sincere affection, and lately every time she was with her she felt almost sick with guilt. When they reached her home, Anna-Maria insisted that Mary come in with her to drink a dish of tea. Tea was the new imported drink that the queen favored, and it had become all the rage at court.

Mary sipped the scalding brew carefully, her lips pursed, and then smiled. "At first I disliked it, but now I confess I am acquiring a taste for it. Drink it, Anna-Maria, it will cure your headache." She began talking about affairs at court, quoting her husband frequently, pride clear in her voice. "Buckingham says—"

Abruptly, without realizing that she was going to do it until she heard the words leaping from her tongue, Anna-Maria said softly, "Mary, I love him, too."

Mary broke off in mid-sentence and stared at Anna-Maria. Her hot tea sloshed in the china dish, and a little spilled onto her skirt. In the confusion of mopping away the stain, both women had a moment to compose themselves. Then Mary straightened in her chair and said, "Tell me."

Anna-Maria leaned forward, entreaty written on her face. "Mary, we have done nothing wrong, committed no sin. But I love him."

Mary's eyes were attentive on Anna-Maria's face as she spoke, weighing, measuring. After a moment she nodded and said heavily, "Aye, and he loves you."

Anna-Maria made a soft exclamation, but Mary cut her off. "I've known of late that Buckingham had finally fallen in love." She looked away, her eyes unseeing as she gazed out the window. "He has always taken women lightly, enjoyed them, then cast them off as casually as a piece of clothing. He thought that he was immune to love, and in truth, so did I. But recently I've known that he has finally fallen in love at last."

She turned back from the window and looked at Anna-Maria thoughtfully. "So, it is you."

There was no reproach in her tone, but Anna-Maria felt tears spring to her eyes. "Mary, we have *not* sinned."

A queer expression that was part contempt and part pity passed over Mary's broad, plain face. "I would not have you deny yourself to him, Anna-Maria."

Anna-Maria gasped, shock clearly written on her face.

Mary measured her for a moment with a look and then asked, "Why did you tell me of your love for my husband?"

Anna-Maria made a feeble little gesture. In truth she didn't know. The impulse had been strong, and she had spoken without thinking. "Because you are my friend. . . ."

Mary's face softened. "Aye, we are friends, and what you have just told me does not change that. I can understand your love for him. In truth, I think any woman a fool who does *not* love him."

Anna-Maria was overcome with gratitude and relief. "I give you my word, Mary, that there will never be anything wrong between us."

"You love a hot-blooded man like my husband, and yet you would deny him what he craves most?"

Anna-Maria stared at her speechlessly.

Mary took a moment to sip her tea, finding the hot liquid a comfort. All Mary's maternal love, denied outlet because of her childlessness, had gone to her husband. She could not bear to see him denied anything.

Slowly she said, "Perhaps I love Buckingham far more than you do, Anna-Maria. If we were not married, *I* would not put my conscience above my love for him. I would give myself to him freely, proudly."

Anna-Maria was on her feet now, her senses reeling. She stared at Mary and then shook her head, dazedly. In a whisper she said, "I don't understand you."

Mary put down her dish of tea with a decided click and rose restlessly. She walked over to the window without speaking and stood fingering the draperies. When she turned, the sun was behind her head so that her face was in shadow, and Anna-Maria could not see her expression.

"Sometimes I don't understand myself," Mary said quietly. "I know only that this business of loving with all your heart, as I love Buckingham, is complex. There are emotions within us that even the poets have not been able to explain." Suddenly her voice was fierce, intense. "I know only that I love Buckingham more than I love myself, that I put his happiness above my own. Whether that is good or evil, I have no way to judge." She paused for a deep breath and then said quietly, "I would not have you deny yourself to Buckingham for my sake."

For a moment the two women stared at each other wordlessly. Then Mary picked up her cloak and put it around her shoulders. She bent and placed a light kiss on Anna-Maria's pale cheek. "I will see you at court, my dear."

When she had gone, Anna-Maria stood frozen in the middle of the room, her mind in a turmoil. What courage Mary had in her loving! How well she fought her jealousy for Buckingham's sake. Shame convulsed Anna-Maria until she thought she would be physically sick from it. She herself had been jealous of every oth-

er woman at court, yet out of cowardice, out of fear
that he would find her lacking, she had denied herself
to Buckingham.

Suddenly she remembered the words Nell had spoken
on stage the evening before. "Thick breath, quick
pulse, and beating of my heart, all sign of some un-
wonted change appear. . . ."

Anna-Maria felt thus when the duke held her in his
arms. Perhaps it showed that a change was taking place
in her, melting the coldness at the center of her being.
Perhaps she could please him after all.

Twenty

That evening she stood in the circle of the duke's arms
as they watched the fading light of sunset. Anna-Maria
reached up and traced the outline of his lips that she
loved so well, her fingers trembling slightly. The duke
smiled and sucked her fingers into his mouth, sending
a shiver running down her spine. She melted into his
arms, wanting to merge entirely with him, and when
their long, passionate kiss was finally ended, she said
softly, "I'm no longer afraid, my love."

She tilted her head so that her dark eyes were looking directly into his and said honestly, "No, that's
not true. I'm still afraid." She dropped her lashes, then
raised them again, exposing herself unflinchingly to his
exploring gaze. Softly she said, "I'm very afraid of not
pleasing you, but I can no longer deny myself to you."

The duke looked down into her upturned face, a
light beginning to blaze in his blue eyes. "My sweet
love!" He crushed her to him.

Anna-Maria thought that he would lift her in his
arms and take her to a secluded place at once, but he
put her away from him. "You tempt me overmuch.
We must plan carefully for our first time together." He
knew that he must deal gently with her, that their first

lovemaking must be flawless if he were not to damage her further.

Anna-Maria looked up at him trustingly. Pulling her to him, he rained kisses on her bright chestnut hair, inhaling deeply as her own particular fragrance rose to his nostrils.

As he held her he was rapidly planning. He and Anna-Maria could not have privacy in either of their homes, and he would not subject her to a cheap room in a tavern. If only they could find themselves sleeping under the same roof, then surely matters could be arranged. Suddenly his arms tightened around her, and he exclaimed, "I will give a house party in the country. A large one. I'll invite many guests, including your husband and yourself. And I'll make the invitation for a sufficiently long period so that we'll have the opportunity to steal many hours together."

Anna-Maria wound her slender white arms around his neck. "I'll do whatever you say, my love."

A day after, Francis proudly showed her an invitation with the duke of Buckingham's crest on it. "He has rented Lord Irvine's mansion in Minster Yard, and he invites us to stay with him for a month." There was a gleam of satisfied ambition in Francis's eyes. Now at last all his hard work was bearing fruit. This invitation from the great duke of Buckingham himself was proof of Francis's growing popularity and importance.

Anna-Maria looked at him, expecting to feel guilt, but found that she felt only a weary distaste. Often when she gazed at Francis, the image of Killigrew was superimposed. If Francis knew the duke of Buckingham had extended this invitation because of *me,* she thought, because I am going to lie in his arms, Francis would no doubt urge me to do it for his ambition's sake.

She began counting the days until the house party. The stolen embraces that she and the duke exchanged were becoming more passionate, more difficult to end. The duke left a week early to prepare for his guests, and Anna-Maria moved through the remaining time in a fever of excitement mingled with apprehension.

When she and Francis finally rode into the courtyard of Lord Irvine's mansion, she scarcely saw the building. Her eyes were clinging to the duke's face as he leaned into the carriage and clasped Francis's hand. When the duke helped Anna-Maria from the carriage, her hand trembled in his, and he looked down with understanding in his eyes. A wordless message of love flashed between them, and Anna-Maria could feel her blood singing in her veins.

The hours between their arrival and nightfall seemed endless, but the duke had arranged a vast number of entertainments, partly to make the hours fly by more quickly and partly to tire his guests. He had left Mary behind at Wallingford House in London and had made all the arrangements himself. Anna-Maria obediently joined in all the diversions, laughing, chatting, flirting automatically with the young fops who clustered around her, but all her senses were straining ahead to the moment when the duke would take her in his arms.

As they were dancing that evening, Buckingham whispered in her ear, "I've given you and Francis separate chambers. Tonight wait for my knock."

His warm breath in her ear set her pulses to pounding, and she looked at him with yearning in her eyes.

He sighed deeply. "Darling, if you look at me so, I'll lift you in my arms now and carry you off in full view of all my guests."

Anna-Maria had to force herself not to raise her lips for his kiss. Instead she moved slightly away from him and fiercely concentrated on the steps of the dance.

When the guests began yawning and departing for their bedchambers, she felt a moment of panic. It had come then, this moment she had been both longing for and dreading. Tonight might mark the end of the duke's love for her, and already she could taste the pain of loss.

She was shaking so badly as she made her toilette that she fumbled often, and it took infinite time. She had left Sarah behind in London with the children, and she wanted no strange maid's company tonight. Over and over she consulted the looking glass, worrying whether or not she was pretty enough to suit the duke. The glass reflected a slim figure in a flowing white nightdress embroidered with miniature pink roses. Her hair tumbled loosely down her back nearly to her waist. She leaned closer to the glass and pinched vigorously at her cheeks, trying to summon forth color.

When the duke's knock finally came, it startled her and she jumped. Her stomach was clenching in apprehension, her pulses pounding as she crossed the room and opened the door to him. Her breath caught in her throat. Suddenly she remembered the first time she had seen him as he rode in the procession, and it seemed impossible that he was standing only inches away from her, that she would lie in his arms this night.

He was looking down at her with so much tenderness in his blue eyes that she felt faint. She would give her life to keep that look in his eyes.

Suddenly he bent and swept her into his arms, still wordless, and then began striding rapidly down the hall, carrying her as lightly as though she were a child. She nestled against him without speaking, feeling that there were no words for this moment.

The great house was very silent, and Anna-Maria drew a deep breath of gratitude, realizing that he had chosen the hour well and that the other guests were deep in sleep.

He had left the door of his chamber standing slightly ajar, and now it opened with the slightest pressure from his foot. An enormous bed dominated the center of the room, and Anna-Maria thought that he would lie her on it immediately. She was bewildered when he deposited her gently in a chair near the fireplace and gave her a light kiss on the top of her head. She looked at him questioningly, and he laughed softly.

"Darling, this is not a rape." He poured a glass of the champagne that she loved and gently folded her fingers over it. "We have the whole night before us. I don't want you to think of anything except the luxury of being able to *kiss* all night, long kisses with no chance of interruption."

He sat on the arm of the chair speaking to her softly and kissing her, and Anna-Maria began to relax, enjoying the sensual pleasure of his touch, the warmth of the fire, the tingle of the champagne as it sang in her veins. They filled their mouths with the wine and then kissed, passing wine from one mouth to another. The delicious intimacy of it sent shivers running through Anna-Maria's body and, lips parted, she clung to him, wordlessly demanding that he intensify the kiss.

He laughed softly, picked her up, then laid her on the bed. For a moment she felt the familiar apprehension, and her muscles involuntarily tightened.

His deep voice was like a caress. "Darling, we are only going to kiss some more. Kiss and hold each other tightly as we've been longing to do."

Still dressed in his breeches and shirt, he lay down beside her and softly grazed her mouth with lingering intimacy. His hands were tangled in her hair, his breath sweet against her lips. Anna-Maria relaxed imperceptibly, her hand reaching out to stroke his cheek. He breathed gently in her ears, whispering words of love, and Anna-Maria felt her senses stirring pleasurably. He commented on the beauty of her features as he kissed her eyes, her nose, her mouth, and traced the line of her cheekbones with his lips. Then he unfastened her nightdress, slowly, gently removing it.

To her surprise he didn't immediately stroke her breasts, but instead bent his blond head and began kissing her arm, blowing softly as he trailed his mouth up her arm until all the fine hairs stood up and she was shivering with pleasure. Reverently, slowly, he kissed the soft inside of her elbow. He turned her on her side and drew her against him until they were lying fully pressed together, her slim, incurving abdomen tight against his muscled stomach.

He was breathing deeply, evenly, and Anna-Maria found her own breath matching his rhythm until she felt that she was melting into him, not even the barrier

of skin left between their bodies. There was a delicious
scalding sensation where their bodies touched, and it
intensified with the rhythm of their breathing. Anna-
Maria held her breath for a moment, filled with the
wonder of it, and then she let out her breath in a long
sigh and strained closer to him. His hand was trailing
up her leg now, gently stroking the satiny skin of her
thigh.

Her nipples were hardening, and it was she who took
her breast and guided it into the duke's mouth, all
self-consciousness lost in desire. She heard him give a
long, indrawn breath of satisfaction, and then his
tongue gently grazed her nipple, his hand coming up
to stroke her other breast. How gentle he was! His
kisses were leaving little flames in their wake, and her
hands went up to tangle in his hair as he alternately
kissed and nibbled at her breasts. There were no bar-
riers to her body now.

He moved away from her for a moment, and she
cried out at the loss, raising her arms beseechingly toward him. He laughed, a tender throaty laugh, and
said, "A moment only, darling."

He pulled off his breeches and shirt and then slipped
into bed again and pulled her tightly against him. She
moaned with pleasure. His naked body against hers
sent waves of pleasure washing through her, and she
wound her slim legs around his muscled ones to bring
him closer.

Her hands caressed his back, and her lips pressed
hard against his in a kiss that stirred her to the depths
of her soul. She wanted him closer, closer.

He was rolling her on her back now, poised above
her. Looking down into her face, soft and open with
wanting, his blue eyes asked a wordless question.

"Oh, yes!" Anna-Maria responded with a long-
drawn sigh of desire.

For the first time she knew what it was to want a
man. She would die if she didn't take him fully; she
strained upward against him, drawing him eagerly closer as he entered her. She began to cry softly, nearly
faint with pleasure. Now, finally, he was close enough,

this beloved being that she had sought all her life. His lips were everywhere as he gave her pleasure—on her shining hair, her tear-damp eyes, her flushed cheeks, and trembling mouth. His strokes on her breast were as light as butterflies' wings, and she strained upward, trying to press her breasts more fully into his seeking hands.

The sheer intimacy of his rhythmic possession of her flooded her with joy. Reaching up, she pulled his lips down to hers in a long kiss, just as the fire that had been building within her exploded, leaving her limp and giddy with pleasure.

For a moment she lay absolutely still, filled with wonder, and then she reached up and tenderly caressed his face.

Her hands moved up to touch his eyes, then gently trace the strong line of his nose, and caress his mouth. She touched him in wonderment, as though for the first time. Then softly, slowly, she murmured, "I loved you with my whole heart. And now—now—I love you with my body as well."

Twenty-One

Anna-Maria spent her days in a fever of anticipation, longing for night to fall so that she could taste the sweet pleasures of lovemaking. Her naked body flamed into desire under Buckingham's skillful caresses, and her responsive ardor delighted both of them.

Sometimes Anna-Maria remembered her earlier fears that she would disappoint him by her coldness, and she laughed softly at her former ignorance. Buckingham had taught her that she was a strongly passionate woman. Her earlier indifference to lovemaking had been only because she had not known a man whose touch could inflame her. The gypsy had terrified her, Francis had left her cool and unaroused, and Killigrew had humiliated and violated her. It was only now—in Buckingham's strong arms—that she found rich, deep delight in her sensual nature.

Often during the day, she would grow weak-kneed at the sight of him, his head thrown back in laughter, and she would melt with longing. Their brief, stolen caresses, a touch on the cheek, a swift movement of hand grazing hand, only served to inflame her desire, and she was trembling by the time he sought her each evening.

The days passed too swiftly, and during the last week, she clung to him, her joy in lovemaking flawed a little because of the impending separation.

"If only we could live together," she whispered longingly.

Buckingham clasped her more tightly in his arms, frowning into the darkness. Divorce was a costly business and almost impossible to obtain. He could remember a single instance of one being granted in England since the time of Henry VIII. He turned his mind from this insoluble problem and wrestled with the more practical problem of how he and Anna-Maria could meet once they were back in London. Finally he sighed and stroked her thick hair, still damp from their lovemaking.

"My sweet?" His voice was uncharacteristically hesitant. "I fear that we can never be together like this in London unless you are willing to meet in a room over a tavern—"

Anna-Maria laughed softly. "And you were afraid that I would be unwilling? My love, I would meet you anywhere, anytime, to lie in your arms like this!"

Marveling at the change in her, swelling with pride because he had created this new, passionate creature, he bent his head and sought her lips. She responded with ardor, tenderly amused to think that he had ever thought to find her unwilling again.

Anna-Maria tried to cling to the hours, then the minutes and seconds, but they poured through her fingers like bits of sand, and the moment came when she found herself seated in a carriage, Francis by her side, bidding adieu to Buckingham. She had great difficulty in keeping her voice from trembling as she bid him farewell, and she turned her head hastily so that Francis would not see the tears in her eyes. Buckingham leaned close to her for a moment's intimacy. In a low, hurried voice, he said, "Till we meet in London, my sweet."

Anna-Maria nodded speechlessly, her eyes clinging to his face, and then turned her face before she could betray herself.

As they neared London, her spirits rose a little. Within an hour she would see the children. Despite her deep happiness in Buckingham's arms, she had been missing them. Once home, she raced into the nursery, eager to see Polly, Charles, and John. They were sleeping and Polly and Charles awoke flushed with wonder to find her bending over them.

"Mama!" Polly held out her arms. "I was dreaming of you!"

Charles, sucking his thumb, sidled up to her, examined her closely, then nodded with satisfaction and scrambled into her lap. John slept on contentedly. Holding them tightly, dividing her kisses between them, Anna-Maria thought suddenly how wonderful it would be if these children were hers and Buckingham's. If only they could all live together, surrounded by warmth and happiness so that she would not constantly be pulled in conflicting directions.

She sang softly to the children until they fell asleep again, and then tiptoed from the room and went to find Sarah. "Let's have a glass of wine and talk for awhile. I've missed you, Sarah."

Sarah, curled in a big chair opposite Anna-Maria, sipped her wine and gave Anna-Maria the details of the children's activities during Anna-Maria's absence, but she seemed distracted and occasionally broke off in mid-sentence, staring into the fireplace.

Anna-Maria, watching her closely, noticed that there was a new softness to Sarah's face, a deepened shine

in her eyes. "And you? Has all been well with you?
You seemed changed."

A slow smile curved Sarah's lips. Putting her glass
down on the table, she leaned forward eagerly. "I *am*
changed. I am no longer a virgin. Oh, Anna-Maria,
I'm so much in love."

"Sarah! Who is he?"

"Sir Joseph Phillips." Merely saying the name
seemed to give Sarah delight. "He is a distant cousin
to your husband—but an impoverished one." For a
moment she seemed troubled, but then she cast her
problems aside, her eyes shining. "He is very tall, very
handsome, and when he kisses me, my bones melt."

"I know. Oh, Sarah, at last I know what it is to enjoy a man's touch." Anna-Maria leaned forward as
eagerly as Sarah, and the two women traded confidences until the candle had burned low. At last Anna-Maria asked, "Where does Sir Joseph live? What
does he do?"

"He acts as secretary to Sir John Talbot, another
cousin of your husband's."

Anna-Maria shivered suddenly, and Sarah looked at
her in concern. "Shall I poke up the fire?"

Anna-Maria shook her head. "Your words frightened me. Buckingham has told me that Sir John Talbot
is one of his strongest enemies. It worries me that you
should love a man who lives in an enemy household."

Sarah's voice was brisk with common sense. "Come
now. You must be overtired and having fancies. My
Joseph is merely a secretary to Talbot. I promise you
that he is no enemy to Buckingham." She stood, picking up the nearly gutted candle and then grinned suddenly. "Do not make this into a high drama. You put
me in mind of that play of Mister William Shake-
speare's, *Romeo and Juliet,* in which the lovers live in
enemy houses."

Anna-Maria smiled reluctantly, but nevertheless she
was still uneasy as she undressed and made ready for
bed.

Sarah, in her own bedroom, was also troubled. She
had told Joseph of her noble birth, and he was eager

to marry her, but since they were both impoverished, the wait promised to be a long one. Sarah sighed and then blew out the candle decisively. It did no good to lie awake, sapping her energy by brooding on problems she could not solve. Joseph was resourceful and ambitious, and she was certain that he would soon find a way out of their difficulties.

She was eager to have Anna-Maria and Joseph like each other. They were the two most important people in her life, and she wanted them to be friends.

The next day she coaxed Anna-Maria into accompanying her to The Golden Unicorn where she was to meet Joseph. Anna-Maria went readily, curious to see the man who had captured Sarah's heart.

He was already seated at a table when they entered the tavern, and as he rose, Anna-Maria was struck by his tallness. He was lean and well-built, with dark blond hair curling over his shoulders.

"He's as handsome as you said," Anna-Maria whispered as they walked toward him. Sarah flushed with pride. Anna-Maria noted approvingly that he dressed well but without ostentation. Apparently he was a man of quiet good sense and did not affect elaborate finery when his pocketbook was lean.

As he took her hand in greeting, she looked into his clear gray eyes and found that she liked him immediately. Her heart lifted. Sarah has made a good choice, she thought, and smiled at him warmly.

It was obvious that he adored Sarah. As they sat over their tankards of hot mulled wine, his eyes were constantly on Sarah's sparkling face as she laughed and chattered. Sarah had never seemed so radiant, so happy, and Anna-Maria warmed at the sight.

Their happiness dimmed for a moment, however, when the subject of the future arose. Joseph flushed and slowly turned the tankard of wine in his hands. "I cannot afford to set up a home for Sarah at present. My family supported the king during the civil war, and they lost everything. . . ."

Anna-Maria, sympathetic to his embarrassment,

leaned forward quickly and put her hand over his. "I understand. My family also lost most of their lands and money. It is nothing to be ashamed of."

Joseph smiled at her gratefully. "Sarah has told you that I am secretary to Sir John Talbot?"

Anna-Maria nodded, a shadow crossing her face at the name.

Joseph drew a deep breath. "He has promised me good prospects for the future if I serve him well. But in the meantime I can see no way that Sarah and I can marry and live under the same roof unless she seeks employment in his household."

Anna-Maria gasped, her eyes flying to Sarah's face. It would be intolerable to lose Sarah.

"Never!" Sarah put her hand over Joseph's and leaned reassuringly toward Anna-Maria. "I'll not leave you."

She turned her face imploringly to Joseph. "What would I do with myself all day in Talbot's household? Sew?" She giggled suddenly. "I should warn you, Joseph, I'm no great hand with a needle or scrubbing laundry, and I certainly don't want to be reduced to the status of a maid. I've been spoiled shamefully in the Shrewsbury household, and I doubt that Lady Talbot would be so generous."

Weak with relief and gratitude, Anna-Maria smiled warmly. "Sarah rules our household and the children, and I would be lost without her." She hesitated and then said slowly, "Couldn't you marry anyway? Sarah could live with us and you with Talbot until you had made your fortune?"

"No." Joseph's tone was emphatic.

Sarah said softly, "His pride forbids it." She reached up and touched Joseph's clenched jaw. "What does it matter, my love? I don't demand marriage immediately. I give myself to you freely." Joseph flushed, and Sarah said quickly, "The countess of Shrewsbury and I have no secrets between us."

Hastily, to relieve Joseph's embarrassment, Anna-Maria interrupted, "There must be a way out of this tangle. If only Francis did not insist on acting as his own secretary, but he swears that he likes the work and trusts no one else."

As she took a sip of her wine, Sarah picked up her own tankard and held it in a toast toward Joseph. "I have faith that Joseph will soon make his fortune."

"I have faith in him also." Anna-Maria smiled at them over the rim of her tankard.

Sarah adroitly turned the talk to Dryden's latest play, and Joseph, visibly relaxing, gave a witty description of the recent performance he had seen. Soon the lovers were so engrossed in each other that Anna-Maria made her excuses, saying that she had promised to visit Nell that afternoon.

As she slipped out of the tavern, she smiled, knowing that soon Sarah and Joseph would seek a room upstairs where they could spend a blissful afternoon in each other's arms. The Golden Unicorn might also be a trysting place for herself and Buckingham. But then she sighed. Several of her acquaintances had greeted her in the tavern, and she realized it was too well-frequented a meeting place to serve her purposes.

When she reached Nell's rooms, she poured out the difficulties she and Buckingham would have in meeting privately once he returned to London.

Nell listened sympathetically, her impish face sober. She mulled over the problem for awhile and then brightened. "The Hare and Hounds where you first took me for supper is perfect. The proprietor is the soul of discretion." She jumped up, her hazel eyes sparkling. "It will not do for the countess of Shrewsbury to be seen too often frequenting the tavern, so you must disguise yourself."

Brushing aside a profusion of objects littering the top of a huge brass-bound chest, she began rummaging through the contents. "I have a trunkful of costumes that have been discarded from the theatre."

Anna-Maria began to laugh. "Oh, Nelly, what would I do without you? You turn everything into an adventure."

Nell began to burrow deeper into the trunk. Soon

the floor was littered with bright bits of clothing, and out of the confusion Nell assembled a shepherdess costume, an oyster vendor, and a splendid outfit worthy of a successful prostitute, complete with a black mask.

Nell began to laugh. "Buckingham will think that he is lying with all women, not one!" She was diving deeper into the trunk, bringing out a blond wig. Anna-Maria was silent thinking that she wished she *were* all women. Soon Buckingham would be back at court where women vied for his attention. A touch of cold fear struck her heart. If he ever preferred another, she would die. Nell was trying to get her attention, dangling a blond wig in front of her.

For a moment Anna-Maria looked at her blankly, and then she smiled. "Nell, what a horror." The wig was matted and unkempt.

Nell looked at it thoughtfully. "It only needs a brushing. Here, sit down." She pushed Anna-Maria onto her dressing table stool.

After a quarter hour's work, Nell had coaxed and curled the wig to her satisfaction, and she began heavily painting Anna-Maria's face. Anna-Maria watched, fascinated, as her face took on an artificiality and a slight coarseness. She looked like a prostitute.

"What do you suppose it must be like, Nell, to give your body to a man for money?" She was wondering if in a paid transaction, the woman would feel any of the delight she found in Buckingham's arms.

Nell shrugged. "My mam had a mind to sell me."

Anna-Maria's eyes widened in shock, but Nell's tone was matter-of-fact. "She sold my older sister Rose to any gentlemen who came to our tavern and took a fancy to her. Henry Killigrew was one of them."

Anna-Maria winced at the name. She had not yet told Nell of Killigrew's rape of her.

Nell was concentrating on outlining Anna-Maria's eye. "I ran when my mam's eye lit on me. I had no fancy to sell myself for a shilling or two." Her mouth twisted in a wry smile. "But then I gave myself to Charles Hart so that I could leave off being an orange girl and become an actress."

Her eyes met Anna-Maria's in the mirror. "That

makes me a prostitute because I gave myself for gain."
Then warmth flooded into her face. "But I swear, Anna-Maria, when I go to the king, I give myself for love.
I refuse the purse he gives me at the end of the evening, but he always presses it on me."

She was off on her favorite topic, and Anna-Maria listened, smiling faintly, as Nell talked of the king.
She knew well how delicious the sensation was of being able to speak a beloved one's name. She only wished that she, herself, could savor that pleasure more often.

A week later she stood outside a wooden door in the upper hall of the Hare and Hounds, her pulses racing.
She took a deep breath and then knocked lightly and entered.

Buckingham was standing at the window, and he turned as she entered, the light from behind making a halo of his blond hair. He started at her appearance, his eyes narrowed, and then he threw back his head in laughter.

"And have you come to sell me a tray of oysters, my sweet? I confess I had other delicacies in mind."

Anna-Maria wrinkled her nose. "Nell made me bring them. And they smell badly." She crossed the room and placed the offending tray near the open window. She pirouetted for his inspection. "Do I please you this way?"

The duke's eyes were widening with desire. "You please me best with no costume at all." His hands were already busy undressing her, and she reached down eagerly to help him. She let out a little cry of pleasure as her breasts sprang free of their restraint.

The duke bent his head and began gently to lick her nipples, sending shocks of pleasure through her body.
She tangled her hands in the back of his hair and arched closer to him, moaning softly. When she could bear no more, he lifted her in his arms and strode rapidly to the bed. There was a new intensity in their lovemaking this afternoon, an intensity born of long starvation. She had come to know his body now, and she greeted each beloved feature with renewed delight,

here the slight scar from an old duel, and here the soft flesh that he loved to have stroked. She could feel love suffusing her, melting through her, and she touched him with reverence and awe, as he touched her.

When they rested later, spent and sleepy with happiness, she looked around and took note of the room for the first time. It was the best chamber of the Hare and Hounds, but still shabby. The embroidered bed hangings had faded to muted shades of rose and green, and the mirror was cracked. Anna-Maria determined to purchase some ornaments to put their personal stamp on the room. "Imagine!" She nestled luxuriously in his arms. "We finally have a private place to ourselves."

The duke looked around the room, and his expression darkened. He looked hastily away so that Anna-Maria would not see it, and his arms tightened around her protectively. He wanted to surround her with all the luxury possible, yet at this moment he could not find a way to give her anything but this. Looking down on her glowing, contented face, he placed a kiss on the tip of her delicate nose. "I love you."

Anna-Maria stretched and pulled his head down to hers, her mouth moving against his lips. "And I you."

When they were dressed and prepared to leave, she looked at the tray of oysters with distaste. "Faugh! The odor is terrible. What shall I do with them?"

The duke laughed at her comical expression, then picked up the tray and decisively tipped it out the window, showering oysters on the cobblestones below. "I have just purchased an entire basket from you. What do I owe you?"

"Kisses," Anna-Maria said. She was still fresh from his lovemaking, but already she yearned for him again. "I'd say there were a thousand oysters in that tray."

The duke pulled her close and began giving her the kisses her upturned face demanded, but then, giving a groan, he pushed her away from him. "Anna-Maria, it grows late."

Hand in hand they walked down the stairway. The duke waited while Anna-Maria went ahead of him into the crowded street. It was several moments before she found an empty public cart, but she mingled easily with the crowd, feeling inconspicuous in her disguise.

She learned to revel in the freedom of the streets, to delight in devising new disguises in which to surprise the duke, who was unfailingly amused by the wit and ingenuity that she put into her various costumes.

It was only when she came one day as a prostitute, wearing a wig, her face heavily painted, and a black mask concealing her eyes, that his face darkened with anger. He snatched the wig from her head and hauled her over to the basin, poured in water, and scrubbed angrily at her face. Anna-Maria, water dripping from her brow, the paint running on her face, realized that she had been tactless and had hurt him. Their situation was too irregular for him to be amused at her appearing as a prostitute.

Then his instinctive protectiveness filled her with a glow, and she was more certain than ever that he loved her deeply.

Twenty-Two

Their stolen moments at court became sweeter than ever because of the knowledge that soon they would be lying in each other's arms. The duke, more practiced in deception than Anna-Maria, and anxious to protect her reputation, was better able to school his expression than she. She wanted to cry aloud to the world, "I love him. He's mine." And though she managed to remain silent, her glowing eyes and swift glances at him were eloquent enough.

Their affair soon began to be the talk of the court, and when Killigrew heard it, his narrow, aristocratic face tightened in anger. Why should Buckingham be receiving as a gift what he had had to take by force? A sullen anger began to build in him, an anger that grew every time he saw Anna-Maria smiling up at the duke. He boasted more and more that he himself had enjoyed the countess of Shrewsbury's favors, implying that she had willingly taken him as a lover. He spoke openly within earshot of Anna-Maria, making her grow pale with anger. Killigrew was cautious enough not to do it in front of Buckingham, and Anna-Maria never mentioned it to the duke, fearing that his quick desire for revenge would do him injury somehow.

One evening Killigrew approached Anna-Maria when the king was standing by her side and asked her to dance. Anna-Maria hesitated, then cast a glance at the king and accepted reluctantly. The touch of Henry's fingers clutching hers made her nauseous, recalling in vivid detail the day he had raped her. There was naked hostility in her eyes when she faced him in the steps of the dance, and the stony cast of her face warned him to be silent.

Henry's lips curled in a sneer. He had not missed the fact that her eyes were repeatedly seeking out the duke of Buckingham. When the steps of the dance brought him close to her ear he whispered, "So the ice maiden has melted at last. The duke of Buckingham tells me that you leave him no peace, that your constant demands for lovemaking are wearying him."

Anna-Maria gasped, her eyes like firebrands in her suddenly white face. Killigrew moved unpleasantly closer to her, and she could smell the stale wine on his breath. "I have not forgotten how your breasts felt cupped in my hands, nor how readily you returned my kisses."

"You beast!" She snatched her hand from Killigrew's grip and stood angrily facing him, her breasts heaving and swelling against her tight, low-cut bodice as she breathed rapidly. Killigrew's eyes lit appreciatively, and he brazenly let his glance trail across her naked shoulders and the delicate swell of her breasts. Her hand raised instinctively. She wanted to rake her nails down his narrow, dissipated face, to draw blood from his sweat-filmed skin. Someone gasped, and she stopped; she realized that they were the center of all eyes. Dropping her hand, she said, in a dangerously calm voice, "Someday I will avenge myself upon you."

She turned and, totally uncaring of etiquette, left him standing in the middle of the dance floor. Buckingham was making his way toward her and intercepted her before she reached the door. "What's amiss, my darling?"

"Nothing. Only that I cannot bear his touch." She could not bring herself to repeat Killigrew's words.

She felt physically ill, to the point of vomiting, and pleaded a headache, avoiding Buckingham's anxious eyes. For several months she had been walking around in a happy dream, conscious only of Buckingham and his love for her. Now it was as though a protective shield had been ripped from her, and she felt again the old pain and humiliation, as well as rage that Killigrew had been able to rape her and go on his way, laughing.

Her face streaked with tears, her eyes wild, she rushed into the bedroom she had once shared with Francis. He was on the point of disrobing, and he looked up, startled. "What are you doing here, Anna-Maria?"

His eyes noted her tear-streaked face, the uncontrollable shudders of her slender body, but he made no move to comfort her.

"Have you no decency, no honor?" Anna-Maria's mouth was trembling, but her words were clearly enunciated. "All these months you have refused to revenge me with Killigrew, and now you and I are both laughingstocks at Whitehall. Killigrew thinks you a coward, thinks that he is safe from revenge at your hands, and it has made him reckless. He swears to everyone that I bestowed my favors on him freely, and he proves his story by describing my nakedness in exact detail! Jane Middleton told me that everyone at court knows of the mole under my right breast, its exact size and shape!"

Francis raised an eyebrow at her but said nothing. He was leisurely drawing off his breeches, exposing pallid, hairy legs.

Anna-Maria's breasts were heaving, her eyes flashing dark fire in the whiteness of her face. Her voice rose nearly to the pitch of a scream.

"Francis! If you don't take some action, Killigrew

will feel free to pull me behind any rose bush and rape me with impunity. So far he has confined himself to insulting me within my earshot, but tonight he insulted me to my face! He is growing more reckless!"

Francis pulled a plum satin dressing gown around him and knotted the sash with careful attention. "What is it that you want of me, Anna-Maria?"

"I want you to do what any husband would feel compelled to do! Defend my honor. Punish Killigrew!"

"Am I then to have all the dangers and responsibilities of a husband and none of the advantages?"

Francis's voice was like ice. He had accepted without comment Anna-Maria moving into a separate bedroom and had not approached her since the night she swore he would never touch her again, but he had been growing increasingly sullen. Now the sight of her, her loveliness heightened by her agitation, inflamed him. He moved toward her slowly.

She backed away as she realized his intention. Softly he said, "There is no rape between husband and wife, Anna-Maria."

His passion suddenly flared at the thought of taking her in violence as Killigrew had done. To his surprise he realized that it would not serve his purpose if she came to him meekly and compliantly as a wife was supposed to do. He enjoyed the fear that was creeping into her eyes, he quickened at the sight of her breasts heaving against the low bodice of her gown.

Without speaking, he reached out, caught his hand in her bodice, and ripped it with one swift motion. Anna-Maria turned to flee, but he was suddenly upon her, seizing her slim waist in two strong hands and pulling her to him. She screamed, and he clapped his hand over her mouth.

Speaking tersely in her ear, he said, "There's no sense to screaming. Even if all the servants rush in, I will merely bid them leave."

He laughed shortly, and the sound frightened her more than anything else in her life had done. "Even the law protects me. No one can interfere with a man taking his pleasure on his wife's body."

Puffing a little, he lifted her, and Anna-Maria had a

fleeting memory of the ease with which Buckingham lifted her into his arms. Frantic, she bit into the flesh of his hand. He let out a short oath and snatched his hand away.

"Francis," her voice was a thin thread of a whisper, "don't do this thing. You are a man, not an animal."

Francis laughed unpleasantly. "All men are animals, my sweet wife. Do you take me for less a man than Killigrew?"

Grunting, he dumped her on the bed and stood over her, his eyes narrowed, his mouth hanging a little slack as he looked at her bared breasts. He reached out to her torn bodice, seized the material in his fist, and pulled strongly until both gown and busk fell away from her. She lay staring up at him, slim and seductive in her frothy petticoats. Groaning, he threw himself on top of her, his mouth seeking to find hers.

Anna-Maria was suddenly swept by anger, a vast, unreasoning anger that came from the depths of her being. All realization that he was her husband, all shared memories faded, and she fought him as she would fight a stranger who attacked her on a dark street. Her sharp nails raked his face, drawing blood, until he seized her two hands in one of his own and twisted them over her head.

She writhed under his body, attempting to kick upward and move his weight from her, but he had her too securely pinned down. When he bent his mouth to hers, she bit his lip until she could feel the taste of his blood on her own lips. To her horror, it only served to increase his passion. He gave a low excited laugh, parted her thighs and entered her. Anna-Maria fought him, writhing and turning frantically, unaware that her movements were only serving to inflame him further. She would kill him, this animal who grunted above her and used her without mercy.

He was done within seconds, finishing with a long-drawn moan that seemed to move upward from his very bowels. He lay on top of her, breathing heavily, and she, close to fainting, lay leaden beneath him. Hatred filled her, seeping into her bones and blood like a poisonous gas.

Finally he rolled off her and turned on his back, staring up at the ceiling. Anna-Maria, released from his weight, moved cautiously, rising from the bed and staring down at him. His face, which she had once thought so gentle and fine, was repulsive to her. It seemed incredible that from this man, these loins, she had gotten her sweet children.

The candle flame danced, sending shadows across her face. "If you attempt to touch me again, I'll kill you."

She escaped to her room and lay staring into the darkness.

She was beyond tears now, dry-eyed, with a hollow feeling in the pit of her stomach. The question kept forming in her mind, "How will I live?" She was Francis's property, his chattel. He could beat her if he liked, have her quietly put to death. She had no money, no property, save what he gave her. For a moment she saw herself running up the steps of Deene, flinging herself into the blessed safety of her parents' arms, but then she realized that they could do nothing for her. Francis could demand her instant return, and her parents would be forced to hand her over. She could imagine her mother's shocked questions. "But Anna-Maria, how did your marriage come to such a pass? It started with such promise. Francis is such a fine gentleman."

Fine gentleman. Anna-Maria's lips curled in the darkness. His air of gentleness and quality had been only a thin veneer, quickly stripped under the onslaught of his ambition and passion. What man of honor allowed his wife to be raped without avenging her?

She thought then of the duke, his blond head bent above her, his blue eyes intense. Suddenly she began to weep frantically. There—there in his arms—lay her only safety. She gave to him freely and joyously what other men took from her by force.

Exhausted, she began to drift into a twilight sleep, beset by nightmares. She moaned frequently and twice sat upright in bed, her hands held out as though to ward off danger. In her dreams Killigrew and Francis merged into one, a faceless menace looming over her, violating her.

The next afternoon she took her own coach to the Hare and Hounds. She wanted no disguise today. It was the countess of Shrewsbury who emerged from the interior, went into the tavern, and walked boldly to the room she shared with Buckingham.

He was not there yet, and she moved restlessly around the room, fingering the objects she had bought to make the place more truly theirs. For the first time she fully noticed the shabbiness of the room, and suddenly shame suffused her. Was this all she was worth? Suddenly meeting Buckingham here didn't seem so romantic anymore, only pathetic and cheap. She was no better than the prostitutes who plied their trade in the London brothels. She had no more protection from a husband than they did; she was as vulnerable to any man's assault as they were.

Buckingham came in at that moment and stopped short. "Anna-Maria, have you lost your senses? You must have been recognized."

Anna-Maria whirled toward him with a look of anger on her face. "Aye, and I'll be judged guilty of my *only* crime—that of loving you. At least it will be an honest judgment!" She laughed bitterly, and the sound shocked Buckingham. "I'm accused of lying with every man at court. Don't you want to join the list, my lord? Or are you ashamed of me?"

Her brittle control broke, and in broken sobs and whispers she repeated the events of the night before —Killigrew's insults and Francis's rape of her. Buckingham let out a string of oaths under his breath.

Anna-Maria looked up at him. "I only want to be with you. No one else. I don't want any other man touching me! I want to live with you freely and openly. To belong only to you."

A look of despair came over Buckingham's face. "Darling, don't you know I want that above all things. But we must be practical. You and I are both married—"

Anna-Maria tore her hands from his grasp and turned away, unwilling to hear what he was saying.

"Anna-Maria, how would we live?"

"We could live very simply in the country. You and I and the children."

"Leave court? Leave politics?"

Her heart sank. He did not love her as she loved him. She would give up everything, risk everything to stand proudly by his side. But she was not the whole of his life. Much of his mind and energies were bound up in politics. "You are as ambitious as Francis," she said angrily.

But anger gave way to acceptance. She didn't love a country farmer, she had fallen in love with one of the most vital and exciting men in the court of Charles the Second. Buckingham had been raised side by side with the prince and had always been part of the great events in England. She turned aside so that he could not read her expression and walked slowly over to the window.

He came up behind her, put his strong hands on her shoulders, and softly kissed the nape of her neck. "Anna-Maria, I swear that you and I will find a way for us to be together, but you must give me a little time. Matters are going well for me now. I think that Charles will soon dismiss the chancellor—and when that is accomplished, I will have more time for my personal life."

Anna-Maria looked at him for a long moment and then nodded. She didn't doubt his sincerity. At this moment he truly believed that he would find a way for them to be together. But she knew that new matters of state would arise and would demand his attention.

He pulled her into his arms, and she went willingly, knowing that his kisses would quiet her pain. But later, as he slept, she grew restless and slipped naked out of bed. She stood idly at the window, scratching at the pane with the diamond from her ring. Then she slipped the ring from her finger so that she could wield it better and began etching her initials, stroking fiercely on the downward stroke of the A. She was working busily when Buckingham awoke three-quarters of an hour later.

He looked over at her and smiled. "What are you doing, my love?"

Her fingers were cramped and stiff, but she still determinedly scratched at the windowpane. She was making something permanent for them in the only way she knew how, leaving a record of their love. "I've drawn our initials," she said softly.

He rose and came to look over her shoulder, smiling as he saw their two sets of initials entwined in a large heart. "Etched for eternity," he murmured approvingly. His voice grew husky, "Just as your image is permanently etched on my heart and mind."

Twenty-Three

Two weeks later Mary Villiers accompanied her husband and Anna-Maria to the theater. " 'Tis best for all three of us to appear together and confound the gossips," Mary said briskly. She had never directly made reference to Anna-Maria's affair with Buckingham since that day in Anna-Maria's house, but she often sent little messages through Anna-Maria to Buckingham in tacit recognition of the relationship. "Tell Buckingham that we are to dine early tonight." Or, "The queen is ill and I will be attending her all night. Tell Buckingham."

Now Anna-Maria put out her hand in an impulsive gesture, but Mary cut her off saying, "Anna-Maria, no gratitude. 'Tis for my pride's sake also that I want to put the best face on matters as possible."

When the three of them entered the box together, there was an audible buzz of interest from the audience. A few of the bolder fops climbed on the seats of their chairs in the pits and raised their quizzing glasses for a better look.

Anna-Maria could feel her cheeks flaming, and she hastily looked at Mary for reassurance. Mary's face was as placid as ever as she returned bows of acknowledgment from acquaintances and friends. Anna-Maria stole a glance at the duke, who was seated on her right. His tension was obvious. Anna-Maria longed to reach out and touch his hand, but she felt constrained in Mary's presence.

She felt as though she were walking through a half dream. It was impossible that she should be in love with a married man, sharing him in tacit agreement with his wife. For weeks, ever since Francis had raped her, she had been drifting. Soon, she knew, she must regain control of her destiny, must make decisions about her future. She could not go on living forever with a man she hated, nor could she exist honorably on the crumbs that fell from Buckingham's bounty. And yet any decision she made must take her away from the sound of his voice and the sight of his face, and she could not bear that.

Taking a deep breath, she raised her head proudly, returning the stares of those who gaped at her. Even the orange girls had paused in hawking their wares and were staring upward at the box occupied by the duke and duchess of Buckingham and the countess of Shrewsbury. This was a rare treat and would serve as fuel for gossip for weeks to come.

Anna-Maria stiffened suddenly as she saw Killigrew entering the box adjoining theirs. He was followed by Lord Rochester, the greatest wit and libertine at court.

Rochester caught sight of the trio and paused in the act of taking snuff. His eyebrows rose high on his handsome face, and he smiled slightly. Leaning forward, he spoke in a low tone to Killigrew, nodding in Anna-Maria's direction. Anna-Maria held her head so stiffly that her neck began to ache. It was monstrous bad luck that Killigrew should have taken the box next to them today of all days, when Mary was with them.

Anna-Maria was relieved when the heavy curtains parted and the action on the stage began. Nell was playing in a revival of *The Mad Couple,* and Anna-Maria had been helping her study her lines for the past few days. She bent intently forward, engrossed as Nell started her first speech. Suddenly the duke stirred at her side. Reaching over, he grasped her arm, his strong fingers digging into her flesh. There was tension in his touch, a communicated warning. Puzzled, Anna-Maria pulled her attention from the action on stage and looked at him. Then her stomach clenched. She became aware of Killigrew's high, affected voice, deliberately pitched to reach the next box.

"I vow, Rochester, that's the drollest sight I've seen this month. Buckingham and his wife and his whore attending the theatre together!"

Anna-Maria heard Mary draw in her breath. Quickly she reached over and touched Mary's arm reassuringly. She forced herself to sit quietly, although she would have liked to have leaped to her feet and attacked Killigrew. She despised giving him the satisfaction, but despite herself she found her head turning in his direction. He was opening an ornately jeweled snuff box, taking a pinch and offering the box to Rochester, who shook his head. His mouth was narrowed unpleasantly. "I confess that I wonder at the duke of Buckingham's tastes. The countess of Shrewsbury has turned her tail to every man at court. Surely Buckingham cannot find fresh pleasure where so many have been before."

Anna-Maria could not repress a little cry, and Buckingham's fingers tightened on her wrist. Leaning toward Killigrew, he said in a low, furious undertone, "Hold your tongue, Killigrew, or it will go ill with you!"

Most of the courtiers feared Buckingham's rare but violent temper, but Killigrew was past sense now. Anna-Maria's face was turned upward toward Buckingham with love clearly written on it, and the sight angered Killigrew even more.

He raised his voice so that it carried down to the pits below. "I but remarked to Rochester, Your Grace, that it amazes me that you content yourself with a whore when so many ladies of the court seek your attentions."

There was a buzz from the pits, and Anna-Maria realized, with a sinking of her heart, that every eye in the theatre was turned in their direction. Her palms were moist, her heart beating unpleasantly fast. Buckingham half rose in his seat and scowled darkly. Many of the people in the theatre were standing on their chairs, craning their heads to get a better view of the action taking place in the boxes. Nell had faltered in her role for a moment and then quickly regained her poise. In an attempt to bring attention back to the stage, she had moved forward until she was in danger of toppling into the pits and was fairly screaming her lines.

Buckingham, keeping his voice low, said to Killigrew, "I warn you! Hold your tongue, or I'll deal harshly with you."

Killigrew scanned the duke's face and paled suddenly. Buckingham's face was murderous, and his hand had gone unconsciously to clap his sword.

Killigrew knew that he was in for a beating at the hands of the duke if nothing more, and he suddenly became inflamed, reckless. He drew his sword, cast off Rochester's restraining arm, then leaped into the next box and brought the flat side of his sword down on Buckingham's head. Mary and Anna-Maria screamed in unison and jumped to their feet.

Killigrew's weak, dissipated face was only inches from Anna-Maria's. She could smell wine on his breath, and the faintly pungent odor of snuff. He brought his face close to hers and spat, "Whore! Common whore!"

"Oh!" Anna-Maria cried out in sheer rage and leaped at him, her fingers clawing at his face, but he was moving in a crablike fashion, scuttling rapidly to get out of the reach of the duke, who was recovering from the blow. Buckingham's eyes were blazing fire.

Mary attempted to seize his arm, but he pulled away from her and set out in chase of Killigrew. Anna-Maria felt on the point of fainting, and she braced herself against the back of her chair to steady herself. Her heart was pounding to the rhythm of "Kill him, kill him."

The entire theatre was in an uproar now, people pushing and shoving each other in an attempt to get a better view of Buckingham's pursuit of Killigrew.

Even Nell had fallen silent on stage and was watching
wide-eyed as Killigrew scrambled over the boxes with
the duke in hot pursuit. Cries of pain followed as
Killigrew or Buckingham knocked spectators aside in
the heat of the chase. Anna-Maria was sick with rage.
To be so publicly exposed and humiliated! Only Killigrew's quick death would serve her now. Killigrew
was slowing, clearly winded. Buckingham cornered
him and knocked him to the floor. Anna-Maria, her
heart fluttering in her throat, waited for Buckingham
to draw his sword and spill Killigrew's blood.

Buckingham kicked viciously at Killigrew, roaring
for him to get on his feet and fight. Instead Killigrew
rolled himself into a ball and writhed to escape the
kicks that were raining on his stomach, chest, and
head. Anna-Maria felt a vicious joy, as though she were
delivering those kicks herself. Killigrew had handled
her body without mercy and without pity. Let him
know how it felt to be exposed and defenseless!

Then Killigrew got up on his knees, begging for
mercy despite the jeers and catcalls of the crowd.
Buckingham gave him another kick in the stomach,
contempt clearly written on his face. "Beg for your
life! Grovel like the coward that you are!"

Killigrew, his face stained with sweat and moist
tears, clasped his shaking hands together. "Your
Grace, I beg you to spare my life."

"No!" The cry was wrung from Anna-Maria's throat
but the crowd roared suddenly and her cry went un-
heard.

Mary's tense hands unclenched, and her breathing
slowed a little as she realized that Buckingham was
safe. As they watched, Killigrew crawled toward an
exit, howling as the duke applied a contemptuous kick
to his buttocks to speed him on his way.

Buckingham came back into their box slightly
winded but smiling cheerfully. Action, the chance to
physically vent his rage on Killigrew, had proved exhilarating.

Anna-Maria looked up at him, her eyes like dark
fire. "Why didn't you kill him?" she whispered.

The duke was dusting off his disarrayed clothing. "Why, Anna-Maria, today's disgrace was worse than death for any man of honor."

"Killigrew *has* no honor." Anna-Maria's voice was a thin thread. "And what of *my* reputation, *my* honor?"

She could feel Mary's soft, restraining touch on her arm, but she shook it off impatiently. Once Killigrew had violated her and gone unpunished. Now he had publicly insulted her before all of London, and still he walked free. The bruises from the kicks Buckingham had inflicted would heal in a few days, but the scars Anna-Maria bore from the humiliation would never heal. Not until Killigrew lay dead.

Anna-Maria was vaguely aware that Mary was murmuring soothingly to her, but she paid no attention to the sound. Head back, eyes blazing, she was looking challengingly at Buckingham. "I feel unclean!" Her voice was passionate, trembling with tears. "And I will never be clean again until I have bathed away the insults with Killigrew's blood!"

Buckingham was distracted and winded by the recent battle, and it made him insensitive to Anna-Maria's state.

She stared at him, feeling as though her breast were being split in two by pain. He cared nothing for her! Just as Killigrew had said, she was nothing but a common whore and Buckingham valued her favors lightly, counting them of little importance because she gave herself so cheaply.

The sounds of the crowd swelled now, threatening to engulf her and she swayed a little. Mary's arm came quickly around her waist to support her, but Buckingham was unaware of her plight. He was accepting congratulations and clasps on the shoulder and hand from the laughing courtiers who pressed around him. His face split in a grin, his blue eyes lit with triumph, he was tossing quips back to his admirers.

Anna-Maria was all relentless pain now, her body tense with it, her heart breaking. She stood without moving a single muscle until Buckingham glanced her way again, and then she held his eyes with her own.

Very clearly, very distinctly, she said, "I have done with loving you, my lord."

Buckingham's blue eyes darkened with bewilderment. He reached out for her, but giving a little sob, she tore from his grasp and ran from the theatre. She was lighter of foot than he, and he was winded from his recent battle. She escaped him easily, running out into the street where she hailed a public cart and climbed into it. Then she dissolved in tears, not caring that passers-by were staring at her, amazed to see a woman of the nobility in a hell cart. There was no lower she could sink, no further depths to her humiliation.

She was frantic to flee London with its prying, jeering laughter, to escape the love that had failed her. As she rode in the cart, she tried to devise a plan. Where could she go—and how? She was too unhappy to plan coherently, but the thought of a ship in full sail suddenly entered her mind, and she felt a rush of longing for the cool purity of it. Then she thought of the convent, and suddenly her decision was made. She would go back to where she began, back to her roots, and there, in the ordered austerity of the convent, she would be able to put her life in order. "Father, I have sinned." She yearned toward the blessed relief of the confessional.

When the public cart bumped to a stop in front of her house, Anna-Maria pressed a handful of coins into the driver's hands without even bothering to count them and then ran into the house calling for Sarah. She began to sob again as she choked out details of the scene at the theatre.

Sarah was horrified at Anna-Maria's decision to flee the country, but Anna-Maria would tolerate no argument. Frantically she flung clothes around the room, packing without thought or care, all her energies bent on immediate escape. "I will not—" she kept muttering between clenched teeth, never finishing the sentence. She would not expose herself to further jeers and hoots of laughter at court. She would not walk the streets of London where Killigrew went unpunished.

She would not live with a husband that she did not love and would not love Buckingham, who held her love cheaply. Sarah, gathering garments as Anna-Maria flung them down, asked, "What about the children?"

Anna-Maria paused, stricken. She had not thought of the children since that horrible experience in the theatre. She felt like a child herself, longing to flee to the comfort of the nuns' arms. She rubbed her hand over and over down the silky texture of the gown she was holding, looking at Sarah with tears welling in her eyes. "If only I could take them with me! But then, where would I go?" She thought of finding a tiny house in the country, but she had no money of her own and doubted that Francis would give her any. "Oh, Sarah —what shall I do?"

Sarah looked at Anna-Maria for a long, thoughtful moment. These last years here in London had been hard on Anna-Maria, and now she was clearly showing the effects. Although she was more beautiful than ever in her new-found sensuality, her eyes were like burning coals, and she moved slowly, as though the effort tired her.

Sarah turned briskly practical. "I've a mind to go with you and take care of you, but it may be best if I stay here with the children. They will be safe with me."

Anna-Maria gave her a glance of relief. Sarah continued, "You badly need the rest that you will get at the convent. No doubt the earl will understand that—" She broke off as Francis came striding through the door, his graying hair disheveled, as though he had just run nervous fingers through it.

He stopped in front of Anna-Maria and surveyed her from head to toe, giving her a long look of contempt. "That was a pretty scene at the theatre this afternoon. You have made us the laughing-stock of all London!"

Sarah gasped, outraged, but Anna-Maria only looked at him indifferently. "I suppose," her voice had no expression in it, "that you do not plan to avenge me for Killigrew's insults."

"Avenge you!" Scowling, Francis strode about the

room. "I've told you repeatedly that you have brought this trouble on yourself. Matters have come to such a state that people are even now saying that you and the duke of Buckingham are lovers. I fear the duke will be offended by the rumors and will withdraw his friendship from me."

Anna-Maria gave a short, bitter laugh. Francis caught sight of the garments strewn about the room, the half-open trunks and asked, "What's this?"

Anna-Maria's voice was totally without inflection. "I'm leaving you, Francis."

He stared at her incredulously, the color draining from his face, then his eyes grew calculating, and he laughed. "How will you live? You have no money." Francis controlled even the small dowry that Anna-Maria's parents had been able to give her.

"I have some jewelry," Anna-Maria said, thinking of the valuable pieces of jewelry that lay in her enameled coffer. "I will sell that, and then I can send for the children when I am settled."

She turned, totally ignoring Francis's blustering arguments. Ranting angrily, he followed her around as she packed. Repeatedly he demanded to know where she was going, but she refused to tell him. The convent was her sanctuary, and she didn't want it violated by Francis. She stuffed items into her trunk without care or forethought and scarcely noticed when Sarah retrieved them and carefully folded them before returning them to the trunk.

Francis, convinced at last that she was going, stepped back a pace when she had finally snapped the trunk lid shut. "And what will I tell the king when he asks why you are no longer coming to court?"

Anna-Maria surveyed him for a long moment. Then, thinking of the king's reaction when Francis delivered the message, she said in an amused voice, "Tell him that I have gone to find my soul."

Twenty-Four

Standing in the bow of the ship, her arms braced on the rail, Anna-Maria tried to keep her thoughts turned ahead to the convent. But always she found herself remembering Buckingham. She felt a strange delight as she thought that even now he must be searching London for her. She pictured him rushing from the theatre after her, then standing frustrated in the street with the bright sunlight making a golden halo of his hair. No doubt he had thought that she would seek him out later at the Hare and Hounds, and when she had not appeared, he had thought to patch up their quarrel the next morning at Whitehall. It was a fierce satisfaction to picture his dismay when he learned that she had disappeared. She savored the thought and then nearly burst into tears, for she had just learned that the reverse side of love was etched with hatred. She was taking vicious delight in picturing the stricken face of the man she loved so deeply. Truly her soul was in need of mending.

She had taken the youngest of her maids, Janet, with her, and in the days that followed, she thought that she would go mad if the girl did not cease her chattering. Janet had an incessant, high-pitched giggle that grated on the ear, and a habit of turning to eye every attractive sailor who passed them on deck.

When they landed on shore in France, Janet suddenly became fearful and clung to Anna-Maria like a limpet, saying she distrusted the French and that they would certainly be murdered in their beds if they stayed at a strange French inn. Anna-Maria was slightly nervous herself. She had never traveled before without her parents or Francis making careful provisions for her safety. Now she was responsible for herself and Janet as well.

She hired a coachman to take them all the way to the convent at Pontoise, fifteen miles outside of Paris, and promised him a reward of a bag of gold coins if he delivered them safely. She had judged from his appearance that he was a good man, a family man, and he proved worthy of her trust. When the gray walls of the convent became visible over the treetops, she felt a vast sense of peace steal over her. Here she could begin again. She smiled and sighed simultaneously, thinking of the young girl she had been when she had ridden away from here six years before. She had been so full of virtuous convictions, so certain that her life would be an honorable one. A shadow passed over her delicate face. Instead, she left behind in London a husband who was half sick with ambition, a lover who did not value her enough to avenge her honor, and a damaged reputation.

The nuns greeted her with open arms, delighted at the return of one of their former pupils so expensively dressed and bearing such a noble title. Anna-Maria had expected to find herself living the quiet, religion-oriented life she had known as a student here; instead, to her bewildered amazement, she found herself ushered to one of a series of special cells, expensively, even luxuriously, furnished, which were reserved for ladies of the French court who wished to go into seclusion for a time.

The nun had withdrawn quietly, and Janet was unpacking Anna-Maria's trunk when there was a light knock at the door, and a very pretty young woman with black tousled curls poked her head through the opening. Her face was vivacious, her mouth wide and very red, her eyes black and sparkling. The visitor entered and introduced herself as Giselle, and it soon became clear during the course of her chatter that she was a person of some consequence at the French court but had fled to the convent for a brief respite from the attentions of her current lover.

"It is wonderful, the effect the convent life has on one's beauty. The plain food,"—Anna-Maria smothered a smile, for Giselle had entered with an ornate box of confections and as she spoke was popping a sweetmeat into her mouth—"the regular hours. Me, I come here at least once every six months, and when I return to court, the other ladies are ill with envy because I am so beautiful."

Anna-Maria was charmed by her. She willingly answered all Giselle's questions about the court of King Charles and in return was regaled with gossip and intimate details of Louis, the French king. Finally Giselle gave Anna-Maria a frank look. "You are very unhappy, ma petite?"

Anna-Maria turned away and sighed, her hands clasping and unclasping nervously. Even though she found Giselle pleasing, she could not bring herself to confide in her. "I merely need a rest," she said.

Giselle tactfully changed the subject, asking about Queen Catherine whom she had heard was very religious and so ugly that it hurt to look upon her.

Anna-Maria protested. Despite the queen's rejection of her as a lady-in-waiting, she still had a fondness for her.

Giselle said shrewdly, "I hear that Lady Castlemaine is triumphant, that the queen has finally accepted her."

Anna-Maria nodded, her face clouding. The queen, weakened by loneliness and lack of friends, had capitulated utterly under the king's pressure and had accepted Lady Castlemaine, admitting the king's mistress to her presence at will.

Giselle was toying with a string of pearls, her face suddenly dreamy. "Tell me of the duke of Buckingham. I saw him often when he was here at court in exile with your King Charles, but although I often put myself in his path, he never noticed me. I wish that he would return for a visit. Now that I am older and more experienced—" She broke off abruptly. Anna-Maria was flushing scarlet, and her eyes had a look of deep pain in them. A fragment of memory, a whisper of gossip, came to Giselle's mind—the countess of Shrewsbury linked with the duke of Buckingham.

Giselle longed to put her hand out in sympathy but something about Anna-Maria's expression stopped her. Instead, with quick tact she turned to a different topic.

No doubt Anna-Maria had had her heart broken by the handsome duke. When in France he had been notorious for the ease with which he won women's hearts and the equally casual ease with which he discarded them.

"Lady Margueritte is giving a small supper in her cell. She'll be delighted if you join us."

Anna-Maria managed a smile. "What of the plain convent food that you said is so good for your beauty?"

"Faugh!" Giselle wrinkled her small nose and made a dismissing gesture, as though waving aside the offending menu. "Once, perhaps twice a week, that is enough. The rest of the time we must be kind to our stomachs."

Anna-Maria laughed with genuine mirth this time. "Thank you, but no. Perhaps another evening." She hesitated and then said slowly. "I was raised in this convent, and of late I've shamefully neglected my religion. I've come here to return to it."

Giselle's eyes widened for a moment, and then she gave a shrug. Broken hearts affected women in strange ways sometimes. For herself, she would prefer to immediately take another lover, but the English had their own ideas on these matters. She slipped gracefully out of the cell door, scattering compliments and future invitations in her wake.

Anna-Maria stretched out on the bed and found it too luxurious. She would have preferred a narrow white cot such as she had known as a child. This bed was large enough to accommodate both herself and the duke, and as she turned on her side, her hand went involuntarily to caress the spot where his head would be lying. For a moment she almost believed she could see him lying there, his eyelashes making dark crescents on his cheeks, and the longing for him was so sharp that she cried aloud from it.

Unable to lie still while her thoughts tore at her, she rose, flung on her cloak, and went to walk in the garden. Sunset was just streaking pink light behind a dark line of poplar trees, and she stopped abruptly. It was at this hour that they stood locked in each other's arms nightly, watching the light of day fade. The sunset seemed naked and uninspiring now, and she turned, sobbing, and fled back inside the convent. Sweet Jesu! Was all her life to be flat, robbed of its pleasure, if she could not share it with him?

In the days that followed, she tried to accustom herself to living without him, and she learned that emotional pain was similar to physical pain. The sharp ache of loss came in waves as had her pain during childbirth. She learned that if she stood still for a moment, letting the pain wash over her, it would ebb after a moment, and she could resume her activity. Some at the convent whispered that the countess of Shrewsbury was suffering a serious illness because she was often seen to turn white and steady herself by grasping the nearest solid object for support. Then she would breathe more deeply, smile, and continue whatever she had been doing.

It was such small, everyday things that brought on the sudden pain. One night they were served a dish of roast lamb, the duke's favorite dish, and Anna-Maria had a sudden memory of his white teeth pulling at the brown meat. Another time it was Giselle's careless mention of a book Anna-Maria and Buckingham had read together, and she caught her breath in anguish at the memory of the way his fingers had caressed hers as they turned the pages. At times she was certain that she would go mad if she had to live the rest of her life without the sight and sound of him, and at other times she convinced herself that she had enough strength within herself to fashion a new life.

To her bewildered disappointment, religion was not the source of strength that she had expected. The priest who heard her confession seemed indifferent to the magnitude of the sins that she confessed to him. Anna-Maria realized that most of the French women who sought temporary refuge at the convent accepted adultery as a matter of course. Were there then two religions—the one that she had been taught as a child and an entirely different one for adults? Or was there one for the rich and one for the peasants?

She sought the answers she needed within herself, walking frequently alone in the convent gardens. Had she truly sinned in loving Buckingham? If it was sin, then why had she felt only deep happiness instead of guilt? When she was virtuous, an innocent victim of Killigrew, pain and humiliation had followed. She remembered the feeling of deep peace, the sense of *rightness* that she had always felt in Buckingham's arms, and her moral confusion deepened. For nearly three months she wrestled with her questions, growing thin and pale under the strain, and then one day she announced abruptly to Janet, "Pack. I must return to London at once."

It was a relief to be in motion, a relief to feel the salt spray against her cheeks as she stood at the rail of the ship. Her hunger to see Buckingham's face was so sharp that she was willing to satisfy it in almost any way—by seeing a glimpse of his lean cheek in a crowd or the sight of the tall crown of his head across a distance. She would take a crumb, *any* crumb, the way a starving beggar would snatch a morsel from the gutters of London.

For the first day at sea she thought no further than of glimpsing Buckingham at a distance. Then the next day she realized that a tantalizing sight of him from a far distance was all that her pride could allow her. He had not counted her of enough importance to revenge her on Killigrew! She could never succumb to her longing to be in his arms again. And certainly she could not return to Francis's house!

Suddenly she dropped her face into her hands and wept. "How will I live?" She was sailing impulsively into an unknown future with no plans to steady her. Then Nell's impish face leaped into her mind, and her tears stopped. "I'll stay with Nelly. And she'll advise me. I can rely on her."

Nell's arms went around Anna-Maria in instant understanding when Anna-Maria appeared white-faced and disheveled on her doorstep. For once Nell did not break into lighthearted chatter but merely held Anna-

Maria quietly while she tried to make sense of Anna-Maria's broken, sobbing whispers. Then she turned her cheerful practicality to the nearest problem at hand. "Of course you may stay with me as long as you like. And I'll keep your secret. No one shall know that you are in London!"

She unfastened the ribbons of Anna-Maria's cloak, settled her into a chair, and pressed a glass of wine into her hand. "There. Drink that and cheer up. You are among friends."

Anna-Maria took a deep swallow of the wine, and a little color began to return to her cheeks. "Nell, I'm ashamed of myself. I'm like a child. I cannot seem to form a coherent plan. I am all emotion and no mind."

Nell leaned forward, cupping her dimpled chin on her hand. "And what do your emotions tell you?"

"That I cannot live any longer without holding my children in my arms." Her voice dropped to a shamed whisper. "And that I *must* catch at least a glimpse of Buckingham. I'm starved for the sight of him."

She took another long drink of the wine and then raised her head defiantly. "And another thing, Nelly. No man shall ever use me again as Killigrew did! No man! Not even my husband. He has lost all right to me by his refusal to protect me!"

Goaded by the memory of Francis's rape of her, she rose abruptly from her chair and began pacing the room angrily. "I must find a way to live where I am dependent on no man!"

Nell's hazel eyes clouded. "What you want is impossible, Anna-Maria. We are women. By our very nature we are dependent on men."

"You're not!" Anna-Maria suddenly whirled about and caught one of Nell's hands in her own. "I admire you so because you earn your own living on the stage. You ask no man to care for you."

Nell started to protest. She accepted many favors from her admirers, both money and jewelry. She had won her earliest parts on the stage by sleeping with Charles Hart. The words of protest died on her lips as an idea was born in her quick brain. "Anna-Maria! You can become an actress!"

As Anna-Maria stared at her, Nell jumped to her feet, planning busily. "What a dolt I was not to think of it on the instant. It will provide a perfect hiding place for you!"

Anna-Maria gasped. "The London stage a hiding place? I'll be exposing myself before the entire populace!"

Nell dimpled, her eyes sparkling with mischief. "Aye, but who would think to look for the countess of Shrewsbury beneath the greasepaint of an actress? You'll be a sensation! You must always keep an air of mystery about you—we'll dye your hair. . . ." She darted about the room, talking quickly and eagerly.

Anna-Maria's hand flew to her gleaming chestnut hair. "Dye my hair?"

Nell stopped and gave her a long, considering look. "Aye, that new white blond color that is so fashionable. And we'll alter the contours of your face a little. Here, look."

She seized Anna-Maria by the shoulders and sat her down on a stool in front of the dressing table. Chattering busily, she began opening one china pot after another, scattering the contents until the dressing table resembled the easel of an artist gone mad.

Anna-Maria had a sudden memory of the first time she had sat before this dressing table with Nell busy disguising her. Then she had been happily planning how she could move freely about the streets of London and meet the duke in safety. She closed her eyes in pain against the sharpness of the memory, and Nell stopped chattering abruptly. "Are you ill?"

Anna-Maria shook her head and attempted a smile. "No. But Nell, you move so quickly that you take my breath away. I don't see how I could ever become an actress. I have no talent."

"Faugh! Talent. What is it? An ability to memorize lines. To move gracefully about a stage looking beautiful." She had her head bent, rummaging in a small carved chest on the dressing table. She gave a quick cry of triumph and held up her find. "Here. Open your mouth."

Startled, Anna-Maria obeyed, and Nell quickly inserted two small, spongelike forms into Anna-Maria's cheeks, deftly smoothing them into place.

"My God! What are you doing?" Anna-Maria found that her voice was slightly indistinct because of the foreign substance crowding her cheeks.

"They are called plumpers. They alter the contours of your face." She stepped back and regarded her handiwork with satisfaction and then gestured toward the mirror. "Look what a difference they make in your appearance!"

Anna-Maria looked into the mirror and then peered more closely in astonishment. Normally the lines of her cheeks were delicate, incurving. Now her cheeks were plumped out, subtly altering her entire expression.

"And a new line for your eyebrows." Nell, her underlip caught between her teeth, was searching for a pair of tweezers. "It's amazing how much difference eyebrows make." She found the tweezers, grasped Anna-Maria's chin in a firm hand, and plucked at the winged curve of her eyebrow.

"Ouch!" Involuntary tears sprang to Anna-Maria's eyes, and she pulled away.

"Hold still." Nell sounded preoccupied but entirely in control, and Anna-Maria saw that it was no use to argue. And indeed, despite the pain of the plucking, it was pleasant to leave all her decisions for the moment in Nell's capable hands.

She endured frequent small stabs of pain stoically, thinking that it was far less severe than her emotional pain. She wondered where Buckingham was at this moment, and she suddenly felt lightheaded, realizing that they were again in the same city. She might even glimpse him this very afternoon.

"There!" Nell gave a sigh of satisfaction. "I vow I could pass you on the street, and I would never know you!"

Anna-Maria looked into the mirror and gasped in astonishment. "I would not know myself!"

Nell had plucked her normally wing-shaped eyebrows into two arched crescents, artificial and somehow cheap looking. Combined with the plumpers in her cheeks, they completely altered her delicate, fine features so that she had the look of a courtesan, at once provocative yet faintly, subtly coarse.

"Nell!" Anna-Maria suddenly whirled on the stool and rose. "I cannot let the children see me like this. They will not know me."

Nell looked dismayed for a moment, and then her brow cleared. "Spit out the plumpers. The children will never notice your altered eyebrows. And after we've dyed your hair, we will make sure you always wear a cap when they are about."

Anna-Maria began to laugh helplessly, although there was a catch in her throat. "Oh, Nell. Life is so complicated. I'd thought it would mean a life in the countryside with my children always about me and now—" She broke off with a gesture that indicated her reflection in the mirror, the room behind them.

Nell said briskly, "I learned early that 'tis best to take life the way you find it and not waste breath nor tears on wishing it were different."

Anna-Maria felt braced by Nell's courage and her air of uncomplaining competence. She gave her a quick hug and asked, "May we send for Sarah to bring the children to me now?"

Nell's eyes softened. "Aye. You must be sorely missing them." Poking her tousled head out the door, she shouted loudly for the footman whom she had recently employed. He was past his prime and slightly crippled by rheumatism, but Nell was vastly proud of him and devised countless errands each day so that he would be seen all over London.

She gave him careful instructions to deliver a message for Sarah's ears alone, impressing on him the importance of secrecy.

Then she bustled back into the room and said to Anna-Maria, "You must eat something. Emotions are always heightened if you experience them on an empty stomach."

She looked about the room expectantly, as though a full-course dinner would appear at her bidding, and then her face fell in dismay. The remnants of last night's supper were scattered about the room, but most of the food was spoiled and clung unpleasantly to the plates. "I had a goodly company here last night—Henry Saville, Babs May, Henry Beck—and all with ravenous appetites. They have picked me as clean as a dog's bone."

"Never mind. I'm not particularly hungry." Anna-Maria had spied a half loaf of stale bread lying abandoned on a pewter dish, and she picked it up and held it out to Nell with a smile. "This will be sufficient."

"Dip it in wine. It will soften it." Nell had often breakfasted on a stale loaf, the remnant of a night's feast.

Anna-Maria did so and then bit into the bread, the wine running down her chin. "Nell, I cannot believe that I will see the children in a few minutes. I missed them so in France that I *had* to come home, even though I knew it was unwise."

She was too impatient to stand still and kept pacing the room, looking anxiously out the window and craning her neck for the first sight of them.

Finally Nell's coach rolled into view, and Anna-Maria felt her heart nearly stop with excitement. She raced down the narrow wooden stairs and nearly collided with Sarah who was just entering, John on her hip and Polly and Charles at her side. "Whew!" Sarah gave Anna-Maria a quick, anxious look, judged that she was in good health, and handed John to her. "Three of them are a handful to take out alone, but I dared not trust any of the maids."

"Sarah! Polly!" Anna-Maria was suddenly flooded with happiness. She buried her face in John's sweet-smelling hair and tried to embrace Sarah, Polly, and Charles all at the same time. It was cramped in the small, dark hallway, and finally Sarah, laughing, pulled the group apart and ushered everyone upstairs. " 'Twill be easier to embrace everyone when you have more space around you."

Sarah and Nell tactfully withdrew to a corner while Anna-Maria kissed and cuddled the children. Quickly, in a low tone, Nell told Sarah of Anna-Maria's arrival and her bewilderment about how to conduct her life without putting herself into Francis's hands. Sarah's eyes widened when Nell spoke of her proposal that Anna-Maria should go on the stage. She thought it over for several moments and then nodded. "I can think of no other plan. But Nell, it is dangerous. If she is discovered, her reputation will be ruined past repairing!"

There was a wry twist to Nell's mouth, and Sarah quickly put a hand on her arm. "I didn't mean—it is different for you to be an actress. It's splendid. But she was born to a different life."

"Aye, and much good it has done her." Nell's eyes were on Anna-Maria who was laughingly fending off young Charles's assault on her curls.

They were both silent a minute, watching Anna-Maria, and then Nell said to Sarah in a low undertone, "Did you know that Killigrew fled to France not long after the scandal in the theatre?"

Anna-Maria had caught the name, and her head came up quickly with the alertness of an animal sensing danger. "Killigrew? What's this about Killigrew?"

The children fell silent, feeling her tension, and Nell moved forward and said soothingly, " 'Tis nothing. Only that he fled to France shortly after you did."

"So," Anna-Maria said slowly, "I shared my refuge with my enemy." She shivered a little and then said matter-of-factly, as though she were discussing the purchase of new hair ribbons, "I shall not rest until he is dead."

Sarah and Nell were silent. The anger in Anna-Maria was deeply rooted and could not be remedied by a few soothing words.

Polly began to beg for a sweetmeat, and Nell, relieved at having an errand, offered to run down to the shop. Left alone with the children, Anna-Maria and Sarah looked at each other for a long, wordless moment. Then Anna-Maria said, with an attempt at a laugh, "Well, Sarah, and how shall you like me as an actress?"

Sarah sat down and lifted John onto her lap. "I don't know what to advise you. Perhaps it is the safest place for you now. No one will think to look for the countess of Shrewsbury in the heart of London. But

Anna-Maria, can you do it? Disguise your walk, your gestures, so that not even the duke will recognize you? Love has keen eyes."

At the mention of the duke, Anna-Maria's brown eyes darkened. She waited a moment until her breathing was under control and then said, "He loves me not, Sarah." Before Sarah could protest, she said, with an attempt at indifference, "Have you seen him lately?"

"He was a wild man when you first left," Sarah said, leaning forward eagerly. "He waited outside the house daily to accost me when I went on my errands, demanding that I tell him your whereabouts."

For a moment hope flared in Anna-Maria's eyes, but then her expression darkened. "Aye, he might seek knowledge of my whereabouts, but when he had the opportunity to kill Killigrew, he did not think me worth the trouble."

She could not bear talking about Buckingham any longer and changed the topic, demanding that Sarah tell her everything about the children's development since she had left. At the conclusion of Sarah's recital, she pressed her hand and said gently, "Sarah, there has never been a better friend in the world than you. Had it not been for your care for the children, I would have bundled them up and taken them with me, and no doubt ended wandering France or England begging for our food."

She buried her face in John's curls and said, "Soon, very soon, I will have money of my own, and then I can set up a household and have my children with me."

Sarah bit back the words that rose to her lips. It seemed unlikely that Anna-Maria would earn a great deal of money on the stage. Most of the actresses were poorly paid, and their real livelihood came from the gentlemen who took them into keeping.

Nell came back in a flurry of laughter and distributed the sweetmeats, pulling Charles onto her lap and gently stroking his curls. "I envy you," she said softly to Anna-Maria. "No matter what troubles beset you, you have these three poppets to comfort you." Nell's hazel eyes were clouded. She longed for motherhood. Then her normally optimistic nature asserted itself. One of her evenings with the king might result in the birth of a child. Imagine if she, little Nelly from the gutters, were to mother a child of royal blood!

The three women talked and played with the children, and Anna-Maria felt as though only minutes were passing. She was startled and dismayed when Sarah suddenly rose and took John from her arms. "We'd best be returning home. It grows late."

Anna-Maria's eyes flew to the window, and she saw that dusk was already threatening. She let out a small cry. "Sarah, will you bring the children to me every day?"

Sarah nodded reassuringly. "Every day that I can manage it without leading your husband to you."

Anna-Maria kept snatching the children to her for one last kiss until Sarah grew firm and took them from her protesting arms. Anna-Maria followed them to the bottom of the stairs, saw them safely into the coach, and then burst into tears. It was not fair! She wanted to be a true mother, to have her children about her day and night.

Wearily she turned and climbed the wooden stairs, moving slowly and reluctantly toward a way of life she had never been fashioned for.

Twenty-Five

"Nell, I'm going to swoon! I cannot do it!" Anna-Maria, her palms damp, stood in the wings of the King's Theatre and hissed into Nell's ear.

"Nonsense!" Nell's voice was impatient, her eyes fixed on the action taking place on the stage. "You have nothing to do but mingle with the crowd."

Anna-Maria tried to swallow and found that her mouth and throat were dry. It was true that she had no lines to speak, but the very thought of stepping onto the stage made her feel faint with fear. For reassurance she looked at Nell's profile, the tilted nose and firm, impudent chin. The play was Massinger's *The Virgin Martyr,* and Nell was dressed in breeches, playing the role of a heavenly messenger sent to watch over the soul of Dorothea, the virgin. When Nell appeared on stage in her tight-fitting breeches, her slim legs clearly outlined, the gallants in the pits had gone wild and had held up the play for several minutes while they stamped their feet and cheered with approval. Nell had remained unruffled, sending impudent grins to her admirers, and now, as she stood waiting to enter the stage again, she showed no sign of nervousness. Anna-Maria marveled at her calm.

"Nell!" Anna-Maria tugged at her friend's arm. "Suppose someone recognizes me?"

Nell turned and whispered calmly, "At this distance? Tom Killigrew has not recognized you, and he has stood closer to you than I am now."

In the darkness offstage Anna-Maria nodded, realizing the sense of Nell's words. Her worst moment had come the past week when Nell had brought her to the theatre and presented her to Tom Killigrew, who had often seen her at court. Tom Killigrew had swept Anna-Maria from the tip of her newly white-blond hair to the toes of her red shoes with a glance in which there was no recognition and had nodded. "We'll use her in the crowd scenes. Later will be time enough to see if she warrants larger parts."

Triumphant, stifling a laugh, Nell had swept Anna-Maria into the life of the dressing room and introduced her to the other actresses. Beck Marshall, who was Nell's chief rival, had been cool to Anna-Maria, but the others had accepted her with easy camaraderie. If Anna-Maria was promoted to larger parts, Nell warned, the easy friendliness would change swiftly to open enmity, but Anna-Maria had protested, "Nell, I want no large parts! I'm content merely to mingle without being recognized."

Now she was uncertain that she even wanted to step

on stage. Suppose she tripped and fell? Suppose she fainted, and the entire theatre howled with laughter?

She heard a flutter of movement as others came up behind her and realized with a sinking of her heart that it was time for the crowd scene of which she was to be a part.

"Go on!" Nell gave her a good-natured shove in the small of her back, and Anna-Maria found herself walking on stage amid a cluster of resplendently dressed actresses.

The flare of the candles was blinding, and she blinked after the sudden shift from the dimness of backstage. Involuntarily she looked down past the stage apron, glancing at the audience. To her relief she could see no one. Beyond the candles was a sea of darkness. The audience might not exist.

She began to breathe more easily and had just raised her fan in a confident gesture when the thought suddenly struck her that Buckingham might be in the audience. She stumbled and would have fallen had not Anne Wallace, who was standing next to her, put a kindly hand under her elbow. "The first time," she whispered, "is always the worst. After that you will feel perfectly at home on stage."

Beck Marshall, who was playing the part of the virgin, threw Anne Wallace a furious glance, looking quite unlike the saintly character she was portraying, and then resumed her sweetly accented speech.

Anne stifled a giggle and then mimed a conversation with Anna-Maria, falling easily back into the minor character she was playing. Anna-Maria felt vastly self-conscious. How absurd it was to be standing here in full view of hundreds of people, pretending to have a conversation that never existed. How often she had watched plays from the other side of the footlights and never dreamed of the high degree of artifice that went into it!

Anne Wallace was still moving her lips, only now words were emerging, so low that they were audible only to Anna-Maria. "I vow I cannot help but fall into laughter every time Beck Marshall plays the virgin. I doubt that there is a man in England who has not enjoyed her favors. Unless he is crippled and lame." She paused for a moment and said thoughtfully. "Even then Becky would have him if he brought a full enough purse."

Anna-Maria felt herself in danger of laughing outright, and she hastily raised her fan to cover her quivering lips. She relaxed suddenly. Really, being on stage was no worse than being at court. There was the sense of being challenged, of being always on display, always on one's guard, but it was a familiar sensation. She remembered how often at court she had felt that she was acting in a play where all the others knew their lines and only she did not. At least here in the theatre she need say nothing unless it was written for her and carefully rehearsed.

By the time her moments on stage were finished, she was moving with genuine ease, her old grace returning, and when she exited, she threw Nell a cheerful grin. Nell winked at her and strode on stage, her legs moving freely in their close-fitting breeches.

Later, in the dressing room, they exchanged an exuberant hug. "You were wonderful!" "And you!" Their voices mingled and broke over each other, and they both paused, laughing.

Beck Marshall threw them a scornful glance. She looked at Anna-Maria. "I see nothing so wonderful in your being able to cross a stage without disgracing yourself. And as for you"—she pointed her comb toward Nell in a threatening gesture—"I've a bone to pick with you, Mistress Gwyn. You attempted to make a fool of me tonight by spoiling my lines."

She had half risen on her stool, but Nell forestalled her. She drawled, " 'Tis no great trick to make a fool of you, Beck. You lend yourself to it readily."

"Why you—!" Beck flung herself toward Nell, her hands upraised as though to seize Nell by the hair.

"Stop!" Horrified, Anna-Maria interposed her slim body between the combatants, but Nell and Becky merely looked amused at her terror. Physical combat was not uncommon among the actresses, and often the two who quarreled liked each other better after the battle.

Anne Wallace poked her head through the door and called softly, "The gentlemen are coming."

Instantly the activity in the room increased, and Beck Marshall turned away, shrugging. She was expecting her latest admirer, and her quarrel with Nell Gwyn could wait for another day.

Concerned, Nell looked at Anna-Maria. "We'd best get you out of here. Buckingham might be among them."

A spasm of jealousy seized Anna-Maria. So Buckingham had joined the throng of men who hovered about the actresses, showering them with presents in return for their favors, buzzing about the dressing room like bees browsing among the flowers. She hated every woman he ever exchanged so much as a word with! She would like to be as free as Beck Marshall and leap openly at her rivals, tearing the very hair from the head of every woman with whom Buckingham exchanged a flirting word.

Nell's tug at her arm was insistent, and Anna-Maria followed obediently, her senses in a turmoil. The rumor had already been spread about the theatre that Anna-Maria was a widowed French woman who had an ailing child at home to whom she was devoted. She had stolen Giselle's name, knowing that lighthearted Giselle would merely be amused, and it was to Madame Giselle that the others called their goodnights as she and Nell left.

At the door of the dressing room, Tom Killigrew stopped them and looked kindly down at Anna-Maria. "Well, madame, and how was your first experience treading the boards? Not too terrifying, I trust?"

Anna-Maria looked at his thin, aristocratic face and marveled for the millionth time that he could be the father of a scoundrel such as Henry Killigrew. She thought of his son, who had ruined her life and brought her to the stage, but forcing a smile, she said, "Not difficult at all, my lord. I quite enjoyed myself."

Tom Killigrew smiled. "We must try you with some

lines soon, my dear." Then he passed by, leaving Anna-Maria staring after him in dismay.

"Nell, I don't *want* to speak lines—" She had started to protest but stopped, realizing that Nell was not heeding her. The king's messenger had entered the theatre and was moving rapidly toward them. He stopped when he reached them and spoke low and rapidly in Nell's ear, and then Nell turned to Anna-Maria with a face that was dazzling in its radiance even in the dimness of the theatre.

"Anna-Maria! The king has sent for me again!" Her hands were touching her hair, her face, smoothing her dress in uncharacteristic self-consciousness. "How do I look? Oh, Anna-Maria, many days I thought I would *die* if I did not lie in his arms again! Do you believe that you can actually die from want of love?"

"Yes! If I never see Buckingham again, I shall die." The words burst from Anna-Maria's lips. It had been months since she had lain in Buckingham's arms and tasted the sweetness of his lips pressed against hers.

Suddenly she felt envious, and then, ashamed, she pressed her cloak upon Nell, a new blue cloak that would enhance the blue of Nell's eyes. Unlike Nell's, it was stained with neither food nor wine and was of a wool so delicate that its touch was like a caress.

"Be happy. Love him well." She settled the cloak around Nell's suddenly shaking shoulders and gave her a kiss. Then, desolate, she watched as Nell ran lightly from the theatre.

If only she herself could run through the streets of London, run without thought or pride until she found Buckingham, then throw herself into his arms. What did her pride matter when she was starved for the touch of his lips, his strong arms cradling her body? She had an image of him picking her up lightly and depositing her on a bed, his tall form bent above her, and she went weak with longing. Had she savored those moments enough? Had she realized how precious they were when they were happening? The past had snatched them away, and now she was left alone in the dimness of this theatre with only the wisps of memory to comfort her.

Leaden, she walked slowly out onto the cobblestoned street and sought out Nell's coach. Once home she flung herself onto the bed, fully dressed, and gave herself over to memories of Buckingham until her body was inflamed with longing, her pillow damp with her tears.

It was an effort to rise the next morning, an effort to listen to Nell's enraptured encounter with the king. How am I to live? she kept thinking. How am I going to live when the world is robbed of all joy?

She forced herself into motion, eating the food Nell set before her, dressing slowly and carefully when it was time to leave for the theatre. Memories constituted the danger, she thought. If she could learn to feel nothing, want nothing, then she could live.

When they arrived at the theatre, she felt no nervousness, only indifference, when Tom Killigrew announced that he was going to allow her to speak a few lines in the next play. "The gallants in the pit have noticed your beauty my dear, and they have demanded to see you further displayed."

Nell was ecstatic on Anna-Maria's behalf and threw her friend a glance of approval, but Anna-Maria found herself hard-pressed to summon a smile. Finally she collected herself and said softly, "I'm gratified at your confidence in me," and then moved away.

Tom Killigrew stared after her in bewilderment. Lack of ambition was a novelty in actresses—he did not understand this beautiful French woman. He shrugged. She was a widow with an ill child, and perhaps her emotions were sapped by her troubles.

Anna-Maria learned her few short lines with indifferent ease. It was good to concentrate totally on the lines, to wipe out all other thoughts. Nell coached her, but often interrupted to tell Anna-Maria a new detail of her most recent evening with the king. "Never was there a man so tender, so sympathetic!"

Ah, yes, there was, Anna-Maria thought and found herself on the verge of tears. Never again would she feel the sweet fire of a kiss, thrill to a touch on her body. She was young, so young, and yet all that was behind her. Loyalty to Nell, tender compassion for her friend, forbade her cutting short Nell's ecstatic recital, yet each word Nell spoke brought forth a flood of memories and was like a knife cutting into her heart.

Finally Nell, her impish face sobering, broke off in the middle of repeating one of the king's remarks and said gently, "You are missing Buckingham."

"Aye." Anna-Maria's face twisted in a spasm of pain. "But do not mind that. Missing Buckingham is woven into the fabric of my life now, and I must accustom myself to it."

Nevertheless, Nell, shooting Anna-Maria a glance from under her thick, dark lashes, kept her memories of the king to herself and began with renewed vigor to coach Anna-Maria in the words and gestures of her part. There was no real interpretation of a part, Anna-Maria learned. No bringing her thoughts and emotions to the character she was to portray and acting spontaneously. The gestures and movements of a tragedienne were highly stylized, and Nell taught them all to her.

Anna-Maria practiced the lines and gestures in front of the mirror at home, and at times she turned away, her mouth twisting wryly. A woman did not act this way when her heart was broken, she thought. Not with large gestures and ringing tones. She moved slowly and carefully—as she herself was doing now—as though a quick movement would bring on tears or worse.

Still, she obediently learned the part as Nell had instructed her and was rewarded on the night of the performance by the gallants in the pit rising as one man and stopping the performance while they cheered her. Afterward, she changed slowly in the dressing room and was still there when they pressed in upon her, persistent in their demands. One gentleman offered her seven thousand pounds a year to go into keeping with him, and another dangled a diamond bracelet before her eyes. Lord Brockhurst, his moon face sweating, swore that he would meet any price if she would only grant him one night with her. Anna-Maria, her mist of indifference clearing for a moment, almost broke into giggles. At least Lord Brockhurst was consistent in his desires. He had followed her about court, peering at her breasts, stealing opportunities to touch her hand. His demands had been less frank and open at court, but his intentions had been almost as transparent. Now he begged her, a trace of saliva drooling from the corner of his mouth, and seemed unaware that the French silver-haired blond that he was lusting after was the same chestnut-haired, delicate-faced countess of Shrewsbury that had so captured his imagination at court.

Nell acted as a small, efficient watchdog, claiming that Giselle spoke very little English, was nursing a broken heart because of her dead husband, and was eager to return to her lodgings to nurse her sick child. Soon, soon, she promised, with a mixture of cajolery and shrugs, Giselle's heart would mend, and she would be eager to entertain offers, but for the moment they must go. Go! She pushed them playfully toward the door.

Soon Anna-Maria found herself alone with the other actresses, a smile on her lips. "At least Buckingham did not seek out the newest face on stage. I could not have borne that."

Nell gave her a worried look. The atmosphere in the dressing room was hostile. The other actresses were creaming their faces, removing their greasepaint, and shooting angry glances in Anna-Maria's direction. They had not liked her success tonight on stage, and they were furious that the gallants had swarmed about her afterwards, ignoring them. The normal camaraderie, the lending of bits of finery, the good-natured rivalry was missing, and they changed and dressed in a dangerously quiet atmosphere.

Nell was anxious to remove Anna-Maria before open hostility broke out, but Anna-Maria was moving

"Come!" As soon as Anna-Maria had creamed her face clean, Nell seized her by the arm. "For once you can wear your costume home."

She bundled Anna-Maria into the coach, and they sat in silence during the ride home. When they reached Nell's lodgings, Anna-Maria went obediently into the bedroom, wearily took off her costume, blew out the candle, and sank into the feather bed.

Most evenings she hid in the bedroom, alone with her memories and thoughts, while Nell entertained company in the next room. It would have been suspicious if the gregarious Nell had suddenly forbidden gallants to visit her in her lodgings, and the only way for Anna-Maria to keep her presence secret was to hide in the bedroom. Anna-Maria had not wanted to spoil Nell's life, to interrupt Nell's free-hearted giving of herself, but Nell had said, her hazel eyes very serious, that she had desired no man since she had met the king and would never again need the privacy of her bedroom since she went to the king at Whitehall.

This evening, as she did night after night, Anna-Maria lay in the darkness, waiting for sleep to come while the thin edge of candlelight crept under the door and the sound of merriment in the next room assaulted her ears.

Nell is more sensible than I, she thought, out there in the next room, dancing with her shoes off, her head thrown back in laughter. And yet I *cannot,* cannot feel laughter, cannot feel life. When I feel anything at all it is love for Buckingham and I cannot bear that.

Once, lying in the darkness, she had curved her hand over her breast as he had done so often and said softly, "My heart still beats." And then the touch of her fingers reminded her of his dear touch, and she drew her hand away, frightened at the remembered emotions she had aroused.

Suddenly her attention was captured by a deep-timbred voice from the other room. She sat up in bed, her hair spilling over her shoulders, her breasts heaving as she strained to listen. It was Buckingham's voice! The sound was like rich honey, and she sobbed suddenly, longing to fling herself out of bed and into his arms.

"Nell, by now you must have heard from her! You are close friends. She would not have let you go all this time without word from her."

Nell's voice was deliberately raised so that if Anna-Maria was awake, she would hear it in the bedroom. "*You* were great friends, my lord, and yet she has not gotten in touch with you."

Nell's tone was cold and a little brittle, and it steadied Anna-Maria. She fought down her impulse to go to Buckingham at once and instead thought of that evening in the theatre when he had allowed Killigrew to go unscathed. The yearning to at least open the door a little and *see* him for a moment was so strong that she clasped her hands together and strained against the temptation. She would not be loved lightly —would not be like a true actress of the theatre who sold herself for a diamond bracelet. Under her breath, addressing the door, she whispered, "If you loved me, you would not allow me to be dishonored."

Suddenly a cold recklessness seized her, and she was filled with pride. She was *not* a common actress, at the mercy of a pair of blue eyes. She was Anna-Maria, a woman who valued herself, and she was not a prey of her own emotions. Unconsciously, in the dark, she raised her head to an arrogant height and listened to Buckingham as he made his farewells of Nell.

"I entreat you—Nell, please—the second you have word of her whereabouts, let me know."

Nell was promising, her voice light, yet sharp, as they moved away from the door.

Anna-Maria, her heart pounding, lay back in the darkness. It had happened at last—she had heard his voice—and she had been stronger than she had believed possible.

When, hours later, Nell crept into the room and lit the candle, Anna-Maria spoke. "I thank you for your loyalty."

"You *did* hear. I thought you might be asleep."

Anna-Maria was pleased at the steadiness of her own voice. "I heard."

Nell's impish face was sober. "Anna-Maria, he loves you truly. I know Buckingham. I know well that his heart is truly engaged."

Anna-Maria turned onto her side, away from Nell. "It is not love that falters when it finds difficulty. It is not love that does not put honor first."

She closed her eyes, and Nell looked at her with despair. "Nevertheless," Nell said softly as she slid out of her petticoats, "he *does* love you."

Anna-Maria feigned sleep until Nell had slid into bed beside her, and then she lay awake staring into the darkness, her pulses pounding. It made no sense that the sound of one voice could so disrupt her life. She had been at ease, not content but at least more at ease recently, and now the sound of Buckingham's voice had ripped apart all her protective coverings, and she was in pain as she had been on the day that she had left him. Simply hearing his voice had made her feel as though he were making love to her. For hours she tossed in the comfortable bed, envying Nell's easy breathing beside her, and then finally she fell into a troubled slumber. Buckingham needed her. . . . He was bending above her imploring her. . . . She was reaching up to him . . .

Nell's light voice brought her fully awake. "Wake up, sleepyhead. We must be at the theatre early today."

She sat up, feeling bereaved at the sudden loss of Buckingham's dear face and blinked at Nell. "What's amiss?"

Nell was flinging on clothes with careless haste. "We've the rehearsal for Ben Jonson's *Catiline*. I'm to speak the prologue."

They dressed and ate rapidly while Nell went over her lines and then set out with Nell still distractedly murmuring her lines.

When they arrived at the theatre, there was a buzz of excitement. The king's mistress, Lady Castlemaine, had come to the theatre to bribe Mrs. Corey, who had the part of the plotting busybody, Sempronia, to act her part in imitation of Lady Elizabeth Harvey.

Mrs. Corey, full of her new importance, was describing her shock at the appearance of the king's red-haired mistress. "I vow I had never thought to see her so near at hand." She turned to accept a flagon of water from one of the younger actresses and then resumed. "She complimented me excessively on my talents and vowed that there was no one else whose skill she would trust in this role."

There was a snort from one of the apprentices, and Mrs. Corey paused in her narration to give him a furious, quelling glance.

"Of course I promised to accommodate Lady Castlemaine."

Nell whispered to Anna-Maria. "Who is Lady Elizabeth Harvey?"

Anna-Maria, familiar with the workings of the court, whispered back, "Her husband, Sir Daniel Harvey, was recently sent as ambassador to Constantinople. Lady Elizabeth is an old enemy of Castlemaine's."

"As am I," Nell said under her breath. She was furiously jealous of Lady Castlemaine, who had held the king's chief interest and love ever since his succession to the throne.

Anna-Maria squeezed Nell's hand sympathetically. "Perhaps the King loves *you* because you have no spite in you. He'll be furious because Castlemaine is using the stage to vent her private quarrels."

On the day of the first performance of *Catiline*, Anna-Maria was as apprehensive as the rest of the company. She stood in the wings as Nell, bravely costumed as an Amazon, strode confidently onto the stage. Nell was attired in a crested helmet set on her chestnut curls and a belted tunic that was cut short above her bare knees. There was an audible response from the pits when Nell strode out, and she had to stand still for a moment before the audience quieted. Bared breasts were no novelty in Restoration England, but it was a rare treat to see beautiful legs displayed as Nell's were now.

Nell stood for a moment, her torso thrust provocatively forward, her head held high, and then swung into her speech. It was a speech perfectly written for Nell's irreverent, impudent humor, a bantering speech destined to put the audience into a receptive mood. Standing taut and slim, Nell made fun of both the play and the playwright. There was a quiver full of arrows slung over Nell's shoulder, and Anna-Maria, fascinated, watched the stillness of the arrows as they rose quietly with the rise and fall of Nell's breath. Nell wasn't nervous at all. She was enjoying herself!

When Anna-Maria had to go on stage, she tried to convince herself that she was as carelessly at home as Nell, but she could never entirely lose her self-consciousness.

Relieved that she had a moment's respite, she stood in the wings as Circiro, on stage, was asked, "What shall you do with Sempronia?" Mrs. Corey had been doing a wickedly accurate imitation of Elizabeth Harvey, and it was clear to all who Sempronia represented. Then she heard a clear, piercing voice from the audience call, "Send her to Constantinople!" Anna-Maria and the rest of the actors in the wings peeked out to see Lady Castlemaine standing proudly in her box.

Bedlam arose in the theatre. Lady Elizabeth Harvey had risen in her own box and was shouting back at Lady Castlemaine. The king, his mouth twitching under his black mustache, had risen to quell the riot, and the gallants in the pits had gone mad, pelting oranges onto the stage and praising Mrs. Corey for her perfect imitation of Lady Elizabeth.

The scene reminded Anna-Maria acutely of the time that Buckingham and Killigrew had disrupted the performance by fighting in this same theatre, and she turned and fled. No matter that the performance might resume in a minute, that she might be wanted on stage —she must be out of this place!

In her haste she stumbled over a coil of wire and would have fallen had not strong arms caught her up.

Breathless, a little bewildered, she looked up and found herself staring into Buckingham's bright blue eyes.

"Oh, Sweet Jesu!" Her breath caught on a sob. So abruptly had this happened, so unprepared was she for his appearance, that she could not collect her thoughts. His arms were like strong cords around her, his breath sweet on her face. Her senses reeled, and for a moment she wanted only to rest herself against his strong chest. She was like a child who has been crying through a nightmare, searching for her mother, and then finally finds herself at home, clasped against strong breasts. She wanted to say, "I've been so lonely for you," and for a moment she was tempted to drop her head against his chest and luxuriate in the sense of homecoming. Then pride steadied her.

She looked up at him. His eyes were very blue, deeply blue even in the dimness of the theatre, and they looked down at her tenderly. He said softly, "So it *was* you! Lately I've not been coming to the theatre, but last night I thought—"

Abruptly he broke off speaking, and his arms tightened around her. "What have you done to your lovely hair?"

Suddenly she was in tears. He *does* love me! she thought, and on a shaking breath she said, "I've dyed it." She scarcely knew what she was saying. She was only aware that his arms were around her again, his heart fast beating under her cheek. Oh, Blessed Virgin, forgive me. I have not been alive in the months since he last held me in his arms. This is life! The sweet closeness of him, his fast-beating pulse under my cheek, his strong arms.

It suddenly seemed impossible that she had moved through days and months without being near him. She had been in exile, and now she was home, and the familiarity of his touch was more real to her than any of her recent past. It all dropped away from her as though she had been another woman living in another time, and she raised her lips to his with a simple naturalness, as though she had been parted from him for only an hour.

"God's body!" Buckingham cursed, and then he

bent his lips, seeking hers. He had been in a raging hunger all these months, and it seemed now as though he could never satisfy it, not if he spent a lifetime tasting the delights of these red lips that quivered and responded to his.

She clung to him, curving her slender body into his, and for a long moment, time ceased to exist for either of them. This was right, this was natural, and this was all of living. Thought fled, everything fled except the eternity of their being together. He was the first to recover and remember the past and their surroundings. He pushed her a little away and asked tersely, "Where have you been?"

Anna-Maria swayed toward him, her eyes still closed. She had been here, she had always been here within the circle of his arms.

"Sweet?"

Her eyes were clouded, and it took a moment to focus. Then she saw him standing tall and angry above her. "I love you." It was the most natural sound in the world for her to make, and she breathed it out.

He held her at arm's length, his expression furious. "And you prove your love by hiding yourself from me for months? I was half mad with worry about you!"

She said dreamily, as though from a great distance, "You didn't care about me. You would not avenge me with Killigrew." At this moment it hardly seemed to matter. She had been starving for so long, and finally she was being fed. His face was inches above hers, his lean body was tantalizingly near. She didn't want to talk or think, merely to experience the closeness of him.

He heaved a sigh that was part exasperation and part longing. "Damn your eyes! You captivate me as no woman has ever done. You've enslaved me!" He swept her into his arms and looked down into her upturned face. "Where shall I take you?"

So long had she waited, and now his face was within reach of her fingertips. She put up a slim hand and touched his clenched jaw, loving his anger as she loved all of him. "To Nell's lodgings. I've been staying with her this past month. The King is angry with Lady Castlemaine and he will surely send for Nell tonight. We'll be alone."

Twenty-Six

In the darkness of the coach she lay in his arms, her face upturned to his, and watched eagerly for each moment when the torches from the street lit up his handsome features.

Buckingham's arms were possessively tight around her, but his jaw was still clenched in anger.

Abruptly he looked down and said, "What have you done to the shape of your face? Do you have plumpers in your cheeks?"

She nodded, feeling sudden jealousy. How did he know so much about the secret devices used by actresses? Perhaps he had once had one in keeping.

"Spit them out!"

Obediently, feeling like a beloved child, Anna-Maria worked her tongue to free the plumpers and then spit them into the duke's waiting palm. He shook his head and pressed his lips against her hair. "Darling, what am I to do with you?"

Anna-Maria tilted her face to his and said softly, "Why—love me."

"Can I help myself? You disappear and leave me wild with worry, you reappear on the London stage with your hair dyed this horrible color—and yet I love you!"

He began kissing her deeply, hungrily, and Anna-Maria pressed upward, thrusting her slim body deeper into his arms.

She was scarcely aware of the jolting of the coach and was surprised when Buckingham raised his head abruptly and pushed her a little away from him. "We are at Nell's lodgings."

Picking her up in his arms, he ran lightly up the

stairs, holding her easily. She buried her face in his neck and marveled that this was actually happening. So often she had descended these stairs, her heart heavy because she had thought never to see him again.

And now—now he was moving swiftly into Nell's bedroom, dropping her lightly onto the bed. "Light the candle!"

Anna-Maria reached over to the bedside table, groped for the candle, and lit it. She examined him by its flare. Wordlessly, she held up her arms, and uttering a small groan, he came to her. "Darling, I thought never to hold you again!"

Anna-Maria touched his hair gently and her voice was faint with wonder. "And I lay awake night after night in this very bed and longed for you."

"And yet you did not send for me." There was an edge of anger in his tone. His voice was muffled against her breast.

"My love, let's not reproach each other." Anna-Maria's mouth was already seeking his.

He teased her, brushing his lips gently against hers but withdrawing a little when she sought to increase the pressure. The light touch was maddening, inflaming. Anna-Maria caught her hands in the hair at the nape of his neck and forced his mouth more deeply against hers, and he gave a low laugh of triumph, knowing that she wanted him as badly as he wanted her.

In a moment his hands and lips were everywhere, on her face, her breasts, her slim throat. She began to ache with sheer joy, responding wildly to his caresses. If this night lasted a thousand years, she would not be able to get enough of the touch and taste of him.

Laughing breathlessly, they rose for a moment to pull off their clothing and then fell naked onto the bed, their limbs moving to intertwine in the old familiar way. Anna-Maria trailed kisses down Buckingham's chest.

"It was not just with my mind and my heart that I missed you—my body craved yours." She curved herself against his belly. "My stomach wanted the sweet fire of your touch, my breasts craved your caress." She moved his hand to cup one of her full white breasts.

He began sucking at her pink nipple. "There is no other woman like you."

Speechless suddenly, because they were both breathless with passion, they communicated with eyes and touch, and when he finally entered her, Anna-Maria cried aloud with pleasure.

If only she could be joined to him like this always! She feared the moment of consummation because she wanted the act of love to go on forever, but when it came, she almost fainted from the sweet intensity of it. Buckingham did not leave her, but only pulled her more tightly to him, and in a moment he resumed his caresses. They made love over and over, until the first pink streaks of dawn lit the window and they heard Nell stealing softly into the next room.

Anna-Maria gave Buckingham a soft kiss, then hastily pulled on a wrapper and went to meet Nell.

"Nell, Buckingham is with me. In the bedroom."

Nell paused in the act of removing her cloak and looked at Anna-Maria with happiness in her eyes. "Thank God. I feared this moment would never come, and if it had not, you would have died for lack of it."

"I know that now," Anna-Maria said simply. "I'll never leave him again."

She remembered suddenly that Nell had been with the king all night. "And you? Are you happy?"

Nell's face glowed and was answer enough. "Aye. But sleepy. I did not close my eyes all night long."

"Nor I." Anna-Maria and Nell both burst out laughing, their faces soft with the aftermath of lovemaking.

Nell gestured at the couch. "I'll finish the night there."

Anna-Maria started to protest that she and Buckingham should not be stealing Nell's bed, but then saw that Nell was perfectly content. She smiled at Nell gratefully and then went back and crawled into bed beside Buckingham. He was almost asleep, his chest rising and falling steadily, but he put out his arm instinctively to cradle her close. She fell asleep to the rhythm of his breathing, a contented smile curving her lips.

It was nearly noon when they awoke fully. Nell had already dressed and gone to a cook-shop, returning with steaming meat pies, buttered shrimp, and several flagons of wine.

Nell gave them a quick grin. "We've got a great deal to celebrate. You've found each other again and the king is angry with Lady Castlemaine and I'm high in his favor." She smiled at Anna-Maria. "You don't even have to worry about Tom Killigrew being angry because you left the theatre. The performance ended right after Lady Castlemaine began shouting and it never resumed."

They made a festivity of eating together, and Anna-Maria thought that food had never tasted so delicious, now that she was sharing it with Buckingham. Nell was full of lively chatter, sitting cross-legged on the couch, cramming a slice of steaming meat pie into her mouth as greedily as a street urchin. She never failed to amuse Buckingham, and Anna-Maria found herself watching him. When he was deeply amused, a whole series of indentations, like a fleet of dimples, appeared briefly at the left corner of his lips. She felt a rush of longing to kiss that spot, to press it with her lips until the dimples disappeared.

Nell, finished with the meat pie, began dipping into a dish of buttered shrimp. She sucked the butter from one slim finger, and then her face sobered. "What will you do now?"

Anna-Maria and Buckingham looked at each other wordlessly. She had never felt so close to anyone as she did at this moment. The world with its practicality was threatening to intrude upon them, but she knew it could not separate them.

She spoke to Buckingham rather than to Nell. "I will never leave you again."

The wordless look from his eyes was more poignant than any speech could have been. Anna-Maria thought, I am like a cloud scuttling across the sky, resting on the security of the sky's blueness. She was so entranced by the moment that Nell's crisply practical voice was like a dash of cold water.

"Will you remain on the stage?"

"No!" Buckingham said with the force of an explosion. Then he looked ashamed. "Sorry Nell, but I don't think it is the life for Anna-Maria."

Very quietly Anna-Maria said, "I will not return to Francis." She looked steadily at Buckingham, and the knowledge flashed between them that if she returned to Francis, he could demand his rights in the marital bed.

Buckingham dropped his head into his hands despairingly. "If only I were not married."

Nell leaned forward and poured more wine into his glass. "But you *are* married, and you'd best plan with that fact in mind."

Anna-Maria moved closer to Buckingham and took his hands between her own. "Could you not buy me a house where I could have the children with me?"

Buckingham drew his breath in sharply. "You would be willing to live openly with me as my mistress?" Incredulous joy flashed in his eyes and then was instantly dimmed. "But Anna-Maria, it would mean the total ruin of your reputation. You would be barred from court forever!"

Anna-Maria wrinkled her nose. "What do I care for life at court? My only interest in it is that you are there." She began to laugh suddenly, a peal of sheer merriment, and both Nell and Buckingham looked at her in bewilderment. "I was just thinking. When I left England, I vowed that I would live through no man, that I would be independent. And here I am, asking you to set me up as your mistress!" Her laughter softened a little, and she looked tenderly at Buckingham. "But you do not seem a man to me—"

"What!" Buckingham's outrage was comical, and Anna-Maria quickly put up her hand. "You are all men, my love. I meant only that you are so much more than that—my closest friend, my true husband. I feel no shame in doing anything that will allow me to be always at your side."

Buckingham reached out and stroked her hair, his brow knit in thought, his expression grave. "I will never let you go again. But we must plan carefully to insure your future. I would not have us make hasty decisions." With all his heart, he longed to protect this woman and cursed himself because he could not give her the ultimate protection of marriage.

His hand paused a moment in his stroking, and he looked at Anna-Maria's blond hair with distaste. "In the meantime, Nelly, please undo the ill work you've done on her hair. It used to be so beautiful, and you've ruined it. It even feels coarse to the touch."

"I'll die it back to its original color," Nell promised. "You'll never know it has been bleached."

Anna-Maria said softly, "I dislike your attitude. I would love you even if you were *bald*."

Buckingham wheeled abruptly and came to her, dropping to his knees. "And I will love you when you are an old woman with no teeth and fallen cheeks. Forgive me, my love. I distract myself with trivialities when my mind is really occupied with plans for our future."

Nell interrupted. "I'd best look to my own future. I'm due at the theatre right now." She left in a flurry of farewells, and Buckingham and Anna-Maria turned to each other and exchanged the kiss that they had been denying themselves for the past hour.

He spoke softly. "If you are quite certain that it is what you want, my darling, we will start looking for a suitable house for you tomorrow. In Pall Mall or—"

"Oh, no!" Anna-Maria moved protestingly in his arms. "I want nothing large or fashionable. Simply a house big enough for me and the children."

Buckingham's arms tightened around her. "Fortunately I'm a very rich man, my love, and if you are going to give up your reputation and your place at court to be my mistress, I will at least see that you suffer as little want as possible."

Anna-Maria sighed and nestled closer in his arms, her head resting on his strong shoulder. She had put her life into his hands, and she would not question any of his decisions.

The next day, Buckingham at her side, Anna-Maria once more emerged onto the streets of London as the countess of Shrewsbury. Nell had announced at the theatre that Giselle had received an urgent message from France and had returned at once.

Anna-Maria smiled at the duke as they rode in his carriage. "Do you think that the London stage has lost a great actress?"

"On the contrary," he said, grinning. "I saw you in but one performance, and I was tempted to throw a rotten orange and hiss you from the stage."

Anna-Maria swung a blow at him, and he ducked, laughing. He had heard of a suitable house in Pall Mall and was in high spirits.

It was a three-story brick mansion with a wide frontage and graceful windows. Anna-Maria sat in the coach for a moment looking at it and then stepped out with Buckingham's assistance. Just as her feet met the ground, she paused and gasped sharply. Sir John Talbot had just pulled his coach up next to theirs and was looking from Anna-Maria to Buckingham with narrowed, alert eyes. Of all the people to meet the first day she went out in London, he was the one she would have feared most.

Talbot, his dark head twisted as he leaned out of the coach window, called softly, "Well, madame. I confess I am amazed to meet you thus. Your husband tells me he has no knowledge of your whereabouts." He raked Buckingham with a glance and then said coolly, "No doubt he should have applied to the duke of Buckingham if he wished your address."

Buckingham, his face darkening, stepped forward in a threatening manner, and Talbot quickly withdrew his head and tapped with the head of his cane on the roof of the coach, urging his coachman to whip up the horses. He had no wish for a hand-to-hand quarrel with the hot-tempered duke. His lips curled in an unpleasant smile. He had at hand a far more satisfactory method of evening his scores with the duke of Buckingham.

Anna-Maria began to shiver, and Buckingham looked down at her with concern. "What's amiss, darling? True, Talbot will hotfoot it to your husband with the news, but we would have had to face him sooner or later."

Anna-Maria nodded miserably. "I know that. It's just because he is such an enemy to you. And he has never liked me overmuch. Alone we might have reasoned with Francis, but I fear that Talbot will stir his anger, will make him cause difficulties for us."

Buckingham's head was thrown back. He looked very tall and very strong as he demanded, "And don't you trust me to protect you no matter what befalls you?"

Anna-Maria looked at him and said, with the intensity of one making a vow, "My life, my soul, my heart are all in your keeping." She put her hand into his, and they walked toward the house.

Neither of them, however, could really concentrate on their inspection of it, and they told the owner they would come back the next day. Returning to Nell's rooms, they had a few hours of lovemaking while Nell was at the theatre, and then Buckingham took his departure so that Nell could sleep in her own bed.

The next morning Buckingham was back, awakening them before daybreak, his face dark with fury. "Your husband has sent me a challenge!"

"Oh, dear God! No!" Anna-Maria's hand clutched at the frill of lace at her throat. "Francis would not even challenge Killigrew when he raped me. It is not possible."

Buckingham's face was like a thundercloud. "It was Talbot's doing. I'm certain of it. He goaded Shrewsbury into making this challenge."

Anna-Maria grasped the back of a chair for support, feeling the room reel around her. Nell sprang instantly to her side and looked uncomprehendingly from Buckingham to Anna-Maria. She had gone to a tavern after the theatre, and her eyes were still heavy with sleep, her wits befuddled.

"But how will John Talbot benefit from such a duel?" Nell asked. "You are far the better swordsman.

Francis will be killed, and Talbot will gain nothing."

Between clenched teeth, Buckingham said, "The challenge is for a duel fought in the French fashion. Talbot is to be Shrewsbury's second and the third is to be Bernard Howard, the eighth son of the lord of Arundel. Talbot is certain that one of their swords will find a resting place in my belly."

Anna-Maria caught her breath sharply, then began to cry wildly, helplessly. Duels fought in the French fashion were cruel, barbaric affairs, a wild melee with three men on each side hacking at each other. If all three on Francis's side concentrated on fighting Buckingham, he would undoubtedly receive a fatal sword thrust. Tears streaming down her face, she murmured brokenly, "This is my punishment—"

Buckingham shook her shoulders lightly, sending her loose hair streaming down her back. "My darling, this has little to do with you and I loving each other. Talbot merely saw his chance and seized it."

Anna-Maria's eyes were wide and dark, staring at imagined horror. "You'll be killed—"

Buckingham's voice was as brisk as a dash of cold water. "Anna-Maria, I will not be killed! Tell her, Nell, that I'm considered the best swordsman in all of England."

"That's true." Nell's voice was unconvincing. She did not see how even Buckingham could go unharmed when fighting three determined swordsmen at one time. As though reading her thoughts, Buckingham said quickly, "Don't forget that I, too, will have two others on my side."

"Choose them well." Nell warned. "This is no time for friendship to affect your choices. You need the finest swordsmen."

Anna-Maria began to tremble. Only two days ago she had sat in this room eating buttered shrimp and listening to Nell and Buckingham trading witticisms, and now they were discussing the duel that would certainly lead to his death. Nell was pacing the room, calling off names to Buckingham as they occurred to her, her brow knitted, her face a study in concentration.

Suddenly Anna-Maria felt vastly ashamed of herself. Nell was so much more of a woman than she, so quick to rise to a challenge. She drew a deep, steadying breath and willed her tears to stop. Tears could not save Buckingham's life. What she needed now was a clear head and courage.

Forcing a smile to her shaking lips, she touched his hand gently. "Tell me how I can best help, my love."

He bent and kissed her. "This is man's work, my sweet. You can do nothing except have confidence in me."

Anna-Maria went to pour wine for him and managed to steady her shaking hands enough so that she spilled only a few drops. I will go to Francis, she thought, and humble myself before him. Beg him to call off this duel.

As she handed Buckingham the brimming glass, she suddenly became furiously angry at Francis. If he was willing to fight Buckingham, then why had he been unwilling to fight Killigrew when she cried out for an avenger?

She stood numbly, tasting hatred like bile in her mouth, while Nell and Buckingham talked calmly. When they paused for a moment, she asked quietly, "When will the duel take place?"

"A week hence." Buckingham took a large swallow of the wine. "Such an elaborate duel takes time to prepare."

Anna-Maria said swiftly, "There will *be* no duel. I'll go to Francis and convince him that this is madness."

For the first time in their lives together, there was coldness in Buckingham's eyes as he looked at Anna-Maria. His voice was like chips of ice falling from a block. "Anna-Maria, I did not think there was anything in this world that could make me stop loving you. But if you attempt to go to Francis, if you rob me of my honor, I will have no love left for you."

Silence fell over the room. Nell stood quietly by, her mouth a little open, as Anna-Maria and Buckingham measured each other with a long look. Anna-Maria felt chilled.

Finally she smiled, a wry twist to her lips. "It's an odd choice, my love. I am to lose you in either case. If I do *not* stop this duel you will be killed, and if I *do* stop it, you will withdraw your love."

Buckingham made no move to touch her. "If I die, at least I will die loving you, with my manhood and my honor intact." His eyes were searching hers, weighing and measuring, and she knew that this was the most difficult test of their life together. Her eyes met his for a long moment, and then she nodded, accepting. He studied her for a moment longer, then he took her in his arms and gave her a kiss in which respect was mingled with passion.

Anna-Maria's lips clung to his, and she wound her arms around him with passionate intensity. Then giving a shaky little laugh, she pulled away slightly. "And now may I make a foolish, feminine request?"

Buckingham grinned. "Of course, darling. I never asked that you be a man—God forbid!—only that you allow me to be one."

"Then"—Anna-Maria fought to keep her voice from trembling—"will you spend every possible moment with me this next week?" Silently, inside herself she was crying: let me have every precious second with you before you are put into the cold ground away from my sight.

Buckingham reached out for her again as Nell spoke. "There is no time for you to find a place together. I'll move into Anne Wallace's lodgings, and this can be your home for the next week."

Anna-Maria and Buckingham both turned toward her with glances of fervent gratitude, and she grinned. "And after the duel, you two can find the finest house in all of London, and I expect to always be a welcome guest."

"Oh, Nelly!" Anna-Maria began to laugh and cry at the same time. "You always make me believe that nothing bad can really happen."

Buckingham poured wine into three glasses and began making a series of toasts. "To Nelly, the finest friend anyone ever had! To the duel! To long lives for all of us!"

Anna-Maria watched the strong column of his throat as the wine slid down it and thought: When I am a very old lady, I'll remember this moment, remember his lean face, his reckless gaiety, his gentleness.

Twenty-Seven

It was not fair! They had been separated for so long, and now that she finally lay in his arms again, it was spoiled by the knowledge that he might be dead at the end of the week. Night after night she lay with him in Nell's bed, all her senses straining to capture him utterly, to make him part of herself so that she could have him for all time. There was no part of him that did not stir her, no surface on his body, no intonation of his voice, no expression that crossed his handsome features.

One night, as he was murmuring to her in his deep, caressing tones, she said suddenly, "I'd like to be able to kiss your voice. It's like rich honey."

He laughed, then pulled her closer into his arms. She protested, "I'm serious. I've kissed every inch of you, tried to make it mine, but I've never kissed your voice."

He parted her delicate red lips with his strong, sensitive mouth and blew his breath down her throat, saying as he did it, "I love you!"

She sucked in his breath hungrily, straining her lips against his.

"Satisfied?" He moved his lips a little away and looked down on her tenderly, his face etched by candlelight.

"Yes." Then Anna-Maria made a little sound that was both a laugh and a cry and wailed, "No! I am never satisfied. I can never get enough of you. Oh, darling, do you think I am greedy?"

Buckingham laughed with rich delight. "I adore your

greed! Don't you know that I have the same desire to absorb you entirely? That when I am away from you I ache with emptiness and my mind keeps returning to the hours we have spent in each other's arms?"

Anna-Maria turned on her side, pulling Buckingham with her, and then stretched her body so that they were lying fully touching, from their toes to the tip of her head, which nestled under his chin. She reached up and clasped their hands over their heads so that their inner arms were meeting, the soft flesh touching and whispered, "Pretend that our skins are melting wherever we touch and that we are flowing into each other. . . ."

Buckingham laughed softly. "I know an even better method for becoming closer." He turned her on her back, a smile playing about his lips, and when she nodded eagerly, he entered her, finding her fully ready. She matched her movements to his, feeling as though her body were weightless, all liquid fire leaping to the touch of a tinder. Yet when it was over and they were lying pressed together, their heavy breathing gradually easing, she began to sob.

"It is not enough! I want to be with you always, be with you wherever you go." She wanted, and she knew it now, to follow him into death if need be and be buried in a mutual grave.

Her tears stopped suddenly as a thought was born. She stole a glance at him from under her lashes. His eyes were closed, his features soft with the aftermath of lovemaking, and she knew that in this mood he could refuse her nothing. Still, lest the lovemaking not be enough, she drove another nail into her argument. Slowly, studying his face in the candlelight, she said, "Remember the day you made me promise not to go to Francis to stop the duel?"

He nodded without opening his eyes, but a look of distaste crossed his sensitive features, and she winced. He was the most tender of men, and when his rare anger flared at her, she almost died, fearing the loss of his love, fearing the loss of life itself. Yet she persisted. "It was a difficult promise for me to make, and yet I gave it to you."

He nodded again, and this time he opened his eyes, looking at her gravely. She breathed a sigh of relief. She could always rely on his fairness, his blessed fairness that was as much a part of his character as his statesmanship or his quick wit.

"Now I am going to ask a difficult promise of *you*." His eyes were very blue in the candlelight, and she looked deeply into them, drawing in her breath with difficulty. "I want you to promise to allow me to come to the duel with you."

He began to sit up in quick protest, but she checked his movement by placing her hand against his chest. "Hear me out. Think what it will be like for me waiting at home for news of the result to be brought to me, knowing that this duel is largely my fault." The muscles under her hand rippled, and she held up her hand, forestalling his speaking.

"Perhaps it is not *my* fault—that what you believe is true. That John Talbot has merely seized an opportunity to rid himself of you. But whatever the reasons for the duel"—she was speaking very slowly now, looking deep into his eyes—"the truth is that it will be *my* husband and *my* lover who are the chief opponents. I cannot wait at home to hear which of you has died."

"I could not wait myself," he said slowly, "to learn whether *you* had lived or died. You must teach me, my love. I have certain expectations for a woman—this is her place—and this. I was not raised to know how to love a woman fully, to allow her to have feelings and imagination and needs just as a man does, but my love for you is opening my eyes. You are not merely a pretty object that I can command, 'Wait until I return.' You are part of my bones and my being, my thinking."

He raised himself up on his elbow and looked at her seriously. "We are no longer separate, my love. I, Buckingham, the male, and you Anna-Maria, the female. Between us we have created an entirely different and beautiful thing—*us*—an indivisible being. If I die during that duel, you will die as well, I know that. You have as much right to be present at our end as I do." He paused and then reached up and with a tender finger traced the outline of her oval face. "A while ago you wished that our skins would melt and allow us to merge into each other. It's happened, my love."

Anna-Maria let out her breath on a sigh. "Each minute I think that no one has ever loved as we do. I think 'I cannot love him any more than I do at this moment.' And the next second I find myself loving you more."

Although she tried to grab at each minute and capture it, the moments of the next week flew by. Buckingham went about the preparations for the duel with calm precision. He had chosen two professional fighting men as his seconds, Sir Robert Holmes, a sailor, and Lieutenant William Jenkins, a soldier who claimed to be an ex-fencing master. Buckingham told Anna-Maria, with satisfaction, "They are aware that Talbot has set it up so that everyone on your husband's side will be trying to kill me, and they are prepared to thwart their efforts."

He seemed exhilarated at the prospect of the duel, and Anna-Maria had to grit her teeth to keep from screaming at him. She had not forgotten the first duel that had been fought over her, the spilling of bright blood into the green grass, and she felt increasingly heavy of heart as the day of the duel grew closer.

On the night before the duel, she and Buckingham lay in each other's arms in Nell's lodgings, and Anna-Maria was prey to such conflicting emotions that she grew ill under the strain. She wanted his kisses, wanted his embraces, and wanted them the more fiercely because she knew this might be their last night together. But if she sapped his strength with her embraces, he might be heavy-eyed with sleepiness tomorrow and might die because of the kiss she was giving him now.

She began to cry, wildly, helplessly and finally choked out, "You must sleep, my love." Buckingham, finding her leaden and unresponsive, finally turned on his side and slept.

Anna-Maria left the candle lit and lay sleepless until just before dawn. Then she rose and began putting on the page's costume that Nell had brought her from the theatre. It was deep hunter's green with tight breeches that outlined her long slender legs, a leather jerkin, and a small cap under which she hid her long hair.

When she was fully dressed, she leaned over Buckingham and marveled at how deeply he slept. Her stomach was clenched with fear, her heart heavy, but he, who might die this morning, lay sleeping peacefully. For a moment she had an impulse to let him sleep on, to ignore the duel as though she knew nothing of it and thus buy him another day of life. But then she checked herself. He would be dishonored if she did such a thing, and his love for her would be marred by it.

Reluctantly she reached out and shook his shoulder. "My love, it is time to awake."

He woke fully and instantly and grinned at her, surveying her from head to toe, a smile playing about his lips. "What a charming lad you make."

Anna-Maria blushed and then hesitantly touched her breasts, flattened by the leather of the jerkin. "Is the disguise good enough? Will anybody know?"

His gaze became more critical. After a moment he shook his head. "I think not. But do not let anyone see your face too closely."

He threw back the muslin sheets and leaped from the bed, his strong legs vigorous in their movements. Anna-Maria felt tears prick her eyelids, and she swallowed rapidly, not wanting to disgrace herself by crying.

Buckingham seemed in high spirits as he hastily pulled on his clothes, but occasionally he slanted a glance in Anna-Maria's direction, and his face sobered. When he was dressed, he put a gentle finger under her chin and tilted her face toward his. "Are you still certain that you want to go? I will not forbid it, but I don't think it is wise for you."

She nodded her head stubbornly, not trusting her voice if she tried to speak.

Buckingham looked deep into her eyes for a moment and then nodded reluctantly. "Very well. But we had best hurry. We must be at Barn Elms before dawn."

The stableboy had the horses already waiting; they were blowing frostily from their nostrils in the pre-dawn chill. There was a thick mist, and Anna-Maria was grateful for it because it meant she had to concentrate all her attention on keeping her horse in view of Buckingham's, leaving her no time for fears. They rode steadily and rapidly, and then, as they neared Barn Elms, Anna-Maria found herself thinking of Francis. She had felt only a black rage toward him, a sick anger that he had dared to jeopardize Buckingham's life, and many times during the past week she had come close to wishing him dead. Now she suddenly remembered the day of their wedding ceremony when she had thought him the best and kindest of men, and tears filled her eyes. She did not wish him dead, she wished death for no one! Guilt assaulted her. She had promised before God to love Francis and be at his side for the rest of her life, and yet now she rode toward this duel at the side of his enemy! It was true that Francis was ill with ambition, that he had used her to further his own ends, and yet, perhaps if she had loved him more . . .

"Buckingham!" Her sweet, carrying voice pierced the chill mist, and he reined his horse to a standstill and waited for her.

When she reached him, she turned her face toward him and said softly, "My love, I flinch from the thought of Francis dying at your hand. He is my husband in the sight of God, the father of my children." She broke off, and her anxious eyes searched his face, mutely begging for understanding.

He said slowly, "I've been giving much thought to that, knowing that if your husband dies at the hands of your lover, it will stain your conscience forever." He reached over and cupped her chin in his hand and said, "I promise you. If it is humanly possible, I will spare his life."

The moment was too intense for Anna-Maria to

speak. She merely looked at him wordlessly with gratitude and love in her eyes, and then they rode on in silence.

Soft, muffled sounds of tied, restless horses reached
them as they neared Barn Elms, and a moment later
Anna-Maria heard low male whispers piercing the pre-
dawn air. The time had come. She threw Buckingham
an anguished look, but he was staring ahead, his
imagination already leaping ahead to the moment of
the duel.

Six men were in the field, and Anna-Maria strained
to identify them. There was Francis in close conference
with John Talbot, both men striding impatiently back
and forth across the damp grass. The man approaching them must be Bernard Howard, a distant
kin to Francis, who was reputed to be a skilled swordsman.

The other two men in the field raised their hands in
greeting and came rapidly toward them as they recognized Buckingham. Tersely, under his breath, Buckingham named them for Anna-Maria. "Sir Robert
Holmes on the left and Lieutenant William Jenkins
is the burly one; the other is a surgeon."

Anna-Maria knew that Jenkins and Holmes were
professional fighting men and the best that Buckingham could have chosen to fight on his side this day.
Their faces were grave, somber, and Anna-Maria bit
her lips to force back a scream. There were only
minutes left now, and there were so many things she
wanted to say to Buckingham, so many words of love
that she wanted to pour out! She could not even kiss
him one more time because Holmes and Jenkins were
beside them now and had merely given her a careless
glance, accepting her as Buckingham's page. She sat
perfectly still on her horse, her hands numb on the
reins until Buckingham gave her a warning glance
and curt instructions to hold his horse's head. Wood-
enly, disbelieving that the moment had really come,
she slipped down from the saddle and obediently held
the horse, her face turned away from Holmes and
Jenkins.

Their voices were keyed up with tension, but Anna-

Maria scarcely heard them. Her attention was fixed on Buckingham's legs as he slipped from his horse and landed lightly beside her. Last night, so many nights, those strong legs had clasped her in a tight embrace, and soon they might be stilled for all eternity. She buried her face in the horse's neck, feeling his warm breath in her ear and began to pray, rapidly, almost mindlessly.

She raised her head and caught Buckingham's eye, and they looked at each other for a long, wordless moment. She raised her hand in a pitiful little gesture, as though to reach out and stroke his face one last time, but then she dropped her hand hopelessly and merely looked at him, her face drained of blood. His eyes were grave, sending her messages of love and reassurance, and then abruptly he turned away and strode across the grass with Jenkins and Holmes at his side.

She wanted to scream and run after him, but she forced herself to stand still, winding her hand deeper into the horses' bridles. White-faced, shaking, slender in her page's costume, she stood holding the heads of the horses while the six men faced each other in the center of the field.

It was barbaric. Inhuman. Living men planning to end each other's lives.

Buckingham and Francis were facing each other, their faces tense, their swords at the ready. Jenkins, by Buckingham's side, was warily watching his opponent, Bernard Howard, and beyond them Holmes faced Sir John Talbot, the instigator of the duel. Anna-Maria spared a fleeting thought to wonder that Talbot had not placed himself nearer to Buckingham since he sought to kill him, but then she reflected bitterly that Talbot was no doubt a coward and feared Buckingham's flashing sword.

A scream broke from her throat, and she began shuddering uncontrollably. The fight had begun, and it was a wild, hacking melee. The clash of blades rent the air, along with grunts and muted cries from the antagonists.

Francis, his graying hair disheveled, his face already

slick with sweat, was searching wildly for an opening in Buckingham's guard. As Anna-Maria watched, her hand at her throat, he suddenly found it, and his sword pierced Buckingham's shoulder, drawing a quick spurt of blood. Anna-Maria screamed, a piercing cry from the heart, and then, fearful of distracting Buckingham, she bit her lips and forced herself to silence.

Buckingham was still on his feet, his shirt streaked with blood, his mouth twisted in a grimace of pain. He lunged so swiftly that Anna-Maria could scarcely follow the motion, his sword catching Francis in the right breast and cutting upward to the shoulder.

Francis, his face suddenly drained white, fell back, clapping his hand to his wounded chest. Instantly redness began to seep through his outspread fingers. Anna-Maria was crying freely now, her vision blurred by the fast-falling tears.

As she strained to watch, Buckingham turned to aid Jenkins, who was fighting by his side, but before he could be of service, Howard ripped Jenkins open with a quick thrust of his blade. At the sight of Jenkins's blood arching in a bright stream onto the grass, Anna-Maria bent double and began to retch helplessly. When the spasm passed, she raised her head and found that Francis was being carried off the field, the surgeon at his side, and Buckingham was coming toward her with a somber look in his brilliant blue eyes.

"Oh, God! Is he dead?" Anna-Maria could barely frame the question.

Buckingham shook his head. "I thrust upward into his shoulder, missing his heart. But this was a bad day's business, my sweet. Holmes took only a cut on the hand, but poor Jenkins is dead."

Anna-Maria no longer heard him. She was staring in horror at the blood that was still spurting from his shoulder, soaking his white sleeve. "You're badly hurt!"

Buckingham, wincing a little, clapped his hand against the wound and forced a laugh. " 'Tis only a scratch."

Anna-Maria began sobbing helplessly, the sight of Buckingham's blood completely unnerving her. How fragile life was—how easily it could spill from flesh on this peaceful English morning!

"Here now, darling." Buckingham reached out for her and then checked himself, darting a quick look around the field. It would seem odd indeed if he suddenly seized his pageboy in his arms, but the others were already in the copse of trees, lifting Francis onto his horse.

He turned and took her into his arms. Her body was shaking with sobs, and she breathed with difficulty, as though she were choking. A quick look of worry passed over Buckingham's face. He must have been mad to let a fragile, highly born female like Anna-Maria witness this morning's barbarism. Lifting her into his arms, he carried her into the nearby barn and gently laid her on the sweet-smelling hay, wanting to get her away from the sight of the blood-stained field.

She lay with her limbs sprawled, as though lifeless. Tossing his sword aside, he lay beside her and began to caress her in an attempt to quiet her sobs. "My love, my sweet, 'tis done now."

At his touch she stirred slightly and opened her eyes. It seemed a miracle to see him bent above her, to know that the blood still pounded in his veins, giving a flush of health to his face. In wonderment, she reached up and began stroking his face, her fingertips grazing his eyelids, the curve of his mouth. She had thought to lose him, and yet he still lived!

He bent and kissed her, a long deep kiss, and she strained toward him, her senses heightened by the danger that they had just passed through. How sweet was the taste of his breath in her mouth, how delicious the way his limbs molded to hers. She sighed deeply as he moved on top of her, pressing her into the sweet-smelling hay. She pulled impatiently at the leather jerkin that covered her breasts, keeping them from his eager touch.

He laughed softly and moved swiftly to help her, and in a moment her breasts sprang free, covered only by the thin gauze of the shirt she wore. "No boy was ever fashioned like this," he murmured, bending his head, his mouth molding the gauze to the rounded shape of her breast.

She arched up toward him and was frantic with impatience until he had taken her fully. The long sleepless night of worry and the horror of the duel had strained her nerves until she was a creature mindless with desire, needing the comfort of his arms to restore her to normalcy. A piercing sweetness consumed her at his touch, and she felt faint, the edges of her vision blurring, the only reality his strong shoulders heaving under her grasping hands. Suddenly he gave a long groan in which there was as much pain as passion, and she opened her eyes and looked at him in bewilderment.

"I'm sorry darling." There was a rueful twist to Buckingham's mouth, and his handsome features were contorted in pain.

Anna-Maria sat up abruptly, horrified. His shoulder wound was bleeding freely, a thick stream of blood staining them both. Buckingham's white shirt was saturated with it. Anna-Maria's delicate face turned deathly white. Lifting her hand, she stared at it in horror. It was covered with blood, her long fingers stained a dark red. Her eyes seemed to grow enormous in her face, and she burst into hysterical sobs.

Buckingham, bewildered by her sudden shift in mood, bent anxiously closer to her. Her eyes were blank with terror.

"The gypsy told me I would have blood on my hands." She began to laugh and cry at the same time. "Blood—I have sinned—the blood will seep into my soul—even hell will not burn it away." She fainted with the last word, and Buckingham looked down in consternation at the limp form in his arms.

Twenty-Eight

He bent over her, frantically shaking her. When her eyes finally opened, they were blank with shock, and then suddenly she began to moan, whipping her head from side to side so that her long hair went spilling across the hay. "No—I never willed death. Not even for Francis—though he hurt me." She put her hand to her mouth and bit on the knuckles, tears spilling from her eyes. "The gypsy—"

Buckingham shook her until her teeth clicked against each other. "Anna-Maria!" He must free her from her torment, or he feared for her sanity. "Francis is not dead! Nor am I! Our spilled blood is not of your doing."

Cradling her in his arms, his voice low and urgent, he repeated over and over, "We both live," until her sobs subsided a little and her eyes cleared.

She moaned softly, "I feel full of sin, as though I were choking on it. It fills my mouth, my nostrils—"

Buckingham's hands grasped her shoulders tightly, his fingers digging into her soft flesh. "You've had a shock. You cannot think clearly at this moment." He suddenly remembered the flask of brandy that he had in his saddlebag for emergencies and left her for a moment while he went to get it.

She sputtered when he poured the fiery liquid down her throat, but after a moment her head cleared, and she managed a feeble smile. "I felt as though I were back in that horrible, smelly caravan with the gypsy mouthing curses at me!"

She had long ago told Buckingham of her experience in the gypsy camp, and now his eyes were filled with understanding. "The gypsy was a foul-mouthed harridan," he said. "She had no skill in foretelling the fu-

249

ture. Your husband lives, Anna-Maria, and so do I."
To prove his point, he took her hand and put it over his
strongly beating heart.

She smiled, and her fingers moved tenderly against
his chest. "We'd best get help for your wound at
once."

Buckingham bent his head and used his teeth to
tear his sleeve from his shirt and then, with Anna-
Maria's help, checked the flow of blood and made a
sling for his arm. "This will serve until I reach a
surgeon."

As they walked out to the waiting horses, Anna-
Maria asked, "Where have they taken Francis?"

"To his home. His wound needs immediate attention, but I doubt that he is in any real danger."

Anna-Maria looked up at him, her face imploring
his understanding. "I must go to him. Nurse him until
he is completely well again. I *am* his wife and—"
Her voice trailed off, but Buckingham was smiling
down at her, nodding his agreement.

His brow knit, and his expression darkened as he
swung onto his horse. With Jenkins dead, this duel had
become a serious matter indeed. According to law, if
one man in a duel was slain, then all the other duelists
were considered guilty of murder. It was on his mind
to speak of the gravity of the situation, but then he
looked at Anna-Maria's pale, drawn face and checked
his tongue. They rode slowly but steadily, not wanting to aggravate Buckingham's wound, and the sun was
well up in the sky by the time they reached the cobblestoned streets of London.

Anna-Maria, anxious to see for herself that Francis
still lived, turned her horse in the direction of the
Strand, but Buckingham reached out and checked her
movements. "Darling, you cannot show up at your
husband's house dressed as a page, covered with blood.
We'll go to Nell's lodgings where you can bathe and
change. Then you can say that a rumor of the duel
reached your ears, and you have hastened to your husband's side."

When they reached the lodgings, Nell was already

there, pacing the floor. "God's body! I never knew hours to drag as they did while I waited for you to return."

Instantly she began to tear muslin into strips to make a fresh bandage for Buckingham's wounds. Deftly she pressed a clean dressing against his shoulder and then turned to Anna-Maria. "Get out of those rags. I'll pour you a hot bath."

Anna-Maria sank gratefully into the steaming tub, wincing a little because she ached in every limb. Buckingham and Nell conferred in low tones, and Anna-Maria, overhearing a word or two, sat up in the tub and called out sharply, "What are you talking about? Who must go into hiding?"

Buckingham stepped closer and looked down at her with pity in his eyes. "I must."

When she moaned, he added hastily, "But only for a short time. I'm certain that Charles will pardon me—"

Anna-Maria interrupted him. "The king pardon *you!* Why?"

Nell and Buckingham exchanged glances, and then Nell said crisply, as though the matter were of small importance, "All who took part in the duel are judged murderers. It needs the king's pardon to clear them."

Anna-Maria nodded slowly, "Because of Jenkins's death." She remembered vividly the moment when his bright blood had spurted onto the grass, and she began to shiver.

Buckingham knelt by the side of the tub, picked up a sponge, and began soaping Anna-Maria's naked shoulders. " 'Tis not so serious as it sounds, my darling. Isn't the king my best friend? And if I fail, there are Nell's charms to persuade him."

He looked up at Nell with a grin, urging her to help him lighten the moment. Nell, ever the actress, responded immediately, throwing Anna-Maria one of her impish grins and doing a pirouette. "If I cannot get so small a thing from the king as a pardon for Buckingham, I'll—" she snapped her fingers, calling for inspiration and then grinned—"I'll go to work in a bawdy house and announce to all and sundry that I've been the mistress of the king. I'll be a great draw."

Despite her heavy heart, Anna-Maria found herself laughing softly. Then she sobered. How could she laugh, for even a moment, on a morning when she had seen a man killed?

Buckingham picked up a thick, fleecy towel and helped her from the tub. "We must hasten."

Anna-Maria, naked under the towel, clung to him for a moment. "How will I live without seeing you?"

Buckingham grinned. "You'll see me. I'll wait outside your house every afternoon between the hours of two and three."

"But you'll be caught!"

Buckingham threw back his head in laughter. "I'll not be caught! I'm a master at disguises. Don't forget that the king and I once escaped across England with a price on our heads." The memory seemed to exhilarate him, and Anna-Maria, suddenly furious, realized that he actually enjoyed danger.

"You laugh while I worry myself sick about you!"

Buckingham placed a lingering kiss on Anna-Maria's trembling lips. "Till tomorrow, my love."

Holding back sobs, Anna-Maria watched him go, then turned to Nell. "I cannot bear to let him out of my sight! This morning I thought to lose him to death, and now he is taken from me by the charge of murder. Oh Nell, why can't he and I live and love quietly without all this danger and secrecy?"

" 'Tis a rare gift to love as you do," Nell said gently, "and such love carries an expensive price." She picked up Anna-Maria's dress and held it toward her. "Don't stay here and fret your bowels to strings. Go to Francis and nurse him, and you'll feel better for action."

Anna-Maria smiled through her tears, then got dressed. When she was ready, she let Nell drape the cloak about her shoulders. She gave Nell a quick kiss and asked, "May I borrow your coach? I'll send it back as soon as I've reached home." She paused and then smiled ruefully. "Home. The word now means *here* to me because Buckingham and I have loved here."

For so long Anna-Maria had been filled with anger

at the very thought of Francis; yet when she entered his bedroom and found him lying ashen-faced on the bed, all her anger dropped away from her, and she fell on her knees beside the bed, taking his cold hand in hers. "Francis, I'm here!"

He turned his head on the pillow and managed a slight smile, his eyes lighting with astonishment at the sight of her. He coughed weakly, bringing up foam flecked with blood. Anna-Maria looked up in panic at the black-suited surgeon who was standing at the head of the bed. "The sword pierced his lung, madam." The surgeon's voice was low and grave.

Anna-Maria's face whitened, and the surgeon hastened to reassure her. "I have no doubt that he will recover, but he will need skillful nursing."

Anna-Maria nodded and tightened her clasp on Francis's hand. "Tell me what must be done."

The surgeon drew her out into the hall and gave her careful instructions, which Anna-Maria memorized rapidly. Then she swiftly changed into an old gown and hurried back to Francis. He had been watching the door, eager for her return, and she went quickly to the side of the bed, feeling a pang of compassion for him.

He reached up and touched her hand. "Forgive me—" The effort brought on another spasm of coughing, and Anna-Maria flinched, fearing that he was jeopardizing his life.

"Hush, Francis, I'm your nurse now, and you must obey my commands." She managed a smile. "The first thing is that you must stop talking, or you will tire yourself."

Francis gave her a look of gratitude and then shut his eyes wearily. Anna-Maria moved quietly about the room, preparing fresh bandages, filling the pewter basin with clean water. There was a tap on the door, and then Sarah poked her blond head through the opening. She shot a look of approval at Anna-Maria and said, "I knew you would come!"

Anna-Maria put her fingers to her lips and gestured for silence. Satisfied that Francis slept peacefully, she slipped through the door and joined Sarah.

Sarah said quickly, "And what of Buckingham?"

"He received a wound in his shoulder, but he swears that it is only a scratch. Oh, Sarah! He will be charged with murder now, they all will, because Jenkins died on the field this morning."

Sarah's face clouded, and then she said, after a moment's thought, "The king will surely pardon him."

Anna-Maria nodded. "He is confident of it. But at the moment he is in hiding. Yet he says he will be outside this house every afternoon between the hours of two and three. Can you relieve me of my nursing duties while I go to meet him?"

Sarah squeezed Anna-Maria's hand. "Of course I will!"

"And will you watch by his bed for a few minutes now while I see the children?"

Sarah smiled, thinking of the children's delight at seeing Anna-Maria at home again, and then she slipped quietly through the door, leaving Anna-Maria free to run to the nursery.

The children were startled at her sudden appearance. "Are we not to visit you at Madame Gwyn's today?" Polly looked disappointed because she dearly loved the ride through the bustling streets of London and the odd shabbiness of Nell's lodgings.

Anna-Maria laughed and hugged her. "I'm going to be here for quite a while. That will be nice, won't it?"

Charles clamored his loud approval, John held up his arms, and Polly smiled after a moment's thought. "It *will* be nice," she admitted. "I like to have you home all the day long, not just see you for a visit."

Anna-Maria felt her heart grow heavy. It was unnatural to live apart from her children. Perhaps when Francis was better, they could leave off their quarreling and make sensible arrangements for their children's care.

Francis was still sleeping when Anna-Maria stole back into the room. Sarah was sitting quietly by his side, and she looked up when Anna-Maria entered. "His breathing is near normal, but I dislike his color."

Together they stood looking down at the bed. "What fools men are!" Anna-Maria whispered angrily. "Yesterday he was hale and hearty, and today he lies here wounded because of his temper."

" 'Twas more like Sir John Talbot's temper," Sarah whispered back. "Joseph is angry with Talbot, although normally he admires him and seems content in his employ." She pressed Anna-Maria's hand and said softly, "Joseph knows well how good you have been to me, and how I love you. He is angry at Talbot for your sake." As always when she spoke of her lover, her face softened and her eyes glowed.

Anna-Maria started to speak and then hesitated. She hated to ask Sarah and her lover to act as spies, and yet she felt goaded by her need to know if Buckingham was in further danger. "Sarah do you think that Talbot has further schemes against Buckingham? Has he—?" She broke off.

Sarah quickly shook her head. "I don't know. He's confided no plans to Joseph." She sighed angrily.

"God's blood. I hate this tangle of conflicts. Why can't people live in peace with one another?"

Anna-Maria looked down at Francis's sleeping form. "I must learn to forgive Francis—both for the duel and for his mistreatment of myself—or else we can never come to terms about how we will take care of the children." She put a gentle hand on Francis's damp forehead. "Francis is weak, but he has no real malice in him."

It was easy, in the days that followed, to be gentle with Francis. His eyes clung to her gratefully as she moved about the room tending him, and often he offered small words of apology for his conduct toward her. The mere fact of *acting* in a loving fashion toward him began to make Anna-Maria feel more kindly toward him. At times he almost seemed one of her children, so needful was he of her care.

The happiest moment of her day, though, was when she stole out of the house to meet Buckingham. Now it was his turn to come to her in disguise, as she had once done with him, and she was endlessly entertained by the wit and imagination he showed. He was invariably keyed up, enjoying the adventure, and it was almost with disappointment that he said to Anna-Maria one afternoon, "The king has relented toward me. He bids me meet him secretly at the duke of Albermarle's lodgings tonight, and I've no doubt but that he intends to pardon me."

"Thank God!" Anna-Maria clung to him, laying her head against his chest. "I've been so frightened. It's been nearly three weeks now, and I'd begun to think that his face was permanently turned against you."

Buckingham laughed, a deep, rich laugh. "Charles can scarcely forget all the boyhood adventures that we shared."

He put his hands on her shoulders and looked down on her upturned face. "When I am pardoned, your husband will automatically be pardoned, too. No doubt the news will speed his recovery."

Anna-Maria's face brightened. Often, when he was feverish, Francis had tossed and turned in the bed, groaning that his career lay in ruins because of the duel. The news would benefit him greatly.

That night, muffled in a dark cloak and disguised by a black periwig, Buckingham secretly met with the king and received his pardon.

When he brought Anna-Maria the news the following day, she cut short her time with him and rushed to Francis's bedside. It was hard to pull herself from Buckingham's enbrace, but the sooner Francis had the news the sooner he would recover and she and Buckingham could be with each other again.

Francis was just awakening from one of his short naps, and Anna-Maria sat on the side of the bed, her face glowing. "Francis, I've just received word that the duke of Buckingham has been pardoned for Jenkins's death!"

Francis sat up in bed excitedly. "Is it true?"

Anna-Maria nodded. "He is fully restored to his former honors. I've heard that he will be at court today as though nothing had happened."

The sudden exertion of sitting up had made Francis cough, but his eyes were bright with relief. "Then I am pardoned, too!"

"Yes. Oh, Francis, now you can stop fretting and concentrate on getting well."

There was a knock, and then the surgeon slid smoothly into the room. "And how are we today, madame?"

"*I* am well," Anna-Maria said with a certain asperity. "As for your patient, you must judge for yourself." She had come to dislike Dr. Lamount, the chief of the surgeons who attended Francis. His manner was too polished, his expression too grave, and Francis always seemed worse after his visits.

Dr. Lamount threw aside his black cloak and set about his daily routine, applying fresh plasters, drawing Francis's blood. As always, Anna-Maria winced and turned away during the bloodletting. Once she had protested to Sarah, "Why does the surgeon daily take more blood from Francis? 'Tis strange to me. Francis lost enough blood from his wound!" Sarah had shrugged. Bloodletting was considered a sovereign remedy for everything from fever to ill humors. Nevertheless, Anna-Maria noticed that Francis was always weaker after the surgeon's visits, and one day she had questioned his practice of bloodletting when the wound Francis had sustained had been so severe. Dr. Lamount had turned on her angrily, assuring her that he had had years of practicing his medical skills and that his judgment was superior to hers. Anna-Maria had bitten her tongue and remained silent.

When Dr. Lamount had gathered up his equipment and taken his leave, Anna-Maria looked after him and made a small moue of distaste. Francis was lying inert, his face nearly as white as the muslin sheets against which he rested. Anna-Maria propped up his head and poured a little of the restorative cordial, a thick reddish mixture, down his throat.

Francis coughed but swallowed as much of it as he could. He was eager now to be well again. Attempting a smile, he said, "The king's pardon has done me more good than any medicine, or any surgeon."

Anna-Maria touched his graying hair, which was damp with sweat. "Soon you'll be up and about again, and everyone at court will be delighted at your return."

Francis took her hand. "Anna-Maria, you've been so good to me, and I don't deserve your kindness. That night that I took you by force—" His words were broken off by a spasm of coughing that left him limp and breathless.

"Hush." Anna-Maria bent and kissed his damp, ashen cheek. "All that is in the past now. From now on, you and I will be better friends."

She sat often at Francis's bedside, his hand in hers, and they talked quietly. A few times she asked him to pray with her, and she felt as though a heavy burden were uncoiling from around her heart. They were both flawed human beings, Francis by his ambition and she by her illicit love, but underneath they were decent people who wanted to live honorably in the sight of God. "We must be kind to each other." She smiled at him tenderly and touched his cheek. She could never love him as she loved Buckingham, but there was no need for them to spend their lives trying to hurt each other.

One day when the tenderness was strong between them, she spoke to him, slowly and quietly, of her love for Buckingham. When she was done, she looked at him for a moment and then said softly, "I *must* live with him, Francis. When you are better, we will make good and decent arrangements for our lives."

There were tears in Francis's eyes, but his expression was steady. "Aye, Anna-Maria. I wronged you from the day I forced you to go to court, and I'm eager to make amends. I'll manage some way that you can live with the duke and have the children with you without damaging your reputation." For a moment he looked perplexed because it would not be easy to make such arrangements. Then his eyes closed in weariness, and he slipped into sleep.

Anna-Maria sat watching him sleep, her heart full of gratitude. How wonderful it was to be free of bitterness at last, to count Francis as a friend when for so long she had felt him an enemy.

She was still sitting by his side when Francis awakened, and he smiled gratefully at her. He began to speak slowly and regretfully of Sir John Talbot, confirming Buckingham's suspicions that Talbot had goaded Francis into the duel. "Talbot is an implacable enemy of Buckingham's and therefore of yours," he warned her. Anna-Maria leaned forward and stroked his head soothingly. "Talbot can do nothing to us without your aid."

Life seemed very sweet again, and during the long afternoons when Francis slept, she sat at his bedside and dreamed of the future. To live openly with Buckingham. To have the children by her side. To be friends with Francis . . .

The surgeons assured her daily that Francis was growing stronger. It was a great shock, therefore, when Francis, near the close of a long afternoon, suddenly rose up on one elbow with startled fear written clearly on his face.

"Anna-Maria!" As he choked out her name, a great gush of blood came rushing from his mouth. As Anna-Maria watched, horrified, it came pouring out in a bright, bubbling stream. Before she could move or think clearly, Francis fell back against the pillows, one hand clawing at the air, his eyes glazing.

Dry-eyed, incredulous, Anna-Maria sat with his lifeless hand in hers, and then she began screaming for the surgeon.

Twenty-Nine

"Murderess!" The news of Shrewsbury's death rocked London. He had been known to be recovering, and now he lay dead. It was common knowledge that the countess of Shrewsbury had sat by his bedside as he died. Rumors began flying. "Perhaps it was the hand of the countess that put him in his grave."

The night of Francis's death, Buckingham came, heavily cloaked and muffled, and demanded admittance to the house. Sarah, her eyes wide and strained in her pale face, flew to the door to learn the cause of the commotion and gasped when Buckingham pulled back his cloak enough to let her recognize his features. He spoke tersely. "Where is she?"

"In his room. His body has been taken away, but she sits staring at the bed. I cannot get her to move."

"Show me!"

Buckingham gave Sarah a small push to hasten her and then followed swiftly as she led the way to the bedroom. The chamber was in gloom, the candles were almost burned down. Anna-Maria sat perfectly still by the bedside like an image carved from stone.

She looked up without surprise when Buckingham burst into the room and said to him, "He died. As I watched—he died." Her voice was wondering, her pale blue gown was stained with Francis's blood.

Buckingham was at her side in an instant, pulling her to her feet and into his arms. She came unresponsively, and her flesh was cold to his touch. He spoke quickly over his shoulder to Sarah. "She's in a state of shock. Bring brandy and warm coverings. I'm taking her to her bedroom."

Sarah showed him the way to Anna-Maria's room and then rushed off for the things he had ordered. Buckingham rapidly stripped Anna-Maria of her blood-stained gown and then bundled her into the bed.

She moved unprotestingly, doing exactly as she was bid, her wide, dark eyes clinging to his face. From time to time she whispered dazedly, "He died," and she seemed to be imploring Buckingham for understanding.

She spluttered and coughed as Buckingham held the brandy to her lips, but she drank obediently. Then one of her hands crept over the bedcoverings and sought Buckingham's. "Why did he die? He was getting better."

"I don't know." Buckingham's tone was curt, his face dark with worry. The rumors had begun scarcely an hour after Francis's death, and Buckingham knew that both he and Anna-Maria were being accused of murder. In her present state, the mere whisper of the word might rob her of her reason.

He turned quickly to Sarah. "Can you keep the other servants out of the room?" When Sarah nodded, he said, "Then I'll spend the night here with her."

Sarah looked shocked, and Buckingham gave her a look of disgust. "Don't be a fool. I wish merely to watch over her. She belongs to me, and I will trust her to no other's care. Not even yours." He gave Sarah a steady glance. "You know what they are saying at Whitehall?"

Sarah gulped and nodded. "And not a word of it is true, as God is my judge," she whispered fiercely.

Buckingham said angrily. "Don't you think I know that! But it is not going to be easy to protect her—" He broke off, giving Anna-Maria a cautious glance. She was watching them quietly, looking from one to another as they spoke, but there was not even a flicker of curiosity on her face. Heaving a sigh of relief, he dismissed Sarah. "Sleep close by. I'll call you if I need you."

He turned to the bed where Anna-Maria lay quietly. Her hair was fanned out over the white pillows, her face very small and white. Yesterday they had stood in each other's arms at the bottom of the garden, watching the play of light over the water of the Thames, and they had both felt keen joy. Francis was recovering, he had promised to be their friend. The future had stretched out rosily before them. And now . . . Buckingham shook his head and busied himself by poking up the fire. This love of theirs was so sweet, so steady a flame, and yet it seemed always to cause Anna-Maria great pain from which he could not protect her.

"My love?" Anna-Maria's whisper pulled him back from his thoughts. She was leaning up on one elbow, her hand held out to him in entreaty. "Will you hold me? I'm so cold. . . ."

In a second Buckingham was on the bed beside her, cradling her in his arms. She nestled against him like a young child, and in a strained whisper sought to tell him of Francis's death. At first he tried to quiet her but then realized that she might find relief in the telling. "I could do nothing to help him. Nothing. It was all over in seconds. . . ." She repeated the tale again and again, her voice disbelieving.

Buckingham knew that after the shock passed, normal grief would follow. Gradually her sobs subsided, and her exhausted body drifted off into sleep. He held her, thinking of the rumors that were flying about Whitehall. This was dirty business indeed. His arms tightened about Anna-Maria protectively. He would demand that Shrewsbury's body be opened and examined by reputable physicians and give the lie to the sly whispers that branded Anna-Maria a murderess.

Shortly after dawn, while Anna-Maria still lay in a heavy sleep, he slipped from her side, roused Sarah and gave her quick instructions, then set out for Whitehall. The king was still in his closet when Buckingham strode in and asked for a private audience.

The king's face was grave as he studied Buckingham. "God's blood! Buckingham, do you know that you are now being accused of Shrewsbury's murder? Although rumor has it that it was actually the fair white hand of the countess that administered the poison."

Buckingham's hand swung up in a swift gesture as though he were going to strike the king, and Charles said quickly, "Calm yourself. I don't believe the rumors. In fact I spent the evening drafting a new pardon, one that clears you of Shrewsbury's death as well as Jenkins's." He nodded toward his writing table where a parchment scroll lay.

The dark scowl cleared from Buckingham's brow, and he clapped Charles on the shoulder. "Forgive me. This latest trouble has left me with a short temper and a murderous rage."

The king looked at him sympathetically, then strode around the room, snapping his fingers nervously.

Buckingham picked up the parchment scroll, examined it, and then said, "I think that the only way to lay to rest the rumors is to have Shrewsbury's body opened. I ask that you order one of your own surgeons to do it so that there can be no question of the results being falsified."

The king shot him a quick glance, realized that in Buckingham's eyes at least, it was no risk at all, and nodded in agreement. He himself had not thought that the gentle countess of Shrewsbury could be capable of murder.

"It shall be done this very afternoon. I'll command several eminent physicians to do so, and a few noblemen who have a reputation for honesty to witness it."

Buckingham gave Charles a hearty handclasp in gratitude and then rushed back to Anna-Maria, anxious to be there before she awakened. He was standing by her bedside when she finally opened her eyes. Her lids lifted lazily, and when she saw him there, she smiled with the same radiance that she had always shown at the sight of him. Then memory returned, and she sat up, giving a little wail. "Francis is dead!"

Instantly he was on his knees by the bed, gathering her into his arms.

He needed her permission to have Shrewsbury's body opened, and swiftly, hurriedly, in a low tone he asked it. She let out a shriek and clutched him more closely, swinging her head back and forth in vehement denial. "I could not bear it. He has suffered enough."

He soothed her, pointing out that Shrewsbury could no longer feel pain, and then, when she continued her frantic denials, he told her in a low voice why it was necessary to learn the reason for Shrewsbury's death.

Anna-Maria stared at him incredulously, her pulses pounding heavily, her head swimming. "They call me a *murderess?* They think that I killed him?"

All the color drained from her face, and she stared at him as though she had taken leave of her senses. "This must be a nightmare." If only she could turn back time to yesterday when Francis had been so full of friendship for her, full of such plans for the future. Only a day had passed, and yet life was once again dark and full of turmoil.

Buckingham already had a glass of brandy in his hand, and he pressed it on her, forcing the goblet against her shaking lips until she drank a little of it. "At first I had thought I could spare you the knowledge, but the rumors are flying so heavily throughout

London that the only way to lay them to rest is through the evidence to be found in Francis's body. Anna-Maria, you must have courage to face this!"

Anna-Maria's head came up swiftly at the challenge, and her breathing steadied. "Once they called me wanton when I was innocent, and I did not know how to fight them. This time I will fight! I will fight them for your dear sake, as well as my own."

"You're magnificent!" Buckingham's eyes were warm with approval as he looked at the courageous set of her shoulders and the firm tilt of her chin.

Tossing back the bedcovers, Anna-Maria climbed from the bed. She felt weary in every bone of her body and less ready to do battle than she ever had been in her life, but Buckingham's approval was sweet, and she would do much to keep that look in his eyes. She could manage, she thought, if she took one step at a time, not looking forward to the days ahead but merely concentrating on the matters at hand.

"I must bathe," she said slowly, "and then"—she flinched—"I must tell the children that their father is dead. Charles will scarcely understand and John not at all. But Polly—oh, dear Lord, Polly."

An hour later she held the sobbing child in her arms, brushing back the damp curls that surrounded Polly's forehead, and then she said softly, "Kneel with me. We will pray for him."

Polly looked up at her. "Do you think he will be happy in heaven?"

Anna-Maria choked back a convulsive sob, her arms tightening about the child. "Yes, dear, very happy."

Oh, God, was it at this very moment that the surgeons were cutting into Francis's body? She prayed frantically, trying to shut out the macabre images that were crowding into her mind. That still body, now at the mercy of the surgeons' knives had once contained the seeds that had given life to this child and to her brothers as well. Memories of Francis kept flooding into her mind—the way he had twirled his wineglass in his fingers and looked at her with longing on the day of their first meeting; Francis, triumphant on his horse, twirling his hat on the day he had told her the king was coming home; Francis studying papers from his black dispatch box.

When she could bear her thoughts no longer, she gave Polly into Sarah's keeping and walked down to the end of the garden. She stood there for nearly an hour, staring out over the Thames, trying to pray coherently, and was startled when she felt Buckingham's touch on her shoulder.

He was wearing an expression of baffled rage. Pulling a sheet of parchment from under his cloak he held it out to her wordlessly. Quickly she scanned the report, reading part of it aloud. "His heart had grown flaccid, his liver and entrails were discolored and decayed." The sheet fluttered in her fingers as she looked up in bewilderment at the duke. "What does it mean?"

Buckingham spoke between clenched teeth. "That the damned surgeons don't *know* why Francis died. I myself think that it was their ministrations that killed him."

Anna-Maria paled. "Then the rumors that I have murdered him will never cease."

Buckingham looked down at her. "I fear not."

She looked out over the water of the Thames for a moment, drew a long breath and then said, "It does not matter. Francis and God know that I am innocent. Let the others say what they will. I shall not let it harm me."

She handed the report back to Buckingham. It seemed cruel, indecent, to be reading about the state of Francis's organs after his death. "I must prepare for the funeral." She turned, the wind whipping her gown about her, and looked up at Buckingham. "I think we must part. I would not have the gossips saying you aided me in murdering my husband."

Buckingham reached out and grasped her by her slender waist, pulling her close. "We can never be parted. Whatever comes, we will face it together. My love for you is as steady and as permanent as the earth beneath our feet."

He shook her lightly. "Do you understand, Anna-Maria? My love for you is the foundation on which you must build your life!"

She leaned back against the strength of his arms and studied his face carefully. Then she nodded. It was as simple as he had said. They belonged together.

Suddenly she realized how much simpler it would be for them to be together now that Francis was dead, and guilt assailed her. Head bent, she pulled herself from his arms, murmuring, "I've much to do."

Buckingham walked back to the house with her and then gave her a quick kiss, promising to return in the evening.

Anna-Maria slipped in through the rear entrance and then stopped, shocked, as she recognized Sir John Talbot's voice coming from the front of the house. He and Sarah were arguing, Talbot's rough tones overriding Sarah's lighter voice. "I will take them with me at once! They cannot remain in the house of a murdering whore!"

Anna-Maria felt anger sweep over her. Francis was barely dead, and already John Talbot had come to pick the corpse clean. What was it that he wanted? Letters? Secret documents that Francis had had in his possession?

She rushed quickly through the house and emerged into the wide entrance hall where Sarah and Sir John were facing each other. Sarah's eyes were blazing, her whole body quivering with defiance. Talbot had a document in his hand and was slapping it angrily against his boot as he spoke. "I tell you I will have them out of here within the hour. Fetch them to me!"

Anna-Maria's cool voice broke in, startling them. "You wish something of my husband's, Sir John? It seems to me that you come in indecent haste."

Talbot whirled to face her, his gray eyes contemptuous. "I come not a minute too soon. I would be a criminal if I left Francis's children under your influence for another hour!"

The children! Anna-Maria fell back a pace, her face whitening. "What do you mean?"

Talbot held out the document he had been slapping against his boot. "Francis gave me guardianship of his daughter and sons."

Anna-Maria reached out and took the document with numbed fingers. Francis's crabbed, familiar signature was distinct below the formally worded order which put his children, Polly, Charles, and John, into the care of Sir John Talbot should Francis die.

The black ink blurred and jumped against the whiteness of the parchment, and she passed her hand across her dazed eyes. It wasn't possible! "Francis promised that he would let me have the children once he was better—he promised."

Sir John's mouth twisted in a snarl, and he nearly spat the words, "The ravings of a man dazed by fever, weakened because you were steadily poisoning him!" He reached out and took the document from Anna-Maria's unresisting fingers. "Madame, I demand that you turn the children over to me at once."

"No!" Anna-Maria came out of her daze with her eyes blazing, her head thrown back defiantly.

Sir John took a menacing step toward her and then checked himself, an unpleasant smile curling his lips. He strode to the heavy entrance door and threw it wide. "I think you have no means to resist me, madame." He nodded toward a group of his men-at-arms who were clustered outside the door.

Anna-Maria gasped. "You would take them by force?"

Sir John looked at her levelly, power in his glance. "If need be."

There was a long moment of silence. Anna-Maria was thinking of how frightened the children would be if there was a fight over physical possession of them. She could summon her own servants, but they were a bare handful compared to Sir John's force, and she doubted that they could lay their hands on weapons at a moment's notice. She had an instant image of the fight that would ensue, the clash of blades and the screams of the children as they were dragged struggling out of the house, and her heart sank.

Then her head went back defiantly. She was deathly pale, but she spoke quietly. "Very well. For the children's sake, I will not have bloodshed in this house.

But I warn you that your victory will be short-lived. I will go to the king, and he will demand that you return my children to me."

Sir John Talbot raked her with a scornful glance. "You do not have any claims at all to Polly. She is not your natural child. And the king is a man who abides by other's legal rights."

Anna-Maria stared at him. From the moment that Polly had run into her arms in the kitchen at Grafton Manor, she had felt that she was Polly's true mother. And Polly herself had forgotten that she had been born to another woman. Surely the king would understand that Polly would be miserable if she was taken from the only mother she had ever known.

Anna-Maria fought down her fear. She would deal with the legal aspects later. Now she must control herself and convince the children that they were about to pay a normal, happy visit to their relatives.

Through clenched teeth she said to Sir John, "Wait outside. I will not have you contaminating my home. I'll bring the children out to you as soon as they are dressed."

Talbot bowed mockingly and withdrew, and Sarah and Anna-Maria stared at each other. Anna-Maria said with ominous quietness, "I do not think I can bear this."

Tears were visible on Sarah's pink cheeks, but she steadied herself and said, "You *must* bear it. It will only be for a few hours, and then the king will demand their return. Above all we must see that the children are not frightened."

"Yes." Anna-Maria steadied herself against the panic that was rising up in her.

Slowly, moving as though she were ill, she began to mount the staircase, Sarah at her side. Sarah said angrily, "If Joseph knew about this and failed to warn me, I'll never forgive him."

Thirty

Half an hour later Anna-Maria lay crumpled on her bed, dissolved in tears. Never before had she known such emptiness, such desolation. Francis lay dead, his body waiting burial, and the children had been snatched from her arms. The house, which had once been overflowing with noise and laughter, now lay silent and barren around her.

She looked up as Sarah slipped through the door. When she noticed that Sarah was wearing her cloak, she wailed piteously, "Are you leaving me also?"

Sarah's heart contracted with pity, and she rushed to the bed and gathered Anna-Maria into her arms. "My poor sweet. I'll stay if you like, but I have an appointment with Joseph at The Golden Unicorn, and he may have knowledge of this business. He can tell us if the children are safe and well."

Anna-Maria sat up and clutched at Sarah's sleeve. "Then go to him quickly." As Sarah stood and straightened her cloak, Anna-Maria asked, "Have you sent word to Buckingham?"

"Aye. I sent one footman to his home and another to Whitehall. He'll come as soon as the message finds him."

Anna-Maria drew a deep, shuddering breath. "I need him so badly, Sarah."

"Nothing will keep him from you," Sarah said reassuringly. As Sarah left the room, Anna-Maria fell into another spasm of sobbing. How dare Talbot kidnap the children—she would see him hang for it! Then fresh terror broke over her. Talbot had seemed so certain that he had a legal right to take the children. Suppose Buckingham and the king could not aid her?

There was a nervous tap at the door, and then a maid entered, her eyes red-rimmed from weeping. "I would not disturb you, madame, but there is a man below who says he has a message about the children."

"The children!" Anna-Maria brushed past the maid and ran down the stairs, breathless when she reached the bottom. A giant of a man, his face half hidden under a dark stubble of beard, was striding impatiently in the hall, his boots scratching the shining parquet. He turned at her step and gave her a bold glance that traveled down her face and lingered on her breasts.

Startled, Anna-Maria stared at him, her hand going nervously to clutch her throat. Surely this brute of a man could not be in the service of anyone she knew.

"You have news of my children?" Her tone was disbelieving.

"Aye." He grinned, his moist lips framed by coarse black stubble. "There was an accident. A gentleman hailed me and gave me a fistful of coins to find a coach and bring ye this message." He thrust a folded sheet of paper at her. "Here ye be."

"An accident!" The words seemed to burn themselves into Anna-Maria's brain, and she unfolded the note with fingers that trembled, her heart beating so rapidly that it shook against her rib cage. She read the words and held back a scream. "My coach overturned in the street, and the children were injured. They are calling for you. Come at once. This man will bring you. Talbot."

Anna-Maria reeled and clung to the handrail for support. Her lips were shaking so, she could barely form the words. "How badly are they hurt?"

"I'm no doctor." The man spoke roughly, impatiently. "I'm to bring you to them."

"Yes. At once." Anna-Maria was unaware that tears were pouring unchecked down her cheeks. She gave no thought to leaving a message for Sarah or Buckingham. Her single impulse was to reach the children, and without pausing to snatch up a cloak, she ran through the front door. Images of Charles with his small limbs twisted and broken, and Polly with blood streaming down her face tortured her mind. And John. He was so fragile.

The man, startled by her swiftness, gave a low curse, snatched up the message that she had let fall to the floor, and then dove after her.

Sobbing, panting, Anna-Maria reached the coach, wrestled the door open, and scrambled inside. The curtains were drawn, and the interior of the coach was nearly black. Before she could accustom herself to the dimness, a blow struck the back of her head, and she plunged into total darkness.

When she came back to consciousness, she was lying on the gritty floor of the coach. Disbelievingly, she struggled to sit up and then fell back as tight bands of pain bit into her wrists and ankles.

A dry voice came out of the darkness, further terrifying her and setting her heart to hammering. "I would advise you to lie still, Lady Shrewsbury. You are securely bound, and any movement will only tighten the ropes and increase your discomfort."

It was Sir John Talbot's voice. Anna-Maria started to cry out and found that she was gagged with a foul-tasting cloth.

The voice came again, amused. "Yes, you are gagged as well. I find that a silent woman is a delightful creature."

Hatred filled Anna-Maria, yet she was tormented with worry about the children. She struggled desperately against the gag, but her cries were choked, and for a moment she felt as though she were suffocating.

Talbot sounded as though he were smiling in the darkness. "You see? Your struggles will only make you ill." He paused and then said smoothly, "But since I'm a humane man, I'll set your worst fears to rest. Your children are perfectly safe. It is only you who is in danger, my dear."

Dear God, thank you, Anna-Maria thought. I don't care what happens to me as long as the children are safe. A sudden jolting of the coach sent her head cracking against the floor, and she fainted.

She was having a nightmare. The children were in terrible danger, and she could not find them because of the evil black mist that enveloped her. She cried out piteously for Buckingham, but he too was lost in the mist. Whimpering angrily, she began turning her head from side to side, and then she swam up into consciousness and gasped as she felt human hair in contact with her cheek, greasy hair that stank. Panic overwhelmed her. She realized that she was still trussed and gagged and was slung over the burly shoulder of the messenger who was carrying her. Talbot walked at their side.

She began to writhe and struggle desperately. Talbot lifted his walking cane and slapped her hard across the buttocks. "Don't be so inconsiderate, my lady. Tom is a strong fellow, but you make his burden uncommonly heavy if you struggle."

Tears began to gush from Anna-Maria's eyes, tears of helplessness and impotent rage. Was Talbot insane? What did he want of her?

She choked out the question as soon as Tom had dumped her on the splintered floor of a hunting lodge and roughly pulled out her gag.

Talbot looked immensely tall and wasp-thin as he stood above her. "You are a nuisance to me, my lady and I do not suffer nuisances gladly. I remove them."

"A nuisance to you? How?" The cords were biting painfully into Anna-Maria's wrists and ankles as she struggled unsuccessfully to raise herself. Her gown was thick with grime from the coach floor, and her hair tumbled over her shoulders.

Talbot raised one eyebrow and spoke as though he were instructing a backward child. "I want the jointure that your husband left you. Francis was good enough to give me legal custody of your children, but I want your jointure as well, and that I must seize illegally. If you die the money will revert to the children—and I'll control it."

Anna-Maria had not thought of her jointure in years. Now she suddenly remembered her father's long hours of negotiation before her marriage. How pleased he had been at securing a vast inheritance for Anna-Maria should Francis die. It would be ironic if all his efforts in her behalf had put her into danger now. But what would Talbot want with her fortune?

Anna-Maria shook her hair out of her eyes and stared at him. "But you have wealth of your own."

"Ah, but not enough. Never enough." Talbot pulled off his gloves, picked up a decanter of wine, and held it invitingly toward her. "Will you take wine?" Anna-Maria shook her head angrily, and he smiled. "No? Then I will indulge alone."

As he poured the wine into a glass, he said, "You see I want power, my dear, and that costs a vast fortune." He sipped at the wine thoughtfully. "Which brings me to another point. Buckingham is a formidable enemy to me. He blocks me in my ambitions. For a time he will be distracted by your disappearance, and he'll search heaven and earth for you—leaving me free to act without hindrance."

The thought of Buckingham revived Anna-Maria. "He'll kill you!"

Talbot smiled unpleasantly, and the sight sent a chill down Anna-Maria's spine. "I think not. There is nothing to connect me with your disappearance. Indeed I will affect to be as horrified as everyone else."

He sat and crossed one leg over the other, studying Anna-Maria as she lay in front of him. "I've been very clever. Tom is not known to be in my service. I employ him from time to time for secret—somewhat unpleasant—matters, but no one knows of the connection between us."

Anna-Maria caught her breath. Why had she left the house so quickly without leaving a message behind? What a fool she had been!

Talbot had been watching her closely, and now he nodded. "Tom carefully retrieved the note I sent you. There is no evidence against me. An unknown messenger arrives at your door, and you rush out cloakless, get into a public coach and"—he snapped his fingers —"disappear. It will be the wonder of London."

Terror flashed through Anna-Maria. She was humiliated by the quaver in her voice but was unable to control it. "What are you going to do with me?"

"I'm not a violent man. I had thought of sending you into a convent and paying to have you kept there for the rest of your life, but then I would live with the fear that somehow you would escape." He twirled the wineglass in his hand and then said slowly, "I fear that you will have to die."

That he said it so coolly, almost casually, as he sipped his wine, made it all the more terrifying. For a moment Anna-Maria simply stared at him, stunned, and then she threw back her head and screamed, the cords in her throat standing out.

Instantly Talbot was on his feet as though to check her, and then he smiled, waving back Tom, who had appeared in the doorway. "We are miles out in the woods. Your outcry will do you no good."

Anna-Maria's screams subsided to soft sobs, and she lay back exhausted. The rope binding her arms was crossed under her heaving breasts, and it threw them into bold relief. A hot gleam appeared in Talbot's eyes, and he bent suddenly, inserted his fingers into her low-cut bodice and ripped the fabric, tearing her gown and delicate undergarments. Anna-Maria's soft, pink-tipped breasts were revealed, and Tom stumbled closer for a better view, his eyes avid in his brutish face.

Talbot laughed, a cruel, chilling sound. "She's a prettier morsel than those you are accustomed to, eh, Tom." He waved at Anna-Maria, a mocking light in his eyes. "Go ahead and kiss her. The lady is in no position to object."

"No, no!" Anna-Maria's frantic cry was cut short as Tom brought his coarse face closer and put his moist lips harshly against hers. Anna-Maria was sickened by the stench of him, by the rough pressure of his kiss, but he held her head tightly in a brutal grip, and she could not avert her lips.

Talbot watched for a moment and then said sharply, as though to a dog, "That's enough, Tom. Leave us."

There was a sullen flare of anger in Tom's eyes, but he rose obediently and left the room, reluctance in his gait.

Anna-Maria was hysterical now. "I pray you, kill me quickly, but do not let that brute have me."

Talbot smiled. "Are you so eager to die? It seems a

waste." He was slowly studying her flushed face, her bright, tumbled hair, her naked breasts.

Anna-Maria recoiled. Lust was clearly written on his narrow features. Dropping to his knees beside her, Talbot bent over her writhing form. Anna-Maria started to shriek a protest, but then she suddenly spied the jeweled dagger at his hip, and an idea was born. The cry died stillborn on her lips. It was the hardest task she had ever set herself, but she willed all her muscles to relax, and when Talbot put his dry lips against hers, she returned the kiss, using all the art and skill she had learned in Buckingham's arms. When he finally raised his lips a little, she murmured huskily, "Unloose me, my lord. I can scarce give you pleasure when my arms and legs are bound."

Talbot sat back on his heels and looked at her suspiciously. Then he gave a short, angry laugh. "You cannot trick me so easily, my dear. Am I to think that you have conceived a sudden passion for me?"

Anna-Maria swept up her long dark eyelashes and looked fully into his eyes with apparent honesty. "No," she said slowly, "but if I give you pleasure you may not be so quick to kill me. Perhaps you will keep me here as your willing prisoner."

The suspicion died on Talbot's face. This was reasoning that he could understand. He laughed. "So. Faced with death, you will trade your virtue for payment like any slut that plies the streets of London."

Anna-Maria stiffened as anger lanced through her, but she managed to drop her eyelids to conceal her murderous expression from him.

"Yes, my lord."

"Very well." Talbot quickly rolled her over and began untying the bonds at her wrists. "But make no attempt to escape. I can easily overpower you, and Tom will come running if I but raise my voice."

Anna-Maria was silent, rubbing her wrists to restore the circulation. She knew that an attempt at escape would be futile, but she was determined that neither Talbot nor that brute Tom would have the pleasure of violating her. She kept her head down and concentrated on massaging the angry red welts that marred her slim wrists. The life *must* come back to her wrists, or she would not be able to strike rapidly.

Talbot grunted slightly as he pulled the ropes free of her ankles, and then, before she could react, he moved over her, pinning her body down as he took her in a long kiss. After her first instinctive recoil, Anna-Maria made herself submissive again. She plied her tongue artfully until she was rewarded by his rapid breathing and increased excitement and knew that his caution had fled. Her hand was already at his side and with a lightning-quick movement, she pulled his dagger free. His body was pressed too tightly to hers for her to reach his heart. She raised the dagger and plunged it into the side of his face, raking it downward with a vicious movement.

He gave an agonized scream and recoiled, then seized her wrist in a brutal grip until her fingers opened and the dagger clattered to the floor.

Then he rose, his expression murderous. His left cheek was laid open in a fearsome wound; blood dripped down onto Anna-Maria's naked breasts.

"You whore! You conniving bitch." He looked demented, his hair wild, his eyes blazing, his cheek a gaping wound.

Anna-Maria was panting with exertion and anger, but she managed to say, "I think I have proved I am no whore," just as Tom burst through the door.

Talbot gestured him back and bent to retrieve the dagger from the floor. "I want the pleasure of killing this bitch myself."

As he poised the dagger over her heart, Anna-Maria arched toward it, her breasts standing out firm and taut. Let him plunge cleanly so that death came quickly.

At her movement Talbot paused and then stepped back, his eyes narrowed. "So you crave a swift death?" He turned and contemptuously tossed away the bloodstained dagger. "Then I shall deny you that."

He motioned to the brute in the doorway. "Tom, bind her again."

Tom moved closer, fascinated, his small, red-rimmed eyes looking from Anna-Maria's naked, blood-stained breasts to the bleeding slash in Talbot's cheek. He fumbled with the ropes, and Talbot said impatiently, "Hurry man. I must get back to London and have this wound attended to. As it is, I'll carry a scar to my grave."

Anna-Maria made no attempt to resist as Tom bound her. For the moment all the will to fight had left her, and she lay limp.

Talbot's face was a mask of evil as he looked down at her. "Your treachery has earned you the cruelest of deaths. You will lie here alone to die slowly of hunger and thirst. Years from now, someone will stumble on your bones, and there will be no clue that you were once the beautiful countess of Shrewsbury."

Then he spat contemptuously, turned angrily on his heel, and strode from the room. Anna-Maria had escaped him by fainting.

She was stiff and cramped. The ropes binding her wrists and ankles were so painful that nausea rose in her throat. Opening her eyes, she stared dully at the cracked, peeling ceiling, and then her memory returned. She looked fearfully around the empty room, expecting to see Talbot or his crude companion, but she listened for a moment, and the dead silence that hung over the hunting lodge reassured her that she was alone. Relief washed over her and was instantly replaced by fear. She would die here. Buckingham and the children would never know that she had not deserted them by choice. She began to struggle against her bonds, but they only cut deeper, and she subsided, sobbing angrily. There was a foul taste in her mouth, the echo of the filthy cloth that had gagged her, and her thirst was almost unbearable. She knew she could live for a considerable period without food, but if she didn't get water soon, she would die in agony.

Goaded by the thought, she looked carefully around the almost barren room for a means to free herself. For a moment she considered the andirons in the fireplace. It was possible that she could loosen the ropes a little by catching them over the shaft of the irons and chafing them until they wore thin. Then her eyes fell on the blood-stained dagger that Talbot had cast away, and hope leaped in her.

It was scarce feet away, but the journey seemed endless. She had to force herself up into a sitting position, then inch along, digging her heels into the floor and sliding on her buttocks. She was damp with sweat and sobbing softly by the time the dagger was within her reach. Despair swept over her—the dagger was useless. How could she wield it when her hands were tied behind her? Defeated, she dropped her head to the rough floor and sobbed. But then anger steadied her. She deserved to die if she lay here bawling like an infant. By sheer effort of will, she checked her tears and forced herself to think clearly. The floorboards were splintered, and cracks gaped between them. If she could wedge the dagger into one of the cracks to steady it. . . . Panting, her hair spilling into her eyes, she backed up to the dagger and after several attempts managed to pick it up, shivering a little as her fingers touched Talbot's crusted blood.

Forcing herself to work slowly and carefully, by touch alone, she inserted the dagger into a crack and tested it. It held steady. She gave a sigh of relief and then began sawing the rope against the dagger's blade. It was slow, tedious work, and she sobbed with impatience. Several times she flinched as the blade bit into her delicate flesh.

The sun was fully up, spilling through the dirty windowpanes, before she felt the first strand of rope part. She gave a small cry of triumph and worked with renewed energy.

When her wrists were finally free, she sat for a moment, dazed by exertion. Her wrists were bruised and circled by angry red welts. She bent and sucked at them to stem the trickles of blood and relieve the pain.

Images of bucketfulls of clear, cold water tantalized her. Her throat and mouth were parched dry, and she trembled with eagerness at the thought of bringing a handful of icy water to her lips.

Forcing her aching wrists into movement, she picked

up the dagger and cut through the ropes binding her ankles.

Tossing the dagger away, she tried to stand, but her numbed ankles collapsed beneath her. She gave a small sob of frustration and then crawled to the table and, holding the edge of the table for support, painfully got to her feet. The wine decanter that Talbot had used caught her eye, and she gave a cry of delight. Putting it to her trembling lips, she poured the wine down her parched throat. She drank greedily, in great, shuddering gulps. When the decanter was empty, she lowered it and stared about a bit dizzily. She must get out of this accursed place.

She stamped her feet repeatedly to make the blood flow freely into her ankles, and then, stumbling a little, she crossed the room and wrenched open the door. The blazing sunlight hurt her eyes, and she stood blinking a moment. The hunting lodge stood in a small clearing, and beyond, on all sides, were dense woods. She wondered if she would ever have the strength to find her way through the forest.

Painfully, slowly, she began making her way toward the faint indication of a path. Crossing the clearing was difficult enough, but when she reached the forest it was much worse. The path was overgrown, and tangled roots caught her feet, making her stumble and fall frequently. Each time the effort of getting to her feet again seemed more impossible.

One fall knocked all the breath out of her. She lay sobbing angrily, wondering whether she had merely exchanged one form of death for another, when a shout caught her attention, and she raised her head disbelievingly.

"Anna-Maria!" Buckingham was riding toward her, his face showing the long night's strain of searching for her, his manner suddenly jubilant as he spotted her.

Anna-Maria's breath caught in her throat. She stared at him incredulously, scarcely daring to believe her eyes. Sir Joseph Phillips, his dark blond hair blowing in the wind, was riding behind Buckingham, and close behind him was Sarah, her small face beginning to light with relief as she caught sight of Anna-Maria. Instinctively, at the sight of Joseph, Anna-Maria crossed her arms against her breasts, ashamed of her half-nakedness.

Buckingham swung from his horse, knelt, and caught Anna-Maria in his arms. She clung to the thick fabric of his cloak, her dark eyes wide. "How did you find me?"

"It was thanks to the quick wit of Joseph," Buckingham said. His gentle hands were going over Anna-Maria's body, searching for injuries. "Did Talbot hurt you?"

"*I* hurt *him*." Anna-Maria gave a small laugh, and Buckingham, thinking she was delirious, put his cloak around her, gathered her in his arms and rose swiftly. Joseph and Sarah were preparing to dismount, but Buckingham checked them. "She needs hot food, a bath, and rest. We'd best ride quickly to that inn we passed."

Anna-Maria felt as though her nightmare had changed into a delicious dream as she rode through the forest with Buckingham's arm clasped tightly around her.

When they reached the inn, Buckingham carried her swiftly upstairs and placed her in the center of a large, soft bed. The sensation seemed strange to Anna-Maria after her night on the bare floor, and she stretched slowly, wincing a little but savoring the moment.

Sarah had already discarded her cloak and was dipping a sponge into a basin of warm water.

Anna-Maria sat up suddenly. "The children! Are they safe?"

Sir Joseph stepped forward. "They are perfectly safe, madame. I was at Talbot's house when he brought them there. They seemed cheerful, thinking that they were to pay a short visit to their relatives." He added in a gentle voice, "Lady Talbot is a good woman. She will care for them."

"Thank God!" Anna-Maria sank back against the pillow and turned her face up to Sarah's ministrations.

Sarah looked exhausted, her eyes like burning coals in her drawn face, but she glowed with exhilaration. "Joseph was wonderful. It is thanks to his sense and courage that we found you."

Buckingham was coming forward with steaming mugs of wine, and he threw a glance of approval in the other man's direction. "Aye, and we'll see that he is rewarded for it."

Anna-Maria took the steaming mug gratefully and sipped from it. Then she looked around at the three faces bent above her. "Tell me."

At first there were false starts with all three talking at once, and then the men, laughing, deferred to Sarah, and she took up the tale.

She had been on her way to meet Joseph at the Golden Unicorn when he had suddenly overtaken her coach, his horse in a lather. He had told her that he feared that the countess of Shrewsbury was in danger, and that there was no time for explanations. Wheeling his horse in the direction of Anna-Maria's house, he had bade Sarah to follow him as quickly as possible.

By the time she had reached the house, Joseph was already questioning the maid, who told him, "A man came to the house with a message about the children. Her ladyship went down to see him. I stayed behind a moment to straighten her bed, and when I came down, she had vanished."

Just then, Buckingham had come striding into the hall, and Joseph quickly told him of the situation. Joseph had been stunned when Talbot had arrived home with the Shrewsbury children in tow and had been suspicious when Talbot locked himself in his office for a short time, then quit the house without explanation. Joseph had searched the office, found a first, spoiled draft of Talbot's note, and instantly realized that Anna-Maria was in danger.

"I've never felt such fear as I did in that moment," Sarah said. She recalled that Buckingham had been enraged. He called for his horse and was determined to set off for Talbot's house at once, but Joseph had forestalled him. "Lady Talbot would never allow Lady Shrewsbury to be brought there by force."

"Where then?" Buckingham had rapped out the question, and Joseph responded immediately. "Talbot has a cargo on a ship that is sailing in the morning for America. Perhaps Lady Shrewsbury is a prisoner aboard."

"When I heard that," Sarah continued, "I raced into the stableyard and ordered a groom to saddle a horse for me. By the time the duke and Joseph came out of the house, I was mounted and waiting. They protested, but I said, 'The gypsies taught me to ride like the wind, bareback if need be, and I'll not be left behind!' "

"She was magnificent," Joseph said, flashing her a look of love and pride.

The three had fruitlessly searched the ship and then turned their horses towards Talbot's country home near Hampton Court Palace. When they met with an equal lack of success there, they had fallen into despair for a moment. "I kept seeing images of your dead, bleeding body." Sarah shuddered.

Then, she continued, Joseph had suddenly remembered once seeing a notation among Talbot's papers about an unused hunting lodge near Richmond. They were exhausted, their horses limping, but they had ridden through the night, "—and we found you," Sarah concluded triumphantly.

Anna-Maria caught Sarah's hand, squeezed it affectionately and held out her free hand toward Joseph. "I owe my life to you. I would never have survived exposure in the woods."

Buckingham clapped Joseph on the shoulder, his face rich with warmth.

"Name your reward. If it is in my power to give it, you shall have it."

Anna-Marie began to laugh softly. "I'll wager I know what he wants most." Swiftly she explained Joseph's and Sarah's longing to marry and live under the same roof.

Buckingham laughed. "That's easily settled. Joseph can be secretary to me if he's willing, and he and Sarah can come to live with us."

Joseph and Sarah turned toward each other, dazed

by their good fortune. Anna-Maria was staring at Buckingham, her lips slightly parted. "Us?"

Buckingham put his arms around her and bent his lips to her hair. Huskily he asked, "Did you think that I would ever let you out of my sight again? Talbot shall not have a second chance at you."

Anna-Maria clung to him, her face radiant. "Feel how rapidly my heart is beating. I think that I shall die of happiness."

Thirty-One

Anna-Maria was too dazed with exhaustion to hear the startled exclamations from the courtiers when they saw the disheveled group riding into the courtyard at Whitehall. Despite her fatigue, she had insisted on going to the king at once and charging Talbot with kidnapping.

When they burst into the king's private closet, he let fall the priceless painting he was holding. "God's fish, Buckingham. What have we here?"

Before replying, Buckingham tenderly helped Anna-Maria into a chair, and she leaned her head back gratefully. Her torn gown was still caught with bits of twigs and leaves, and her face was deathly pale against the framework of her hair. Sarah and Joseph, suddenly shy in the presence of the king, hovered near the doorway.

Striding angrily around the room, his boots making staccato noises on the parquet flooring, Buckingham told the king of Talbot's treachery. The king listened closely, his intelligent dark eyes kindling. Midway through the tale, he interrupted Buckingham, went to the door, and spoke in a low tone to a footman. Returning, he explained, "I've sent for Talbot so you can confront him."

Anna-Maria felt a shiver of fear. Then she straightened. Here in this quiet room with the king, Sarah, Joseph, and Buckingham all protecting her, she was perfectly safe. It was Talbot who needed to fear for his life now!

The king took a survey of the group and said sympathetically, "You all look the worse for your night's work." He placed his hand under Sarah's arm and helped her into a chair. Sighing, she sank into it and looked up at him with awe and gratitude.

The king poured wine into tall crystal glasses and began serving them himself. Despite her anxiety and fatigue, Anna-Maria smiled. Part of the king's charm was his humanity, his lack of formality.

She turned suddenly, spilling drops of wine onto her gown as Talbot was announced. He strode aggressively into the room, clad in a suit of black velvet, his cheek heavily bandaged.

As he caught sight of Anna-Maria, shock blazed in his eyes, and for a moment he checked his stride. Then, instantly, a mask of composure slid over his features. Anna-Maria felt Buckingham's hand on her shoulder, gripping her reassuringly.

There was a moment's silence, which the king let spin out, hoping to make Talbot uncomfortable, and then he asked, "You've been injured, Talbot?"

Involuntarily, Talbot swung his head until he caught Anna-Maria's eyes. His expression was murderous, but he managed to say smoothly, "Yes, Your Majesty. I was set upon by a highwayman last night." He touched his bandaged cheek. "I killed the fellow, but unfortunately his dagger made its mark first."

Anna-Maria gasped at his bland lie. The shock of finding her alive in the king's chambers must have been overwhelming, but he was acting the role of innocence with the assurance of any actor on the stage.

Buckingham's angry voice bit through the air. "Your lies are futile, Talbot. Lady Shrewsbury has already informed the king that you kidnapped her and attempted to murder her."

Talbot's plucked eyebrows arched until they almost disappeared into his hairline. He turned toward the king. "An unusual tale, Your Majesty, but scarce one that you will credit."

Talbot's insolent tone made clear that he didn't care whether the king believed the tale or not. The real power in England, Talbot felt, was in the hands of Parliament, and if the king proved troublesome, he could be disposed of, as his father had been.

The king's face darkened. "You'll be charged for your crimes, Talbot."

Talbot leisurely opened a jeweled snuff box, extracted a pinch, and held it to his nostrils before replying smoothly, "I think not, Your Majesty. If I am to be charged with these crimes, there must be credible witnesses against me." He gestured around the room. "Are these your witnesses? Buckingham is my acknowledged enemy. His word against mine will carry no weight. Nor will that of his mistress or her maidservant. As for my secretary, he is in love with Lady Shrewsbury's maidservant, and no doubt by now he is in Buckingham's employ. If these are the only witnesses—and I assure you that there are no others—then the court will surely drop the charges as a scheme concocted by Buckingham's wily brain."

Anna-Maria shivered. The implication was obvious —Talbot had killed the brute, Tom, so that there would be no living witness to his crimes.

The eyes of Buckingham and the king locked across the small distance between them, and there was defeat in their glances.

The king spoke quickly. "Do you deny that you kidnapped Lady Shrewsbury's children and that they are at your home now?"

There was a gleam of mockery in Talbot's eyes. "I do not deny it, Your Majesty. My cousin Francis left his children in my care, and I have every legal right to them." He reached into his black velvet doublet and brought forth a parchment. "Would you care to examine the legal documents?"

The king took the documents, moved over to his writing table and laid them flat. The hiss and sputter of the fire was audible in the quiet room as he read. The king had his lips pursed in a soundless whistle.

His eyes moved to the bottom of the document, and then he sighed and read it again, as though reluctant to believe its import. Then he raised his head and looked at Anna-Maria with compassion in his eyes. Her heart began to skip and flutter in her breast, and she clutched the arms of her chair.

The king looked at Anna-Maria with pity. "I'm sorry, my dear, but these papers are in order, and they legally place your children in Talbot's custody." He sighed heavily. "Even the king cannot flout the laws of England."

Anna-Maria's eyes were dark with shock, and tears began to spill down her face. She heard Sarah give a low wail behind her and was conscious of Buckingham's fingers gripping her shoulder.

Before Buckingham could leap for Talbot's throat, the king raised his voice. "These papers give you no control of Lady Shrewsbury's jointure, yet I understand you have seized it. Turn her fortune over to her by this hour tomorrow, or I *will* have legal grounds for clapping you in prison."

He paused a moment and then said between clenched teeth, "Nothing would give me greater pleasure than to see you hanging in irons against the damp walls of a cell." He nearly spat the next words. "Leave us now."

Talbot bowed mockingly. "Your Majesty," he said, then turned to Anna-Maria. "Your servant, madame." He strode jauntily from the room.

Anna-Maria began to sob. "Talbot can *keep* my children?" There was disbelief in her voice and an edge of hysteria.

Buckingham had his hand on his dagger's hilt. "He won't be alive to keep them, my love. I'll kill him."

Anna-Maria clenched her fists, her tears subsiding. "A quick death is too merciful for Talbot. Last night he denied me the swift end that I craved. He left me to die slowly and painfully. Worse than death for Talbot would be the end of his ambitions, the loss of the power he holds so dear."

Buckingham and the king exchanged glances, and then the king nodded, putting his hand on Buckingham's tense arm. "If you kill Talbot, there is nothing to prevent another of his family from seizing custody of the children in his name. But if you strip him of his power, he will be at your mercy."

Buckingham's hand fell from his dagger. "Your cool head has stayed me many a time from a foolish action." He gripped his friend's shoulder affectionately. "I thank you."

He turned to Anna-Maria. "It will mean a wait until you have the children again."

Anna-Maria's voice was trembling, but she said resolutely, "I want Talbot forced to turn over *legal* custody so that I don't have to live in fear that they can be snatched from my arms again."

Joseph stepped forward, his voice heavy with pity. "Lady Talbot is a good woman. She will see that the children are well cared for."

Anna-Maria swayed with fatigue, and Buckingham sprang forward to catch her. "You're overstrained, darling. I'm taking you home before you get ill."

He turned to Joseph. "If you return to Talbot's house, your life will be in danger. You'd best move into Wallingford House with us today." For a moment a grin touched his mouth. "Since Sarah will be there, you'll scarce find it a hardship."

The king gave a startled exclamation. "You are going to take Anna-Maria to live with your wife?"

"It's the only way to be certain she is safe," Buckingham said tersely. He was already lifting Anna-Maria into his arms.

The king shook his head dubiously. "If your wife permits Anna-Maria to enter her home, she will lose favor with the queen."

"Then I'll send Mary into the country," Buckingham said impatiently. "Nothing on heaven or earth is going to part me from Anna-Maria again!"

Mary, her hand flying to her throat, stared at the bedraggled cluster of people who had just entered Wallingford House. Anna-Maria had fallen asleep in Buckingham's arms. Her long chestnut hair, caught with bits of leaves, spilled over his shoulder. Her face was pale, marked by tear stains. Her maidservant, whom Mary recognized, hovered nearby. Mary looked questioningly at the tall, dark-blond stranger who stood beside her, and then her glance flew to Buckingham's, begging for an explanation.

"Have rooms prepared at once." Buckingham spoke rapidly, certain of her swift understanding. "Anna-Maria must be put to bed. Give Sarah a room next to hers." He nodded at Joseph. "Sir Joseph Phillips is my new secretary. He will need accommodations."

Questions flew to Mary's lips, but she bit them back. She felt a flash of pride as she realized how completely Buckingham trusted her to act like a woman of sense.

She clapped for the servants and bid them to prepare rooms instantly, then followed Buckingham as he carried Anna-Maria up to a large, elaborately decorated chamber. One maid was already lighting the fire, and another was pulling the window hangings closed so that no shaft of sun would disturb Anna-Maria's sleep. Buckingham gently put Anna-Maria onto the bed. A sigh escaped Anna-Maria's lips. She rolled over and hugged the softness of the pillow to her.

Mary whispered, "Does she need a doctor?"

Buckingham shook his head. "She's merely exhausted. Come below with me, and I'll explain matters to you."

As they descended the staircase, he put his arm affectionately around Mary's waist, and she felt a thrill of excitement. His nearness always set her pulses to racing. She turned her head hastily lest he notice her quickened breathing and feel pity for her. When they entered the small room he used as an office, he dropped his arm from her waist, and she felt suddenly bereft. The casual contact that stirred her senses meant nothing to him.

She hid her disappointment and smiled up at him as she took the glass of wine that he poured and held out. His blue eyes gave her a glance of warm approval, and for a moment she stared at him wordlessly, feeling flushed with pleasure. She would brave fire and flood to bring that look of approval to his eyes.

Buckingham said, "Sit down, Mary," and led her to a chair, then dropped to a footstool at her feet. He slowly turned the goblet of wine in his hand. "I scarce know where to begin." Hesitantly at first, then speaking more rapidly as he warmed to his tale, he told her of the seizure of the children and Talbot's kidnapping of Anna-Maria and his attempt to murder her. At the conclusion he said simply, "So you see, I *had* to bring her here for protection."

Mary's mind was whirling, and she clung to the arms of her chair for support. When she could find her voice, she said, "Of *course* you had to bring Anna-Maria here. She is my friend, too. Did you think that I would object?"

Buckingham placed his hand over hers. "I know full well the extent of your kindness, Mary. But the situation is more difficult than you realize. The king has warned me that if you and Anna-Maria remain under the same roof, the queen will be angry."

Mary nodded reluctantly. "The queen believes the ugly rumors that Anna-Maria poisoned her husband." She put her hand tenderly on Buckingham's head. "I don't care if the queen is angry with me." She sighed unconsciously. She loved her duties at court and would miss them sorely if the queen dismissed her.

Buckingham leaned over and brushed the corner of her mouth with a kiss. "Ah, Mary, if you only had a husband more worthy of your love!" Mary's lips trembled. It took all her self-control to keep from pulling his head to hers and deepening the kiss.

They were silent for a moment, and the silence lay heavy with the knowledge of her love for him and his regret. Then Buckingham squeezed her hands with decision. "You must go immediately to your father's at Nun Appleton. I'll let it be known that you fled this house in high indignation, and the queen will be pleased with you."

Mary searched his face for a long moment, and then she sighed. "It will never be the same again, will it?"

Buckingham looked at her with compassion in his

eyes, hesitating. He had not intended to tell her of his plans so soon, to heap blow upon blow. Her gaze was very steady, her brown eyes clear and honest in her broad face. He owed her no less than the truth.

"I am going to find a house in London where Anna-Maria and I can live openly together." He seized her two hands in his as he spoke, as though to give her courage.

The shock and the pain were so great that for a moment Mary stopped breathing. She had lost him entirely! Then anguish filled her. He would come to hate her. As long as she lived, she would be the barrier that prevented him from marrying Anna-Maria. The thought of killing herself before he began to despise her filled her mind, and then she bent her face into her hands, weeping. Her voice came up muffled, ashamed.

"My love is not as great as I thought. I would die for you gladly, but I am too much of a coward to die by my own hand. Suicide is a grievous mortal sin, and I shrink from the thought of an eternity of hell-fire."

Horrified, Buckingham gathered her into his arms, stroking her hair. "Mary, I swear before God that neither Anna-Maria nor I wish you dead. She loves you as I do." He turned her face up towards his, and speaking very distinctly, his eyes holding hers, he said, "If you died by your own hand, neither Anna-Maria nor I would know a moment's happiness."

Mary searched his eyes, read the truth there, then nodded and dropped her head again to his shoulder. There was a bittersweet happiness in being held in his arms one last time, and she nestled against him as her sobs subsided. Her fingers touched the velvet of his doublet, and she was conscious of his cheek so near her own. Memories of the nights he had held her in his arms, attempting to father an heir, flashed through her mind. She had responded to him with passion, nearly fainting with pleasure, and now he would never touch her again except as a sister or a loved friend. For a long moment she clung to him, knowing that from this moment on, she must learn to live with her unfulfilled longing for his touch. Then she raised her head and smiled bravely. "I'd best start my packing."

There was admiration in Buckingham's eyes, and the memory of it steadied her as she left the room, summoned a maid, and began packing. She vowed that she would never give him cause for that look of admiration to fade.

When her trunks were ready, she picked up her cloak and slipped into Anna-Maria's room. Anna-Maria was just awakening, looking about her in bewilderment, and when she spied Mary, she held out her arms and gave a little wail.

Mary moved swiftly to the bed and put a comforting arm around her. "You are out of danger now. Rest quietly until you regain your strength." She smoothed Anna-Maria's hair, then stood and began pulling on her gloves. "I'm going to stay with my father at Nun Appleton. Buckingham feels that there will be too much gossip if you and I stay under the same roof."

She paused and then said quietly, "Buckingham has told me of your plans to live together."

"Oh!" Anna-Maria struggled to sit upright, pity showing in her eyes. She started to speak, but Mary gently put the tip of her finger against Anna-Maria's lips. "Hush. Let me speak. You need feel no guilt on my account. I know that there is no evil in either you or my husband. The love that has flamed between you is beyond our understanding, a natural force of nature like fire or flood." She drew a deep breath. "It is senseless to protest against fate, so we must try to accept it with dignity."

Anna-Maria looked at her speechlessly, her eyes shining with tears.

Mary said softly, "Love him well, Anna-Maria—as I do." Drawing her cloak around her, she said, half to herself, "I shall love him all my life." Then she bent swiftly, kissed Anna-Maria, and was gone.

Thirty-Two

The wind blew in gusts across the ground, scattering dust into the open grave. Anna-Maria stood shivering but dry-eyed when Francis's body was lowered into the ground. Conscious of eyes upon her, she looked up and found Talbot staring at her across the yawning grave. She drew her cloak more tightly around her and moved closer to Buckingham. If Talbot had succeeded, she would be a corpse herself.

For a moment she held Talbot's eyes, hatred and defiance on her face, but then she shut her eyes and concentrated on praying for Francis's soul. For an instant, bitterness touched her because he had given his children's custody into Talbot's greedy hands, but she forced herself to remember the last days of Francis's life when she had tended him during his illness. They had forgiven each other and drawn closer in those hours, and she was certain that had he been less weak, he would have remembered to destroy the document.

She whispered a last goodbye to Francis as the dirt was scattered over his grave and then turned away. As she and Buckingham moved toward their horses, the hiss of "murderess" followed them, audible in the clear, crisp air.

Buckingham's hand was under Anna-Maria's elbow. When he heard the whisper, his grip tightened so much that she winced at the sudden pain. Under her breath she said swiftly, "Ignore it, or you will only make matters worse," and Buckingham nodded and strode on, although his chest was heaving with the force of his anger.

When they reached Wallingford House, his mood suddenly lightened. As they sat in front of the fire, he smiled and picked up a gleaming tendril of Anna-Maria's hair, winding it about his finger. "I've good news for you, my love."

Anna-Maria had been staring into the flames, thinking of Francis. She turned, the firelight playing over her delicate features. "Good news? What is it?"

Buckingham looked triumphant. "The king sent for Talbot this morning and commanded him to let you visit your children daily." The king had called Talbot to his private chambers and pointed out that even though Talbot had legal custody of the children, he had no grounds on which to forbid visits by their mother. Talbot had shrugged, willing to concede a minor battle as long as he won the war. There was no point in needlessly provoking the king.

Anna-Maria cried out in delight and then leaped from her chair, calling for Sarah. Within half an hour she was in the nursery at Lady Talbot's house, John in her arms, Charles and Polly pressed close to her knee. She felt as though she had been starving and had finally been fed. She could not get enough of the touch and feel of the children.

Charles tugged at his mother's skirt. "Will my father come back from heaven?"

A sob caught in Anna-Maria's throat. "No, darling, he never will." Tears hung on her long eyelashes, but her voice was steady. She caught him close to her. "Perhaps one day you will have a new father." Her heart leaped, thinking of the children in Buckingham's arms.

When Lady Talbot glided into the nursery Anna-Maria rose, feeling conflicting emotions. She put John down and faced Lady Talbot. "I would be a liar if I pretended that having the children here is not making me desperately unhappy. I warn you, I will do everything in my power to have them returned to me. However, they seem well taken care of and happy, and for that I must thank you."

A smile touched Lady Talbot's thin lips, and her low voice was sympathetic. "My heart goes out to you. I do not approve of my husband's actions, but I have no influence over him. I promise you that the children will not suffer under my care." She looked at the children affectionately. "Indeed, I have already grown fond of them."

Anna-Maria pressed her hand in a silent thank you and then hurriedly promised the children she would see them the next morning and left, Sarah following.

As the coach swung through the streets of London, Sarah chatted excitedly in an attempt to raise Anna-Maria's spirits. "It has been less than a week, but I vow Polly has grown an inch." Anna-Maria began to smile. She would never be completely happy until the children were living under her roof, but it was more than she had hoped for to be able to see them every day, and Lady Talbot's kindness was reassuring.

She chatted idly with Sarah for a moment and then broke off to say, "Isn't it time we began planning your wedding?"

Sarah's cheeks, already flushed with pleasure from seeing the children grew even rosier. "Joseph and I have been hoping we could wed soon. The duke of Buckingham was so generous in taking Joseph into his service that we scarce know how to repay him."

Anna-Maria squeezed Sarah's hand. "It was Joseph's quick wit and your courage that saved my life. We are in *your* debt."

She smiled gaily. "How quickly do you think Mrs. Muggs can make you a wedding gown?"

Sarah dimpled. "Within the month I would think. Oh, Anna-Maria, I want the most beautiful wedding gown ever created!" Excitedly she began describing the gown, sketching it in the air.

Anna-Maria, delighted by the happiness on Sarah's face, hugged her. "Then the banns must be announced at once."

She began to laugh softly. "Think how dumb-founded all the gossips will be when they find that my serving woman is actually a lady in her own right. Your high birth has been the best-kept secret in London."

Sarah gave a sigh of deep contentment. "It's wonderful not to have to fear my father any longer. Even if he learns of my marriage, there's nothing that he can do. Joseph's blood is as fine as my own—even though he has not the wealth that my father lusted after."

When they reached the house, Sarah ran to find Joseph and flung herself into his arms. He laughed and caught her, reeling a little under the sudden impact, then smiled down into her upturned face. Sarah stood on tiptoe to reach his mouth and gave him a long kiss.

Then, a little breathless, she said, "We can be married before the month is out. I've just spoken to Anna-Maria, and she and the duke want us to be married in the chapel here at Wallingford House, and we've already planned the decorations and—" She broke off, laughing shakily. "Oh, Joseph, I cannot believe our good fortune."

"Nor can I," Joseph murmured huskily, his lips seeking hers. "I never dreamed such a woman as you existed, Sarah. And now to have found you, to have you be my wife. . . ." His arms tightened hungrily around her.

Three weeks later, hands clasped tightly together, they stood in front of the minister in the small chapel at Wallingford House. Tears of happiness misted Sarah's eyes. It had been a long and difficult journey she had made to reach Joseph's side. Sudden memories of the quarrels she had had with her father and of her life with the gypsies tumbled through her mind. Suppose she had broken under the force of her father's wrath and married that ancient nobleman? She would never have known happiness. Her hand began to tremble in Joseph's, and he turned and gave her a smile of tenderness and pride. His voice husky with emotion, he made his vows to her, and Sarah, her eyes shining, answered him in her clear young voice.

Anna-Maria's eyes stung with tears, and she fumbled at her side until her hand met Buckingham's. Her own lips were silently shaping the beautiful words of the vows, and she looked at Buckingham with longing in her eyes, wishing desperately that she could make those same vows to him. His answering glance was full of understanding and pain.

The next day Buckingham suggested that they start searching for a house. The third house they examined seemed perfect to Anna-Maria. Buckingham rapped on the walls and gave a critical eye to its state of repair, but Anna-Maria stood in the long drawing room and saw only its graceful proportions and the lovely line of the windows, which extended from floor to ceiling. In her mind she was already placing furniture, and she turned to Buckingham with a face that was suddenly radiant. "We will be happy here, my love."

He smiled and shook his head simultaneously, marveling at her. How resilient she was! Already she was casting aside her troubles and planning for the future.

He caught her close to him. "I love you—your grace, your laughter, your courage—" His voice was charged with longing, his lips suddenly demanding. In a moment, she knew, they would be at a point at which they could not stop, and she pushed him away a little. They both looked at the barren room, the bare wooden floor and then burst into laughter at the absurdity of the situation. As they left the room, Anna-Maria felt lighthearted because they had baptized it with laughter.

For the next few weeks, she was in a fever of hectic activity, furnishing the house. Each item she bought filled her with joy. "He will sit in this chair." And, "It is here at this table that we will dine together."

Despite her impatience to have the children living with them, she found that she was happy. Never before had she had the experience of going to bed at night with the certainty that Buckingham would be at her side in the morning and all the mornings to come. To actually *live* with him was a heady experience indeed. Often, in the evenings, she would neglect her tapestry and merely sit watching his face as he read, the candlelight casting shadows across his sensitive, strongly masculine features. She found that he was unfailingly good humored with her and that rich laughter and warm caresses were hers on instant demand.

When the house was finished, they moved in, and Mary was summoned to return from Nun Appleton to Wallingford House. It was agreed among the three of them that Buckingham would live with Anna-Maria, but for appearances' sake, he would appear frequently at Wallingford House and even entertain there occasionally.

"I would not have the gossips saying that you are a deserted wife," he said to Mary. "You know well that you have my respect and affection always."

Mary's plain face lit with happiness. If he would only go on smiling at her the way he was smiling now, she would be content.

Anna-Maria and Buckingham entertained frequently, and Anna-Maria began to be confident of her success as a hostess. Despite the cloud of scandal that hung over their household, the courtiers fought for an invitation to her table and went away boasting of the good food and fine company. Anna-Maria selected their guests carefully, and many were chosen simply because she and Buckingham wanted to influence them against Talbot. Slowly, steadily, Buckingham was adding to his already enormous power. But sometimes he felt helpless because Anna-Maria had sacrificed so much for his sake, and he could do so little in return.

One night, as they were undressing for bed, he was unusually quiet and morose. Anna-Maria had been chattering about the evening's entertainment, but she broke off and looked at him anxiously. "What's wrong, my love?"

His voice leaden with pain, he said, "Anna-Maria, now that Francis is dead, you are free to marry. You have a vast fortune, you are beautiful—"

Anna-Maria interrupted quickly. "And my reputation is in shreds."

Buckingham waved aside her objection. "There's no woman at Whitehall who has not had a scandal to live down. If I leave you now, if you live quietly for a time, you will be able to marry anyone you wish."

The room was so quiet that for a moment Anna-Maria could hear the birds singing in the garden outside. He was right, she knew. In a year or so everything would be forgotten in the overlay of fresh scandals that rocked London daily. She could marry again, someone of her own rank, and have the life she had dreamed of as a young girl. A quiet, respectable life in the country. For a moment she was tempted, and then she looked at Buckingham, and her spirit rushed toward him in an irresistible tide. She said softly, "I need you as I need the blood that flows through my veins, as I need the beat of my heart. If they stopped, I would die. So, too, would I die if you and I parted."

She spoke without passion, in a simple, matter-of-fact tone that was more convincing than any emotional entreaty.

"I'm not a humble man, my love. I'm often criticized for overweening pride. But your love humbles me." He wasn't touching her except with his voice and his eyes.

"You'll stay with me?" Anna-Maria's voice was uninflected, but her posture betrayed that her life hung in the balance.

"I will stay as long as we both shall live."

It was as though Buckingham spoke his marriage vows. She put out her hand and curled it into his. Both had tears stinging their eyes. It was a moment beyond words, and they were too emotional to speak. Buckingham finally broke the spell by bending and kissing her bare shoulder.

In the weeks that followed, Anna-Maria's happiness increased. She believed that the worst of the scandal attached to her was the label of murderess and that, in time, it would be forgotten. In the meantime, life was sweet indeed. She saw the children daily, she visited and gossiped with Nell, shopped at the Royal Exchange, and went to the theatre. And always, always, Buckingham was by her side, his eyes meeting hers in a shared joke, his understanding ear always ready for her confidences.

After several months had passed, she noticed that people no longer made a sign to ward off evil when her coach passed them in the street and that not in several weeks had the hissing whisper "murderess" followed her as she moved from stall to stall at the Royal Exchange.

Her days took on a quiet rhythm that was a balm to her wounded spirit. She felt that she had finally sailed into a safe, happy harbor. Each morning she awoke with her head pillowed on Buckingham's chest, his deep breathing a contented sound beneath her ear. As they ate, bathed, and dressed, there was a constant exchange of laughter and kisses. Often Buckingham reversed the process in the middle of dressing and took her back to bed for another hour or two. When he had finally dressed and left her, Anna-Maria would find her mind leaping ahead to the moment of his return. His absence would have been unbearable save that, in imagination, she kept him always by her side. It was for his sake that she consulted the cook about the evening's menu, for his pleasure that she arranged fresh flowers throughout the rooms.

For years, ever since first going to court, she had been keyed up, alert for a sign of danger. Now she relaxed entirely, blissfully happy.

Thirty-Three

Nell, her small face alight with happiness, had confided to Anna-Maria that she was carrying the king's child, but there was no hint of it yet as she stood on the stage in the King's Theatre, playing Almahide in Dryden's *The Conquest of Granada by the Spaniards*. Anna-Maria leaned forward in her box and studied Nell's form with a critical, discerning eye. Nell's waist was still a mere handspan, her hips as slim as ever. Yet Anna-Maria fancied there was a new fullness to Nell's face, a bloom to her complexion.

Anna-Maria turned to whisper to Buckingham and then froze, feeling as though ice water were plunging through her veins. At her left, on the far side of the theatre, she could swear that she saw Henry Killigrew seated next to Lord Brockhurst. Her posture was so rigid, her face so white, that Buckingham noticed it and became instantly alarmed. "Are you ill?"

"No!" Anna-Maria shook her head in impatient denial and then whispered back. "My eyes are playing me uncomfortable tricks. I could swear that was Henry Killigrew in Brockhurst's box."

Buckingham followed the direction of her pointing finger. He examined the distant figure for a moment and then said, "Aye, it is. I wonder that he dares return from France."

Anna-Maria could not speak, she was so choked with rage. It was Killigrew who had first damaged her reputation, Killigrew who had created the scene in this very theatre that had caused her break with both Buckingham and Francis. If Killigrew had not caused the scene, Francis might be alive today and she would have her children with her. She would not have fled to France, would not have returned openly to Buckingham's arms, there would have been no duel. . . .

She was tearing at the silk fabric of her fan, shredding it as she would have liked to tear Killigrew's flesh. Buckingham's eyes were worried as he watched her. "Shall I challenge Killigrew and kill him?"

"No." Anna-Maria said it dully. The mere fact that he had to *ask* was a disappointment to her. She knew that Buckingham had never fully understood her wish to see Killigrew's blood shed. He had felt victorious the day that he had trounced Killigrew in this theatre. His lack of understanding weighed heavily on her heart, and she wanted no repetition of the quarrel that had sent her fleeing to France.

"Sssh." She leaned forward as though she were intent on the action taking place on stage, and Buckingham settled back in his chair, occasionally sending guarded glances at her. Lately Anna-Maria had been coming to court with him again, and he hoped that Killigrew's reappearance would not send her flying back to the safety of their home.

Anna-Maria fought back the tears that were threatening to choke her. She reacted to Killigrew's appearance with the same fear and revulsion she would have felt if she had suddenly confronted the devil reaching for her from the pits of hell. These last months had been so peaceful, so full of happiness and now . . .

Although she kept her eyes resolutely fixed on the stage, she saw nothing of the action that was taking place there. She was startled when loud clapping broke out, marking the end of the performance. She had to be an actress herself to respond to Buckingham's comments on the play.

Never before in their life together had she failed to confide in him, yet now she felt that there was a vast wall between them and she could not scale it. He does not understand what Killigrew did to me, she thought. No man understands what it is to be a woman, to lie helpless while a man takes his brutal pleasure on your violated body.

Buckingham was more aware of her feelings than she had thought, and when they reached the privacy of their bedchamber, he said softly, "Tell me what you are thinking."

She kept a distance between them, giving him the careless, practiced smile of a courtesan. "I am thinking of nothing, my love, except what pleasure it will be to dance in your arms tonight."

She pulled away, murmuring an excuse that time was short and she must bathe. The king was giving a large ball that evening, and everyone of importance at court would be in attendance. It was one of the affairs to which Queen Catherine could not refuse Anna-Maria admittance, and Buckingham had been eager for her to attend.

Anna-Maria drew false courage from the beauty of her gown. It was of gold cloth with an overskirt of tissue lace in the same rich shade. As Sarah helped her into it, Anna-Maria said shakily, "I feel as nervous as I did on the first day you dressed me to go to Whitehall."

Sarah's face was sympathetic. She had gloried in the last months when Anna-Maria had been so content, so carelessly happy with the duke, and she was as dismayed as Anna-Maria at Killigrew's return. Smoothing a fold of the glimmering skirt into place, she stood back to regard her handiwork. "Perhaps Killigrew has learned discretion at last. He's cooled his heels in France all these months, and I doubt that he wants to incur the king's disfavor again."

Anna-Maria picked up her gold lace fan and regarded her reflection in the mirror. Sarah had arranged Anna-Maria's hair into long curls that hung below her shoulders, with shorter curls caressing her forehead and cheeks. Near her left eye was a beauty patch, shaped in the letter B to honor Buckingham. It drew attention to the beauty of her eyes. Her bust rose full and enticing over the tight-fitting bodice of her gown, and her waist was a mere handspan beneath. Below that the full skirt of her elaborate gown billowed out and rustled as she moved. She gave the appearance of being a sophisticated lady of the court of Charles the Second, and no one could have known by looking at her that her palms were moist with nervousness, her stomach clenched with fear.

Buckingham let out a long, low whistle of approval when she twirled for his inspection. He was flirtatious and deferential, as though he had met her for the first time, as he handed her into the coach. Anna-Maria's heart lifted. Even though she and Buckingham lived together day and night now, they had never fallen into the attitude of indifferent complacency toward each other that befell so many men and women. Each night that he returned home, she felt her face grow radiant, her pulses fluttering. Every time they made love, he treated her as though it were the first time, as though he were overcome with the wonder of winning her.

Nothing, not even Killigrew, can mar what we have built between us, Anna-Maria thought, as their coach wound its way through the darkness toward the brightly lit palace of Whitehall. When they entered the palace, she was still full of soaring confidence, and she answered greetings and sallies with a ready wit.

The musicians, she noted, were in fine form tonight, and she tapped her foot impatiently, eager for the dancing to begin. When she danced with Buckingham, she felt as though she were a bird on the wing, so perfectly were their steps matched. She felt cheated each time someone else claimed her as a partner. Since she was popular, the times she was whirled from Buckingham's arms were frequent, and she found herself longing for the privacy of their bedchamber. The musicians would be absent, but she was just thinking that she and Buckingham could hum the tune and fit their steps in the privacy of candlelight and firelight, when she suddenly found Henry Killigrew bending over her hand. She gasped and would have drawn her hand away, but he had it in a firm grip, his smile sardonic. "You have the fine white hand of an Italian," he murmured.

Anna-Maria felt her cheeks flame indignantly. Italians were notorious for their skills with poisons, and she did not miss the allusion.

She felt her breath coming short, her eyes blazing as he rose from his bow and surveyed her with a look that stripped her of her clothing. If only she had a dagger to plunge into his evil heart!

"I understand that you are under the protection of the duke of Buckingham now," Killigrew said smoothly. "How the virtuous have fallen! When I fled England, you were still a married woman, protesting your innocence, and I return to find you a kept woman, as notorious as Nell Gwyn."

Anna-Maria could feel the blood beating in her veins. It was a moment before she could summon her voice, and then she said, between clenched teeth, "If you ever speak to me again, ever approach me, I will kill you!"

Killigrew's lips twisted. " 'Tis a threat that I must take seriously. All of London knows that you are capable of murder. I understand that your husband lies uneasy in his grave, his soul crying out for vengeance."

Anna-Maria was so angry now that she had lost all sense of time, place, or reason. She would have sprung at Killigrew, intending to claw his eyes out, had not the king's voice sounded at her side.

"I crave the privilege of dancing with the most graceful woman in the room."

She should have been honored. Etiquette demanded that the ladies of the court invite the king to dance, and this was a singular privilege that he had sought her out and asked *her*. She was aware of envious eyes as he led her out onto the floor, but it meant nothing to her. Her eyes were black with anger, and her breath came in little, indignant gasps.

The king was aware of her state and set himself to charming her into a semblance of calm. Anna-Maria, grateful for his kindness, forced herself to respond, and after a minute felt herself becoming calmer. When she could trust her voice, she looked at the king and said angrily, "The rumors that I poisoned my husband have been forgotten these past months. I fear that Killigrew will start them up afresh."

She was upset chiefly because she had hoped that soon she could demand the children's return. Londoners had begun to accept her irregular situation with Buckingham, and Talbot's argument that she was notorious would have less and less weight.

The king nodded sympathetically. "I'll have a private word with Killigrew."

Anna-Maria's answering smile was an instant reward for him. "Your Majesty, you are the best of friends. Buckingham and I have much to thank you for."

When the dance ended, she swept him a deep curtsy, the ample folds of her gown billowing out around her. She saw the king stride across the room and tap Killigrew on the shoulder. They withdrew to a corner of the vast room, and the king spoke quickly and decisively while Killigrew nodded. Anna-Maria's heart lightened. Killigrew would learn to hold his tongue still in his head or he would answer to his monarch!

In the weeks that followed, she found that the king's influence on Killigrew was less strong than she had thought. Killigrew, who was certain that the king could never stay angry with him for long, returned to slyly tormenting Anna-Maria. He would insinuate himself into a position near her, breathe a low insult into her ear, and then move away before she had time to turn and confront him. He was careful, however, never to do it when Buckingham was within earshot, and Anna-Maria found that she did not want to tell Buckingham about it. Once she had seen Buckingham face another man in a duel for her sake, had seen blood streaming from his body, and she could not bear it again. She had thought that she wanted Buckingham to kill Killigrew, yet now she felt herself flinching from the prospect of a duel. Buckingham was by far the better swordsman, but in every duel there was the chance of an error. Suppose Buckingham slipped on wet grass or was blinded by the sun? Killigrew's sword could rip into his flesh in that instant, and she would be left bereft, with the knowledge that his death was of her own making.

She began to have nightmares. Once again she was back in the tavern with Killigrew's hot, heavy body pressing her into the bed. Again and again he assaulted her, his face mocking, until she awoke sobbing with helpless rage, to find Buckingham bending over her anxiously. "What is it, my love?" Each time she excused her nightmare on the grounds of having too rich food before sleeping. Buckingham, alarmed at the frequency of the nightmares, began watching over her diet, insisting that she eat only bland foods during the evening. But the nightmares continued, and Anna-Maria found herself fearing sleep. She lay awake in the darkness, staring. Killigrew would give her no peace as long as he lived.

The long nights of sleeplessness began to take their toll. She grew thin, strained, and nervously irritable. Buckingham thought that she was ill, and Anna-Maria seized on the excuse to stay away from court for a time. "I confess that I have a sick headache, my love, and it does not seem to get better. If I rested a few days . . ."

Buckingham was instantly concerned, and Anna-Maria felt a twinge of guilt at lying to him. Nevertheless, it was a relief to have him tuck her into bed and ride off to court without her.

She lay quietly, with a vinegar-soaked cloth that he had applied before he left on her forehead, and tried to read. Killigrew's mocking image kept superimposing itself on the page, and eventually she tossed the book away in disgust. For nearly a week she stayed away from court, and gradually the peace and quiet of her own home served as a balm.

On the afternoon of the fifth day, she was sitting quietly in front of the fire, staring into the flames, when the footman entered and held out a note on a silver tray. "This was just delivered, madam."

Anna-Maria thought it must be one of Nell's lively, ill-spelled messages, and she took it with a look of pleasure. Smiling she unfolded the single page and scanned it, then recoiled with a look of horror. It was a badly rhymed couplet, unsigned, that reviled her as a whore and a murderess. Unable to help herself, she read it again and again with sick fascination, the words seeming to burn into her brain. Killigrew! No one else's hand could have penned such obscenity.

She began to shake. Abruptly she rose and tossed the page into the fireplace, then began stabbing at it with the poker, as though it were Killigrew's face. If only she were a man so that she could challenge Killigrew herself! He thought her a helpless woman so he dared treat her as he would treat no man! If Buckingham were to challenge him, Killigrew would disclaim all authorship of the couplet and would raise his eyebrow in surprise at Anna-Maria's accusations that he was constantly whispering vile insults to her. And in any case she could not put Buckingham's life in danger for her sake.

She wanted to take action herself, to slash at Killigrew the way she was slashing now with this poker. Suddenly she had an idea. She could not openly challenge Killigrew to a duel. It would be absurd, and she knew nothing of swordsmanship. But she could waylay him in the dark of night and thus avenge herself.

Suddenly she felt less helpless, less vulnerable. She wanted to set out that very night to seek out Killigrew, but she knew that she must plan carefully.

When Buckingham returned, he was delighted to find that the color was back in Anna-Maria's face, her energy fully returned. She was eager to accompany him to court the next day and the days that followed. She used the opportunity to study Killigrew's habits and discovered that each night he followed the same route to his home at Turham Green.

Now, when he sidled up to her at court and delivered one of his low-voiced insults, she merely smiled indifferently. Killigrew studied her in puzzlement, his eyes narrowed, but Anna-Maria gave no hint of her scheme.

Thirty-Four

Anna-Maria's palms were damp, and her heart kept rhythm with the pounding of the horse's hoofs as the black coach moved through the moonlit night. She had not dared to take her own coach on tonight's errand lest it be recognized, and when she went to hire a coach she had been seized by an impulse and chosen a black mourning coach. It's the perfect symbolism, she thought. I'm mourning my ruined reputation, my dead husband, my lost children.

She could hear the low voices of the four footmen who were accompanying her. They were a rough breed. She had selected them for their strong physiques and for their reputation for keeping a still tongue in their heads, warning them that it would go ill with all of them if this night's work became known.

"Oh, Sweet Jesu!" The coach was stopping now,

pulling to a halt in the shadows of the highway. They would remain hidden, waiting, until Killigrew passed. As she sat in the darkness of the coach, Anna-Maria's resolution almost faltered. She had never deliberately struck another human being in her life, never willingly inflicted pain. She rubbed her gloved hand nervously against the leather of the seat and wished that her heart were not beating so rapidly; she felt as though she were suffocating. She had only to tap on the roof of the coach and order the footmen to turn back. Her hand half lifted in the gesture, and then she checked it, steeling herself to resolution. She deliberately recalled Killigrew's raping her, his persistent and relentless persecution, his sly insults, his cruel slanders. He had used her without a humane feeling, and she would show him none now!

A lust for revenge swept through her, and she leaned forward, eager for action. Suddenly she heard one of the footmen give a low-voiced warning that Killigrew's coach was approaching.

Anna-Maria leaned out of the window and strained to catch a glimpse of the coach. It was lumbering down the center of the dirt highway, the coachman half asleep atop the box. As it drew near them, Anna-Maria's hired footmen leaped out of the darkness. The tallest of them ran to stop the horses, and the coachman came awake with a start.

"Here now! What's amiss?"

As he spoke, another of the footmen leaped nimbly onto the seat beside him and swiftly bound and gagged him.

It was Killigrew she wanted! She watched breathlessly as two of the footmen jerked open the door of the coach and dragged Killigrew into the dust of the road. Killigrew was screaming protests in which there was a high note of fear. The sound sped along Anna-Maria's nerves, further inflamed her as she remembered her own screams when Killigrew had raped her.

Leaping from the black mourning coach, the sound of her heartbeat loud in her ears, she looked down with satisfaction at Killigrew sprawled in the dust. His doublet had been ripped as the footmen dragged him from his coach, and his hair was already thick with mire from the road. Her footmen stood above him, their knives and cudgels upraised, their moonlit faces already revealing a lust for his blood, but Anna-Maria waved them back. This moment was for herself and Killigrew alone.

Killigrew was cursing frantically and struggling to regain his feet, meanwhile glancing in every direction to gauge the number of his enemies. His weak face was slack with terror, and the sight stimulated Anna-Maria.

Slowly, deliberately, she dropped the hood of her cloak so that her long chestnut hair streamed down her back and her delicate face was clearly visible in the moonlight.

Killigrew paused in his effort to rise and dropped back on one elbow, his face stupid with surprise. "Anna-Maria!"

Anna-Maria stood looking down at him for a long moment, savoring her sense of victory. Then she said softly, almost gently, "I'm going to cut out your malicious tongue. No other woman's reputation will suffer from your lies as mine has done."

Killigrew remained motionless, searching her face. Some of his fear was beginning to ebb away. No doubt Anna-Maria had a score to settle with him, but she was a gently born lady and would do him no real harm.

He made the mistake of smiling in his relief, and Anna-Maria's control snapped. "You scurvy dog! Fiend from the lowest pit of hell!"

She snatched a dagger from the nearest footman and held it over Killigrew, the blade glinting in the moonlight. The handle was heavily carved, and she could feel its indentations against her palm. A sense of triumph spread through her as she saw fear springing into Killigrew's eyes.

"Once, in that tavern, you thrust and thrust into my body, although I implored you to stop. I was helpless, just as you are now. Learn how it feels, Killigrew, to be at someone's mercy. Your body is going to be violated as mine was, and you can do nothing to prevent it! Are you as humiliated as I was?" She was panting, unaware of the tears that were streaming down her cheeks. Hatred filled her so that she was choking on it. "Now *I've* a mind to thrust into you, Killigrew."

She thrust the dagger downward, aiming for Killigrew's heart. The moonlight flashed along the blade. She saw the stark horror in Killigrew's bulging eyes. At the last second, with a despairing sob, she deflected the blade and sent it plunging into his leg. The slicing of the dagger into soft flesh was sickening, and involuntarily she released the blade and jumped back with her hand to her mouth, fighting nausea. For a long moment, she and Killigrew stared at each other. Death hung between them. For a moment she wanted to turn and flee.

As she watched, Killigrew's face hardened into a desperate rage, and he struggled to his feet, pulling his dagger free. "You whoring bitch, you'll die now!"

He lunged at Anna-Maria, and she stood frozen, unable to move, certain that in a second she would feel the bite of the blade in her heart. Then her footmen encircled Killigrew and set upon him. The dagger in his hand, Killigrew fought them with the savagery of a bear being baited, his weak face twisted with rage, his eyes murderous. The air rang with oaths, cries of rage, and the sound of cudgels against flesh.

Anna-Maria's voice pierced the clear air. "Beat him!" Her cries mingled with the sounds of battle, and then suddenly silence fell, and the footmen stepped back. Anna-Maria's cry was bitten off. Killigrew was lying senseless in the dust; the footmen's cudgels dangled at their sides.

Anna-Maria stared down at Killigrew's blood oozing into dark shapes in the dust. She could feel her fierce anger slipping away as swiftly as Killigrew's blood was slipping from his body. Fear replaced it. In a hoarse, dazed whisper, she asked, "Is he dead?"

The largest of the footmen seized her by the waist and hoisted her unceremoniously into the black coach. "I don't know, my lady, but we had best flee. You said to beat him, not kill him, but in the heat of battle —" He shook his head and gave a dubious backwards glance at Killigrew's still form.

Anna-Maria huddled in the back of the coach, biting on her knuckles, hating herself for her female weakness. For so long she had wanted Killigrew dead, and now her heart was shaking with fear lest she have the stain of murder on her soul. A man would not have deflected the dagger as she had done, he would have driven it straight into Killigrew's heart and gone away with triumphant laughter on his lips.

She wanted nothing in the world as much as the comfort of Buckingham's strong arms, and the journey back seemed interminable. She was drenched with perspiration and deathly white by the time they reached her home. Forcing herself to appear calm, she handed the footmen a purse fat with gold coins.

Then she picked up her dusty skirts and ran into the house. Buckingham was asleep, his arm thrown across his eyes, and it took a moment to rouse him. He blinked in the candlelight, bewildered to find Anna-Maria fully dressed and in a state of panic. In a voice thick with sleep, he asked, "What is it, my love?"

"I've killed Killigrew." Anna-Maria looked nearly witless with fear.

Buckingham shook his head to clear it, his expression incredulous. For a moment he thought that she was having another nightmare, but her dusty garments and the scent of damp air that clung about her spoke of her having been out.

With the alertness of a man trained for the battlefield, Buckingham woke fully. Anna-Maria's teeth were chattering, and the slight clicking sound convinced him instantly of the urgency of her fear. He threw back the bedcovers and took her into his arms. "Tell me!"

"He has been tormenting me—taunting me at court, reviling me with insults, calling me a whore and a murderess." Her words were indistinct because she was shaking so hard, and Buckingham had to use all his wits to decipher her meaning. Gradually he pieced the story together—the hiring of the mourning coach and the four footmen, the scene that had taken place on the moonlit highway. He was caught between admiration for her courage and fear for her safety.

"Are you certain he is dead?" His fingers gripped

her shoulders, rousing her from her self-absorbed terror.

Anna-Maria shook her head, her hair spilling across her face. "No. The footmen pushed me into the coach before we could be certain." She began to scrub her hand over and over against the fabric of her cloak. "If he dies, I will be a murderess." She was remembering the sickening feel of the knife as it sliced into Killigrew's flesh.

"Killigrew deserved death at your hands." Buckingham tried to rekindle some of the anger that had prompted her action, but Anna-Maria swayed limply in his arms, and he could rouse no fighting spirit in her. He picked her up and laid her on the bed, then began chafing her cold wrists.

"Sleep, my love. In the morning I will send to find if he still lives."

Had she fainted or had normal exhaustion overcome her? He studied her pale face anxiously. Her lashes lay heavy on her pale cheeks, but her breathing was even. He lay awake, only one candle dancing in the gloom of the room, and pondered the problem.

Buckingham was dressed and out before dawn, and by the time Anna-Maria awakened, he had returned with the news that Killigrew had sustained serious wounds but still clung to life, although he was in such a weakened condition that the surgeons expected him to die at any moment. Anna-Maria remembered the moonlit night, the tall, silhouetted figures ringing Killigrew, their cudgels rising and falling relentlessly. She shivered and whispered, "God help me! I must have been insane!"

When she looked into Buckingham's face, she felt a chill of fear settle in her bones. He had always been so strong, so certain before, and now, although he tried to mask it, she could see that he was desperately worried. He forced her to eat, spooning the food into her mouth with his own hands, before saying, "Killigrew has sworn information against you, and the lord chief justice has begun to make inquiries. You must go into hiding for a time."

Anna-Maria looked around her desperately, like a hunted animal. "Hide? Where?"

"Nell's?" Buckingham was turning the idea over in his mind.

Anna-Maria shook her head, numb with misery. "Killigrew knows of my friendship with Nell. He'll send the lord chief justice there."

"If this house only had a priest hole!" Buckingham was fingering the handle of his dagger, frowning in concentration. Finally he said reluctantly, "There's no help for it. It will have to be in public lodgings—a room over an inn."

Anna-Maria brushed away the apologetic note in his voice. "I do not care where I hide. It's the reason for hiding that is so terrible to me." Putting her hands to her slim white throat, she felt her pulse leap erratically against her fingertips. "I will be executed for murder, and my soul will go straight to hell!" Her fear was almost a tangible presence in the room.

"My love!" Buckingham's voice was raised as he fought to bring her back from the visions that were tormenting her. "You will not be executed, I swear it! And God himself must understand that Killigrew goaded you beyond endurance."

"I was so angry," Anna-Maria whispered, "that I gave no thought to the gravity of what I was doing—"

"You did exactly what I would have done." If Buckingham lived to be a hundred years old, he would never fully understand this complicated woman that he loved. Underneath his fear for her was a glowing pride that she had taken such bold action against her enemy.

An uncharacteristically cynical smile touched Anna-Maria's delicate lips. "Aye, but since you are a man, you could have challenged him openly, with your honor intact. I had to attack him secretly—" Suddenly much of her fear disappeared, and her head went back defiantly. "I did it in the only way open to me, and I must take the consequences."

Thirty-Five

Sarah had prudently taken rooms in an inn in one of the poorer sections of London, a place where the innkeeper displayed little curiosity about his guests, wisely turning a deaf ear to their activities.

Anna-Maria stood in the middle of the shabby room and slowly inspected it, while Sarah apologized. "I felt that the lord chief justice would never look for the countess of Shrewsbury *here.*" She flinched and jumped back as a loud bellow of coarse laughter rang out in the hall. She looked anxiously at the door to see if it was securely fastened. "But there may be worse dangers here."

Anna-Maria laughed for the first time in forty-eight hours. "No doubt I am sharing this inn with highwaymen and pickpockets. Which is fitting since I've become a highwayman myself."

She poked a finger into the lumpy bed. "If my tender conscience is not enough to keep me sleepless, this bed will be."

She began to unpack her few possessions, placing her books atop a crude wooden chest and her embroidery on the arm of the one chair. The few gowns she had brought with her belonged to one of her serving women, who had been both baffled and honored when the countess had begged to borrow them.

Sarah marveled at her calm, but Anna-Maria knew that her composure could crack at any second, and she busied herself with small details to keep herself from thinking. At this very moment Killigrew might be gasping his last breath. For a moment the thought of the gypsy flickered through her mind. Was it true that her future was written on her palm? Had it been destiny that some day she would shed a man's blood?

"Sarah, my rosary beads! I've forgotten them!" She began to search frantically, but the mother-of-pearl beads were nowhere in her possession. "I want to pray for Killigrew's life. And my soul." The irony of it struck her with the force of a blow. She had wanted nothing in the world so much as Killigrew's death, and now, with the same intensity, she wanted him to live.

Sarah fished the rosary beads out of the depths of her voluminous skirts and held them out. "I thought that you would want them."

"I've been so blessed in my life. To have a friend with your depth of understanding—" She broke off, but her expression was more eloquent than any speech, and Sarah hugged her tightly. She wanted to share Anna-Maria's vigil, but Anna-Maria urged her to go home where she would be able to learn instantly if Killigrew lived or died.

When Sarah had gone, Anna-Maria knelt on the splintery floor, unrelieved by the softness of a rug, and began to pray. She knelt for hours, until her knees ached and the evening shadows began massing in the corners of the room. She had just risen and was lighting a candle when Buckingham slipped into the room, his face impassive but his eyes burning with anger.

Anna-Maria turned to look at him, the candle in her upraised hand. Her expression asked the question that her trembling lips could not form.

Buckingham took off his hat and threw it onto the bed. "Killigrew still lives."

Anna-Maria let out her breath in a long sigh of relief.

Buckingham looked around the room, and his mouth twisted in distaste. "It grieves me to see you in such a place."

Anna-Maria shrugged and looked around her indifferently. "It's a refuge."

Buckingham nodded. "The lord chief justice came with a warrant for you today and searched the house."

She gasped and began trembling.

Buckingham caught her hands in his. "I will keep you safe, my love."

He had been closeted with the king all afternoon, trying to find a way to protect Anna-Maria. The king had been sympathetic to her. He knew that above all women at court she had been sorely beset, and he could not blame her for hating Killigrew. The king's lips had twitched under his black mustache in a grin he could not repress. "The black mourning coach was a picturesque touch." Nevertheless, he could do nothing until they learned whether or not the charge would be murder. Killigrew's life hung in the balance, and they must all wait.

Buckingham bent and gently kissed Anna-Maria's trembling lips. "I'll go to the cookshops and bring back a light supper for us."

Anna-Maria started to protest that she had no appetite, but Buckingham had already picked up his plumed hat and was halfway out the door.

He returned with his arms laden, and she hastened to relieve him of his burden. There was only one small table in the room, its surface marred and scratched, and Buckingham was obliged to put one of Anna-Maria's slim, leather-bound books under the table leg to keep it from wobbling. Anna-Maria thought of the care with which she had furnished their sumptuous home, and she was caught between laughter and tears.

Buckingham, sensing the direction of her thoughts, smiled at her. "I have only one requirement for a home, my love—that you grace it with your presence." He picked up a leg of roasted chicken and bit into it. "The rest"—he waved his hand around the meager room—"doesn't matter to me."

Anna-Maria felt tears spring into her eyes. "How kind you are," she said softly.

"Kind?" He cocked an eye at her. "I'm a man in love. That's an entirely different matter."

He insisted that she eat, and in a few moments she found herself biting into a chicken leg with genuine enjoyment. Her worries seemed to slip away into the shadows as she watched his face. "Love is a miracle, isn't it?" There was awe in her voice. "When I'm with you I care about nothing else."

He held her hand during the rest of the meal, and they shared a wineglass, Anna-Maria taking care to place her lips in the exact spot his had touched.

When the meal was finished, Buckingham rose and tested the bed as Anna-Maria had done earlier. He grinned broadly. "There is no chance of *sleeping* on this flea-infested, lump-ridden mattress. How do you suppose we can occupy ourselves through the long night?"

Anna-Maria moved slowly toward him. Her voice husky, she looked at him from under her dark lashes. "I rely on your wit and intelligence to find a pastime to divert us, my lord."

In the morning the room seemed less shabby to her. She was not even acutely lonely because she knew that Buckingham would be returning in the evening, and the room seemed filled with his voice, his laughter. She set a routine for herself to while away the hours —so much time for prayer, for embroidery, for leisurely reading. Always, underneath, was the haunting fear that at any moment Sarah or Buckingham might appear and announce that Killigrew was dead.

If Killigrew died, she would be hanged as a murderess. Anna-Maria had once passed Tyburn Hill just as a hanging was taking place. The avid crowd had hemmed her in so that she was forced to stay and watch the execution. The condemned man had put up a frenzied fight for his life, and Anna-Maria had never forgotten the look of stark horror on his face. When the rope broke his neck, he was still screaming protests, his eyes bulging. He had worn that expression of frozen fear into eternity, and it was still engraved on Anna-Maria's mind.

She looked up, terrified, when Buckingham appeared unexpectedly at midday near the end of the week. She jumped to her feet and stood facing him, her fear so great that it welled up in her throat and forced a low moan from her lips.

"There's nothing to fear, my sweet. Killigrew is out

of danger. In fact, he is so well that he received visitors this morning, and I was the first of them!"

"You went to Killigrew?" Anna-Maria was laughing and crying simultaneously, the tears hanging like diamonds on her dark lashes.

"Aye." Buckingham grinned at her with enormous satisfaction. "He has agreed to drop the charges against you. You are free to come home, my love!"

"But why—?" The thought of home rushed through her like a clean wind.

Buckingham had his hand clapped victoriously on the hilt of his sword. "I told Killigrew that if he did not drop the charges I would deal with him myself and this time he would of a certainty find himself in his grave."

Buckingham began to laugh. "I also think that he fears *you,* my sweet. He'd thought you a helpless female, but now he bears scars from the wounds you dealt him, and he will be wary of you in the future." He took off his hat and swept her a deep bow. "Madame, I congratulate you!"

"Oh, do not joke about it!" It was a reprieve, a wonderful reprieve, but she could not so quickly forget all the days she had spent locked in this room, certain that the stain of murder would soon be on her soul.

"Hurry." Buckingham was already moving about the room, packing her meager possessions, but she stayed him with a swift gesture.

"Will you wait?" she asked quietly. "It was here in this room that I implored God to spare Killigrew, and it is here that I must give thanks."

He nodded, his blue eyes filled with understanding. When she knelt, he knelt beside her, and they prayed together. At the conclusion, still kneeling, Anna-Maria turned and kissed him tenderly.

He rose and helped her to her feet, and then brushed ruefully at his dust-covered knees. Anna-Maria found herself laughing, giddy from the release of tension.

When they emerged into the London air, she breathed deeply of freedom, not caring that the air was foul with the smoke from the tanneries and the odor of human refuse. How wonderful it was to know herself free! The commonplace sights of the streets delighted her, and she pointed them out to Buckingham as though they were novelties. He was as lighthearted as she, and by the time they reached home, they were both weak with laughter, their faces glowing.

Sarah was loitering in the hall, eager to be on hand to welcome Anna-Maria home. Anna-Maria hugged her so exuberantly that Sarah pulled away, protesting.

"I vow that you have broken two of my ribs!"

That, too, struck Buckingham and Anna-Maria as funny, and they caught each other's eyes and shook with laughter.

Sarah looked from one to the other with mock indignation; she was also feeling the release after the long week of terror, and she vented it in the form of affectionate scolding. "You look a fair disgrace in those rags!"

She bundled Anna-Maria off to bathe and change while Anna-Maria called laughingly over her shoulder to Buckingham, "You see. I have been given into the hands of a jailer after all."

The next few weeks were idyllic. One night, lying in Buckingham's arms, Anna-Maria said, "We should always live our lives as though we might die tomorrow. I thought to be executed as a murderess, and now that I have been reprieved, everything seems the sweeter because I had thought to lose it." With her finger she was tracing the outline of a heart on his naked chest. She had wonderful news to tell him, and she was pondering the best way to do so.

Buckingham noticed her abstracted expression and asked, "What are you thinking of, my love?"

When she raised her head, he caught his breath in admiration. Her eyes were so filled with happiness that they looked golden in the flare of the candlelight. Anna-Maria suddenly discarded all her carefully rehearsed speeches and said simply, "We are to have a child."

Buckingham looked stunned, disbelieving. The deepest sorrow of his life had been that he had never fathered a child. The simple pleasure that was given to any peasant working in a field had been denied to the great Villiers, duke of Buckingham, and his pride had suffered a sore blow. Often he had suspected darkly that the fault lay not with his wife, Mary, but with himself. And now Anna-Maria, who had given him so much, was giving him this priceless gift.

He leaned on one elbow, his joy blazing in every line of his features.

She smiled, asking unnecessarily, "You are happy, my love?"

"Happy!" He found his voice at last and pulled her to him. "To have a son at last. . . ."

Anna-Maria leaned back slightly so she could look into his face. "I feared—" She hesitated and then took a deep breath. "The baby will not be legitimate."

Buckingham's arms tightened around her; she could feel his powerful muscles rippling. "He will be *my son*, a Villiers, and none shall dare call him a bastard."

Anna-Maria relaxed suddenly, nestling against his chest. Giving birth had always seemed a miracle to her, but never had she felt it more keenly than at this moment. For a woman to bear a child to a man she loved as deeply as she loved Buckingham must be the ultimate happiness. "He will be a young god," she murmured, "an Apollo fashioned by our love."

Buckingham, his cheek against her soft hair, was planning busily. Already in his mind the child was old enough to sit on a horse and Buckingham was instructing him. . . .

"When?" he asked, and Anna-Maria said dreamily, "By my reckoning, he will be born sometime in February."

They murmured plans while the firelight died and the candles burned down, neither aware of the swift passage of the night. When the fire had sunk to glowing embers, Buckingham rose to kindle it.

Anna-Maria sat up in bed watching him. The white lace of her nightdress had fallen from one shoulder, and she pulled it up absently, then said, her voice hesitant, "The only flaw in my happiness is Mary's pain when we tell her you are finally to have a child. She wanted so badly to give you one."

Buckingham's expression was instantly sympathetic,

regretful. "She is the best of wives, and I have brought her nothing but unhappiness." They were both silent for a moment, and then he said heavily, "I will tell her in the morn. It's best that she hears it immediately from my own lips."

In the morning Buckingham rode to Wallingford House, and Anna-Maria, busy about her tasks, found her imagination straining to picture the scene that was taking place with Mary.

When Buckingham returned, she flew into his arms and scanned his face anxiously. He looked bemused, shaking his head and saying, "I begin to believe that Mary is a saint. She vowed that she was happy for me, for you also, and I swear, Anna-Maria, that her emotion was genuine."

"How generous she is." Anna-Maria's voice was filled with gratitude and wonder. Could she be as generous if another woman was bearing Buckingham's child? At the thought her eyes squeezed shut in a spasm of jealousy, and she clung to him, her fingers tangled in the cloth of his cloak. Intensity was in her voice as she begged, "Swear to me that you will never leave me."

"Never!" Buckingham bent his head and sought her mouth.

Thirty-Six

"The king is sending me to France." Buckingham's face was bitterly unhappy.

"Oh, no!" Anna-Maria stood up, the book she had been holding dropping from her suddenly nerveless fingers.

"Minette is dead."

"Oh, dear God!" Anna-Maria was seized with pain. Minette was the king's adored younger sister. She had recently visited England, and Anna-Maria, like everyone who came in contact with Minette, had adored her instantly. "How did she die?"

"She drank iced chickory water, was stricken with severe pain—and died."

Anna-Maria felt tears misting her eyes. All that bright laughter, that young joy, gone. "The poor king," she murmured pityingly. She knew well that the king loved his younger sister above all people in the world.

"He is wild with grief." Buckingham sounded heartbroken. "For a few hours I feared for his sanity. The worst part is that there is a suspicion that Philippe had her poisoned."

"Sweet Jesu!" Anna-Maria put her hand to her throat, horror in her eyes. Minette's husband, Philippe, the younger brother of the king of France, was an effeminate, mean-spirited man who painted his face and affected women's clothing in secret. He had always been bitterly jealous of his young, beautiful wife who so easily won the love and adulation he craved but never received.

Buckingham was angrily beating his fist into his palm. When he and the king had been in exile in France, they had made a pet of Minette, and Buckingham had been half in love with the gentle, high-spirited girl.

Anna-Maria touched his hand sympathetically and remained silent. After a moment he collected himself and looked down at her regretfully. "I hate to leave you, darling. Especially when you are pregnant."

Anna-Maria fought with herself to be brave. After all, she was alive and well. It was Minette who lay stilled beneath the cold earth. Looking at him levelly, she said, "I will be fine."

"Good girl." Buckingham gave her a look of approval and then went back to pacing the floor restlessly. He would like to be in France this very moment with his hands around Philippe's smooth, effeminate throat. "If he has caused her death, I'll kill him myself," he vowed.

Anna-Maria wrestled with the feeling of loss that

was overwhelming her. When she could trust her voice, she asked, "When will you leave?"

"Tonight. As soon as I can pack and be on my way."

"Then let me help you." Anna-Maria was proud of the ease with which she spoke the words. There would be time enough when he was gone to indulge in tears. Now he needed her to be steady and calm.

She would not let the serving women pack his trunk. She wanted to handle each of his garments herself, stroking them with loving care before folding them. Her fingers were trembling, but she tried to keep Buckingham from noticing. Once her eyes fell on their bed, and she felt grief overwhelm her. How many nights would she lie there without him? Already she felt the ache of loss, and she stole quick glances at him as he moved around the room, memorizing each line of his strong face.

An hour before he left, she sent for Mary so that she too could make her farewells. Mary stepped over the threshold and flashed Anna-Maria a look of gratitude, thanking her for her thoughtfulness. She knew that her husband would have set off posthaste for France and sent her word later had not Anna-Maria intervened.

"I know how grieved you must be at Minette's death. You'll help the king greatly by going to France and determining the truth." She put her hand on Buckingham's sleeve and looked up at him, her face very grave.

Buckingham covered her hand with his own. "It's a bad business, Mary."

Mary nodded. She had been at court this morning and knew a great deal about the matter. She said gently, "My dear, be certain that it *was* murder before you punish Philippe. Let your cool head rule you instead of your hot temper."

Anna-Maria, standing by quietly watching, was struck anew by how much there was of motherliness in Mary's attitude toward her husband.

Buckingham nodded his head in tacit promise and Mary, standing on tiptoe, placed a kiss on his cheek.

Buckingham took her face gently in his hands. "Will

you make me a promise, my dear? Will you take care of Anna-Maria while I am gone?"

Mary nodded, her eyes clinging to his, and gave him her soft-voiced promise. Anna-Maria felt tears prickling beneath her eyelids. If only Mary could find a man who loved her deeply. But Mary claimed to be content with her life as it was now, to have Buckingham's respectful affection, Anna-Maria's friendship. She seemed genuinely happy about the baby and had already begun sewing small, intricately worked garments.

Mary tactfully withdrew, saying she was expected back at court, so that Anna-Maria and Buckingham could make their farewells alone. Despite her resolutions, Anna-Maria found herself clinging to Buckingham. Life was very uncertain. One day Minette had been alive, laughing, and the next day they were preparing her for burial. Buckingham's ship could be lost at sea, his horse could throw him. . . .

Tears were wending a damp trail down her cheeks, although she made no sound. Buckingham groaned and pulled her so tightly against him that she could not breathe. "My love, don't look at me like that. Your eyes are like a wounded deer's."

Anna-Maria forced a smile onto her trembling lips. She didn't want him to ride off with a tearful image of her. He kissed her with such passionate intensity that her lips were bruised, and then, suddenly, he was gone.

The house seemed very silent when he had left. Anna-Maria wandered disconsolately through the rooms, watching as the sunlight caught the dust particles in the air. She must set up a rigid schedule, must fill her days with so much activity that she had no time for wistful longing for Buckingham. She wanted to stay cheerful and healthy for the baby's sake.

She lived for the hastily scrawled messages that came from Buckingham, telling her of the course of his investigation—and of his love. At last, he wrote that Minette had died from natural causes, of cholera morbus, and that she had been so brave during her illness that no one had known of the pain she was experiencing, although she must have been secretly ill for a very long time.

Anna-Maria remembered suddenly that during her visit to England, Minette had often turned pale, her hand flying to her stomach, but no word of complaint had ever escaped her lips. Anna-Maria heaved a sigh of relief that Minette had not been poisoned by her husband and read on. Suddenly her face flushed with joy. Buckingham was on his way home!

The letter fluttered from her hand as she rose and began pacing the room, in a fever of impatience to see him. It was maddening to wait here quietly. A plan came to her, and she hastily threw on her cloak and went to see Mary at Wallingford House. "Mary, he is on his way home! Let's ride to meet him. We can take a ship and meet him at Calais on the French shore! Won't it be a wonderful surprise for him?"

Mary was taken aback. She studied Anna-Maria to see if she was serious, and her heart sank when she realized that she was indeed.

As gently as possible she said, "Anna-Maria, it's a foolish, dangerous prospect. Two women traveling alone? There are highwaymen and thieves all over on the roads."

Anna-Maria waved her hand impatiently. "We'll travel with a score of male servants. We'll be perfectly safe."

Poor Mary was inevitably seasick, and her heart failed her when she thought of crossing the rough English Channel on the small ships that made the trip between Dover and Calais.

"Oh, *please*, Mary." Anna-Maria seized the older woman's hand and begged.

Mary hesitated. "It may be dangerous for you in your condition."

Anna-Maria played her trump card. It was well-known that pregnant women must be given whatever they fancy lest the child be injured. "It's precisely because I *am* pregnant that you must not refuse me."

Mary heaved a sigh and capitulated. She immediately found herself caught up in the whirlwind of Anna-Maria's enthusiasm. Before she could fully catch her breath, she found herself on the highway the next day, Anna-Maria at her side, chattering happily, dozens of servants riding beside them for their protection. Anna-Maria was so happy that she scarcely noticed the discomfort of the rough, flea-infested inns where they rested, and Mary suffered in silence.

When they boarded the ship at Dover, Anna-Maria felt that her spirit was filling with pure joy, just as the ship's white sails were billowing with clean salt air. To feel the touch of his lips again, his strong arms around her body!

She leaned against the railing and laughed delightedly as the salt spray splashed against her face. Mary's face turned an unhealthy greenish pallor, and she hastily excused herself. A storm blew up, and Anna-Maria found herself glorying in it. She was completely without fear, watching the thick green-gray boiling sea, although the ship was listing alarmingly and her hands often slipped on the wet rail. But the storm played her a false trick. The captain declared that it was impossible to make the voyage across the channel safely, and he turned the ship back.

Sick with disappointment, Anna-Maria found herself back in Dover again, and this time Mary was unmovable. She announced firmly that they would wait in Dover, that never again would she set foot aboard a ship of any kind, large or small.

Anna-Maria fumed, but she could not sway Mary in her decision. They settled down for the wait, Mary calmly occupying herself with her embroidery while Anna-Maria spent long hours impatiently pacing the shore. Her heart began to race each time a ship sailed into port, and she was repeatedly disappointed, turning away dejectedly when Buckingham did not appear.

And then, finally, one morning, she saw him, lean and handsome, just stepping onto the beach. She began running across the pebbled beach, stumbling a little, completely forgetting her pregnant condition. Buckingham, his expression incredulous, raced to meet her. She half fell into his arms, laughing and crying simultaneously, too breathless to speak.

For a few minutes there was a confusion of explanations, interspersed with kisses, and then Buckingham held her at arm's length and said, "I swear there has never been a woman like you before. To make that dangerous journey and in your condition—" He broke off, seeking her lips.

Anna-Maria could feel the sunlight beating down on her bare head, the crunch of sand beneath her feet. Buckingham's lips tasted slightly salty, and she wished that the moment could go on forever.

Then the sailors began calling out good-natured jeers, and they broke apart, blushing but smiling. Buckingham put his arm around her thickening waist and began helping her across the sand.

She could not take her eyes off him, and she kept touching him to make certain that he was really there. He told her of his anxiety to return to her, that he had worn out two horses in his swift ride from Paris to Calais. "We'll never be parted again, my love. I swear it!"

Mary's greeting was more restrained, but her gray eyes were shining brightly as they lingered on Buckingham's face.

They set a quick pace for London. Buckingham was anxious to sleep in his own bed again, and Anna-Maria wanted to see her children.

As they neared the outskirts of London, Buckingham suddenly clapped his hand to his forehead. "Damn, I forgot the female!"

"What female?" Anna-Maria was instantly jealous, and her eyes snapped angrily.

Buckingham laughed. "Not so fierce, my love. The female is Charles's fancy, not mine. Remember Minette's lady-in-waiting who captured Charles's interest when Minette visited England?"

Anna-Maria nodded. "Louise de Kéroualle." Louise was a haughty blond, and Anna-Maria had not thought her particularly pretty. The king, however, had been taken by her and had suggested that Minette leave her in England under his royal protection. But Minette had protested that she was responsible to Louise's parents for the girl and must return her safely to France.

Buckingham explained, "The king of France is sending her to visit Charles, and he pressed me into service as her escort. We started the journey together, but she drove me near to distraction. I sent her on to Dieppe while I galloped for Calais. And I forgot to send a ship for her. She must still be cooling her heels there!"

Anna-Maria laughed, a trifle scandalized. It was dreadful to think of Louise waiting for a ship that did not arrive, but it warmed Anna-Maria's heart to know that Buckingham had been so impatient to reach her.

As soon as they arrived in London, Buckingham made arrangements for the remainder of Louise's journey and then forgot the matter. Neither he nor Anna-Maria had the slightest premonition that Louise would never forget Buckingham's insult to her and that her enmity could be dangerous.

Thirty-Seven

Anna-Maria watched with detached, amused interest as the king fell in love with Louise de Kéroualle. She still considered Louise haughty, unattractive, and completely lacking in grace, but the king was blind to her flaws, and acted like a man totally besotted. It was true, Anna-Maria admitted grudgingly, that Louise was extremely intelligent. Buckingham suspected that the French king had hidden motives in sending her to Charles, that Louise's first loyalty was to France and to French interests.

Nell was sick with jealousy and kept referring to Louise both publicly and privately as "the French whore." The English public, who detested the French, supported Nell in her rivalry and heartily cheered her when she rode through the streets in her coach.

Anna-Maria, her pregnancy advancing, found herself less and less interested in court gossip, and in matters of politics. Buckingham, as usual, often talked of his schemes and ambitions, and she listened to him only because she loved him.

Her back often ached, and she was mildly resentful when Buckingham insisted that she accompany him for the racing at Newmarket. But she held her tongue and forestalled any words of reproach because she realized that if she was to hold his love, she could not cage him. He was like one of the falcons that flew in the sky over England, and he would sicken and die in captivity.

Buckingham had placed heavy wagers at Newmarket, and Anna-Maria, catching the spirit of the event, stood elbow to elbow with him at the rail and cheered his horses to victory. The one unpleasant aspect was that they were to spend the night at Lord Arlington's great country mansion with other members of the court. She had no stomach for watching the king in his futile pursuit of Louise. Louise was driving the king half insane by her refusal to bed with him, and Anna-Maria, who liked the king, found it degrading to watch him make a fool of himself.

Louise was more provocative than usual that evening, her breasts nearly spilling from her low-cut gown, her manner wanton as she flirted shamelessly with the king. Anna-Maria was within earshot as Charles, seated in a curtained window alcove with Louise, seized her plump hands in his and poured out entreaties and promises. Embarrassed to be overhearing such a private conversation, she moved away hastily, but not before hearing Louise say, "I cannot be a whore for any man. I must have the dignity of a wife."

As she crossed the room, Anna-Maria wondered exactly what Louise's scheme was. Did she expect the king to have his barren queen secreted off to a convent the way many had suggested he do? Anna-Maria walked out into the garden and was taking a deep breath of the clean, crisp night air when Buckingham found her. There was an odd expression on his face. "Anna-Maria, the king is going through a marriage ceremony with Louise tonight."

"What?" Anna-Maria was so startled that she turned abruptly, twisting her ankle.

Buckingham reached out and caught her under the elbow. "Louise will not bed with the king unless she has the dignity of a wife." He waved his hand in dismissal, "Oh, the ceremony will not be legal—they both know that. But it shows what honor Charles is willing to accord her."

Anna-Maria shook her head incredulously.

Buckingham smiled. "Arlington is even arguing that if the law allows most men one wife, then the king, who is above the law, should certainly be allowed two."

As they entered the house, they found the guests in a high state of excitement. Arlington was to officiate as "priest," and he had already gone to seek out proper robes. The king's dark eyes were sparkling, every line of his body betraying his excitement and tension. He had waited a long time to bed Louise, and he was jubilant now that the moment was at hand.

Anna-Maria smiled faintly at his pleasure, but she was grieved to think what a sore blow the news would be to Nell. At least Nell had the king's child in her belly, and perhaps that would comfort her. Anna-Maria put her hand on her own curving stomach and sighed. Both she and Nell were bearing bastards, and yet, because they were both so deeply in love, they counted themselves fortunate.

Louise sailed back into the room with a triumphant smile on her thin lips. She had changed into a more demure gown, high-necked and virginally white, as befitted a bride. There was a moment's confusion as they assigned themselves positions, Louise and the king facing Arlington in his priest's robes, the guests forming a semicircle around them. Then Arlington, looking very self-important, began reading an abbreviated version of the wedding ceremony.

Buckingham and Anna-Maria had forgotten to close the long windows as they came in from the garden, and a breeze swept through the room, sending the candle

flames to swaying. Buckingham stepped back from Anna-Maria's side and quietly pulled the window shut
just as Arlington closed his prayer book and smiled at
the king and Louise. The king, his arm tight around
Louise's waist, smilingly invited congratulations, and
the courtiers swept toward them. When Buckingham
and Anna-Maria reached them, Louise gave Buckingham a look of deep anger as dangerous as a dagger's
thrust. Now, her look seemed to say, now you will
see what influence I have with the king. I will repay
you for your insult to me. Anna-Maria shivered, but
Buckingham seemed oblivious to the ominous warning.

The king was anxious to take Louise off to bed,
and once the guests had laughingly seen them to
their chamber, the great house fell silent. Buckingham
studied Anna-Maria's pensive face as she was undressing. He thought her even more beautiful now in the
bloom of her pregnancy. "What is troubling you, my
love?"

Anna-Maria stepped out of her frothy petticoats and
said slowly, "I fear Louise. She truly hates you, and
I am afraid that she will use her influence with the
king to harm you in some way."

Buckingham laughed. "Nonsense. Charles is infatuated with her, but his blood will cool once he has
had her. In any case he would never let a woman affect our friendship. Come here, darling, and let me
kiss those worried lines from your forehead."

Anna-Maria went obediently into his arms and let
him finish undressing her, but later, as he lay sleeping
quietly by her side, she stared into the fire, remembering the malevolent look that Louise had shot at
Buckingham.

When they rose in the morning, they found that the
king was more infatuated with Louise than ever, and
Anna-Maria felt an ominous weight settle on her heart.
Louise was clever, and she would slowly edge herself
deeper and deeper into the king's favor, and Anna-
Maria feared that Buckingham would suffer for it.

Several times, in the months that followed, she tried

to warn him, but he always dismissed her fears lightly. He was heavily engaged in politics and was confident of the king's support in all his schemes. Anna-Maria tried to stop fretting and instead threw herself into preparations for Christmas. It was wonderful to fill the house with scented pine branches, to hang waxy white mistletoe in the doorways. Buckingham, bending his tall frame to clear the doors would invariably grin, seize her in a kiss, and comment approvingly on the custom. "It would please me if we had mistletoe hanging all the year round."

Anna-Maria teased him. "When do you ever need an *excuse* to win a kiss from me?" She was lavish in her spending for Christmas presents. Buckingham was generous with her, she had her vast jointure at her command, and what more pleasant way to spend money than on those she loved? Laughing in the cold December air, she piled presents into her coachman's arms until he protested that there was scarcely room for *her* inside the coach. She bought recklessly for the children, Nell, Mary, Sarah, Joseph, and lingered over her choices for Buckingham.

On Christmas morning she sat on the floor, leaning against his knees, deeply happy. Around her neck was a magnificent diamond necklace, and her slim fingers went often to caress its coolness. "You were too generous," she protested to Buckingham. She waved at the profusion of other gifts heaped on the floor. Scented gloves, a fur muff, rich lengths of fabric, flagons of perfume.

"And all the presents you bought for the baby!" She began to laugh. Buckingham had purchased enough gifts for the unborn baby to last him until he was ten years old, at least. "I marvel only that you did not buy him a pony as well!"

Buckingham grinned a bit sheepishly and placed his lips on the top of her soft hair. "A man must be allowed to be a little foolish over his first son."

Anna-Maria turned until she could look up into his face. "Will you be very disappointed if the baby is a daughter?"

Buckingham, innately truthful, was silent for a second and then forced himself to say no, but Anna-Maria read the truth in his expression, and she began to pray with increased fervor that she would give him the son he so craved.

She thought of Nell's new infant, young Charles, and smiled. Nell was rapturous in her motherhood, proud of her achievement. She had not sent for Anna-Maria until she had been in labor for several hours, and when Anna-Maria had entered the room and found Nell haggard looking and writhing with pain, she had been frightened for a moment. But Nell, irrepressible Nell, had managed a grin, blowing a damp strand of hair off her forehead. "I begin to think I might be a lady after all since I'm having such difficulty in giving birth. It's very aristocratic of me, don't you think?"

Anna-Maria had found herself laughing helplessly, saying, "Oh, Nell, don't you ever take anything seriously?" She had sat next to Nell the long afternoon, lending the midwife a hand when she could, and she had been present when the king's son had come fighting his way out of Nell's slim body. Daily she rode over to visit with Nell and marvel over the new achievements of the infant Nell declared to be the finest baby ever born.

Nell was ecstatic these days. The king had set her up in a fine new house in Pall Mall and was generous in his presents to her so that she could furnish lavishly. "I'm certain now that he loves me," she confided to Anna-Maria. "He rides over almost daily and he has promised to give our son a dukedom. Imagine, me, Nell Gwyn from the Coleyard, being the mother of a duke of England."

Buckingham watched Anna-Maria's face as she looked into the fire, a tender smile curving her lips, and asked, "What are you thinking?"

"About Nell. She is so happy with her baby. My love, I cannot wait to hold *our* child in my arms."

Buckingham picked a pine cone from the iron basket and tossed it into the fire. Slowly he said, "I've been thinking, my sweet. Before the baby is born, I would like to regularize our union—"

"How?" Anna-Maria looked up in bewilderment. As long as Mary lived, they could never be married. She sent a hasty prayer speeding to heaven. She loved Mary and wished her no ill. "How?" she repeated, looking up at him in confusion.

Buckingham began stroking her hair slowly, staring into the fire. "I've been talking to Dr. Sprat, my chaplain, and he has agreed to officiate while we vow our love to each other in the sight of God." He paused and then added, "When Charles and Louise went through that ceremony, it gave me the idea. I, too, want to honor you." Hastily he put up his hand as though to ward off objection. "That was a mock ceremony, and I did not find it beautiful. But ours will be, my love. Meaningful in both the sight of God and man."

Anna-Maria felt love for him flooding through her, and she nestled her hand in his without speaking, too full of emotion for words. Lately she had been wistful that she and Buckingham were to have a child without the benefit of clergy. She put her hand on the swelling of her stomach and found her voice at last. "Oh yes," she said softly, "I would love that."

Buckingham's hand was on the nape of her neck now, lightly stroking it. His voice was deep with regret. "You know that above all things I wish I could give you a legal marriage."

"Hush." Anna-Maria tilted her head to look at him. "We have so much—it would be a sin to wish for more."

They began to talk quietly about the ceremony, agreeing that they would have only those that they loved best and who would understand their need to make such vows. Anna-Maria began ticking them off on her fingers. "Nell, Sarah." She sighed and wished that she could invite her parents, but they had turned a blind eye to her union with Buckingham, preferring to pretend ignorance of it.

"And the king," Buckingham reminded her.

"I shall have a new gown made," she said dreamily.

Buckingham threw back his head and laughed, and she sat up indignantly. "How can you laugh? I want to look beautiful for you."

A smile teased Buckingham's lips. "I find you *most* beautiful when you are naked, but I fear the chaplain might object."

Anna-Maria stuck her tongue out at him, then she put her hand up and implored, "Help me up, please!" These days she found it difficult to rise from the floor without assistance. "I must find Sarah at once and tell her."

Sarah nodded her head approvingly when Anna-Maria poured out the plans. She found the idea romantic. "We'll keep Mrs. Muggs sewing day and night to finish the gown." Then she added quickly, *"Madame Julie,* I mean," giving the name the same accent as the dressmaker affected, and they both burst into laughter.

Anna-Maria was a romantic vision in the finished gown. Madame Julie had found silk in the palest possible shade of blue, and she had pressed into service the finest seamstresses in London to aid her in thickly embroidering the skirt with flowers until the result was a veritable English garden. Anna-Maria, touching a yellow primrose with a reverent finger, began to laugh shakily.

"Oh, Sarah, I truly feel like a bride. As though I have never been married before, never borne children."

Sarah, her mouth full of gold bodkins, was twisting Anna-Maria's curls into place. She herself was already dressed in her best gown of deep green satin. Anna-Maria had refused to let Buckingham see her gown before the ceremony, and now she smoothed its folds and anxiously wondered if he would find her lovely.

The quick light that leaped into his eyes when she walked slowly into the small, intimate chamber they had selected was answer enough for her. Nell was already there, her arm tucked through the king's, and Dr. Sprat stood behind a small table that served as an altar. Anna-Maria saw none of them. Her eyes were linked with Buckingham's, and she suddenly remembered the first time she had seen him as he rode into London. Their eyes had met in the same fashion

then, and it was at that moment that her destiny had
been decided. Joy rushed through her, and she smiled
at him with such a radiance of love that the others in
the room caught their breaths and felt slightly embarrassed, as though they were present at a too-intimate
moment.

Buckingham moved forward to meet her and when
he stood in front of her, Anna-Maria said softly, "Hel-
lo, my love."

His eyes darkened with emotion, and he stood
looking at her wordlessly. Then he took her hand, and
they walked slowly toward Dr. Sprat.

Twice before, in the civil and religious ceremonies
with Francis, Anna-Maria had made her vows, but
both times seemed dim and remote to her now.
Now it is with all my heart, she kept thinking. This
was the first time that she was able to vow love with
every fiber of her being, and she felt gratitude welling
up in her heart that she had not gone through life
empty, cheated of love. Buckingham who was skilled
with his pen, had written the ceremony himself, drawing partially from the marriage ritual and partially
from his own inventiveness, and now Dr. Sprat guided
them through it. Anna-Maria and Buckingham joined
their lives to each other although the word marriage
was never spoken.

Buckingham took Anna-Maria's hand and placed a
heavy gold ring on her fourth finger. Conscious of its
weight, she looked down and saw that two ruby hearts
were set into the twisted gold.

Buckingham's voice was very deep, very rich.
"With this ring I pledge you my love for our lifetime
and for all eternity to follow."

Anna-Maria was suffused with love for him. Without
waiting for Dr. Sprat's prompting, she spoke simply,
directly, from her heart. "I shall love you always." Her
voice was very clear, very confident, and she heard a
sigh escape from one of the witnesses.

Her eyes glowed like jewels, the candlelight picking
out the golden highlights in their brown depths. Her
mouth was red and sweetly curved, and Buckingham
could wait no longer. He tilted her face towards his

and kissed her as the chaplain was reading the last words of the service.

Thirty-Eight

The sharp February wind was blowing with the force of a gale, moaning under the eaves of the house and trying to fight its way indoors. Anna-Maria, a thick fur covering her knees, sat huddled near the fire, her hands too chilled to hold a book or an embroidery needle.

The baby was moving and kicking vigorously, and she often shifted in her chair, trying to find a more comfortable position. Her time was near, and the mid-wife had already been ensconced in the house. Buckingham tried to conceal his impatience for the birth, but Anna-Maria was aware of it in his restless movements and in the sidelong expectant glances he kept giving her. She gave a sigh of relief that he was at court this afternoon. It was far easier to relax without his anxious scrutiny.

She heard a small commotion in the hall and then Nell's quick, light voice. Nell bustled into the room, her small impish face glowing from the cold and framed by the thick luxurious fur of her hood. "I've come to cheer you. These last days of waiting are the hardest to bear!" She moved quickly to the fire and held out her hands to warm them. "That cold air cuts like a knife!"

Anna-Maria was delighted to have a visitor. "Nell, how good of you to come! Sit down. Tell me all the latest gossip."

Nell plumped herself in the chair opposite Anna-Maria and grinned. "I will if you'll give me some hot mulled wine. I vow my throat is clogged with ice."

Anna-Maria smiled, rang for a servant, and ordered the drink. Nell, without waiting for the remedy for her throat, plunged into a ribald tale, and Anna-Maria laughed until the tears were running down her cheeks. "Nell, you are as good as a tonic!"

Nell grinned and accepted the pewter mug of wine that the servant had just brought. She blew on it a moment to cool it and then took a deep swallow. Anna-Maria also accepted a mug but sipped it more cautiously. "Tell me more," she urged.

Nell rummaged around in her fertile mind for a moment, and then a faintly malicious look crossed her normally good-natured face. "They say that Jane Middleton is *paying* her lovers now."

"Surely not!" Anna-Maria was scandalized by the idea, but she found herself giggling. Then her laughter broke off abruptly as a sudden pain seized her. The pewter mug tipped in her hand, and a little of the wine splashed onto the fur covering her knees. "Nell! I think my time has come."

Nell, forgetting her own mug of wine, leaped from the chair, spilling wine in dark rivulets onto the shining floor and raced to the hall, bellowing for the midwife. Then she returned to Anna-Maria's side, uttering reassurances. Anna-Maria smiled up at her. "Nell, I've *had* two babies already. I'm not frightened."

The midwife entered the room on a run. The midwife that Anna-Maria had used for her first two children had died, but this one, Mrs. Spragg, was highly recommended. Sarah followed quickly on the midwife's heels, and the three women soon had Anna-Maria out of the chair and upstairs to her bed.

The pains began coming at steady intervals, and Nell said that Buckingham should be sent for. Anna-Maria protested. "He will have nothing to do but pace the floor and worry, poor darling. I'd rather he came home to find his son delivered and waiting for him."

Nell wrinkled her nose. "Men. They have their pleasure giving you the child, and then they disappear when the rough patch comes."

Anna-Maria said softly, "Buckingham would have this baby *for* me if he could. I know that he fears I will suffer and that is why I don't want him here—" She broke off with a gasp as another pain assailed her.

"They are coming so quickly. With my other two babies, it was hours before the pains came so close together."

Mrs. Spragg sounded pleased. "Each child comes more quickly and easily than the one before." She gently ran her fingers over Anna-Maria's stomach, then turned and gave instructions to Sarah.

Nell suggested a game of cards to while away the time, and they played until Anna-Maria could concentrate no longer. She was in a fever of anticipation to see the baby, to actually hold him in her arms. She said to Nell, "We are giving him such a wonderful legacy! He may be a bastard—" she hesitated a moment over the word, "but he will be rich in knowing that his parents loved each other above all things!"

Nell laughed cheerfully. "If our sons are bastards, at least we took care that they were of noble blood." The king had promised that as soon as it was possible, he would give his son by Nell a title, and Nell was awed by the prospect of being the mother of a duke.

Anna-Maria winced as a new pain struck, and then a shadow crossed her face. "I do not mind for myself," she said with difficulty, "but I fear that Buckingham grieves because his only child will not be legitimate. He is such a proud man, and he has longed all his life to have a son."

"Aye." Nell's impish face grew sober in its turn. "He and the king are both unfortunate in that respect. I know the king loves our child—indeed he loves all his bastards—but he will not be content until the queen gives him a legitimate heir to the throne."

As fresh pain assailed Anna-Maria, she welcomed it, glorying in the fact that she was not barren like the poor queen or Mary. Truly it was worth this agony to have a new life emerge from her body.

Nell dipped a cloth in vinegar and gently wiped Anna-Maria's forehead. Sarah and Mrs. Spragg had gone downstairs because Anna-Maria had insisted that she might take hours yet, and they had best eat something while they could.

Anna-Maria smiled at Nell gratefully. "It's so kind of you to sit with me this long while. It cannot be very entertaining for you—" She stopped abruptly, sweat beginning to bead on her forehead.

"Nonsense." Nell wrung out the cloth and returned it to the side of the basin. "You kept me company while my baby was being born."

Anna-Maria was leaning back against the high-banked pillows, her eyes shut. She said dreamily, "When I am giving birth, I feel like the river Thames."

Nell, startled, touched Anna-Maria's cheek, thinking she was feverish. Anna-Maria smiled and opened her eyes. "I mean the rhythm. The childbirth pains ebb and flow like the tide in the Thames. And lovemaking itself is similar—the rising swells."

She broke off, blushing slightly.

It was not seemly to discuss intimate details even with so close a friend as Nell. And perhaps it was different for Nell. She might not experience the ever-rising swells of passion that ultimately peaked, leaving Anna-Maria drenched with ecstasy. She paused to collect her thoughts.

"When a baby nurses at my breast, there is the same feeling of ebb and flow." She sat up, resting on one elbow, looking earnestly at Nell. "It reaffirms my belief in God because there is such a *pattern* to it all."

Nell began to laugh softly, shaking her head. "You never fail to amaze me. When *I* gave birth, I had no desire to philosophize about it. The only thought I gave to God was to implore him to deliver the baby safely and quickly."

Anna-Maria sat fully upright, her hands clutching nervously at the bedcovers. "Nell, you'd best call Mrs. Spragg," she gasped. Her eyes looked enormous, and she was biting on her lower lip. Nell ran to the bedroom door and, in her stage voice, bellowed for Mrs. Spragg.

The midwife and Sarah came running, and for the next hour there was an ordered confusion in the room —Mrs. Spragg's low-voiced commands, Sarah and Nell's answering replies, and, to Anna-Maria's shame, occasional groans that she could not repress. Near the end she shrieked once, a long piercing cry, just as

Mrs. Spragg said with satisfaction, "I've got it now!" and delivered the baby.

The voices of Nell and Sarah tumbled over each other in their eagerness to give Anna-Maria the joyous news. "It's a boy!" "You have your son!"

"Oh, thank God!" It was a cry straight from Anna-Maria's heart, a spontaneous prayer. Now she was on fire with impatience for Buckingham to come home, to see the joy on his face.

She refused to rest and instead scandalized Mrs. Spragg by insisting that she be cleansed and perfumed immediately and her hair dressed so that Buckingham would find her beautiful. Mrs. Spragg, tending the baby and emptying basins, muttered her disapproval as Nell and Sarah gently sponge-bathed Anna-Maria and coaxed her damp hair into soft curls.

She was lying back against the pillows, exhausted, when she heard Buckingham's feet striking loudly against the polished bare wood of the stairs. As he reached the doorway, she sat up and cried out the news that he had been longing to hear. "We have a son."

He stopped abruptly as though the breath had been knocked from his body, and then his eyes began to blaze with an inner light.

The expression of wonder and gratitude on his face was the most beautiful sight she had ever seen, and Anna-Maria felt that she would have gone through fire and flood to bring him the son he craved.

He moved toward her slowly, picked up her hand, and stroked it. "Anna-Maria, there are no words—"

She raised her face. "Then kiss me instead." There was a bubble of laughter in her voice. At this moment she felt more truly a woman than she had ever felt before in her life.

As Buckingham's lips met hers, there was a faint wail from the cradle near the fireplace, and Buckingham straightened, looking stunned. Anna-Maria understood. It was awesome to realize that there was new life in the room.

"Go and make the acquaintance of your son," she urged gently. Looking dazed, Buckingham moved over to the cradle. For a moment he merely gazed downward, then bent and gently touched the cradle's occupant. "Hold him if you like," Anna-Maria whispered, "only do it quickly before Mrs. Spragg returns."

Buckingham, normally graceful in all his movements, looked a bit uncertain and clumsy as he picked up his son, and Anna-Maria laughed softly. "Bring him here. Lie him on the bed next to me."

Moving gingerly, seeming to hold his breath, Buckingham crossed the room with his son in his arms. Anna-Maria held up her arms, laughing a little, and, with an expression of relief, Buckingham gave the infant to her.

Once the baby was safe in Anna-Maria's arms, Buckingham felt free to lean down and examine it closely. His voice expressed awe as he whispered, "He is so tiny, so fragile!"

Anna-Maria pretended indignation. "Did you expect me to present you with a full-grown soldier?"

Buckingham grinned. His fingers lightly touched the top of the baby's head, bald except for a faint, light-colored fuzz.

Sounding pleased, Anna-Maria said, "He will have hair the shade of yours." She imagined the child playing in the garden with the sunlight turning his hair to gold the way it did Buckingham's, and she was happy.

Buckingham had finished his scrutiny of his son for a moment and was searching Anna-Maria's face anxiously. "Are you well? Was it very bad?"

Anna-Maria had forgotten the pain she had just experienced. She smiled up at him. "It was so easy that I think I will demand that you give me a baby every year."

Buckingham grinned. "Nothing would give me more pleasure." Then a look of consternation crossed his face. "I almost forgot. I have something else to give you." He reached into his doublet and pulled out an exquisite ruby necklace and dangled it so that it sparkled in the firelight. She caught her breath. "It's beautiful!" Then she protested, "But you need give me nothing—"

"My love, don't deny me this pleasure. For years I envied men when their wives bore them children. Now I want to savor each small delight—giving you a birth gift, watching you as you lay there with my son in your arms."

Instantly understanding, Anna-Maria reached up, and their fingers touched. Softly she asked, "Will you put it about my neck?"

As his fingers were busy at the back of her neck, fastening the clasp, she looked down at the baby, sleeping peacefully, and her arms tightened about him. Happiness flooded through her, and when she looked up at Buckingham, her eyes were filled with tears. "We are so fortunate. Life has given us so much."

In the days that followed, she felt such happiness welling up in her that she often fancied it was spilling from her fingertips, shining from her eyes.

Buckingham's immense pride in his new offspring was a never-ending source of delight to her. He wanted to heap the baby with riches and honors immediately, and Anna-Maria, laughing, had to restrain him from buying wildly inappropriate presents.

She had never liked Buckingham's Christian name, George, and had never used it in speaking to him, but she knew that he would be brokenhearted if his son did not bear his name, so she suggested it herself. Buckingham had every legal right to give his illegitimate son his own family name, and the infant was christened George Villiers III. Reckless in his pride for his son, Buckingham took a further, illegal step and bestowed on the baby the title he himself had held at his birth, the earl of Coventry.

"I'm certain that the king will confirm the title in time," he assured Anna-Maria with easy confidence.

But she was not so confident as he. The king had stood godfather to the infant, but his manner to Buckingham had been markedly cool, and Anna-Maria suspected that Louise's influence was at work.

Thirty-Nine

The nursery window stood half open to the March gale, and the wind was coming in with angry spurts, scattering rain over the cradle where the infant lay.

"Oh, my God!" For a moment Anna-Maria stood transfixed in the doorway, staring in horror. Then she sped across the room and wrestled to close the window. Angrily she began shouting over her shoulder, bringing the servants on the run. One of the footmen sprang to her aid and succeeded in pulling the window shut.

Anna-Maria snatched the baby from the cradle, screaming incoherently, "Who is responsible for this? Why was the baby left unattended?"

The servants had never seen the gentle Lady Shrewsbury in a rage before, and they stood clustered together looking from one to another. Prompted by a push in the small of her back, the newest of the nursery maids moved forward from the group, clutching a large pile of linens in her arms. "I left him only for a moment, my lady, to get fresh bedding. The storm blew the window open while I was out of the room."

"He should never have been left alone. Never." Anna-Maria was frantically taking off George's soaked garments. "Someone poke up the fire. And you—" she said, pointing at one of the footmen, "fetch a doctor immediately. The rest of you may go."

Tears of anger and worry filmed Anna-Maria's eyes as she changed the baby. George was not as robust as her other two children, and already he was coughing weakly. Oh, if only Sarah had not chosen to go visiting this afternoon! If only . . .

She pushed the fruitless speculations aside and carried George closer to the fire, gently drying his fuzz of hair. In his short life he had been coddled and pam-

pered and never before had he been cold or wet.
Anna-Maria kissed his soft cheek and vowed fiercely
that nothing would ever hurt him again. She loved
this child with an intensity that almost frightened her.
He was herself, he was Buckingham, he was the result
of their love, the mingling of their blood.

The door banged open, and the doctor entered,
shaking drops of rain from his hat. "This weather is
dreadful." He tossed off his cloak and came over to
examine the baby. "Some fool of a nursemaid let the
rain blow in on him?"

Anna-Maria nodded, her eyes dark with anger. The
doctor took the infant from her and examined him
carefully. Then he straightened and said, "It is really
too soon to tell if any damage has been done. Keep him
warm and dry. Send for me if he begins to cough or
run a fever."

Anna-Maria thanked him and then sat down in a
chair near the fire, holding George protectively. She
was sitting there, crooning softly to him, when Sarah
returned home.

Sarah was so full of self-blame that Anna-Maria
hadn't the heart to reproach her. Sarah said furiously,
"That girl swore to me that she had had a great deal
of experience in nursing babies else I would never have
left her in charge. I had her here with me in the nursery this past week, and she seemed competent."

Anna-Maria held George more closely. "No doubt
she knows how to change a baby and tend to his needs,
but her judgment was poor." She knew that Sarah
needed an affirmation of her trust in her, so she smiled
and said, "Will you hold him for a while? My arms are
beginning to cramp."

Gratitude and deep relief lit Sarah's face as she
took the infant. Anna-Maria remembered the years of
Sarah's friendship, her fierce loyalty, and she touched
Sarah's hair gently. "Do not reproach yourself, Sarah. And look! He is sleeping peacefully. No harm has
come to him."

Anna-Maria and Sarah both stayed in the nursery
all afternoon, reluctant to leave George's side. When
Buckingham came home Anna-Maria gave the baby a

lingering kiss and then went to join the duke. She was in the habit of telling him all the small incidents of her day, but she held her tongue this time. There was no reason to alarm him needlessly.

When Buckingham spoke of his son, full of enthusiasm and plans, Anna-Maria smiled. "One of *my* dearest hopes for him is that his eyes remain blue. It will be wonderful. When you are away from me during the day, I can look into his eyes and feel that a part of you is still with me."

Buckingham threw back his head and laughed. "You are a romantic." He picked up his glass of wine and drank. "I have more practical ambitions for him, Anna-Maria. I work with a new fervor now because I am building a future for my son. Before he was born, I sometimes felt a futility in all that I did. I built up a fortune, honors, but when I died, all would die with me." He set the goblet down on the table and looked at her tenderly. "You have given me immortality."

His eyes were so rich with love as he looked at her that she felt dizzy with happiness.

She was delighted when he said that they need not go to Whitehall that night but could spend a quiet evening at home. They dined alone, heaping the choicest tidbits onto each other's plates, sharing a single wineglass. At dinner's conclusion they went hand in hand to see the sleeping baby. Anna-Maria's eyes winged an anxious question to Sarah, and she heaved a sigh of relief when Sarah gave her a reassuring nod. The baby was sleeping peacefully, his breathing even and regular. Buckingham touched his son's cheek with his finger, and Anna-Maria caught her breath with pleasure.

Anna-Maria had been pronounced completely recovered from childbirth, and she and Buckingham had been able to resume lovemaking earlier in the week. It was all the sweeter because of their time of abstinence, and she went readily into his arms once they had reached their own chamber. Her breasts were rich with milk, taut and white-skinned with faint blue veins etched on the creamy surface, and Buckingham exclaimed at their beauty. He clasped his hands around her slender waist. "My son has not swelled your shape, for which I thank him."

She laughed and turned her face up for a kiss. Her breathing quickened as he lifted her lightly in his arms and carried her over to the bed.

If possible, they were even closer than ever these days because their lovemaking had resulted in a child. The baby's birth had made them complete. Each night Anna-Maria thought that she had reached the heights of her ardor and then found that the more they shared, the more she craved his touch.

He was trailing kisses down her body, when suddenly there was a loud pounding at the door. Frightened, Anna-Maria sat upright, her eyes widening, her hair falling forward to cover her bare breasts. "What is it?"

Buckingham was already on his feet, racing across the room and yanking the door open. The youngest of their footmen stood there. His eyes widened as he caught sight of Anna-Maria naked, her exquisite beauty heightened by the candlelight. He hastily lowered his eyes and said, " 'Tis the baby, my lord. You'd best come at once."

"Oh, no!" Anna-Maria cried. Buckingham spoke tersely to the footman. "We'll be there at once."

Closing the door, he quickly began to dress, while Anna-Maria pulled a dressing gown around her, crying softly. In snatched half-sentences, she told Buckingham of the nursemaid's carelessness, and his face darkened.

"I'll wring her neck with my own hands." He was thrusting his arms into his shirt as he spoke, and in a moment he had reached for Anna-Maria's hand and was pulling her down the corridor toward the nursery.

Sarah, bent over the cradle, looked up as they came in. "I've already sent for the doctor."

She stood aside so that they could see the baby. He was deeply flushed with fever, his breath a rattle in his throat. Buckingham gave vent to a worried oath, and

Anna-Maria snatched the infant from the cradle and held him to her breast, her lips feeling scalded as they touched his burning forehead.

Buckingham turned and began swearing angrily at Sarah, but the girl looked on the verge of collapse, and his face softened. "Here, sit down." He guided her to a chair and seated her. "I know that you love the baby, but Sarah, *why* did you leave him to the mercies of that fool of a nursemaid?"

Sarah was crying helplessly, unable to respond, and Buckingham said, "Forgive me. I know that you cannot be in the nursery day and night I—" He broke off, flinging out his hand in a gesture of helplessness. He needed someone on whom to vent his anger, needed action to relieve his anxiety. He began pacing the room, his bare feet soundless on the floor.

Anna-Maria held the child's fragile body and suffered with him as he labored for breath, the effort shaking his tiny chest. The doctor came in, grumbling at the lateness of the hour, and then stopped abruptly as he saw the duke's face. Instantly he was all professional competence, gravely taking the baby from Anna-Maria.

When he straightened from his examination, his eyes were worried, although he fought to hide his expression. He began giving instructions in a low, hurried voice and they listened anxiously, their eyes searching his face for reassurance. It was Buckingham who held the infant's head steady while the doctor spooned medicine between the already bluish lips.

Sarah went to wake the kitchen staff to tell them that they must stay up all night, boiling pots of water so that the steam could be used to ease the baby's breathing. Anna-Maria and Buckingham sat opposite each other across the cradle and tried to give each other strength. Once, as Buckingham asked the doctor a question, his voice broke, and he paused until he could steady it. Anna-Maria's heart ached for him. She took comfort in praying, her hands clasped lightly together, her eyes never leaving her son's face.

After an hour the baby's breathing seemed somewhat easier, and the doctor stretched and yawned. "I must sleep for a short while, or I will be useless. Call me if there is the slightest change."

He asked for a bed close at hand, and as Sarah was about to lead him out of the room, Anna-Maria said, "Sarah, you must also get some sleep so that you will be fresh in the morning. I will care for the baby during the night."

Alone, with only the hiss and crackle of the fire and the sound of the baby's breathing to break the silence, Buckingham and Anna-Maria looked at each other. She stretched her hand across the crib and stroked his cheek. "Have faith, my love."

He took her hand and tenderly dropped a kiss into her palm. His mouth still against her hand, he said, "If we lose our son—"

"Hush!" There was frantic denial in Anna-Maria's whisper. "Do not even think of such a thing. God would not be so cruel!"

They spoke in soft whispers for a short time and then fell silent, leaden with fatigue and anxiety. An hour passed, and then another, as they kept vigil. It was toward dawn, just as the sky was beginning to lighten a little, that the rhythm of the baby's breathing changed again, becoming harsh and labored. Anna-Maria started up in fright. She was just reaching into the cradle to pick him up when he made a convulsive movement, his tiny back arching. There was a rattling sound deep in his throat, the most terrifying sound Anna-Maria had ever heard, and then abruptly his breathing ceased.

Anna-Maria stared at him for a moment, disbelieving, then her eyes met Buckingham's. "Oh, Sweet Jesu! No!" Her cry split the air like the shriek of a wounded animal.

Buckingham was insane with grief and rage. When the doctor, summoned on the run, shook his head hopelessly, Buckingham looked down on the small corpse and let out a bellow of torment that froze Anna-Maria's blood. Before she could reach out to him, he had flung himself out of the room.

When she caught up with him, he was in the lower hall, his hands around the throat of the young nursemaid who had let the wind and rain blow in on his son. The girl's eyes were bulging, and her face was beginning to turn blue and red as she fought for breath. Buckingham was cursing mindlessly, his face twisted in anger.

Anna-Maria seized his arm. "No! Buckingham, do not kill her!"

Buckingham, his eyes blank, seemed unaware of Anna-Maria's frantic cries. In desperation, she bent and bit into his hand, and the sudden pain startled him into looking at her.

Her face was contorted with grief, tears streaming down her cheeks, and he dropped his stranglehold on the nursemaid and reached out for her. "My darling!" His words were choked, and he said no more, merely cradling her in his arms. Long, racking sobs shook his body, and she held his lean frame close to her, seeking for a way to comfort him. She was still stunned, unable to believe that their son lay dead in a room above them. Surely this was a nightmare, and in a moment she would wake and put it behind her.

Buckingham's sobs were convulsive, and Anna-Maria began to be frightened. He had always been so strong, so perfectly in control, that to see him broken like this was terrifying. She began to urge him toward the privacy of their room. As they passed the nursemaid, the girl retreated, her hands to her throat where red welts were already forming.

Anna-Maria turned her head to whisper quickly, "You'd best leave this house before he notices you again."

Buckingham leaned on her heavily as they mounted the stairs, and Anna-Maria found herself panting under his weight. When they reached their bedchamber, she looked around it and felt fresh sobs welling up in her throat. Only a few hours ago they had lain in this bed full of the sweet fire of lovemaking, and now their lives had been ripped apart. Nothing would ever be the same again.

Buckingham was beating his fist into his palm, asking, "Why?" over and over until it became a monotonous, grief-stricken chant.

Anna-Maria struggled for her faith, but she could find no answer for him. Her own deep grief was thrust aside for the moment as she tried to minister to him. Finally, in desperation, she sent for a bottle of brandy, hoping to dull his senses until the first edge wore off his grief. He drank obediently when she held the glass to his lips. Then he pushed it aside and sought to regain some of his usual strength. *"I* should be comforting *you,"* he protested.

Anna-Maria said steadily, "I am comforted because you are with me." Suddenly the realization came to her that she had three other children, but he had lost his *only* child. She knelt down in front of him and urged him to finish the brandy. There were lines in his handsome face that had not been there earlier, and his eyes were still blind with shock. She fought down the remembrance of the feel of the baby in her arms and knelt in front of him, clasping him about the knees.

Buckingham began brokenly to talk about his son, recalling in detail each moment of his short life. By the time the brandy bottle was half empty, his words were slurring a little, and some of the tension was gone from his body. Anna-Maria called one of the footmen to help her get him into bed and then stood looking down at him as he lay relaxed in sleep. He had never known defeat before in his proud, arrogant life, and now he had been beaten by a force he could not control. Love for him rose up in her, and she vowed that she would be strong enough to put her own loss behind her and ease his pain. She bent and touched his forehead with her lips and then went to find Sarah.

Sarah's eyes were red-rimmed, her face chalky pale. She burst into a wail when she saw Anna-Maria. "It was all my fault. I—"

Anna-Maria held her hands over Sarah's lips to check her words. "It was God's will," she said firmly, "and we must accept it." Tears were running from the corners of her eyes, but her voice was steady.

She managed to keep her composure during the long hours that followed, although she became increasingly afraid for Buckingham. He stayed in their bedchamber all through the night and well into the next day, drinking steadily. At intervals he would fling open the door, bellow for another bottle of brandy, and then retire back to his isolated grief.

Finally, at dusk on the second day, Anna-Maria went to him. His face was covered with a stubble of blond beard, his eyes red, his hands shaking. Compassion filled her but she fought to keep her voice matter of fact. "My love, our son must be buried."

Buckingham flinched at the words, but after a moment he steadied himself. "Aye, and he shall be buried with the full honors due to him."

Words of protest rose to Anna-Maria's lips. The baby was illegitimate, yet Buckingham, his voice low and hurried, was making plans to have him buried with full pomp in Westminster Abbey. Suddenly she realized that he had a driving need to give the baby in death all the honor and titles he would have bestowed on him in life, and she was silent. If it gave him comfort to have an elaborate funeral, she would not hinder his plans. Quietly she stood by as Buckingham, now bathed, shaved, and dressed in somber garments, made the arrangements.

On the day of the burial, she stood in Westminster Abbey, her hand clasped in Buckingham's, and watched as they put the tiny coffin of her son in the duke of Buckingham's family vault. Her every instinct made her want to leap forward and snatch back the coffin. It was intolerable to think of her baby being walled up in the blackness of that vault for all eternity, his sweet flesh falling from his bones until only a tiny skeleton remained. She had the irrational conviction that if only she could nurse him again, give him nourishment from her own body, she could restore him to life. Her breasts were aching with the milk that he would never take from her.

Buckingham was dry-eyed, his face set into grim, stony lines. When Anna-Maria broke into tears, he put his arms around her and cradled her. She had her eyes tightly closed.

"I cannot watch," she whispered brokenly. "I cannot bear him to be shut into that darkness!"

His arms tightened convulsively around her. "Hush, darling. 'Tis only his poor body that lies here. His soul roams happily in heaven."

Anna-Maria was startled because he had never been as religious as she. His words were like a sudden ray of light piercing the gloom, and she began to pray, ashamed of her lack of faith.

Neither of them could sleep that night, and they lay huddled together, talking in whispers, weeping. Buckingham cried with the difficulty of a proud man unaccustomed to tears, in a choked, labored fashion, and Anna-Maria's heart ached for him. A few times during the night she fancied she heard the baby cry and sat up in bed, straining to hear.

Buckingham comforted her and then said, " 'Tis best if we get away from this house for a time. It is too full of memories for us now."

She clung to him in grateful assent. Perhaps if they went to the country for a time, the sharpest edge of their grief would blunt a little.

She was up before dawn, packing hastily, and by mid-afternoon they were in Buckingham's lovely country home in Kent. They stayed there until mid-April, taking long walks through the countryside, relaxing more and more as the air grew gentle and took on a hint of spring.

One afternoon Anna-Maria spied an early primrose, and she picked it with a suddenly lightening heart and held it out to Buckingham. Softly she said, "Spring promises the renewal of life—that nothing ever really dies."

He twirled the flower between his fingers, and a faint smile lit his face. That afternoon they made love in a sheltered dell, and when they were finished, the same hope showed on both their faces.

Anna-Maria would have been content never to return to the grime and foul odors of London, except that she craved the sight of her children, but she noticed the first signs of Buckingham's restlessness. Before the death of their son, he had been embroiled in a great many political matters, and she knew that he would forget his grief more quickly if he plunged into action again. She suggested that they go back to London and was rewarded by his quick look of relief.

Anna-Maria hesitated outside the door of their house on the Strand, dreading the first moment of stepping inside, dreading the reminder of the small life that was missing from it now, but she steeled herself. Once inside, she made a low-voiced excuse to Buckingham and went to the nursery. She found her eyes wet with tears when she discovered that Sarah, dear Sarah, had had the baby's cradle removed and all his small garments packed away. Anna-Maria knew that she could not have faced folding the tiny items of clothing, remembering the feel of him in her arms when he had worn them. She turned away from the nursery with a fervent prayer that it would soon be filled again.

Nell arrived shortly after they did, delighted to have Anna-Maria back in London again. She searched Anna-Maria's face with a keen glance to gauge the extent of her recovery and then plunged into a series of lighthearted stories about court and theatre doings.

In the days that followed, Nell sought to keep Anna-Maria constantly busy, urging her to shop and attend the theatre. "It's a fair treat to sit in a box and *watch* instead of strutting the stage myself," she said comfortably and popped a sweetmeat into her mouth, grinning happily.

After they had been home a week or two, Anna-Maria noticed that Buckingham was tense and preoccupied. A few times she awoke during the night to find him missing from her side. When she sought him out, she found him in his office, scowling over thick sheafs of papers. But despite her repeated questions, he refused to tell her what was troubling him. Finally she sought Nell's advice. "It's more than the death of our baby, I'm certain of that. He's more worried than grieved."

Nell hesitated, biting her lower lip. Since Anna-

Maria had returned to London, Nell had tried to keep unpleasant gossip from her, but there was no point in keeping her in ignorance if she was going to fret anyhow.

She took a deep breath and plunged in. "Buckingham's enemies—Clifford, Arlington, Talbot—are beginning to close in on him. They are using your baby's funeral to fire tempers against him."

"Our baby's *funeral?* How?" Anna-Maria thought Nell had taken leave of her wits.

Nell sighed and tried to tread delicately. "My dear —" she hesitated, "the baby was buried with all the pomp that befits royalty—as though he were Buckingham's *legitimate* son." She paused as Anna-Maria winced and then went on. She had gone this far, and there was no sense in turning back. "Many say that Buckingham's pride is so overweening that he believes himself to be above the law. He ennobled the baby by making him earl of Coventry when the baby had no legal right to the title."

Anna-Maria turned away, her heart full of pain. She whispered, "What does it matter whether or not the baby has the title? He lies dead in Westminster Abbey and will never use it."

Nell shook her head impatiently. "You don't understand. By giving him the title illegally, Buckingham made a mockery of the peerage. His enemies use it as an example to illustrate Buckingham's dangerous pride!"

Anna-Maria was fumbling in her pocket to find her handkerchief, tears beginning to form in her eyes. "How can they hound him so? He has suffered enough."

Nell embraced her in quick sympathy. "You both have suffered! You must warn Buckingham so he treads more softly for a time. Now that he has lost the king's favor—" She broke off as though she had said more than she had intended.

Panicked, Anna-Maria clutched at Nell's arm. "What do you mean?"

"It's the doing of the French whore," Nell said uncomfortably. "She is influencing the king against

Buckingham. More and more he has been deserting Buckingham, refusing to throw his support behind him."

"Oh, if we could only leave all this and live quietly in the country!" Even as she said the words, she realized that it was hopeless.

Nell shook her head with pity and a touch of asperity. "Anna-Maria, Buckingham is first and foremost a statesman. He needs the great stage of London to strut across. If you tried to make him into a country gentleman, he would either stop loving you, or he would grow ill and die of boredom."

Anna-Maria's smile held a mingling of pride and sadness. "The first time I ever saw Buckingham, Francis pointed him out as one of the most important men in England. So I knew from the beginning that it was no ordinary man that I loved." She put her hand out imploringly toward Nell. "How can I best help him?"

"Urge him to caution for a time," Nell said earnestly. "Even Buckingham's friends are turned against him now because of the rich trappings of the baby's funeral. But after a time it will be forgotten if he does not provoke them again."

That evening she broached the subject to Buckingham as they were undressing. For a moment he stared at her, then he threw back his handsome head and laughed. "My love, you cannot be serious. I do not fear that pack of scoundrels. I have plans for England—glorious plans—and no one is going to stop me!"

Forty

Adultery! The word hung on the air between them.

Anna-Maria shook her head dazedly, as though to clear it and then said haltingly, "I don't understand."

Buckingham, murderously angry, had his hand on the hilt of his sword, as though he were about to draw it. "Talbot has sunk to the lowest depths in his attempt to disgrace me. He is using my love for you as a weapon against me."

"But adultery is no crime!" Anna-Maria, suddenly frightened, was struggling through a mist of bewilderment.

There was a bitter twist to Buckingham's lips as he laughed shortly. "It's a punishable offense, but if the law were ever enforced, all the nobles at court would be in trouble."

His face darkened. "Talbot dares to treat me like a common peasant, dragged before the constable with a whore in tow."

She winced as though he had struck her, and instantly his face softened. He took her into his arms. "Don't look like that, my darling. I'll not allow Talbot to harm us."

"Tell me the entire story," Anna-Maria begged. His first version of the tale had been so angrily spoken, so incoherent, that she had not understood one word in three.

Making a visible effort, Buckingham calmed himself and then sat down, pulling her onto his knee. He began stroking her hair. "I fear that this will wound you, my love. But by tomorrow all London will be talking about it, and there is no way to keep it from your ears." He studied her troubled expression for a moment and then said, as gently as possible, "Today Talbot rose in the House of Lords and presented a petition from the kin and trustees of your son, the young earl of Shrewsbury."

"Charles?" Anna-Maria's thoughts flew instantly to her beloved oldest son. "But why?"

Buckingham sighed heavily. He knew he could plunge a dagger into her breast and it would wound her less than the words he must speak. "They claim that as Charles grows older, he becomes deplorably upset about the manner of his father's death."

Her hand flew to her throat. The old charge of murder would never die.

Buckingham continued, "They say that each day he is increasingly aware of the disgraceful and scandalous life his mother leads by living openly with the duke of Buckingham."

"This is monstrous! My poor child. To use him as a weapon against me!"

She jumped up and walked rapidly across the room, her skirts rustling angrily. Then she pressed her face against the window pane and began to cry. At first she was angry for her son's sake, hating that he was being forced to hurt her without understanding how he was being used. But then a terrible thought struck her, and she turned and asked pitifully, "You don't think that Charles *believes* that I murdered his father, do you?"

Buckingham shook his head impatiently. "He is too young! At his age murder is merely a word to him. Besides, he loves you well."

He slapped a hand angrily against his knee. "They seem to favor using children as weapons. The petition would never have been brought, they said, if we had not buried our son in Westminster Abbey with full rites and ceremonies. They claimed it was proof of our flagrant disrespect of the laws of God and man."

She felt as though she must be dying. Each word he spoke was a thrust directly to her heart, bringing forth blood. She had been stripped naked in public, her private life laid bare to unfriendly eyes, and she could not bear the humiliation of it.

Brokenly she whispered, "And what of our love? We love each other faithfully. We loved our son, and we buried him with honors."

Buckingham laughed with icy bitterness. "They care nothing for love. Talbot wants to embarrass me."

"But what will happen now?" Anna-Maria fought to control the tears that were threatening to overwhelm her.

"They seek to make me a laughingstock!" Buckingham fumed. "They can censure me for conduct unbecoming to a member of the House of Lords."

His eyes fell on her, and he was appalled at his thoughtlessness. His anger had been so great that he had poured out his rage when he had intended to be gentle. She was tormented by the idea that her own son was being used as an instrument against her.

Taking her into his arms, he found that all her muscles were taut, her body rigid. Her eyes were tightly closed, and he bent and licked away the tears that were spilling from under her eyelids. "My love, we have lived down gossip before! We'll do it again." His face suddenly became grim with determination. "And then Talbot and the rest shall feel the weight of my revenge!"

Anna-Maria clung to him. She wished that she could bury her face against his strong chest and never face the world again. How often they had fought for the right to simply love each other! She drew on all her courage, and raised her head, forcing a smile onto her lips. "I do not care about the gossip. As long as you return to me each evening, hold me in your arms all night, I can face anything!"

Buckingham bent his mouth to her quivering red lips. "In all the world, my love, there is not another woman like you." He kissed her with passionate intensity, and she clung to him. His eyes darkened with desire, and he crossed the room with rapid strides and dropped her onto the softness of the bed. He gave her a questioning glance, and she nodded, stretching her arms toward him. At this moment she wanted to be as close to him as possible, to blot out the world with the sweetness of their lovemaking.

Their long hours of lovemaking had a calming effect and she fell into a deep, sweet sleep. In the morning she sent Buckingham off with a sound of her soft laughter ringing in his ears, then turned to her household duties.

She was pleased when her footman announced the duchess of Buckingham, and she rushed to the entrance hall to greet Mary, then stopped in consternation. Mary's hair was disheveled, her face was suddenly old and lined.

"Anna-Maria, I have come to warn you!" Mary shot a look at the footman and then pulled Anna-Maria out of the hall and into a long reception room.

"Buckingham's enemies seek to destroy him utterly."

Anna-Maria took Mary's shaking, cold hands into her own warm ones. "Hush, my dear. Buckingham says it is not so serious. There will be gossip again for a time but—"

She broke off as a bewigged, portly stranger bustled into the room without announcement, ignoring the footman's protests. He looked swiftly from one woman to the other and then fastened his prominent gray eyes on Anna-Maria. "You are the countess of Shrewsbury?"

Anna-Maria was too startled to feel anger at the intrusion. She nodded.

"Then, madame, I have this petition to hand you." He thrust a document at her, bowed perfunctorily and backed out of the room.

Anna-Maria stared at the document in bewilderment.

"Oh, dear God! I feared this!" Mary pressed the back of one hand to her trembling mouth. Anna-Maria looked at her uncomprehendingly and slowly unfolded the parchment. She scanned it quickly and then dropped it as though it were a burning brand.

Mary bent and snatched it from the floor, then read it rapidly. She nodded unhappily as though her fears had been confirmed. The parchment was a copy of the petition that had been read in the House of Lords.

Anna-Maria found her voice. "It says that I am to be banished and the full amount of my jointure returned to my husband's estate!"

Mary made an abrupt, angry gesture. "That is Talbot's doing. The rest of them have no real interest in you. They are using your liaison with Buckingham against him, and they don't care one way or another if Talbot takes the opportunity to seize your fortune. I have spent the whole morning pleading with the king, and it availed me nothing. I even went to Talbot himself." She blushed deeply. Mary knew that she had been a pathetic, comic spectacle—the wronged wife asking for mercy for her husband and his mistress. But she had cared nothing about her own pride; only Buckingham's safety was important.

Anna-Maria trembled. The pupils of her eyes were dilated with shock, her voice blurred. "They will hound me out of England as though I were a criminal, unfit to live on English soil." The humiliation struck so deep that she felt nauseated by it, and she turned away, groping for a chair.

Mary sprang to help her and was just settling her into the chair when they heard Buckingham's deep voice, and the sound of his boots striking the parquet floor.

When he entered the room, he seemed unaware for a moment that Mary was there. His eyes flew straight to Anna-Maria, his face angry and worried. "Were you served with a petition this morning?"

She nodded. "They are going to banish me."

Buckingham swore, his string of oaths the crude ones that men used on battlefields. Mary silently handed him the parchment. He looked at her and then read the document. Suddenly he ripped it across violently, as though he were laying his hands on his enemies, and tossed the fragments into the fire.

"I was handed mine as I was walking down the Stone Gallery at Whitehall. That pack of jackals! They do not fight like men." He began to swear again, too angry to temper his language in front of Anna-Maria and Mary.

Anna-Maria's eyes were suddenly dry, her posture alert. "But what is it that they *want?*"

Buckingham answered tersely, "They want us to stand surety that we will never see each other again. We must send our answers in writing to the House of Lords within the week."

"Never see each other again!" Anna-Maria felt as though she had heard her own death knell.

Mary made an inarticulate sound of compassion, but all Anna-Maria's attention was fixed on Buckingham, and she did not even turn to Mary.

Buckingham seized Anna-Maria's cold hands between his. "My love, it's far more serious than I had first thought. They don't merely mean to make a laughingstock of me—they seek to ruin me entirely."

"I don't understand." Anna-Maria's voice was a thin wail, and she was shaking uncontrollably.

"Here!" Buckingham turned to a small, inlaid table on which there was a decanter of wine and several glasses. He was silent as he poured the wine and handed glasses to Anna-Maria and Mary. Anna-Maria gripped the stem of her glass with both hands and fought to control her shaking.

Buckingham began to speak very slowly, as though to make himself crystal clear. "My enemies circled me in their minds, looking for a weakness through which they could attack me." His blue eyes met Anna-Maria's, and they were lit with tenderness. "They found that I am vulnerable because of my love for you."

Anna-Maria made a choked sound of anguish.

Buckingham continued, "My sweet, I don't consider it a weakness. My love for you is the strength of my life." He paused a moment, running his finger around the rim of his glass. "The House of Lords has the power to punish me for adultery. They can fine me heavily or send me to the Tower for an indefinite stay—"

Mary let out her breath on a long sigh. It was exactly as she had feared. She had gone that morning to beg the king's word that he would interfere if Buckingham was sent to the Tower, but the king had said coolly, "It might prove beneficial for Buckingham to cool his heels for a time."

Quickly Mary told Buckingham of her interview with the king.

Anna-Maria understood now that her love for Buckingham was going to do him irreparable damage, and the pain of the knowledge was so unbearable that she felt she would suffocate under its weight.

Buckingham nodded heavily when Mary had concluded her story. "That French bitch! She has Charles under petticoat rule now, and he has forgotten our long friendship."

This too was her fault, Anna-Maria thought. If

Buckingham had not been in such haste to return to her, he would not have dealt Louise the insult of leaving her on the French shore. She had wanted to give him nothing but joy in life, yet her love was a dagger pointed straight at Buckingham's heart!

Mary stood up, retrieved her cloak from the back of the chair where she had flung it, and pulled it around herself with decision. "I'm going to the queen. If the king will not help you, then she must."

They all knew that it might prove a futile effort. The queen had little liking for Buckingham and only small influence with the king.

Mary bent and touched Anna-Maria's cheek gently with her lips. "Be of good heart!" The anxiety on her face belied her words.

Anna-Maria sat silently, feeling weakness in her every muscle, as Mary made her departure, escorted by Buckingham.

He came back and stood looking down at Anna-Maria for a long moment without speaking. Then he said gravely, "My love, there is worse news. Are you strong enough to bear it?"

She looked up at him and then nodded slowly, tightening the muscle of her jaw. She knew now what a man must feel when he was fighting a duel, the sword thrusts coming so rapidly at him that he did not have time to catch his breath.

"They seek to strip me of my offices." Buckingham's voice was bleak, a man facing ruin after long years of ambition and hard work.

"How?" She clenched her hands together until the knuckles showed white.

"If I do not separate from you, they threaten to apply the old ecclesiastical laws against adultery and excommunicate me. According to the new Test Act, if I cannot take communion according to the Anglican rites, I cannot hold public office."

"But that law was designed to keep *Catholics* from holding public office!" Anna-Maria protested.

"Aye, but if I am excommunicated from the Anglican Church for adultery, the law will apply to me also."

"Then we must separate," she said softly. Even as she spoke the words, they had no reality for her. She could not picture living without him.

"Never!" He swept her into his arms. His muscles were taut under her fingers. "Let them strip me of my offices if they can. I'll never give you up."

Anna-Maria suddenly remembered the petition. "Suppose Talbot succeeds in having me banished?"

Buckingham pulled her more tightly against him. "Then I shall leave England by your side."

Forty-One

The candlelight flickered, sending shadows across Buckingham's naked body. Anna-Maria slowly stroked his taut belly, shivering deliciously as her fingertips touched his warm skin. She bent her head and nestled against him, her lips seeking his throat, her long hair spilling over his chest. He picked up a fragrant strand and passed it across his lips, smiling faintly as it tickled him. For hours they had not spoken except for the small murmurs of lovemaking.

Anna-Maria sighed and leaned on one elbow, looking gravely down into his face. "My love, we must talk."

"Must we?" He smiled teasingly and cupped one of her breasts in his hand.

She put her own hand over his to still his caressing movements. Her voice was very low and determined as she said, "We can no longer evade our problems."

During the sweet hours of lovemaking, they had sought to push their troubles out of their minds, but underneath had been a gnawing despair. It was certain now that Anna-Maria was to be banished from England, and the thought made her feel unclean, as though she were a criminal or a leper. Talbot had not yet succeeded in seizing her jointure, but he would no doubt make the attempt within a few days, and they must make immediate plans if they were to save her fortune.

A shadow darkened Buckingham's face, and he sighed heavily. All week he had made frantic efforts to win support to his side and had failed.

"We will go to America," he said slowly.

Anna-Maria bent her head so that her hair swung forward, hiding her face from his keen eyes. "When I am banished—I do not want you to go with me."

Buckingham gave a cry that had the explosive force of an oath and sat up, seizing her angrily by the shoulders. "I will not be parted from you!"

She winced as his fingers bruised her flesh, but she tossed back her hair and faced him bravely. "I don't want to be the instrument by which you are ruined, your career wrecked."

Buckingham's face was sad, but his voice was resolute. "I care only about you, nothing else."

"I cannot let you sacrifice yourself for me." Pain was cruelly twisting Anna-Maria's heart, and she knew that if she looked into his eyes, her resolution would falter.

"We'll sail for America, and there we'll build a new life together." Buckingham tried to force enthusiasm into his voice. "They say that America is a fine place. Vast forests, more land than any man has ever dreamed of. My love, we'll carve a home for ourselves out of the wilderness, and in a few short years we'll have entirely forgotten England!"

For a moment Anna-Maria was tempted. She had a sudden vision of Buckingham shirtless, his muscles rippling under the sunlight as he planted a crop. She would cook for him with her own hands, and at night they would lie in each other's arms, spent with exertion but proud of their industry. Then she realized how foolish the notion was. Buckingham was not a man of the soil, he was a statesman. She feared that his love for her would fade and die if he left England in disgrace, his life's work in ruins around him.

She began to shake her head slowly. She loved him so much that she could not bear to see him hurt. "I fear that one day you would come to resent me because of all that your love for me had cost you." Her voice held the hint of tears, but her expression was firm and resolute.

Suddenly, for his sake, she was on fire with determination to persuade him. "My love, let me go to France alone. It will not be for long. Once I am gone, your enemies will have lost one of their greatest weapons against you. The charge of adultery against you will have to be dropped. Soon you can rise to power again—and then you can send for me!"

A spark of interest flared in Buckingham's eyes. There was a great deal of sense in what Anna-Maria said. Then he thought of life without her, and he groaned, crushing her to him. "I cannot bear even the shortest separation from you."

A choked sob escaped Anna-Maria. She had not forgotten the last time she had gone to France, the sleepless nights of longing for him, the restless, empty days. She clung to him wordlessly for a moment, inhaling deeply as though she could absorb some essential part of him and take it for herself. At this moment she realized the full measure of her love for him. She was willing to endure pain and loneliness for his dear sake.

Raising her head, she faced him with a challenging smile on her lips, instinctively knowing it was the surest way to win his agreement. "Where is the courage for which you are so justly famous? You have gone into battle for England's sake, risked your very life, spent years in exile and poverty. Surely you can sacrifice your mistress for a few months for the sake of your country!"

Buckingham's head went back, and he stared at her, shocked by her unexpected challenge. "You are serious about wanting to part from me?" There was deep hurt in his eyes, as though she had just declared that she no longer loved him.

A small cry escaped from Anna-Maria's lips, and she fell against him, frantic to comfort him. "My love, my dear love. I want to leave you for *your* sake. And for our future. We will have more children, and I want them to grow up in England, to inherit all that you have built for them. Surely you would not have them raised as savages in a strange land!"

She could see capitulation in his eyes even before his arms tightened around her. "It would only be a matter of months," he agreed. Plans were already beginning to form in his mind.

Anna-Maria released her breath, suddenly exhausted. She lay back against his shoulder, and watched his face as the candlelight played over it. Soon —too soon—she would be lying awake and lonely at night, returning in imagination to his side. "Tomorrow I shall pack. And then—" she drew a difficult breath, "I'd like to set out for Dover immediately."

A look of consternation crossed Buckingham's face. "So soon?"

Anna-Maria forced herself to speak unemotionally. "If I hesitate, it will give Talbot time to seize my jointure. Besides, I would rather leave England with dignity than be removed by *force*. By leaving secretly, at once, I can forestall the humiliation of banishment."

Buckingham nodded; her pride was similar to his own. "I'll send Simpson ahead to hire a boat for you." Although it was past midnight, he slipped from the bed, found his manservant, and ordered him to set out for Dover within the hour.

When he returned to the vast bed, he pulled Anna-Maria against him, almost crushing her with the intensity of his embrace. "My sweet, how will I face the long nights without you?" He began kissing her upturned face. "Did I ever tell you that the sweetness of your eyes captured me the first moment I ever saw you?"

Anna-Maria, too, found her mind racing back over their years together, memories tumbling one upon the other. The way the sun had glinted off his golden hair when she first saw him in the king's triumphant procession into London; his quick understanding of her shyness at court and his efforts to put her at ease, their long hours of lovemaking during which she had learned the delicious joys of being a woman; the intimate nights when they had talked until dawn, never tiring of exploring each other's minds. When she thought of their son, buried in Westminster Abbey, tears wet her cheeks. Buckingham, sensing her thoughts, kissed her passionately, and they made love with a frantic intensity, storing up more memories against the long loneliness that was to follow.

When she woke the next morning, she found that pain had coiled itself around her heart. This was to be her last morning in this beloved house, and she lay still for a long time, conscious of Buckingham's sleeping form beside her, memorizing the details of the furniture that she had selected with such care. Finally she rose and went to find Sarah, who was in the buttery scolding one of the housemaids for carelessness. Sarah broke off her tirade when she caught sight of Anna-Maria's strained face. Hurriedly she dismissed the tearful maid and asked Anna-Maria, "What is it that makes you look so?"

Anna-Maria poured out her plans rapidly, as though the words were painful on her tongue and she wanted to rid herself of them quickly.

Sarah listened closely, trying to follow the hurried rush of speech and then she nodded. "Perhaps it is best. I will go with you."

A smile illuminated Anna-Maria's face. "Sarah, will you? I dared not ask it of you. It will be a strange country."

Sarah dismissed that briskly. "Joseph can come to protect us. Surely the duke will want that. When will we leave?"

"Today." At the look of consternation on Sarah's face, she said quickly, "There's no other choice. If we linger, Talbot will have time to seize my jointure."

"Then we must make haste." Sarah bustled into action, calling the footmen to remove all the trunks from the storage rooms and the housemaids to stop their other chores and lend a hand with the packing.

Buckingham was half dressed when Anna-Maria reentered the room. For a moment she paused on the threshold. Suddenly the commonplace act of his dressing seemed beautiful and poignant to her.

His expression was tender as he caught sight of her,

and they exchanged a look of understanding. Buckingham said, "I'll be out all day, securing your fortune."

Anna-Maria nodded. A portion of her jointure was in the house, a massive pile of gold coins safely hidden against emergencies. But the bulk of it was deposited with various money lenders around London. "Will you have difficulty getting it at such short notice?"

Buckingham shook his head, looking pleased with himself. "If I had deposited the entire amount with one goldsmith, the poor fellow would have been hard pressed to return it on such short demand. That's why I took the precaution of depositing it with several money lenders—there should be no difficulty."

Anna-Maria picked up his plumed hat and handed it to him, smiling at him. He clapped it on his head, gave her a prolonged kiss, and then strode out the door.

Anna-Maria was relieved that the hours flew so quickly. There were a thousand decisions to be made about what to pack and what to leave behind, as well as letters of farewell to pen to Mary and Nell. She begged them both to send her word of the children and asked Mary to visit the children at the Talbot house occasionally. Surely Talbot would not dare refuse the duchess of Buckingham, who was in such high favor with the queen. Anna-Maria's hand shook so that occasionally she had to lay down her quill lest she blot the pages.

By the time twilight had fallen, the hall was full of trunks, the horses and carriages waiting outside the door. Anna-Maria walked slowly through the rooms of the house, making her last farewell. She went alone, leaving Buckingham to supervise the loading of the trunks into the carriages. The rooms seemed vast and suddenly very silent. Once they had rung to the sound of their laughter and the sweet piercing cry of the baby's hungry wail.

She turned abruptly and left without looking back.

Several of her servants broke into open sobbing as she climbed into the coach, and Anna-Maria had to clench her teeth to keep back her own tears. Sarah and Joseph were riding in the rear coach with the luggage so that Anna-Maria and Buckingham could share a coach in privacy.

He followed her inside, ducking his head to clear the low doorway, looking at her anxiously. She smiled reassuringly at him. "I'm fine, my love."

As they drove out of London, she hung out of the coach window eager for the last sights of the dirty, endlessly fascinating city. She kept her hand tucked in Buckingham's all during the journey, and they alternately talked and fell silent, murmuring of her plans, of their shared memories.

They broke their journey at the least disreputable looking of the roadside inns, but Buckingham snorted with contempt when he saw the lumpy bed, the dirt-stained walls. Anna-Maria only laughed and held out her arms to him. She was on fire with desire to be close in his arms, to feel his lean body stretched against hers.

They were up before dawn, setting a fast pace toward Dover. Anna-Maria became frantic to seize time in her hands and drag it back. The hours were speeding past too quickly, and they were taking Buckingham away from her. She could not keep her eyes from him, and often she lost the thread of what she was saying, so intent was she in memorizing his handsome face.

Once they drew the curtains over the coach windows and attempted to make love, but the jolting motion made it awkward and sent them tumbling to the floor. Anna-Maria pushed at her hair, which had come tumbling down, and laughed a bit shakily. After a moment Buckingham also began to laugh at the absurdity of the situation, and their laughter lightened the sadness that hung heavy between them. They were not far outside Dover now, and he tapped on the roof of the coach, directing the coachman to the nearest inn. "I vow that if this inn is as bad as the last, I will set fire to it with my own hands."

Anna-Maria smiled sweetly. "Did you notice dis-

comfort, my lord? Then you are not the ardent lover
I had thought you."

Buckingham gave a mock scowl. "You find me
lacking in ardor? I must redouble my efforts tonight."

They ordered supper sent to their chamber and
then left it untouched on the crude table while they
lay in bed, sharing a glass of wine. Anna-Maria had
decided that she would not spoil these moments by
tears or by thinking of the future. Buckingham was
here beside her, and she wanted to live these moments fully.

When he was kissing her, she forgot that this was
their last night together, and she lost herself in ec-
stacy. Neither of them slept, and when the room was
fully awash with light the next morning, they rose
reluctantly, suddenly silent. They shared the intima-
cies of dressing and Anna-Maria thought, I'll never
be able to fasten my bodice without remembering how
his fingers looked as they carefully tied my laces. . . .

The coaches had already gone ahead with the
trunks to load them on the ship, and Sarah and Joseph had gone to supervise. There were two spirited
horses waiting for Anna-Maria and Buckingham. The
fast pace the horses set made talking impossible, and
they rode side by side with the wind streaming in
their faces.

Anna-Maria had a feeling of unreality. Surely this
could not be the last time they rode together; it
was impossible that at nightfall she would not be in
his arms. All around them were the chalky white
cliffs of Dover, and Anna-Maria remembered how she
had paced these shores, waiting for Buckingham to
return to her.

They were on the beach now, their horses' feet
scattering the small pebbles. Buckingham swung down
from his saddle and turned to lift Anna-Maria to the
ground. Dear God, it's actually happening, she
thought, and a terrible fear gripped her. She had
known it was to come—as one knows that death must
come at the end of life—but until this moment she
had not truly believed in the reality of it. She felt a

cry of protest swell in her throat. Already he was turned away from her, his face raised toward the sailors who were loading the last of her trunks. For this last dear moment, she had his loving care, his instructions for her comfort, and then no more. Then desolation.

Suddenly he turned, and his gaze held hers. Reaching out, he gently traced the outline of her cheek, and the gesture was so infinitely affectionate that she felt weak with love.

He concentrated on her totally. Even the sounds from the sailors and servants seemed muted, and they stood alone in their silence as they had on the first day they had met. At this moment of parting, she felt closer to him than ever before.

He reached out and pulled her against him, gently, without passion. It was a moment for raising her lips to his, but she knew that she could not bear the sweet, searing fire of a kiss. Instead she rubbed her cheek against his shoulder, trying to absorb some of his strength. It was a moment of wordless companionship. Between them were all the small, intimate moments that had made up their years of loving. Thousands of filaments had been woven from one to the other, and they were bound together for all eternity.

The master of the ship was calling to them to hurry, his voice sharp with urgency. Without thinking, Anna-Maria obeyed the summons, moving away from Buckingham and then stood still as pain sliced through her. She had taken the first step on her long journey away from him. The small strip of sand between them suddenly seemed an unbridgable gulf.

He made a move as though to stop her and then checked himself. "Write to me, darling. Let me know that you are safe. Our parting will not be for long. . . ." His voice was rich with love, promising that he would always be with her in some fashion, would always be thinking of her, protecting her.

She looked at his blue eyes, his sensitive, firm mouth that had always attracted her. Even if this were not their final parting, some day it would come.

Life ended, one of them would die. A great swell of sadness and loneliness rose up in her. How unfair of God to have made life so brief! Then her mind flashed back over their few years together, and she was instantly flooded with a radiant joy. How much they had been given! Understanding broke over her, and she moved a step closer to him, feeling the sand crunch beneath her feet. She looked deeply into his eyes, her voice very steady.

"No matter what happens in the future, I will always thank God for giving you to me. Most people live empty lives. They feel mild affection and call it love. Life has cheated them. But you and I have been given the greatest of all gifts. Each day we shared, I felt 'my cup runneth over,' and I was bathed in the overspill of love."

Buckingham was watching her intently. "You have given up everything for me, your reputation, your children, your place at court, and now you are being banished for my sake. Is my love worth it?"

Anna-Maria tilted her head to look up at him, and searched his handsome face as though she were memorizing every line of it. "Once," she said tenderly, "a gypsy told me that I would love one man for all my life and for him I would give up everything." She smiled, lit by an inner light. "The prophesy came true. And yes, my love, it is worth it!"

ABOUT THE AUTHOR

PATRICIA CAMPBELL HORTON grew up in Glen Cove, Long Island. She enrolled in a nursing program at Adelphi College, but left before completing her degree in order to write. A public relations job provided Ms. Horton with valuable experience, and after the birth of her first child, she decided to start a newspaper. Sea Cliff, Long Island, hadn't had a newspaper for forty years—Pat Horton had chosen the perfect spot to settle. The *Sea Cliff-Glen Head Times* is now in its sixth year. When her busy schedule permits, Ms. Horton works on her novels. TENDER FIRE, the result of years of careful research, is her second published novel.

a Special Preview of
the colorful opening pages of
the newest novel by
the author of LA BELLE

BLOOD
RED
ROSES

by Elizabeth Boatwright Coker

One

Everything was upside down at Cedar Grove Plantation in Albemarle County, Virginia, on the 13th day of October, 1860. My whole delightful, wonderful world was about to come to a bad end suddenly as Aunt Dell had constantly warned me it would when I was over-excited as a child. Ironically this was going to happen because of my noble gesture: agreeing to Aunt Dell's velvet-veiled suggestions that I immediately marry a rich man who will adore me enough to pay off Uncle Jim's tobacco and racing debts, saving his honor as well as the plantation.

It was my duty to do this awful thing. Papa put me in Aunt Dell's arms minutes after I was born. Barely hesitating to give the farewell kiss to her younger sister's corpse, Aunt Dell rushed out of the room, to show me to Uncle Jim, who was Papa's elder brother. I don't believe it ever occurred to them thereafter that they hadn't conceived me themselves.

Oh, how I will hate that rich husband. Aunt Dell insists that if he isn't a thoroughly bad hat I will learn to like him well enough after the children start coming. My precious little half-sister, Amun, who is frail, can be the one of us to marry for love.

Misfortune struck The Cedars this past May when Uncle Jim wagered a great part of the plantation on one of his racehorses. In the match the gallant animal broke his leg and had to be destroyed. In July the tobacco crop was shredded by hail. Then in August the cider house burned down and the apple harvest rotted on the ground. In September a heavy storm broke in the night. The

James River roared like the ocean and went over its banks. Rain filled the outbuildings and barns and fields. The boats were all swimming in the boathouse. An enormous oak tree upended and crushed the whiskey still. Six skilled tobacco field slaves ran away.

To cap his bad luck Uncle Jim was so exhilarated by the way the "Chosen," wealthy Mr. Monk, of the Eastern Shore of Maryland, looked at me at supper last night that he drank so many bumpers of wine on top of brandy, hallooing and toasting first the hunt, then jolly Mr. Page, the Master, then Mr. Monk's racehorses, one after another, that on finally setting out to resume his chair at the head of the table, he misjudged the distance and fell hard on the floor.

After silently watching him make a few unsuccessful tries at rising, Aunt Dell languidly summoned Great Peter, our head house Negro, to carry him off. Great Peter laid him on his four poster bed from which in this October daydawn he was shouting orders.

I was dressed in my expensive new green velvet riding habit, determined to make the most of Mr. Monk's interest, even though he is a full head shorter than I and one of his eyes rolls around in its socket.

Mr. Page, Uncle Jim's best friend, aware of his financial difficulties, arranged this hunt today just so Mr. Monk could watch me take Parasol, my peppery mare, over the fences. If anything will sell me besides my looks it will be my horsemanship. I am more exciting in the saddle than in the waltz for, though fine-boned and graceful, I am almost six feet which is a trifle too tall for most gentlemen to be able to look down into my eyes.

As I finished adjusting my plumed hat and a sheer veil over my face I heard our horsekeeper, Jason Jenks, in Uncle Jim's room. I flew down. Jenks was saying it had to be today or never. Bonnie Bet had fooled him. This could be the end of her heat, not the beginning. He'd turned the teaser horse into the next run to get her frolicky and excited, ready for *her* chosen: the big bay stallion, which Uncle Jim had mortgaged the now-extinct tobacco crop to obtain to stand for a season. The bay was in the pen raring to go, said Jenks. A wonder we hadn't heard him neighing in the night.

"What's happening?" In my haste I stumbled over my long skirttrail.

"You're supposed to hook it over your wrist," Aunt Dell's voice came from somewhere in the dim room.

Uncle Jim shouted, "What's happening indeed! This clod, Jenks, has had the gall to suggest that if I can't walk, you give up hunting and cope with the teaser when Bonnie Bet is taken from him to the bay. My proud beauty! What villain would deprive the huntsmen of such a vision?"

Jenks stood staunchly on his thick young legs. "There'll be two hunts a week, Mr. Burwell, from now until late spring. Miss Angel's the only one the teaser won't harm at such a time as today, you excepting, of course, sir."

"Just give me a minute to take off this endless riding habit, Jenks."

"Do." Uncle Jim wrathfully lifted his bushy salt and pepper head from the pillow. "I've changed my mind. If we miss breeding Bonnie Bet we're out of the racing and the tobacco business."

"Don't fret, darling. I'll enjoy taking part." I was already unpinning my hat.

I could see Aunt Dell now, rocking in a cane chair by the wood fire, nightcapped and wrappered in flowered flannel. She said how could I, her own niece, think of taking part in a going-on like that. I said I didn't intend to take part in the actual going-on but what if our teaser got out of control and jumped the fence and got to Bonnie Bet as he was so capable of doing? Was Aunt Dell eager to go to the poorhouse?

Uncle Jim said, "Don't argue with that fool girl, Mrs. Burwell. She's well aware of what's expected of her. But the crazy way she is about the teaser she'll probably open the gate and slip him to Bet first. Her pity for the underdog will be the ruin of her yet. Help me up, Jenks. God damn you—my back's broken for sure." He fell back, groaning.

Great Peter tiptoed in with a silver mug of warm rye

whiskey and sugar water and supported Uncle Jim while he drank. "Be gentle now, Master. Miss Angel knows what's fitten for a lady. She won't go no further than the run; not Miss Angel."

Jenks, his yellow whiskers standing out from his rosy cherub cheeks, spoke to me across the bed. "He's slipped a joint, Miss Angel. This ain't the first time. Usually he manages to hide it from you all. We rub him with liniment at the stables and loosen him up. But today he's worse than I've ever seen him. You take off that pretty green skirt and put on something real old. The runs are a bog of mud."

Uncle Jim waved his hand. It was trembling. I took it and squeezed it hard, saying, "Mr. Monk wouldn't do for me, Uncle Jim. You might as well know that I saw him nodding when I played the Chopin waltzes after supper. I'll be very careful around dear Teaser."

"I don't trust you, Angelica. Not when your emotions are involved. You're too much like your father. He could always be counted on to behave rashly and grieve about it later."

"If you don't trust Angelica, Mr. Burwell, tell her to pin her hat back on and gallop to the Inn where the hunt is this minute assembling." Aunt Dell had risen and put her arm around my waist. She was a tall listless looking lady with marked remains of beauty. She was listless because she never took any exercise. Her green eyes glittered when lighted with interest, which was seldom. Most of the time she had a vague stare whether she was talking or not. Today was no exception.

Jenks was going out through the door into the hall. "I say, Mr. Burwell, I'll not let Miss Angel nowhere near the pen. The teaser needs her."

"And *I* say, Mr. Burwell," Aunt Dell's eyes were staring at nothing in the fringed bed canopy, "Mr. Monk and his money are more important to Angelica *and* us than the teaser."

Assuaged by his hot toddy, Uncle Jim raised up on his elbow, "And *I* say, Mrs. Burwell, that unknown to you I've wagered everything on a successful crop of foals next year. A get of Bonnie Bet and the Sir Archy bay, unrun, will bring enough to pay off the wager on The Cedars. Once the colt runs, Angelica can be an old maid and spend her life with the teaser if she so chooses. Hurry, girl, they are waiting for you at the stables."

A light frost had fallen in the night. The ridge horizon was robed in a haze of dream-stuff blue. I heard the melody of the huntsman's sweet-toned copper horn and the belling of the hounds. As the hunt distanced I thought, well, there goes the best chance I'll probably ever have to pay the bills for my fine coming-out clothes and help Uncle Jim settle his debts. When Mr. Monk vanishes there's nobody around here rich enough for me to set my cap for. We'll be bankrupt by New Year's whether we breed Bonnie Bet or not . . .

Teaser had impeccable bloodlines but Uncle Jim had a horror of a white colt with blue eyes. Teaser had been an accident that befell Silver Star, full sister to Kitty Fisher. Silver Star was one of Uncle Jim's most prolific grey brood mares. Five years ago, a grey hunter of Mr. Randolph's ran away and vaulted the six-foot fence surrounding the east pasture where Silver Star was trotting along with her two-week-old black filly. Jenks had found her and the hunter there grazing together but no one suspected what had gone on before until Silver Star began making nests in the hay in her stall a week before she dropped Teaser.

One look at the poor shivery little creature had been enough for Uncle Jim. The two greys had made an albino! The best fate I was able to bargain for him doomed him to frustration whenever the breeding pen was active.

But every now and then I loaned him to Farmer Grundy, who considered himself lucky to get, free of charge, white colts descended from the great Eclipse. Teaser was the swiftest moving, boldest jumper in our entire stable.

There was a lot of commotion beyond the near barn where the breeding pen was set up. This was the nearest I'd ever come to the "going-on" as Aunt Dell called it. Hog killing and horse breeding were secret rites. Ladies and children stayed behind drawn curtains at such times.

If Jenks saw me so near he'd order me back to the house. I picked my path through the mud and into the barn, staying close against the stalls.

Through the light at the end of the runway I saw Jenks and four black men coming with the big bay. The stallion was plunging and throwing his head, snorting clouds of steam through his dilated nostrils. His eyes were fiery, his breathing loud. He struck the soft earth with his hard hoofs. Bonnie Bet, held by two black stablehands, was kicking with her back feet and thrashing her well-set flaxen tail back and forth in the stallion's face; suddenly she threw her tail far to one side.

He was just about to——

"Angelica! Hurry!"

I could have killed the beloved caller. "Amun! What are you doing here? Don't you know what's taking place? Get back to the house."

"Aunt Dell and Uncle Jim want you at once. It's an emergency."

I caught the hand my tiny blonde half-sister held out and fled with her to the rambling old strawberry-colored brick house . . .

Amun kept chattering about a letter as we ran through the weedy, formal garden hedged with unclipped cedars. I hadn't listened but was aware that great news had come when I saw Aunt Dell in a close-bordered tarleton cap, seated at the head of the dining table. She was wearing her widest hoop under her least-shiny grey taffeta day gown. Her green eyes glittered as she waved some rumpled sheets of paper in my direction.

"We're saved!"

"Let's go into Uncle Jim's room. I'd rather hear about it when he does."

"He's savored every word already. Great Peter is shaving him now. He's going to make an heroic effort to put his trousers on and be brought out into the drawing room."

Two

My dear Adelia,

There is only one subject discussed a days in Charleston, SECESSION! The resolution to quit these United States consumes everybody. Throughout South Carolina men of all stations in life sit together under spreading oaks talking about it. I doubt you could find more than a handful of Up Country souls who agree with Mr. Pettigrew and Mr. Calhoun that we should put up with Yankee meddling in our private affairs any longer. What impudence! In *their* sailing ships *they* fetched the blacks here from Africa. Now that they've pocketed *our* money their pious preachers demand that *we* set them free! To the devil with them, as dear Papa would have said. . . .

Baynard Elliott Berrien of Cotton Hall Plantation on Hilton Head, S. C., sailed into town about a month ago and took up residence at the Charleston Hotel. He resembles his late father, our Cousin Hazzard, being six and a half feet high and considering Hilton Head Island more important than Charleston. Have you ever known such gall?

But, lacking Hazzard's rude conceit, Beau, as he is called, possesses an almost royal presence heightened by the rufous coloring and the bold hooked nose that have been in the Berrien family since the Crusades. His fiery brown eyes give him alternately the look of a sly fox or a swooping hawk. It's difficult to describe him. He's different from anybody we ever had in the family before.

The ladies flock after him, those from the uptown back streets as well as ones of our kind. Tales of his wildness where wine and women (including his young stepmother) are concerned have been whispered behind fans ever since he returned from his studies at Harvard College six years ago. He never noticeably refuses the role gossiped about; if folks choose to be shocked he generally obliges. But since his father's death and his inheritance of the Berrien fortune, his eccentricities are called quaint and amusing. His friends say that under the dwindling bouts of carryings-on he has improved, changed considerably, except for being unpredictable.

Aged twenty-five, he plants cotton on Hilton Head Island and St. Helena Island and Fripp Island and along the River May. Lord knows the extent of the Berrien holdings in blacks *and* cotton land in Mississippi.

He possesses parts as well. His peers speak him as the finest deer and waterfowl shot in the Low Country, a magnificent horse rider, a careful father 'in locus' to his three younger brothers, and properly proud of his Huguenot heritage.

Did Beau hold the reputation for being too often in his cups or for cruelty to his slaves as did his father I would not be writing you. As you know, our Cousin Julia, this boy's mother, broke her heart and health over it. They say the second Mrs. Berrien knew how to cope with Hazzard. She rarely, if ever, set foot on a sea island plantation, and let her husband lie wherever his drinking flung him. Beaufort keeps an aloof distance, she having managed to make enemies of every family connection. So far as I know Hazzard only brought her to one Ball in Charleston. I was serving the oyster stew that night so merely glimpsed her. Mainly I remember that she had too much hair and the way she kept fidgeting with her diamonds and her raspy Northern voice complaining that Southern ladies didn't appeal to her.

I mention this because it struck me as odd for Beau, on his first visit, to bluntly state his reason for calling: I must help him find a suitable bride! Have you ever? He is anxious to marry and settle down before war clouds darken the horizon.

"War?" I asked.

"Of course, Madame," he answered firmly. "You aren't under the illusion that the North will let South Carolina depart in peace, are you?"

Not caring to pursue unpleasant subjects I returned

to his request. "Why me, rather than your stepmother?"

"Frankly because I don't want Elsa to know a damn thing about it."

He chose me as his mentor having often heard his mother speak of me as THE Grand Dame of Charleston!

Flattered, I arranged dinners and teas for him in the best houses and he went through all the motions of the proper courtier. Ten days ago he gave me his reaction to the Misses Ravenel, Middleton, Chisolm, Prioleau, Stoney, Heyward and Alston: though Miss R had gorgeous blue eyes she also had brown spots on her teeth; Miss M fell off her horse and cried; Miss C affronted him, reading aloud vulgar poems by a fellow named Whitman; Miss P pretended to faint when he bit the tip of her ear as they were waltzing; Miss S constantly fanned and giggled; Miss H had an offensive odor; and Miss A had thick ankles.

I was about to send him packing. After all I'd spent the better part of a month at his disposal and so far he'd only presented me with a silver rice spoon. But suddenly I thought of you. Angelica's heron-like beauty has been carefully reported in Charleston by several young gentlemen who have recently hunted in your area. Already I have received six requests for the pleasure of escorting her to my Oyster Roast at the Cooper River Plantation in February!

However, knowing that things have not gone well for you and Jim of late, I have given Beau Berrien directions about arriving at The Cedars and have been advised that he left on the cars for Richmond October 6, thinking to procure a mount from his Cousin Harrison there and ride on to you. Expect him on the 13th or 14th . . .

> Fondly,
> Rebecca Bacot

"Your mother and I played with Beau's aunt in his grand house in Beaufort when we were children. I would love for you to be mistress there."

I could feel my hair slipping down from its net. "I simply *must* put Teaser into his stall."

"Don't go back out there, darling, you look worn out."

"I've been running ever since dawn. What time is it now?"

"Ten o'clock. Do make haste. The South Carolina Hamptons are stopping by for dinner on their way from White Sulphur Springs after visiting the Prestons. Mr. Page has sent word that Mr. Monk was so disappointed at your not showing up for the hunt he's going to stay over and hunt tomorrow. They will be here for dinner, along with Azilee and Lizora Bizarre. You'll have to watch out for that Lizora. She looks stunning in riding dress and she's poor too. Oh, everything is working out perfectly. The Walkers are here already, playing whist in the drawing room."

"Lizora Bizarre makes me feel awkward. She knows it and always stands close to me to show off my tallness by her littleness."

"That makes thirteen people at table, Aunt Dell," Amun said.

"Then you'll eat in the kitchen, Miss Puss."

"If the rich fox gets here in time *he* will save me." Amun nodded her round little head shining with cropped flaxen hair, she having had typhoid fever last summer.

Aunt Dell airily waved a silver teaspoon. "He'll get here. I've got one of my hunches. If he isn't here by three I'll delay dinner till four then five then six o'clock. I've ordered Great Peter to fill the gentlemen up with grog and the ladies with a concoction of brandy and sugar water. Competition between Beau and Mr. Monk will turn the trick. You must wear Mrs. Meriweather's blue silk, Angelica. It makes your eyes glisten like morning glories."

I had never seen Aunt Dell so enthusiastic. Nor have I ever felt more wretchedly desolate. "He won't like Chopin and I don't like pompous asses."

"His mother played for Chopin in Paris when she was a girl. And Chopin listened! He rarely did, you know."

"I'll tell Dinah to fix you a bath in the big tub. You've got to smell good. You smell pukey now." Amun was jigging around excitedly on her skinny legs.

"You go on like a jackanapes." Aunt Dell tapped

Amun's sharp little shoulder with the spoon. Her eyes took on the glittery look again. "Hepzibah is boiling our last three-year-old forty-pound ham. There's a white-faced sheep on the fire and all those wild geese and ducks you and Jenks shot day before yesterday; *and* a turkey gobbler and a dozen pullets and hominy and sweet potatoes and syllabub and lemon ice cream."

I couldn't stand any more. I rushed away through the kitchen, which was filled with chattering black women and quick little mulatto serving boys in white long-sleeved aprons, with red and white turbans on their heads. They were egg whipping, butter creaming, meat basting, raisin stoning, salad chopping, sugar pounding, biscuit beating, fowl picking, silver polishing, napkin folding, wine cooling and things like that.

There was no doubt about it, Aunt Dell had executive talent. She had put everybody, except me, to a task they could happily accomplish. In her book, today was one of life's great occasions to which, without appearing to do anything at all, she planned to rise superbly. It was maddening.

When I reached the lot it was obvious that Teaser was determined not to be put into his stall. His game of catch-me-if-you-can had a peculiar effect on me. Being on the edge of hysteria, I burst out laughing. Recklessly jumping up to catch his halter I stepped on my skirt and tore it half off. Still laughing I admired my shapely leg and didn't duck away from a clod of mud Teaser's fore-foot kicked up. It smeared all over my forehead. This was the last straw.

"Come here, you damned demon!"

The unfamiliar, screaming tone of my voice arrested him. He quieted, nuzzling my shoulder with his long soft lips.

"You funny old horse." Exhausted, I leant my cheek against his lathered neck. "You poor funny old horse."

Three

"No funnier than you."

I recognized him immediately up there against the sky, looking like an over-life-sized equestrian statue in an exaggerated stovepipe hat. Did he go all the way up into the hat? Apparently he did for when he lifted it off he was still the tallest human I'd ever seen in a saddle.

Dismounting, he bowed smartly, "Baynard Berrien, at your service, dear lady."

Teaser tensed, pricked up his new-moon ears and neighed angrily. As the giant secured his mount to a post and, waving his hat, headed toward the gate, Teaser wheeled away from me and galloped along the rail, sending mud and stones flying right and left as he went.

"Climb through the fence quick, you idiot. I've panicked him."

The gate opened and Teaser made for the space to escape.

"Hoa, there. Hoa, you scoundrel," the newcomer roared, jamming his hat back on.

Teaser was on his way to freedom. I kept running and calling, "Mr. Berrien! Mr. Berrien!" knowing Teaser saw only the open gate and not the man blocking his escape.

The thought of those powerful hoofs and huge hard teeth crumbling that magnificent specimen into a muddy-bloody mess undid me. I kept on shrieking and screaming. Teaser was upon him. I froze, paralyzed. For a few seconds of hideous noises it was man against horse. Then a yell; then a squeal; a jerk; and it was all over.

Teaser snorted and kicked and snapped his teeth like castanets. Flecks of foam exploded from his nostrils.

The Chevalier Berrien, his whole powerful body turning flexibly, iron arms taut, Wellington boots planted ankle-deep in the mud, hung on to the halter as the stallion plunged and reared.

"You're killing him," I gasped, stumbling and slipping as I ran, "you're killing him."

"Better him than me," he shouted. His linen shirt frill was ruined; his cravat gone; his sleeves torn from the shoulder seams of his tight fitting fawn broadcloth coat.

As I reached up to snatch the rope away from him my hand came in contact with a hairy wrist above a sodden chamois glove. Flame from the bare reddish flesh darted into my fingers, ran up my arm, through my armpits, tightening and thrusting my breasts toward this wild man. He was the fox! I heard his rapid heartbeats; and mine.

"What in blazes were you doing fooling around with this crazy stallion. Do you work here?" he asked, breathing heavily.

He thought I was a stable hand! My weariness vanished. My audacity and courage returned. "My uncle works here. I was on a special assignment to lock up the teaser. They're breeding the finest Burwell mare over beyond the big barn. Teaser wouldn't hurt me. He loves me."

"Which goes to show you know nothing of the male sex when he is deprived of his rights. Where the hell are my cigars? In the mud, dammit. Come on, I'll lock him up. Lead the way to his stall. He won't make any more trouble. He's met his match and knows it."

Teaser did too. Capriciously he snapped at a mass of flying russet hair. My rich prospect was about to be scalped! But, not liking the taste, Teaser let go and whickering, head down, gave a playful hoist of his back feet and lightly picked his way behind us through the muck toward his stall.

As the bolt dropped into place the newcomer said, "Even in this disheveled state I must present my compliments to the Burwells. First, I'll stable my dull mount, than I'll look in on the breeding. See if the horses are as ill cared for as the land. Then I'll be forced to endure an endless dinner full of conversation about Virginia people I never heard of. After that I'll slip away and take tea with you."

"How will you find me?"

"Your uncle will direct me. I'll make friends with him

at the breeding pen. Don't worry; I'll not divulge my wicked designs on you. I'll tell him I might drop in on him later and talk horses."

"You can't miss him. He has yellow hair and bushy yellow sideburns. His name is Jenks. The stall on the end is empty. I'll see that your horse is fed."

Angelica's meeting with Beau leads them to build a life together. However all of their plans are threatened by the onrushing events of the Civil War.

The complete Bantam Book will be available May 24th, on sale wherever paperbacks are sold.

RELAX!
SIT DOWN
and Catch Up On Your Reading!

DON'T MISS
THESE CURRENT
Bantam Bestsellers